THE
BLOOD
RACE

K.A. Emmons

PROLOGUE
Sunrise

They said I was born with the markings: black stains that wrapped my upper arms like mourning bands. But no one had witnessed my birth—I would never know if that was true. I was the dark horse, the unlabeled package, the unwanted child thrown to the back of the classroom to feed and fester in the shadows.

My name was spoken in whispers, in shadows, in the places where the fearful gathered to chant. I was the foundling, the mystery, the curse. I was different, they said. The markings were an omen; the devil lived inside me.

I couldn't understand what he meant when his gentle voice told me he had been looking for me, watching since I was a child. The words came out of his mouth like velvet to touch my bruised flesh. I shook beneath their weight; I avoided his bright sky eyes. His voice was like a mother's, and his face was like the sun. His skin was satin, diamonds, gold, everything from which I'd been restrained.

He told me that I was like the dawn. When I asked what he meant, he told me that heaven and earth existed between a soul torn in two. A sunrise marred by the fruits of the world as it was, and a sunset marked by all that it could become. One, he said, that would mark the beginning of a harvest, and another that would mark its culmination.

"How can this be?" I asked. "I don't even know who I am. Where I've come from."

"I know who you are," he told me. "I designed you."

"Who are you?"

"Does it matter?"

"It does," I replied. "It does to me—I have to know if I can trust you."

"Trust is earned, dear one."

"I don't understand."

"I'm a protector of that which is to come," he replied.

"That which is to come, sir?"

"I am not 'sir'; I am your teacher," he said. "You have a greater mission than I."

I stared at him through the shafts of early morning sun, searching for something behind the blue in his eyes. "A mission?"

He looked at me, then nodded. "To find the other half of who you are."

CHAPTER ONE

"You're literally going eighty?" West almost choked.

"There's no one out here."

"We're going to get pulled over."

"We won't if you just *shut up* and let me concentrate."

I saw West fighting with the seatbelt in my peripheral vision, throwing glances over his shoulder like there was an ax murderer in the backseat.

"Relax," I told him, leaning back in the seat. "I know what I'm doing."

West shook his head and Ruger, in the backseat, blew out a laugh.

"Where did you say you were from again, West?" Ruger asked, leaning forward. "Phoenix?"

"Tucson," West corrected, beginning to sound a little out of breath.

"That's not quite under a rock," Ruger submitted. "What gives?"

West shrugged. "I don't know. Maybe I don't drive like an animal?"

The girl seated beside Ruger in the backseat laughed. "Everyone drives like an animal here. You'll get used to it."

I gave my side-view mirror a quick glance. I could see the orange blaze that ran up and over the hood of Riley's car, where there was an airbrushed painting of his girlfriend. Half of her face was normal—stunning, like it was in real life—while the opposing half was zombified, with the bone structure exposed.

Checking my mirror again, I cursed under my breath and leaned into the gas a little more. "He's gaining."

"What's your speed?" Ruger peered impatiently over my shoulder. "Ninety?"

"Ninety-five," I corrected, flexing my finger joints. "Just scratching the surface."

I felt Ruger's elbow on the back of my seat. "Are you ever going to let me try her out?"

I shook my head, watching the red needle steadily climb the speedometer.

"Oh, come *on*."

I shrugged one shoulder. "You're drunk all the time, Ruger. Do you know how much I paid for this?"

"I'm *not* drunk all the time—"

"An arm and a friggin' leg," I finished, ignoring his defense. "Did you literally not even notice that I'm missing limbs? Now quit leaning on my seat."

"Ion, you *suck*."

I checked the mirrors again.

Maybe it had been a stupid bet to make; I couldn't decide. Standing in the parking lot of Club Scorpio earlier that night, watching Riley play with that stupid chain around his neck while he raved on about how fast the zombie-mobile could fly, it had been too irresistible of an idea to leave alone. So I'd thrown out the name of a local break where I knew Riley surfed. I'd seen him there on several occasions.

"Whoever pulls in last forks over two hundred. Deal?"

Riley had shrugged, twisting the chain. "Deal."

I knew the only way I could win the bet was if I really focused, and that was hard with West riding shotgun.

"Zombie's getting close," the girl in the backseat announced, letting her window down. The air swept in like a hurricane.

Riley's car shot ahead before I had a chance to react. I heard West curse and mutter something about how we were all going to die.

I stepped hard on the gas. "No one's dying but Riley."

West leaned back into the headrest. "Why the hell am I living with you guys?"

I heard Ruger laugh under his breath. "I was about to ask the same question."

My focus shot to the speedometer again. One ten and I was still staring into taillights.

"Come on," I muttered, resting my forearms on the steering wheel as I waited for the long familiar stretch I knew was coming up. I was counting down the seconds in my head, watching the lights edge tauntingly ahead.

"Dude, you're losing him."

"I'll have him back after this stretch. Shut up."

I wasn't convinced, but I tried to sound the part. I started watching for my exit; the expressway lights were turning into star trails around us. West's breathing was beginning to sound suspiciously pre–heart attack.

"I hope you brought cash." I felt Ruger's elbow again. "How much was this one?"

I would have reached back and smacked him had I not been so focused on the taillights in front of me.

I hated those taillights. I hated how I always seemed to be just a step behind Riley, whether in races or in life. I hated the feeling of inadequacy that was slowly rising in my chest. I was maxing out the engine of my beautiful car, and I could tell she didn't appreciate it.

I squinted at the rear window of Riley's car in front of me. I could vaguely see his silhouette. I tried to divert my thoughts, to concentrate. I was going as fast as the engine would allow, yet I could still feel her accelerating.

I glanced down at the speedometer, watching the needle waver slightly, then sink steadily back to a docile ninety. Eighty, seventy. Then back up to one ten.

"How fast are you going?" West was starting to panic.

I didn't respond to his question. The sound of his voice faded and died along with everything else, abandoning my heartbeat to center stage. I snapped out of it just in time to make the exit—bulleting past Riley.

Ruger let out a low whistle. "That, gentlemen, is how it's done."

I lost my head for the rest of the ride. My concentration zeroed in on slowing us down enough to stop. My speedometer was at five miles per hour when I must have been going seventy. Thankfully I was the only one who noticed. Ruger was drunk and West had his head between his knees.

Silently coaching myself to relax, I cut sharply into the beach parking lot. I let out the breath I'd been holding as I shifted into park. I could feel my heartbeat warring inside my chest.

Riley pulled up alongside me, getting out after a long hesitation. I rolled my window down as soon as I had caught my breath.

"What the hell was that?" he said, throwing his arms vaguely in no particular direction. "How fast were you going?"

"I wasn't paying attention," I replied, steadying my voice. "But you owe me two hundred bucks."

Riley stared me down with narrowed eyes, but after a moment he fished a couple hundred-dollar bills out of his pocket and threw them at me.

"Whatever." He took a couple of steps backward. "That thing isn't street legal, is it?"

"Didn't your momma ever teach you to lose with dignity?"

"Did yours ever teach you to shut the hell up?"

Ruger laughed as I put the window up again. I could still feel Riley's gaze burning holes in the back of my head when I pulled out of the sand-sprayed parking lot and onto the street.

"That was so sick," Ruger drawled, elbowing my seat. "The look on his face."

I didn't reply, trying to focus as I navigated the narrow streets.

"How fast were you going anyway?" he asked. "I thought this thing maxed at one thirteen?"

"It does."

"Then what the—"

"Riley must have let off by accident or something." I cut Ruger off before he could finish, feeling a mild sweat beginning to prickle across my spine. "Illusionary speed."

"Illusionary," he reiterated, sounding skeptical. "Sure."

My heart rate had calmed slightly when I pulled into the driveway of the house we were renting. Dawn was slowly making its entrance across the skyline, washing the city in a shade of indigo. It reminded me of how physically taxed I was—how attractive sleep sounded.

The trance was only momentary. The car jolted, yanking me back into the present and choreographing the disheartening sound of steel against steel.

"How could you miss that?" West hissed, tearing off his seatbelt.

I swore under my breath and got out to evaluate the damage. West followed suit.

I stared silently for a few moments before simply saying, "I didn't see it."

West turned and gaped at me. "You didn't *see it?*"

"I was *distracted.*"

I had made a mental note when we'd first moved in to never cross the neurotic old guy who lived next door. I knew nothing about him beyond the fact that he kept an eye on us. Now I was standing there in the driveway, staring down at the ugly crater my Mustang had just punched into the rear bumper of his sandy-brown station wagon.

West exhaled in disgust, adjusting his glasses. "Well, have fun explaining that to the old man. You're on your own."

I swore and kicked my front tire. Visions of the red needle came darting back into my mind's eye, the unnatural way it had danced over the various speeds, accelerating beyond what I knew the car was capable of. My roommates had vanished indoors, though I scarcely noticed that they had left. Ruger's date paused on the porch steps.

"Hey," she said quietly. "You okay, Ion?"

I gave a nod, refocusing.

"Yeah," I said. "Yeah, I'm fine."

There was a pause. I heard her soft footsteps a second later as she ascended the rest of the stairs, then the door sighing closed, leaving me standing alone in the driveway.

When I looked down at my hands, they were shaking.

CHAPTER TWO

The window above the kitchen sink overlooked our neighbor's front yard. I found myself standing in front of it the morning following the accident, staring out as the coffee brewed quietly.

In contrast to the sandpit that was our front lawn, the old man's yard was meticulous. A white fence ran along the edges of his manicured lawn, wisteria spiraled up into a trellis at one end, and a bed of vegetables grew alongside it. My roommates and I occasionally stole tomatoes over the fence when he wasn't around. That was actually how I had met him. He'd caught me sneaking a beefsteak and asked where I was from. I'd answered "northern California" and apologized for stealing, though he didn't seem to care. He had asked my name and whether I was a student at the college. Odd as it was, I hadn't asked a thing in return, not even his name. Later I realized that there was a question I wish I *had* asked.

Every other morning a girl who looked around my age came and watered his front lawn. I would see her through the window, standing there with a garden hose in her hand. She entered and exited the house like she lived there, but as far as any of us knew, she didn't. No one saw her otherwise. Ruger had suggested once that maybe she was the guy's illegitimate child, but I wasn't convinced.

Whatever the case, she was a thing to behold, standing there in the seven a.m. sunlight with her thumb pressed over the opening of the garden hose, sending up a spray. I'd never had an excuse to approach her until that morning. Fender benders don't necessarily make for great conversation starters, but I gave it my best shot. I walked over to the fence, cup of coffee in hand.

"Hey," I said, clearing my throat. "I, uh, I came to apologize to your father. I hit his car last night."

She didn't look away from the grass.

"It was really late. I was tired," I continued. "I guess I didn't see it until the last second. I was hoping to talk to him—is he around?"

"He's not," she replied bluntly. "But he asked me to give you a message."

I felt one of my eyebrows rise. "He did?"

"He asked that you come by later to talk."

"I have classes this afternoon." I paused. "Is tonight okay? Maybe seven?"

She nodded.

"How did he know I would be over here talking to you?"

"It's not important," she said, and finally glanced in my direction. "And he's not my father."

I studied the tattoos around her biceps. She must have noticed, because after a second she looked away again.

"Sorry, I just assumed he was—"

"I understand." She refocused on the grass.

I glanced down at the mug in my hands. "What's his name?"

"You can call him Sensei," she said.

"Sensei?"

She simply nodded.

"And, uh," I faltered, "what's your name?"

She had made her way over to the spigot, where she leaned down to turn the water off. Her glistening cocoa brown hair slipped to her left shoulder. "You ask a lot of questions."

I could tell she was just about done, but I thought I would take my chances. "Can you give me a heads-up—is he totally irate over it?"

"Over the car?"

"Yeah. I mean, it's a pretty bad dent," I said. "I wouldn't blame him, but I do want to stay intact."

She didn't seem amused. "I've never seen Sensei irate."

I squinted at her through the sunshine. "Why is he called Sensei?"

"Because he's a teacher."

"What does he teach?"

She started coiling the hose around her arm like a long green boa constrictor. "If you have questions, why not just ask him?"

"Maybe I think you have better answers?" I fumbled lamely.

"Answers don't change if they're truthful," she said, switching the coil to the opposite arm. "They're the same from my lips or his. And it would be better for you to hear about it from him."

I didn't understand why it was a big deal *who* I heard it from, but I complied.

"I'll let him know you'll be here," she said, in a tone that told me the discussion was over.

West was in the kitchen when I let myself back into the house. He looked up from where he was hunched at the table.

"Where have you been?" he asked, not sounding particularly interested. "Your coffee sucks, by the way."

I threw myself down into a chair across from him. "I was next door, talking to the girl."

"*The* girl?"

I nodded.

"And?"

I shrugged. "She's not his daughter, but it sounds like she lives there."

"Is she related to him?"

"No idea. I didn't even get her name."

West shot me a look. "Aren't you smooth."

"She wouldn't give it to me," I said. "I went over there to talk to the dude about his car."

"Did you get *his* name?"

"Sensei."

"Is that a name or a title?"

"Your guess is as good as mine," I said, getting up to refill my mug. "I'm assuming I'll find out tonight. I have to go back over there to talk to him about the car."

"Does he work during the day or something?"

I shrugged again, pouring the coffee. "Who knows. His car was still there, so unless he walks…"

"Strange."

I stole a glance through the window again, but this time she was gone. The wet lawn glistened in the sunlight.

"Yeah," I said finally. "It is kind of weird."

I didn't have time to think about it after that. I spent the rest of the morning locked in my room, bent over an agglomeration of papers at my desk.

"You're normal," I told myself under my breath. "You are normal, Ion. Your life is normal. Nothing is going to happen."

My thoughts were a contradiction. They swelled like furious waves and threw themselves against the inside of my chest. It was an all-out battle to keep my mind from wandering back to the night before: the red needle, the bipolar speeds, the inconsistencies, the cold sweats. I tried to block it all out, but it was next to impossible. There was no option for coexistence—it was me or them. I would either win or die trying. I left for campus that afternoon with an exhausted mind, but a will of iron. I focused in class, went through the motions, and came out unscathed. For a little while I felt like I could breathe again.

As I cut back across campus, a pair of clicking high heels fell into sync with my gait. When I looked up, recognition came flooding in immediately— even if her face wasn't half undead.

"Quite a show you put on last night, Ion." Mel, Riley's girlfriend, grinned like it pleased her that my voice had just committed suicide in my throat.

I felt my spine tense up at the mention of the night before. "How do you mean?"

"Don't give me that," she said. "I was riding with Riley. I saw the whole thing."

"I didn't see you in the car with him."

"Riley was breathing murder on the way home."

I laughed uncomfortably. "He's also going to put me through a blender if he catches us talking."

Mel laughed a little. "I don't think you realize how much you get under his skin."

"Yeah? Well, we're even, then."

"Are you jealous of him?" she asked.

I shook my head.

"Well, he's jealous of you."

I glanced over at her as she tossed her long dark hair over her shoulder.

"He thinks I'm attracted to you."

I considered this for a moment. "How accurate is this suspicion of his?"

Mel gave me her soft doe eyes for a fleeting moment before shrugging her shoulders. "I don't know, Ion. Last night sort of clinched it."

I subconsciously scanned the crowd as we walked. Riley was the last person on earth that I wanted to accidentally run into. So without saying a word, I deviated from the walkway. The green was dotted elegantly with some ancient-looking oak trees, which offered us some cover.

"Do you have any plans tonight?" she asked.

My mind was reeling. Only moments before, everything had been relatively normal, and now I was staring down the possibility of a date with one of the finest girls on campus. Everything inside me said yes, except the waves behind my rib cage. I could feel a storm brewing there.

"Uh, I kind of have…" I dug my hand back through my hair, thinking fast. "Homework."

Mel looked taken aback. "Can't you do that, like… later?"

Of course I could do it later. What was wrong with me?

"I, um…" I swallowed back the rest of the sentence before it had a chance to come out. "Wow, yes. Of course. I'm sorry, my brain is just kind of shot right now. What do you have in mind?"

"We could hang out at your place…"

I grabbed glances out of my peripheral vision as my steps slowed and halted. We were concealed behind the enormity of an oak. The leaves whispered overhead as I turned and looked at her; the low light filtered down in tired pastels.

"Mel, Riley's going to kill you."

"Would you quit thinking about Riley?" She sighed. "You're obsessed."

"I'm not obsessed, I'm realistic," I corrected.

The corners of her lips curved into a smile. "Then stop being realistic."

Mel was fairly tiny, but her heels brought her up to almost my height, making it easy for her to lean in and push a taunting kiss onto my lips. I felt her fingers closing around the collar of my shirt.

"I have something at seven," I said when she pulled back and separated us again. "Do you mind waiting at my place?"

"Do you mind giving me a ride?"

"Oh, I totally mind."

She laughed, and I felt my hesitation start to crumble.

I checked the time on my phone. I was assuming the meeting next door would be quick—and once that was behind me, I would have the rest of the night with Mel. The plan seemed safe—not to mention highly appealing. I was just hoping she didn't ask why I was going over to the neighbor's house, because the fender bender would be an embarrassing explanation.

"So where do you live?" she asked as we entered the coolness of the parking garage. "I hardly ever see you around."

We headed for the aisle where I had parked. The sounds of our footsteps intertwined and echoed off the cement walls around us.

"I rent a place with a couple of friends," I explained. "A few miles from here."

I spotted my Mustang. Mel began a reply as we approached my car, but I stopped listening, coming to an abrupt halt as the sudden feeling of a presence behind me drifted into my consciousness. As I turned, a hand clamped down on the back of my neck and threw me face-first into the hood of the car next to me; the air came rushing out of my lungs as I impacted, and I heard Mel scream. Two hands twisted my arms hard behind my back, and for a second I was too winded to react, but then I threw myself backwards, body-slamming my attacker up against the car that was parked alongside mine.

He swore, shoving me forward. Mel inserted herself between us before he could reach for me again.

"Riley, just stop it, okay?" she yelled, getting in his face. "My god—do you *ever* quit?"

Riley shook his head. "Mel, you don't understand—you have no idea what you're getting yourself into."

She back-stepped closer to me as if I would somehow prove to be a fortress. I was afraid to let her get that close. I could feel the vibration coming into my hands again.

"Mel, listen to me." He stepped closer, putting a hand on her shoulder. She pushed it away. "You can't go with him."

Mel let out a cool, sarcastic laugh. "Who do you think you are, Riley? You can't tell me what to do."

"Mel, you don't know what he's like." Riley's eyes locked on mine. A sick feeling was beginning in the pit of my stomach.

"No." Mel gave her boyfriend a shove. "*You* don't know him."

"That's my point!" he retorted. "No one does."

I nudged Mel gently out of the way. "That's a lie. Lots of people know me."

"Yeah? Then why doesn't anyone know where the hell you come from?" he asked.

"I'm from northern California," I replied, trying to keep my voice down.

"Really?"

I nodded.

Riley stared at me. "Because you're entered in the university's system as being from New York."

My heart plummeted in my chest. Mel turned to give me a look.

"The story changes all the time, doesn't it, Ion?" Riley looked steadily into my face. I glanced away. "I knew from day one there was something strange about you. You've never given anyone a straight answer about anything."

I closed my eyes, pulling in a breath. I could feel heat making its way up into my face. "There's nothing wrong with me."

"You sure about that?" Riley's voice rose as he took a step closer. "Because I've heard otherwise."

I opened my eyes again and my gaze locked on his.

He nodded. "I know why they kicked you out of the last school."

"Riley, please." Mel's voice was unsteady. "*Stop.*"

"I wasn't going to make a big deal out of it—I wasn't going to be 'that guy.'" He brought his voice down slightly. "But I asked questions. I know what you did."

"Asked who?"

"You don't need to know."

I felt my jaw tighten. "You don't know *anything* about what happened there."

He was close—too close. I looked away again, trying to keep my brain distracted, but it was impossible.

"I know that someone almost died," he said. "And I also know that if you do something to Mel—if you hurt her? So help me, I will kill you."

I took a step closer. "Mel has a right to choose who she wants to be with. Maybe that person isn't you."

"You're changing the subject."

I shook my head. "I'm calling this what it is—you're jealous."

Mel had slipped a little closer to the Mustang, which was parked only a couple of cars away. All I had to do was maintain my cool long enough to get out of there.

"Jealous?" Riley reiterated the word like it was foreign. "Jealous of *you?*"

I felt Mel's eyes on the back of my neck.

Riley's lip curled into a cold smile. "Why would I be jealous of a freak like you?"

The word hit its intended target like a bullet. That word I'd heard over and over again all my life.

Freak.

I felt the softness of Mel's hand on my lower back, I heard the beginnings of her telling me that we should go. But it faded to an inaudible blend of white noise and then nothing. The darkness inside Riley's eyes absorbed my focus—it locked there.

Almost of its own accord, my arm drew back and I felt my fist launch forward into his face. It landed on his jaw.

The impact should have been hard, yes. It should have sent his body into the car behind him. It should have left a few bruises. But instead, the force sent Riley over the hood of the car and hurtling into the windshield of the one parked behind it, blowing out the glass.

CHAPTER THREE
Hawk

I could feel the light filtering down across my face and shoulders, pooling in warm patches to offset the coolness of the sheets. The softness of a familiar hand settled onto my shoulder, but I made no effort to open my eyes. I knew whose hand it was.

"You did well today," he said, aware of my consciousness. "You intrigued him."

"He seemed a little intimidated, to be honest with you," I murmured. "But I gave it my best shot."

"You were very normal."

A laugh slipped past my lips. "I wouldn't go that far. He's a flirt, and my skills in that area are a little rusty—I haven't done it in the past century."

"He agreed to the meeting," Sensei continued. "You were successful."

I rolled over onto my back, opening my eyes to take in the softness of his familiar face. Asian, slightly tousled dark hair, and eyes as blue and bright as the sky beyond the window. His lips were turned into a warm smile.

Sensei—*my* Sensei. We all saw him differently, each one of us. We were students, we were learning, and so he met each of us where we were. But this was how I saw him.

"Well, he's yours now, so enjoy." I mumbled.

"You're not quite finished with him yet." He said. "I have a new assignment for you."

My eyelids closed again. "Sensei…"

"When I meet with him tonight," Sensei went on before I could say more. "I'm going to ask him to come by the house tomorrow morning."

"To test him?"

He nodded, rising from the edge of my mattress where he had been seated. "I think you should be the one to do it."

I opened my eyes. "Must I?"

"It's entirely your decision."

I threw my sheets aside. "Why can't Fin do it? Or Gaia?"

"Because I am asking *you*."

I swung my feet to the floor and sat on the edge of the bed for a moment. "What do you want me to do with him? Can I light something on fire?"

Sensei opened the window. The birds were calling louder now. "I think you overestimate his current abilities."

I grunted. "So you're giving me a complete fledgling—not even."

"Ion is an opportunity for you to exercise gentleness, Hawk," he said. "Be gentle but be firm. I trust you to make the decision."

"But why me?" I asked. "You're the one who got him this far. You're the one who set up the accident and created the obligation for him to see you."

Sensei was quiet for a moment. "Are you intimidated by making the decision yourself?"

"I am," I said.

"Good." Sensei turned from the window to look at me. "Then you're ready."

I heaved a sigh. "That line sounds better in fiction, Sensei. I have no experience in slider identification. I *train* students; I don't go find them."

For a moment Sensei merely looked at me, saying nothing verbally, yet almost everything under the sun with his eyes.

"What is experience?"

"Practical contact with and observation of facts or events," I recited, exhaling the words. "And something I'm fresh out of when it comes to selection."

"Then we will create experience for you, dear one." Sensei smiled. "I suggest you wash, dress, and meet me on the platform."

At length I nodded, and Sensei let himself quietly out of the room. I sat there for a moment longer before going to the window to watch him descend, but he had already gone. The narrow mossy strip that separated my apartment from the drop was void of life. A wind washed up from the abyss below, running its fingers through the chimes that hung from the woodwork.

I crossed the room, casting a brief glance in the direction of the wardrobe standing opposite. The doors eased obediently open as I approached. I dressed and paused in front of the glass wall to tame my hair. Eyes that couldn't decide if they wanted to be green or hazel brown scrutinized me from the other side of the glass.

Sensei had told me there was something beyond the inconsistency of those eyes. Something beyond my skin and my hair and my tattoos. Something he called "the warrior within"; something I looked for each morning in the glass, but could never seem to find.

I went to the large window Sensei had opened and slipped my legs over the sill. I sat there for a moment, feeling the breeze rushing across my skin. Out of habit, my eyes started scoping out the drop yawning beneath my bare feet, the various levels carved into the cliff side below, and the amount of activity on each protruding platform. I could see the dormitory, a collection of basketlike pods woven together by sets of rope bridges several hundred feet below. The students scurried from each like tiny indistinguishable ants, making their way toward the large thatched roof that covered the training platform. I heard the wind as it met the tree line twelve yards below, a sound like the quiet sighs of a violin.

I closed my eyes, focused in, and let my body leave the sill.

The free fall rushed up around me like a hurricane, howling in my ears like a soul lost in the darkness as my skin caught fire. My hidden identity, whatever that actually looked like, seemed to stretch its wings, finding some whisper of expression in those moments. A melting sensation swept in with the distortion of trees as I plummeted past them, falling parallel with the cliff side that now seemed to rocket above me. The sound of the wind slicing through the spaces between my fingers softened to a delicate whisper, and the warmth fled my body as quickly as it had captured it.

I burst into the updraft.

Everything was still when I opened my eyes and gazed downward again. Everything was sharp, defined. The wind wove softly through my feathers and pressed my body upwards. I spotted the training platform again and turned to cut down toward it. The pure, thin air parted around me like water as I landed on the railing, talons first.

Fin was kneeling beside the rail farther down, hunched over a tray of fresh soil. I noticed a scattering of seeds in his cupped hand. He looked up as I landed.

"Taking your time today," he said. His warm Irish accent took the edge off his words.

I tilted my head to the side, giving him a questioning look.

Fin motioned vaguely with his elbow. "Sensei was here waiting for you, but he left."

I watched as he began pushing seeds into the soil with his thumb, creating a staggered row, and then lightly covering the holes.

"I said, 'Sensei, are you waiting around for Hawk again?' and he said, 'As always, Fin.'" He began slowly twirling his index finger over the places where the seeds were. "I said, 'Can't you get a cage for that bird of yours, Sensei? It would be a little more convenient.' He said I was a genius, but I told him I was already aware of the fact."

I watched him bite back a crafty grin and wanted to roll my eyes.

"Seriously, though, he *was* looking for you." He cleared his throat. "He was headed for the portal. Something about the LA house."

I glanced in the direction he was referencing, having learned nothing new from the information he'd sprinkled into his satire.

"He's been talking about that place a lot lately." Fin was still looping his finger around in the air just above the tray, where small seedlings were beginning to break the surface. "It sounds like something is going on there."

I shot him a pointed look.

"Oh, come on, Hawk," he drawled, and spun his finger faster over one seedling in particular, giving it an impressive growth spurt. "I'm just curious."

I stretched my wings back and allowed the same sensation that had overtaken me in the air to come flooding back in. I slipped down off the railing and shook my legs slightly as my once-again human feet met the platform.

"Then don't be curious," I said, wiggling my toes. "Because I can't answer you."

Fin's finger froze in its hover over one of the sprouts as he gazed intently at me.

"What are you staring at?"

Fin refocused. "Oh, I don't know. The whole... human-bird thing—it still kind of gets me."

"*Shifting*, Fin."

"Yes." He grinned. "That."

I smiled a little and turned to leave.

"So you're literally not going to even give me a hint?" he said to my retreating back.

"No."

"You're involved this time, though?"

"Perhaps."

"Hawk—"

I lifted a hand. "Enjoy your gardening, Fin."

The rest of the platform was buzzing with activity. Most of the students were present and sectioned off into their appropriate groups for the day, sorted by rank of experience. I greeted my fellow students with a polite nod. At the end of the platform there was a hall lined with windows on either side, and at the end of the hall there was a single, unglamorous door with a brass handle.

The space inside was more like a cave than anything else, a small but ancient cavern that had been hewn into the cliff side. Geodes of no fiscal value studded the rough stone walls like upholstery nails in fabric, reflecting prisms of cool, white light as I slipped into the tiny empty space and shut the door behind me.

I closed my eyes and breathed for a moment, listening to the sound echo in the hollowness of the space. I began pacing my inhales.

"Focus."

California. Los Angeles, California. Sun-bleached streets and palm-lined avenues. Melbourne Street, six houses down. The sandy-brown station wagon parked in the driveway.

"Inside the house—"

White walls and empty space with almost no furniture. An empty living room, a deserted kitchen with only a table and chairs, and then a vacant hallway. At the end of the hallway, the broom-less broom closet...

"—with one bare bulb suspended from the ceiling."

Without opening my eyes, I reached up and grabbed the drawstring. I tugged, and the warmth of yellow tungsten light flooded down on me.

When I opened my eyes, I was in the broom closet. In the house in Los Angeles.

My hand went to the brass knob, and I let myself out into the hallway.

Sensei was a minimalist when it came to lodgings, furniture, clothes, and other commodities, but where food was concerned, his minimalism ended. The kitchen was, by habit, my first stop, and I found the refrigerator stuffed with exotic things like mac and cheese, pizza slices, Japanese takeout, and tubs of artificial "whipped topping." For someone who didn't require food consumption for survival, he had certainly acquired a taste for it.

"Hoarder," I muttered, and snatched one of the plastic containers of white foam. I found myself a spoon and wandered out into the front yard. Sensei was gathering tomatoes into a basket.

"Is the kid home from school yet?" I asked, squinting at the neighboring house through the late afternoon sunlight.

"His name is Ion," Sensei said. "And no, he's not yet back from his classes. Why do you ask?"

"Because I'm about to stand here and consume a container of whipped topping, and that might be awkward for him to watch," I explained, prying at the container. "And he does watch—I've seen him."

"He watches because he is curious."

"He watches because he's a simple-minded, non-transdimensional male."

Sensei chuckled beneath his broad sunhat. He placed another tomato into the basket.

"He only ever sees me when I'm watering the lawn," I went on. "Not exactly intriguing stuff."

"You disapprove of Ion."

"I neither approve nor disapprove of him, Sensei," I said. "I don't know him. But I know you, so I trust your judgment."

"Stay with me tonight and evaluate him for yourself."

I succeeded finally with the lid. "I would rather not have to put up with him tonight, since I'll have to deal with him shortly anyway. Tomorrow morning California time, right?"

"If he agrees, yes."

"How are you going to set this up, exactly?"

"What would you suggest?"

I cautiously sampled the white foam. "Didn't he steal some tomatoes once? Maybe you could have him harvest some. Plant new ones. Something like that."

"It's a bit late for planting, but that has potential."

"I guess I can wait around for him with you," I said eventually, swirling the spoon around in the container. "I can't promise I'll stay human, though."

"Hawk."

"*Kidding.*"

"Choose one, and stick with it." He moved the basket to the next plant. "You shouldn't want to frighten him."

I couldn't help but grin slightly. "I know, Sensei."

A pause inserted itself for a moment. I ate the whipped topping in contemplative silence.

"If he really is a slider," I said finally, "shouldn't he be used to the unexpected by now?"

Sensei straightened, dusting off his hands.

"One cannot grow used to something they've yet to acknowledge," he said. "And how can one acknowledge something they've been told is an impossibility?"

I studied my teacher's face for a moment before slowly shaking my head. I sank down onto the lawn and sat cross-legged.

"In this dimension, it wasn't long ago that it was believed an impossibility to run a mile in less than four minutes," Sensei continued, mopping his brow. "Until someone did."

I squinted up at him. "And?"

"*And* less than fifty days later, someone else did the same," he replied. "And then someone else, ad infinitum. Something is only impossible in one's mind until it is achieved, and then it is no longer impossible."

He paused here, seeming to consider the matter. "It was never impossible to begin with."

CHAPTER FOUR

Ion

The sound of shattering glass shook me out of my stupor. I heard Mel let go of an exhale behind me.

Riley rolled over the hood of the car and hit the ground on the opposite side, propelled by the momentum the punch had created. His lip was split open, and his face was bloody. Splatters of crimson soaked through his T-shirt.

I wanted to say that I hadn't meant to do it, but that would have been a lie. I wanted to run, but I couldn't seem to move.

"Riley, I—"

He cut me off before I could go on. "Are you talking to me? Seriously?" His words sounded thick.

"Riley, I didn't—"

Riley grabbed a handful of broken glass and hurled it in my direction, apparently oblivious to the new cuts that opened on his hand. My thoughts were coming to me as if through water, and because of it I ducked too late. A glinting shard sliced down across my brow like the blade of a knife.

"Riley, *stop!*" Mel screamed as my hands instinctively covered my face.

"Stop?" Riley was livid. "Mel, did you see what he just did?"

The outburst must have attracted some attention, because I heard a new voice asking what was going on, then Riley yelling a reply, but I couldn't make out the exact words. The sounds around me were blending together, distorting. I had melted to my knees, my energy going down like lights in a storm.

In the chaos, I was able to somehow make out fragments of a voice announcing that they were calling for security, and the next thing I felt was two hands on my shoulders. Two soft, small hands.

"Ion, get up."

I couldn't process the words—I had no idea who was talking to me. My body was there, but my mind was somewhere else.

"Get up."

The hands pulled me to my feet and started guiding me forward. I squinted through the blood that was beginning to blur my vision, then finally shut my eyes altogether. I heard a car door open and a second later I fell into the passenger seat—I could feel that there was no steering wheel in front of me. Someone got in on the driver's side.

"Give me the keys."

"They're in my pocket."

One of the hands reached in and dug them out. I heard the engine start.

I reached back over my shoulder blades and pulled off my shirt, using it to soak up the blood that was still spilling from the cut across my face. I felt sunlight on my skin after only a few moments of motion, telling me we were out of the parking garage. Voices outside yelled for us to stop, but we didn't.

I swore under my breath; my senses were returning just enough that I could finally feel the pain in my face. I shot a glance in the direction of the hands on the steering wheel.

"Why are you helping me?"

Mel didn't answer right away; instead she asked a question. "Where do you live?"

I gave her the directions as she drove, keeping the balled-up shirt pressed to the left side of my brow. For a while she didn't speak, but when we stopped at the first red light, she exploded.

"What the hell went on back there, Ion?" She stared at me as if she'd never seen me before. "You could have killed Riley—do you realize that? He could have *died.*"

"I know," I said quietly. "I'm sorry."

Mel relaxed back into the driver's seat. "Ion, tell me what's going on."

"I can't, Mel."

The light went green and she stepped on the gas. "Why not?"

"It's not…" The words were splattered everywhere on the inside of my skull. I couldn't find anything I was looking for. "I don't know why. It's not something you could understand—it's not something anyone could understand."

She glanced over at me again, her eyes still whirlwinds. "Ion, is there… really something wrong with you?"

My body tensed up at the question. I had no idea how to respond.

"Why are you helping me?" I asked again. "Aren't you afraid of…" I didn't finish.

"I probably should be." Mel slipped the steering wheel into a smooth turn. "But I'm not."

I couldn't decide if she was brave or stupid. Either way, I was afraid of being in the car with her—being close to her. I was afraid of what could happen if she touched me. I was *terrified.*

"Riley was calling security," she said finally as she turned down my street. "I didn't want them to find you like that."

"Why? I deserved it."

"Yeah, I know," she agreed. "But I like you, so I'll do something stupid for you."

Mel slowed the Mustang halfway down the street and asked which house was mine. I pointed it out, and she pulled into the driveway with a little more grace than I had the previous night. As she killed the engine, I felt my body relax for the first time since I'd seen Riley catapult over the hood of the car.

"Let me see your cut—" Mel turned and reached for my face.

"Don't." I pulled away. "Don't touch me."

She said nothing for a few seconds, though I could feel her eyes on me.

"Are your roommates home?"

"Not this early."

Mel opened the driver's side door and got out. I heard her footsteps coming around to my side and a moment later my door popped open.

"Come on," she said, nodding for me to get out of the car. "Let's get you cleaned up."

I dropped my house key into her hand as we approached the front door. I glanced over my shoulder to the neighbor's to see if anyone had observed us, but to my relief all was still quiet. The curtains were drawn shut over the windows.

Mel opened the door and stepped inside, prompting me to follow. I gave the house next door one last glance before I closed the door behind us.

The kitchen was bathed in sunlight. Quiet and completely vacant.

I pulled one of the chairs out from the table and fell into it while Mel soaked a handful of paper towels under the faucet.

"Is it still bleeding?"

I pulled the shirt away from my face slightly to check. I started thinking about the possibility of stitches when I noticed how much blood had soaked into the fabric.

"Yeah."

Mel wrung out the wad of paper towels and walked over to the table, pulling up a seat directly in front of me.

"Let me see."

I shifted my gaze up to meet hers. "Just... don't touch."

Mel gave me a look. "What is it with this 'no touch' thing?"

"Didn't you see what happened in the parking garage?" I dropped the balled-up shirt into my lap. "You saw what happened."

"But you *punched* Riley."

"That's not the point."

"You might need stitches," She said, gently pressing the paper towels to my forehead. "I'm touching you, by the way... I'm so scared."

She gave me that grin again, and I rolled my eyes.

"It doesn't always happen," I told her as she brushed the hair back off my forehead. "I just don't want to hurt you, okay?"

"Would you hurt me?"

"Not on purpose."

The vibration had finally left my hands. For her sake, I was grateful that my brain was too exhausted to focus.

"You're not going to tell me, are you?" she said.

I studied her face for a moment before replying. Her eyes were close to mine and they were huge. They were the kind of eyes that tried to bring shipwrecks to the surface.

"There's nothing I can tell you, Mel," I said finally. "I just…"

I didn't finish and Mel didn't push me for an answer. I started becoming aware of her hand still on my forehead. Then the noises of cars passing outside.

Cars.

My mind went back to the ugly dent in the station wagon and the appointment I had with my neighbor. I kicked myself inwardly.

"What time is it?" I was almost afraid to hear the answer.

I took the paper towels in my own hand so Mel could check her phone.

"Seven."

"Have I stopped bleeding?"

Mel shook her head.

"I have to go talk to my neighbor about something real quick," I said cautiously. "Could you tape me up enough to go do that?"

For a second she just stared. "Are you serious right now?"

"Yeah. It's… uh…" I trailed off, searching for the right words. "It's kind of important."

———————

When I rang the old man's doorbell, it was half past seven. It wasn't a normal doorbell; it was a long weathered rope attached to a misshapen iron bell that hung from an overhead support beam. I was doubtful that anyone inside would hear the low clangs it produced, but after a second a shrill, animalistic cry erupted from the other side of the door.

I heard the sound of a bolt retracting, wings flapping, and then the door creaked open on its hinges.

"What made you late?" His voice was flat, completely unsympathetic, even when he noticed my face. "Fight?"

Sensei was average in height, but somehow still managed to loom over me with an Everest presence. He was Asian, with a gray, receding hairline, bare feet, and faded attire—practically the definition of nonaggressive, yet there was something about the steadiness of his gaze that sent my confidence running for cover. There was a hawk perched on his right shoulder.

"Yes," I replied. "Sorry."

He motioned for me to follow him inside.

"There is no excuse for lateness," he said, leading me past the small empty living room and into the kitchen. "You could have been on time if you had desired."

"Well, I'm sorry, sir," I said, squinting in the dimness. "I was busy getting my face slit open."

Sensei didn't respond to this comment. He sat down at the head of the table, the hawk still on his shoulder, and motioned for me to follow suit. He leaned back, folded his hands over his stomach, and studied me for what felt like a small eternity before saying anything.

"Ion, correct?"

I nodded, trying not to stare at the hawk still perched on his shoulder.

"Ion." He repeated my name. "You hit my car."

He announced this as if it would be a revelation—like I wasn't already aware that I had plowed into his station wagon the night before.

"Yes, sir." I gave a meager nod. "I'm aware. In fact, I'm here to discuss that with you."

I leaned forward slightly to reach into my back pocket. "I have my insurance information—"

"That will not be necessary."

I paused. "What will not be?"

Sensei gestured with his hand. "The papers—your information. I do not need it."

"You don't need it?" I repeated. "What do you mean? I thought—"

"I already took care of the dent."

I was the one staring now. "What is it that you want from me, then? I'm confused."

"You and your friends have taken tomatoes from my garden, yes?"

"Tomatoes? Uh, well—"

Sensei lifted a hand to stop me. "Yes or no?"

I rubbed the back of my neck awkwardly. "Yes."

"I have a place in the backyard where the soil is turned," he said. "To repay me, you will plant tomatoes there."

"Are you serious?"

Sensei nodded. "I have a dozen plants that I have started from seed. Come back tomorrow morning and transplant them."

"That's all you want me to do—plant tomatoes?"

He nodded.

I couldn't believe what he was telling me. I was getting off so easy, it was almost sad.

I leaned back in my seat. "Alright, sir. If that's what you want."

The hawk made a small throaty noise and adjusted its perch on Sensei's shoulder.

"My student will be here tomorrow," he continued formally. "She will assist."

"Your student?"

He nodded, and my mind immediately flashed back to that morning. The girl who had watered the front lawn. The girl with the tattoos, who had neither answered my questions nor given me her name.

The mystery.

"Sensei, your student…" I began. "Does she live here?"

He didn't answer right away. I could practically feel his eyes burning into the cut across my eyebrow.

"She does," he replied finally.

"She said you were a teacher. Is that true?"

Sensei was still staring at my face. My injury felt magnified under the intensity of his gaze. "Yes, it is."

"What is it that you teach?"

"What is it you need to learn?"

I felt myself laugh slightly. "Oh, I don't need to learn anything. I was just curious."

Sensei lifted the hawk off his shoulder and onto his hand, stroking its head. "Everyone needs to learn something."

"Yes," I answered slowly. "I know."

He was still looking at the bird. "Then what is it you need to learn?"

I thought about what he was saying for a second before opening my mouth to reply, but words didn't come. So I just sat there like an arrogant fool.

He smiled slightly, his attention not having diverted from the hawk. "Learning yourself would be a start."

I wasn't sure how to respond. Things were getting off track and I wasn't in the mood to listen to the advice of some strange old man who spoke in riddles and had a bird perched on his hand.

"What time should I come tomorrow?" I asked.

He reached up to stroke the bird's chest, looking at it like it would provide him with an answer.

"Dawn," he replied finally.

"Dawn?" I repeated, feeling suddenly half dead.

Sensei nodded. "Dawn."

I was mentally rehearsing what excuse I would give as I made my way back across the driveway. I couldn't remember the last time I had gotten myself out of bed at dawn, and I wasn't exactly excited to break that streak. Ruger's car was parked beside the house now, and our paths crossed as he was coming out of the house.

"Dude, where have you been?" he asked. "Some random girl broke in while you were out."

I rolled my eyes, passing him to head for the front door.

"Seriously, though," he continued over his shoulder. "You were over at the old guy's house again? What's up with that?"

"I hit his car, in case you forgot," I told him, taking the steps two at a time. "I had to, uh, go over insurance stuff with him."

There was no way I was telling him about the tomato thing. I slipped into the house before Ruger could continue the inquisition.

Mel was at the kitchen table, leaning on her elbows as she browsed her phone, one of her perfect legs draped over the other at the knee. She looked up as soon as I came in.

"How did it go?"

I paused at the sink to fill a glass. "Alright."

"What was so urgent?"

I'd been so preoccupied that I had forgotten she was bound to ask. My brain couldn't process anything fast enough to give her a normal answer.

"My neighbor's going away for a couple weeks and wanted to know if I would water his plants while he's gone," I lied, in the most pathetic way possible. "I promised I would tell him whether I could or not by tonight… so…"

I could feel Mel's stare.

"Your lying skills suck, you know."

I shut off the tap. "I'm aware."

I heard her push back her chair, then her approaching footsteps. I set the glass down on the countertop and turned around to let her loop her arms around my neck.

"Ruger told me how you hit your neighbor's car last night," she said, resting her forehead lightly on my chest.

"Of course he did."

She laughed a little.

"I was stupid," I said after a pause, gently resting my chin on the crown of her head. "I am stupid. I will probably continue to be stupid."

"You're not stupid."

I exhaled a neutral laugh. "Mel, I like you—really, I do. And because I do, I strongly suggest that you don't get mixed up with someone like me."

She looked up to meet my gaze. "What qualifies as getting mixed up with you?"

"Pretty much everything you're doing right now," I said, my voice coming out slightly quieter.

She bit her lower lip, grinning. "Yeah?"

I nodded slightly. Her immense brown eyes softened as they stared up into mine, and I started getting distracted by the contrast between her lashes and her skin. Then her expression changed.

"Ion, what happened to your face?" Mel's voice came out barely above a whisper.

I felt one of my eyebrows rise a little. "What do you mean what happened? You saw what happened."

"That's not what I mean." She reached up and touched the place where she'd bandaged my forehead. I felt her fingertips against my skin. "It's gone."

"What's gone?"

"Your cut," she said. "The bandage, the place where the glass hit—it's not there anymore."

I felt my muscles freeze up. "What?"

Mel shook her head, backing off slightly. "I don't know, Ion. This is weird."

I reached up and touched the place where the bandage covering the gash should have been, checking my fingertips for blood. They came back clean.

"Ion…"

I met Mel's gaze again. She was still staring at my forehead, searching for words. I didn't wait for her to finish.

Brushing past her, I cut across the room and started down the hall. When I reached my bedroom, I flung open the door and flipped on the lights to check myself in the mirror.

Mel was right—the cut was gone. There wasn't even a scratch.

"Ion, what's going on?" Mel's voice was quiet as she hesitated in the doorway. "How did—"

"I don't know, okay?" I cut her off before she could finish.

"How can you not know?"

"I need you to promise me something."

"What?"

She was in the room now, closer than I had expected. I took a step back to space us out.

"Mel, I don't…" I trailed off, struggling to think straight. "I don't know what's happening to me. But I need you to promise me that you won't tell anyone about this. No one can know. You have to promise me."

She was standing in front of me with that same expression I couldn't read, looking at me like I was a word she didn't know how to pronounce. "I'll promise if you answer me something first."

I said nothing and waited for her to continue.

"Where are you really from?" she asked, almost as if she was afraid to. "And why did you transfer?"

I felt my muscles tense again.

"Do you want the truth, Mel?" I asked. "Or do you want me to make up something that will preserve your image of who you think I am?"

I hadn't really expected her to respond, and she didn't. She waited for me to continue.

"To answer your first question," I began, pulling in a deep breath. "I honestly don't know where exactly I'm from."

For an instant there was a deathly silence. When Mel finally did speak, her voice sounded exactly as I would have imagined it.

"Ion, what are you talking about?"

Her eyes had wild things inside them.

"To answer your second question," I continued, ignoring her almost terrified expression. "You heard what Riley said. I transferred because I almost killed someone."

Mel didn't respond.

I turned back to look into the mirror, breaking the lock between our eyes. "Any other questions?"

CHAPTER FIVE
Hawk

After the conversation with Ion had ended and the door had closed behind him, two things happened. I shifted back into human form, and Sensei ordered Japanese food.

"Have you formed an opinion, Hawk?" he asked when we had finished and the dishes had been cleared.

I sucked in a breath and blew it back out again. "He's a little arrogant. But then, that's to be expected. He is, after all, a non-transdimensional male, as I pointed out before."

"That sounds more akin to judgment, dear one."

"Perhaps," I admitted. "But the dilemma remains that I know nothing about him beyond my prejudices, and I honestly can't understand what you see in him."

"I know, Hawk."

"You're the one who has been guarding him all these years," I said, leaning my elbows on the table. "Why is it so important that I be the one to make the decision?"

"Because it is."

I decided not to question him further.

"I'll do whatever you wish me to do, Sensei," I told him. "But I'll need something from you."

"Ask it."

"Everything you know about Ion," I said, putting heavy emphasis on the first word. "Where he's from, where he goes, whom he associates with, to whom he speaks and what he says—all of it. I want to know him as if he were my own son. That's the only way it can work."

Sensei nodded slowly. "I can give you all that I have."

"Give?"

This time he rose to retrieve something from a drawer, returning after a moment with a folder in his hands.

"Everything you want to know has been included here," he explained as I flipped it open. "Photographs, notations, paperwork, and so forth."

My gaze shot up to his. "You made this collection for your own reference? Over all these years?"

Sensei shook his head. "I do not require sight for analysis. But I knew you would not move unless you saw—hawk by nature."

I exhaled a tired laugh. "I'm underwhelmed by your opinion of my faith."

"You are a student, Hawk," he said. "Doubt is commendable."

Inside the folder I found an agglomeration of photos assembled linearly. Ion from age ten through nineteen. Tanned skin, messy dark brown hair, icy blue eyes, and never a smile. He was the kind that looked older than he actually was, according to human terms.

"A serious face," I commented, thumbing through the images. "Birthplace... unknown?" I shot Sensei a questioning glance.

"He was found."

I felt my eyebrows rise slightly. "Found?"

"A car was found abandoned in a ditch off a rural dirt road," Sensei explained. "The car had the appearance of one that had recently been in an accident, but there was no driver. The vehicle was empty, with the exception of the child that was found in the backseat."

The story was more colorful than I had anticipated.

"So he was a foundling, essentially," I concluded, turning to the next page. "How did he get from there to where he now finds himself?"

"His history is well recorded," Sensei said. "I will let it speak for itself."

I didn't argue. Instead I let him leave without further questioning and dug into the information he had provided me with.

The various notes and copies of legal documents explained that Ion had been taken in by foster parents, but then brought up in an institution for troubled youth in Detroit due to "complications with the family situation."

I stopped reading, feeling a chill breaking out over my skin. The story sounded all too familiar.

"Completed high school… earned a scholarship…" I spoke under my breath as I skimmed. "Began college in Chicago. Transferred due to complications. Resumed semester in New York. Transferred due to violent incident…"

Violent incident?

I flipped through the pages, but found no information or notes as to what this "incident" involved. That was where his story abruptly ended, leaving him in a mediocre school in good old LA.

I turned to a page labeled "Profile."

"Ion 'Jacobs'… biological surname unknown. Interests include parkour, Greek mythology, automobiles and pretty, young women." I paused to roll my eyes. That was predictable.

What I didn't predict was the next section.

"Incident history… injuries to students by thought perpetration." I continued reading, muttering aloud. "Abnormal behavior by self-induced thought perpetration; vehicle operation anomalies, minor object levitation, e.g., paper clips, basketballs. Healings of animals… note: cannot self-induce healings…"

So that was why Sensei had healed his face. Ion couldn't do it himself.

"Interesting…"

I snapped the folder shut and rose to my feet, pushing back the kitchen chair.

Somehow, I would need to find out what was involved in the incident that had prompted his last transfer, but for the time being I had all the information I needed. Now I had to come up with a game plan.

Sensei had told us that there was a certain secret to slider selection, one that would make it impossible to mistakenly identify a slider. To my knowledge, no one had yet discovered this ancient key, but at this point I was almost certain that Ion was one of us. No ordinary human had a backstory like that. The question that remained was simply whether he had what it took to *realize* he was one of us. It was my job to figure that out.

It was late by the time I finally stepped into the broom closet. I shut the door behind me and snapped off the light. When I let myself out again, I was in the long familiar hallway lined with windows. The last rays of evening light bled through the glass and spread out over the floor like a sheet.

'Time,' as humans called it, passed differently here. The rusty gold sunset would not fade into a star-filled twilight, but into another immediate dawn.

Evening, dawn, evening...

And similarly, what felt like only an hour or two in the Dimension could very well be a day or more in the human world. Time seemed to sweep past like a rushing river there when I was here.

Fin had promised me a lesson in channeling that evening. I wasn't ashamed to admit that I was an amateur in that area, while he was a guru. It was his natural tendency. I was horribly late by this point, but when I arrived on the platform, he was still there.

He stood several yards away, facing the railing where a row of cairns had been lined up. The sound of my approach attracted his gaze and he smiled.

"Hey."

"I'm unacceptably late." I stopped beside him. "I can't believe you waited for me."

Fin smiled. "I felt like getting some practice in anyway."

I felt one of my eyebrows arch. His gaze shifted back to the empty space he was balancing between his hands like a ball.

"Where were you, anyway?"

I opened my mouth, but the words didn't come right away.

Fin wound his arms back over his left shoulder and hurled what looked like nothing at all across the platform. The cairn in the center dissipated. "Or can't I know?"

I cleared my throat. "I was in a meeting."

"A meeting?"

"Yes, a meeting."

"And what was this 'meeting' about?" Fin turned to give me a look.

I returned it unreservedly. "It's between Sensei and myself," I stated a little too coolly. "I don't feel the need to discuss it with anyone other than him."

"Fair enough," he conceded. "You don't have to talk about it if you would rather not. I already know what it's about anyway."

"Did Sensei tell you?"

Fin squinted at the two remaining rocks silhouetted against the rust-colored glow beyond the rail. "No. But I know you."

I nudged him aside and took my place in front of the rail, bringing my hands in front of me to start forming an orb. Fin watched.

"Sensei's been guarding someone—this guy in LA," I began slowly. "He's an anomaly. Sensei's been watching him since he was a kid."

"And he wants you to test him?"

I nodded.

"So… what is the issue, then?" Fin questioned. "I'm not sure that I follow."

I rotated my hands slightly. "The issue is that I've never tested anyone before. I've never had to call the shots about something this important."

"Do you believe he's one of us?"

"I have very little doubt."

"Then go for it."

I started moving the energy from side to side, kneading it gently between my hands. "It's not that simple. I can't just abduct him into it—I have to see that he's willing. That he actually has what it takes to be who he really is. To be dedicated and not just betray us."

"The test will give you the answer to that question."

I focused on one of the cairns. "I know. I just hate to be the one to decide."

"Why?" Fin asked. "You doubt yourself?"

I wound my arms back and threw. I missed.

"Apparently so." I sighed. "How do you make this look so easy?"

"Insomnia." Fin stepped up beside me. "And practice."

I slipped a space back between my hands.

"Keep it loose. You're not supposed to be squeezing it," Fin said, nudging a little more emptiness into my palms. "You're just holding it in place. Let it develop on its own."

I focused on the cairn again, rolling the tension out of my shoulder blades.

"So when is the test?"

"Dawn," I answered, rotating my hands. "His time."

"What's he like?"

"Self-important," I said, taking aim. "And very irritating."

I threw. The first few rocks tumbled off the top of the left cairn as it impacted.

Fin nodded his approval. "Better."

I pulled in a breath and extended my hands to start forming another orb.

"But he grew up in an orphanage—or a home, as they call it now," I continued after a moment. "So I guess I should feel like I can relate. But to be honest, I can barely remember my life in that world. It's a smudge left by an eraser."

I could feel Fin's eyes. "You don't remember any of it?"

I shook my head, swallowing back a tension in my throat. I took aim and threw. I missed.

"You're getting tight." Fin stepped up beside me again. "Relax."

His hands came up onto my arms, coaching my elbows to loosen. He gently spaced my hands farther apart, and for a split second his fingers paused against my own. I suddenly became aware of his body's closeness.

I pulled back.

"I've got it." My voice came out sharper than I had intended. "I don't need help."

His expression was as confused as I expected it to be, but it was still gentle. I reached up and wiped away the sweat that had begun to bead my brow.

"You okay?"

I snapped out of it, pulling my gaze back up to his. "I'm sorry, Fin," I fumbled. "I have a lot on my mind."

He looked at me for a moment. "Are you sure that's all it is?"

I nodded, getting back into stance. Fin took a step back.

"Focus," he coached, crossing his arms loosely. "Try to stay relaxed. Sorry I threw you off."

"Forget about it," I said, trying to shrug it off.

I was the one who wanted to forget about it. I could still feel a tingling sensation wreaking havoc on my nervous system as I let the energy build up. I pulled my left hand a little farther to the left side and felt a slight pull on my right hand, like my palms were joined by a string.

Without giving myself time to hesitate, I brought my hands back and hurled the ball of energy across the platform. It blew out the cairn to the left, dispersing the rocks like bullets and taking a large portion of the railing with it.

When I glanced over at Fin, his eyes were wide.

"That was something," he commented hesitantly, trying to sound positive. "Slightly too… aggressive. But we can work on that."

I reached up to massage my forehead. "Right."

He squinted out at the rail, sizing up the amount of damage I'd done. "What were you thinking about when you threw? Anything in particular?"

I felt my jaw tighten at the question.

"No," I lied. "Nothing in particular."

Fin cast me a glance, but didn't ask anything further.

"I think I need a break." I said, brushing my hair back. "I have to be back in LA shortly, and I still have to run through this test in my mind."

He nodded and there was another pause between us. I turned to walk away but then faltered and turned back to him.

"Fin?"

He looked up.

"Can I ask you a strange question?"

His usual half smile started fighting its way back onto his lips. "Go for it."

"When you look in the mirror…" I began slowly. "What do you see?"

He grinned. "An Irish boy with a peculiarly green thumb."

I smiled a little. "But past that. Do you ever see anything… underneath it all?"

Fin's gaze narrowed contemplatively. "What do you see underneath all of you?"

I hadn't expected him to turn the tables.

"I can't say that I see anything," I said quietly after a pause. "There's a hollow spot—not unlike the ravine below us."

A hesitation filled the silence between us. I could hear the birds beginning to awaken with the dawn.

"You know, Hawk," he said, "though no one has ever been to the bottom of the ravine, it doesn't mean it's nonexistent."

I back-stepped without breaking his gaze. "But no one knows for sure."

He brought his hands up in front of him to channel a mass of energy between his palms. "Don't you trust me?"

I bit back the impending smile. "Trust isn't particularly my forte."

He rolled his eyes, though a grin was still teasing the corners of his mouth, and threw the invisible ball at me. I threw myself over the edge before it could get close and free-fell into the colors of dawn.

CHAPTER SIX
Ion

I set my alarm for dawn and got up with the sun. If the events of the previous night hadn't been breathing down the back of my neck, it might have felt peaceful to be the only one up.

I zipped on a hoodie and slipped out into the driveway. Sensei's student emerged from the house as soon as I came to a stop at the gate leading into their yard.

"On time today," she commented as she unlatched the gate.

"You weren't even here last night," I said as I entered. "How did you know I was late?"

She shrugged.

I narrowed my eyes. "Do you ever actually answer questions?"

"When I feel like it."

She closed the gate behind us and motioned for me to follow. We walked down a tall row of arborvitaes that ran the length of the house; their tops bent toward the roof, creating what looked like an evergreen tunnel.

"Is this strictly business, or is small talk allowed?" I asked, trying to keep pace. "Because if it's okay, I'm going to ask what your name is again."

"I would prefer that you didn't."

"And if you give me your name," I continued, "I'll probably ask how your day is going or something like that."

She was in black skinny jeans and a matching tank top. Her brown, razor-cut hair just brushed against her shoulders, and the sunlight was flirting with the black bands that curved around her biceps. She shot me a look.

"I don't do small talk," she said. "You're here to do a job, not to talk to me."

"Is it hard to pronounce?"

She slowed up slightly. "What?"

"Your name," I clarified. "Is it hard to pronounce? Is that why you won't tell me?"

"It has nothing to do with pronunciation."

She was too hard; it was too early. I was done.

We stopped beside a large rectangular patch of disturbed ground. The soil was rich and purplish. Beside it was a plastic tray containing a dozen straggly tomato plants.

"Isn't it kind of late in the season to be planting these?" I asked, shielding my eyes with my hand.

She didn't seem particularly impressed by the question.

"Didn't Sensei ask you to plant these?" She raised an eyebrow.

I nodded slowly.

"Then it doesn't matter." She took a step back. "Get to it."

I wasn't about to make her say it twice. There was a shovel leaning up against a nearby tree, so I took it and started digging holes. I had no idea how to plant tomatoes, or anything else for that matter, but I kept my ignorance buried deep. It couldn't be that hard. I could feel her eyes on me for a few moments as I worked; then I heard the door open and close as she went back inside.

The sky was cloudless and ablaze with the sun's wake-up tantrums, coaxing me out of my hoodie and shirt to let her warmth race down my back, leaving beads of sweat.

About halfway through the ordeal, I noticed Sensei's hawk perched on the tree branch overhead.

"Who let you out here?" I squinted up at it as it looked down on me like an overseer would a slave.

Naturally, it didn't answer. It just sat there, poised, with its talons sinking into the tree's tender bark.

"So the old man lets you out sometimes, huh?"

It tilted its head slightly to the left and then looked away.

"Kind of wish you could talk," I said. "I think you could answer quite a few of my questions about that guy—and especially the girl."

This had to be a new all-time low. I was gardening in someone else's yard, talking to a bird.

"She intrigues me," I went on. "Can't put my finger on what it is exactly."

I stepped the shovel down into the soft ground again as an arid breeze wafted its way in from the south. It was the kind of heat that left you wishing you could peel out of your own skin, and it wasn't even seven o'clock yet.

The wind was gentle at first, but it rapidly became more substantial, messing with the leaves overhead like a hand caught up in hair. I was bending down to take the last plant out of the tray when I heard the sound of a branch cracking and falling to its death. I drew back instinctively, unsure of where it would crash-land, but apparently the hawk wasn't as quick to react.

A medium-sized branch had broken from a higher point and taken the bird down with it like an oversized set of claws. The hawk shrieked and crashed to the ground like a comet in a chaos of flapping wings. It landed with an audible thump and began screeching what must have been curse words if translated to human language.

I watched from a safe distance as it fought itself free from the branch, which took some effort. Its left wing had been torn, and there were feathers missing where a streak of crimson now flowed.

I glanced back over my shoulder towards the door, checking to see if anyone had emerged from the house because of the outburst, but there was no sign of movement. The curtains were still drawn shut.

I began to debate whether I should go find Sensei's student and let her know what had happened. I wasn't unaware of how bad it would look if the bird died on my watch—what had already unfolded was bad enough.

I took a few steps in the direction of the door, but the hawk's trilling screams were like weights in my footsteps. I turned back around to find that it had moved forward slightly, clawing at the grass where the blood was beginning to spread.

I cursed under my breath, glancing toward the door, then to the hawk again. *The front yard.* Someone had to be in the front yard—*someone* had to have let the hawk outside. I gave the injured bird one last glance and then took off running. I wound my way back through the long row of bending arborvitaes, each murmuring in a way that was almost otherworldly as I raced past them. The closer I came to the front of the house, the taller they seemed to become. It was like the trim evergreen tunnel I'd entered was transforming into a cone, getting wider and rising higher the farther I went. I slowed my pace and then came to a complete stop.

"What the…"

I gazed up overhead, looking for some sign in the sky that was now being swallowed up by the treetops. As far as my sight would allow there were evergreens—tendons of trees hell-bent on destroying whatever I had left of my sanity.

The tunnel curved ahead, and when I arrived at that point, it curved again. I couldn't see the end.

I could feel the sweat eating its way down my spine and across my forehead. Distantly I heard the hawk's cries, though now they sounded like they were reverberating through water. I was still staring in the direction of where the tunnel should have opened up to the front yard, feeling my heartbeat up in my throat, but after one more echoing wail from the other side, I turned around and rapidly retraced my steps.

The bird was still there, though now it was splayed out on the grass, propped up on its opposite wing.

I tried the back door, but it was locked, and no one came to answer it when I knocked. I felt the sweetness of normality quietly slipping through my white-knuckled grasp.

There was blood all over the grass where the bird was lying. I knelt down beside it. The broken branch next it was bristling with thorns.

"That must have felt good," I said sarcastically. The hawk had its eyes trained on me as I extended a hand toward it. For a moment, I almost thought it would let me get away with it, but at the last second it lurched forward.

It bit down hard into the flesh between my thumb and forefinger, its tomial tooth sinking into my skin like a knife through butter. It released me when I cursed, and blood started spurting from the puncture like wine from an uncorked bottle. Now we matched.

"Dirtbag," I renamed it through gritted teeth. "Do you want me to help you or not?"

It stared at me as if it wanted to cuss me out.

I pressed my fingers to the hole in my hand, blocking the blood flow while I studied the hawk's wing. It grumbled threatening trills at the back of its throat.

The gash that ran along its wing wasn't as deep as I would have guessed it to be; like a facial wound, it just bled a lot.

I threw a glance over my shoulder in the direction of the evergreen tunnel to nowhere. My mind was still feeling like it had just been through a blender. When I turned back to the hawk, it had calmed to a dead stillness. I reached out and touched it, and this time it didn't scream—it didn't bite me, it didn't move. My hands shook as I took the bird's wing between them, pressing my thumb down at the top of the gash. It tried to jerk away, but I held it still.

I pressed down hard and slowly dragged my thumb down the length of the wound, leaving a trail of clean, uninjured flesh behind it.

At length, I drew my hands back, exhaling heavily. I felt strangely drained. The hawk pulled its wing back and I could hear it trilling. A wave of vertigo was taking over, making it impossible to comprehend anything else. I felt like I was going to be sick, and by the time my focus cleared enough to take in my surroundings again, the hawk was gone. I was alone in the back-yard.

For a few seconds, I was soaked in quiet nothing. The only sound was that of my pulse pounding in my skull. Then I heard the back door creak open.

"Hey." The voice was female and familiar. "What are you doing?"

I shook my head despondently, still trying to slow my breathing to its normal pace. "Nothing."

"I can see that." I heard the door shut and a second later her descending footsteps. "Why did you stop? You have one plant left."

I wanted to reply, but I couldn't. I still hadn't turned to look at her. My brain felt numb.

She pulled in a breath. I could sense her right behind me now. "Never mind it."

"I can finish," I told her, pushing myself up to my feet. "I was just—"

"It's not necessary," she said. "Have you had anything to eat?"

"Today?"

She looked at me, stupefied. "No, yesterday."

I felt a blush break out over my cheeks.

"Do you want to come in and have some breakfast?"

The invitation caught me off guard, but I said, "Okay."

She turned and gestured for me to follow her, which I did without question. We went up the back steps and inside. The rear of the house was just as sparse as the front had been on my first visit, making it hard to believe that anyone actually lived there.

"I can get you something for that cut," she said as we entered the kitchen. "How did it happen?"

"Kind of a long story—where's Sensei?" I said, smoothly evading her question.

She gestured for me to sit down at the table, turning up the radio that was playing softly on the counter. Apparently she liked explicit rap music.

"He's not here."

I could tell by the tone of her voice that I wouldn't be getting an explanation beyond that, but I decided to pry anyway.

"Does he have a day job?"

She kept her back to me as she retrieved something from a cabinet. "You could say that."

She tossed me a box of Band-Aids with some antiseptic ointment. The feeling of déjà vu was strong as I bandaged up my hand. Less than twenty-four hours ago, I had been doing the same thing to my face. Thinking about it sent chills down my spine.

"Does he teach at a school close by or something?" I asked. "He wasn't exactly clear."

"Clarity isn't his forte," she replied, setting a plate down in front of me. "I hope you like eggs."

I didn't particularly, but I wasn't about to be *that* guy.

"Thanks."

She sat down across from me, that same scrutinizing look in her greenish brown eyes. I wasn't sure which was more distracting—that or the music.

"Am I ever going to know your name?" I asked after what felt like an awkward amount of time had passed.

"You have a thing about names, don't you?"

"Most people like to know someone's name."

She pondered this, resting her elbows on the table. "I'll give you a name, then."

I could tell by the way she said it that whatever followed would be anything but her real name.

"Hawk."

"Hawk is your name?" I started poking at the eggs with my fork. "Like the bird?"

"Sure."

There was something incredibly irritating about her. I couldn't put my finger on what it was. The music was still throwing me off.

"You're making this up," I told her finally. "I can tell by how you're acting."

For the first time her expression seemed vaguely amused. "You don't know me, so you have no basis for what my norm is," she said. "There's no way for you to know whether I'm lying or telling you the truth."

"It doesn't matter." I took a bite of food. "I only cared because flirting is easier when you know someone's name."

"Is it really." She didn't say it like a question, and I could tell it wasn't one.

"Could you possibly turn that down?" I asked, glancing in the direction of the radio.

She raised an eyebrow. "Why, so you can flirt with me?"

"No, it's just a little too loud," I said. "But I could make the flirting thing happen too."

"You don't like this music?"

"Not particularly," I said, swallowing another bite. "It's a little annoying."

"Why do you think it's annoying?"

"I don't know," I said, my voice trailing off, and she put up a hand for me to stop. There was a thin circular tattoo wrapping her ring finger.

"Shh."

"What?"

She motioned with her hand again. "Listen. Listen to it."

For a moment I did, without even asking why. I set the fork down on the plate and pushed it away quietly. Her eyes met mine from across the table.

"Describe what it is you don't like, exactly."

I thought about her strange question.

I didn't like the music, I didn't like the beat, and I didn't like the sound of his voice or the lyrics. There was, in fact, nothing about the song that I liked, but her question still brought my attention to every detail. I was starting to become aware that this was dangerous ground.

"The lyrics."

"What about them?"

"Nothing particularly," I said. "I just don't like them."

"Does it sound louder to you now than it did before?" Hawk asked, still not breaking eye contact. "Did you hear the volume change at all?"

I opened my mouth to reply but closed it again before any words could come out, listening.

The volume *had* changed. It *was* louder now.

"It sounds the same," I lied, trying to ignore the intensity of her gaze.

"Are you sure about that?"

I nodded vigorously.

"What about—"

I cut her off before she could say anything else. I had no idea how she had found out about me, but I knew where she was taking this.

"Just stop, okay?" My voice rose as my hands went unconsciously up over my ears. "Don't make me focus on it—I don't want to think about it."

I felt my heartbeat starting to pick up. When my hands fell away, the room was completely silent.

"That was strange, wasn't it?" she asked slowly. "It suddenly stopped."

"You turned it off," I corrected.

"No." She shook her head slowly. "I didn't."

I pulled in a sharp breath. "Look, I have to go."

"Why?" she asked, folding her hands on the table in front of her. "Are you scared?"

"Of course not." I tried to level out my voice. "What are you talking about?"

She looked at me hard for a moment before saying anything. "I think you know."

I shook my head, but she persisted.

"Come back tonight, Ion."

I stared at her for a moment. "Why?"

"Don't ask why," she said, rising. "Either come or don't."

I was beginning to feel like I was living out an episode of *The Twilight Zone*.

"I didn't even finish with the tomatoes," I said, clinging to the few shards of my life that still made a little sense. "Why did you invite me in? Why do you want me to come back?"

She took a few steps forward to pause in front of me.

"Don't worry about it. You finished everything that you needed to," she said. "Now do you want to come back tonight or not?"

"Of course I don't want to," I said finally, still trying to process everything. "But I will."

CHAPTER SEVEN

Ion

Mel sent me a text that afternoon to ask if I was alright. I replied and told her that I was fine, and she responded with a monologue.

Ion, I don't understand what the hell is going on with you, but I promise I won't say anything. I have no idea why I'm doing this for you… If I were you, I'd try to lie low for now. They're still reviewing the security recording and they might want to question you. Riley's making a pretty big deal out of it.

And then, in a separate text:

And just so you know… I'm here for you if you need me.

I hadn't even thought about the surveillance recording until then. Of course that would be the first thing they would check—what was wrong with me? I texted back to thank her for everything, and in turn she asked if I was doing anything that night. I said that I had to help my neighbor with something, which must have sounded like the lamest excuse ever, but I candy-coated it with an invitation to go out the following night. She accepted, and that was the end of the conversation.

I had to keep Mel pacified. She knew more about me than she should, and I had to make sure she didn't drop off my radar.

Mel had been in the wrong place at the wrong time, and because of it she knew something was wrong with me. Hawk, if that was even her real name, hadn't been witness to *anything*—she hadn't seen me more than a couple of times, yet somehow she had figured me out.

———

I was back at Sensei's at half past eight. He was nowhere in sight; Hawk greeted me at the door.

"Where's Sensei?" I asked when I realized we were once again alone. "Didn't you say he would be here?"

I was sitting across from her at the kitchen table while she ate what looked like a bowl of ramen noodles in broth. Her hair was slightly tousled, and she was wearing the same black clothes from earlier that morning.

"He's not here, nor did I say he would be," she replied.

"But I thought you—"

Hawk cut me off as she lifted a hand. "I told you to come if you wanted to, and you came. You didn't ask for details."

"Well, I'm asking for them now."

"Which is why you're sitting here with me for a while before I take you any further," she said coolly. "I knew you would have questions to work out of your system—so go for it."

"Who said you were taking me anywhere?" I shot her a glance. "I don't even know you."

"I know you don't. Which is why I invited you over—isn't that what people do? Invite people over and talk to them?"

"Sort of," I replied slowly. "I don't really think you have the hang of it, though. I take it you're not hugely social."

She laughed slightly, twirling her chopsticks around in the bowl of noodles. "I was supposed to go easy on you and let you bring it up, but apparently this tactic isn't going to work out."

"Tactic?" I reiterated, confused. "What are you talking about?"

"The music today," Hawk replied flatly. "The bird's wing. Why are you afraid to talk about them?"

"How did you know about the bird?"

"Never mind how I know," Hawk said. "Do you want to talk about it? If so, get it out now while you can still talk. Because from here onward you're going to have to get used to keeping your mouth shut and your ears open if you want anything to actually change."

"What makes you think I want anything in my life to change?"

"You're here, aren't you?"

I opened my mouth to reply, but no words came. A thick silence hung in the air like a sheet between us.

"You have until I finish these noodles to talk," she said, picking up the chopsticks she had set down. "So either do that, or sit there and watch me stuff my face. Your choice."

I took a deep breath, trying to keep my focus. If it was questions she wanted, questions I would give.

"Is Hawk really your name?"

"It wasn't always."

"How did you find out about—" I trailed off, groping for the right words. "—everything?"

"I haven't found out about everything," she replied. "I actually know very little about the universe in its entirety."

"You know what I mean," I said. "About my abilities."

"Your abilities?"

I searched again for the right words. "Disruption of normality?"

"Sensei told me."

I stared at her. "How did *he* know?"

She studied the tangle of noodles between her chopsticks. "Because he's been watching you."

"He's been *watching me?*"

"Unnerving, isn't it?"

I felt a tension across my collarbone. "Look, I don't know what kind of game this is you're playing with me, but I want it to end right now."

"Game?"

"Yes, game."

"Is a game like flirting?"

I leaned forward on the table, looking her in the eyes. "If you don't tell me what's going on, I will literally force it out of you."

She twirled her chopsticks around in the bowl of noodles. "Is that a threat? That sounds like a threat."

"Bingo."

"Then go for it," she said, pausing to drink the rest of the broth out of the bowl. "Force it out of me."

Her nonchalant attitude was nothing short of infuriating. I had no idea how to respond, and when I didn't, she raised an eyebrow.

"What? Are you afraid to?" she asked.

The answer was yes, so I didn't reply.

Hawk pushed aside the items in front of her and extended her left arm on the surface of the table. She nodded toward a knife I hadn't noticed before, laid in front of an empty seat.

"See that knife?"

I nodded.

"Pick it up."

My gaze shifted to hers. "Why?"

"Just do it."

For a moment I did nothing. Then, slowly, I lifted it.

"Now stab me," she said, her eyes flicking to the palm of her upturned hand.

"What the f—? Are you out of your mind?"

Her gaze hardened. "You passed the first two tests. Do you want to fail the third?"

If I hadn't been lost before, I most certainly was now.

"Tests? What are—"

"No," she cut me off. "You've exhausted your questions. Either do as I say, or leave."

My gaze dropped to the knife in my hand. There was no way I could do what she was asking.

"You're out of your mind," I said. "I can't do that."

"Yes, you can." Her gaze was still sharp on my skin. "In fact, you want to—you don't even like me."

"So? I don't like a lot of people—that doesn't mean I stab them."

"Really?"

I nodded.

"I think you're used to hurting people," she continued, her voice a little lower than before. "You're so used to it, in fact, that you do it without knowing it—you don't even know how to stop."

It was like cold water in my face. My mind raced, searching for a defense.

"I have no idea—"

"You have *every idea* what I'm talking about." She cut me off again. Her palm was still lying face up on the surface of the table. "It's your very ideas that control you, Ion. It's your ideas that make you dangerous—that make you an anomaly."

Anomaly.

Everything in me froze. A numbness washed over me, and I could tell that Hawk noticed. A smile twitched at the corners of her mouth.

Before my mind could process what was happening, my fingers curled around the handle of the knife, pulled it back and drove it down into the center of her open palm. The tip sliced through her flesh and nailed into the table beneath her hand. She didn't flinch. When I let go of the blade, it stayed standing on its own, a pool of crimson forming on the plateau from which it arose. My hand was shaking.

Hawk released a shallow sigh, lifting her gaze from her pierced hand. "That took twice as long as it should have."

I watched wordlessly as she reached for the handle of the knife and firmly pulled it up from her palm, sending droplets of blood scattering across the table's surface. A stream of crimson immediately began to flow down the length of her forearm as she lifted her hand. Her eyes followed its progression.

"Next time I tell you to do something, do it without question," Hawk said, her voice as calm and neutral as it had been before. "If you can't do that, this entire endeavor will prove to be pointless—"

Her eyes focused on the trail of blood, which had now stopped. I watched in silence as it reversed its progression and crawled slowly back up into the puncture wound, where it congealed and then closed up, returning her skin to its normal, unmodified state.

"—for both of us," she finished, looking back at me.

By that point, any words I'd considered saying had been siphoned away, so I said nothing. She rose from her chair and took her empty bowl to the kitchen sink.

"Any other questions, Ion?"

I shook my head.

"Good." She turned and started towards the hallway. "Then follow me."

We left the kitchen, and Hawk led me down the short, run-down hallway that led in the direction of the backyard. We stopped at a less prominent door about halfway down, which I identified as a sort of utility closet. Hawk opened the door and gestured toward the vacant interior. The space was illuminated by a bare bulb; it was about six by six feet and completely empty.

"Get in."

"You're joking with me, right?" I turned to stare at her blankly. "You want me to get into the closet?"

"Are you not hearing me the first time around?" she asked, irritated. "You had your chance to ask questions."

"That's not fair—you didn't want to lock me in a closet until now."

"I'm not locking you in."

Hawk stepped into the closet, grabbed me by the arm, and dragged me in after her, closing the door. It was the last thing I'd been expecting.

"You are *highly* unusual, you know that?" I was still short of breath from the ordeal at the kitchen table, and my panting was audible in the smallness of the space.

Hawk reached up for the pull chain. "Speak for yourself."

Touché.

The closet went dark.

"Most people would consider this suggestive behavior on your part," I pointed out. "Is this experience going to be at all sensual?"

"It will have the opposite effect, I assure you."

I heaved an exhale of mock disappointment, and she kicked my shin in the darkness—slightly harder than I'd been expecting.

"Ow—"

"Shhhh, would you?" She shoved some distance between us. "I can't focus."

"Focus on what? What are we doing?"

Her hand clamped fiercely down over my mouth, slamming the back of my head into the wall. "Close your eyes and be quiet."

Her hand tasted vaguely of saffron. I had no idea what she was doing, but after what felt like only a few seconds, she opened the door again.

Her hand went down to my forearm. It felt warmer now, in contrast to the air, which now seemed strangely cold. I heard the mechanical clicking of the tumblers as she twisted the doorknob. White light streamed in through the open door and into the tiny space. Half of her face remained hidden in shadow as she turned to look at me. Oddly, her voice echoed slightly when she spoke.

"Follow."

We stepped out of the closet and into a hallway—an entirely different hallway from the one we had been in only moments before. Enormously tall windows rose up around us, letting the light pour in. Beyond the glass, a massive ravine was visible. I halted and glanced back over my shoulder towards the closet from which we had just emerged, catching glimpses of geodes lining the walls as Hawk swept the door shut.

"What the hell is going on?" I turned my full attention to her, eyes wide. "What did you do—where are we?"

She took me by the shoulders and turned me back around to face forward, not saying a word. I had no idea where we were, or what kind of transformation had occurred. My heart rate had risen significantly, but I didn't resist her as she steered me down the hallway and out onto a large crowded platform. Along the edges ran wooden rails and posts that rose up to support a massive thatched roof. Beyond the edge of the platform was a steep drop into what looked like an abyss.

My eyes immediately began scanning the crowd for Sensei. At last I spotted him standing towards the front of the platform. The sight of him calmed me, strangely. Almost involuntarily, I took a step towards him, but Hawk stopped me with a glance before I could get any farther. Aside from Sensei, everyone else was either a teenager or a twenty-something, representing a multitude of ethnic backgrounds. There were probably close to a hundred of us, both male and female. Some chatted quietly among themselves while others stood silently, as if awaiting a command.

Sensei gestured for everyone to sit down. Hawk sat cross-legged, so I followed suit. She didn't seem particularly impressed by the gesture. I shimmied closer to her for further inquisition before Sensei began speaking, but she only slid farther away, shooting me an irritated glance.

"Today we welcome several new students into the Dimension," Sensei said. He had remained standing at the front of the platform, close to the rail. "This being the case, I would like to begin this session with an introduction, though this will undoubtedly benefit all of you."

Half of my brain was at high attention, waiting for him to give at least something of an explanation, but the other half was still stuck on the word *dimension*.

"You may be wondering why you are here and how you've come to be here, for that matter," Sensei began. "You may be wondering why *you* are here and not someone else—why it seems almost as though you have been chosen…"

He paused, and for a moment his eyes found mine in the crowd of teenagers.

"That is because you *have* been chosen," he continued finally, seeming to pull his gaze from mine. "You are not here by chance, but because you have been especially selected for this place—through the test you have taken, you have proven that you have what it takes to become a protector, those of us who are different from the rest of the world. You have shown that you are one of the anomalies of earth—those of us who cannot fit in because we have awakened to something beyond the walls the world built around us. You see things that others cannot, and you find yourself doing things beyond what you can intellectually comprehend."

I listened intently—wondering if everyone else could relate as much as I could.

"I have guarded each of you since the day you came into your natural worlds," Sensei continued, beginning to walk slowly among us as he spoke. "I have watched you grow and learn and struggle with the very things that have set you apart from everyone else. Though you have not seen me, I have seen *you.*"

He gestured around us.

"This place, this Dimension… it was created for you," he said. "To protect you and to provide you with a place of training, where you may learn to embrace your differences and stop running away from them. Where you may discover who it is that you are… and that all you have ever needed is already within you."

When he said this, he seemed to look at me. But his eyes moved so swiftly I could hardly tell.

"Those who have not awakened, though they do not understand you, will need you," Sensei said, raising his voice. "There is a darkness that lies ahead of them that they will be unable to rescue themselves from. Having lived so long without the light, the darkness will seem more familiar to them. But the future is not theirs to claim for darkness—it is yours to reclaim for light. And that is why I have brought you here."

A soft murmuring arose from the audience of students. I was still attempting to get my head around "the darkness that lies ahead" when Sensei spoke again, this time shifting to a new topic.

"We will begin by moving into a gentle *pranayama*," he said, glancing towards the back of the crowd to meet my gaze momentarily. "This will help you to understand why you are here."

I felt my forehead creasing in puzzlement. I turned to shoot Hawk a glance. "What's a pranayama?" I hissed.

She placed a finger to her lips, refusing to acknowledge me with her gaze.

Apparently, I wasn't the only one who was apprehensive about this. Whispers rose up from various clusters of students.

"I know that for many of you, control of breath is not your natural tendency," Sensei continued, seeming to sense the hesitance among the more cynical of us. "But you are capable of mastering it just as you would any other ability. It simply hinges on focus. It is no different from channeling, shifting, cognitive reading, or healing."

I felt my ears perk up at the mention of the last item. Flashbacks to blood and feathers.

"Breath is our most essential and primal tendency," Sensei went on as he began to slowly cross the platform. "We breathe; thus we survive. The very fabric of your survival is dependent upon your next inhale and exhale. When we control the breath within the body, we control its energy, choosing to lock it either in or out."

I watched him closely as he made his way slowly through the crowd, his feet still bare. I could glimpse his crystal blue eyes occasionally.

"The concept of pranayama is ancient within human culture, and its purpose is to control each breath and consciously utilize the energy therein howsoever you choose. Humans have utilized it to a fraction of its potential, but in its entirety, it is channeling in its purest form."

Sensei paused again and then nodded in Hawk's direction. It seemed to be a signal only she understood. He cast me one more glance before he returned to the front of the platform, beckoning the students to stand again. The apparently newer enrollees hesitated slightly.

"This session will be guided."

I was still lost. In fact, I understood almost nothing, but somehow I kept my cool. Maybe I was just used to life reaching fairly high levels of abnormality.

Sensei continued his explanation. The body was an empty glass, and the oxygen was the water with which it would be filled. "An inhale is a filling of the entire body," he said, "and an exhale a total emptying."

In essence, he taught us to breathe, coaching us calmly on inhales and exhales, instructing us to hold, or "lock," the air within the body. These pauses lasted only several seconds.

"Breathe slowly in… and hold."

And so we did.

"Engage your focus."

At first it felt like nothing. The first "round," as Sensei called it, was cake. We stood there and breathed. I didn't grasp the concept; I didn't understand how this was difficult or remotely important.

Hawk nudged me back to attention as Sensei began speaking again, guiding us into what I could only guess to be round two, which turned out to be identical to the first aside from one small hitch.

At first I didn't notice; I was still too overwhelmed by my surroundings. But after a while, I noticed an increasing feeling of lightheadedness, which alerted me to the fact that the amount of time between each inhale and exhale was increasing. It had begun as mere seconds; now it was pushing a minute.

Still listening to Sensei's calm instructions, I slowly filled my lungs with air from the bottom up, drawing it in deeply and pinning it down until it burned. My mind was getting foggier. On an exhale, I glanced over at Hawk to check her expression. She seemed unperturbed—which didn't necessarily surprise me—but when I stole a glance at the other students around me, I realized that I was the only one who was struggling.

Shit, shit, shit…

I shook my head almost imperceptibly and focused on Sensei's voice.

"Breathe deeply in, engage."

We were holding our breath for almost two minutes at a time, then three, pushing four. I was keeping count now. I could feel my heart racing against my rib cage. I closed my eyes and coached myself to relax. If Hawk could do it, if everyone around me could do it, there was no reason why I couldn't. I had done stranger things before. I had this.

Or maybe not…

In spite of what I tried to tell myself, my lungs were screaming for air. My head was throbbing with the blood that was rocketing to my skull. When I opened my eyes again, my vision was distorted.

Fighting to keep it together, I turned and looked at Hawk once more. Her expression, though blurred, still looked neutral. I couldn't believe it.

A cloud of yellow sparks swept in, soft as doves, blurring my vision. Hawk twisted and swirled, changing color as the yellow turned to gray and I was borne away into soft, dark unconsciousness.

CHAPTER EIGHT

Ion

I felt like I was in an oversized basket. The walls were woven from something like wicker, narrowing above my head and leaving only a small, tipi-like gap at the very top where I could see a fragment of a blue-green sky. I reached up to massage my forehead with my fingertips, becoming aware of the mattress beneath me, the coolness of the sheets on my skin.

As basketlike as the interior seemed, it was a fairly large room. Two sets of bunk beds were stacked up against the walls, and at the far end there was a desk occupied by a guy who looked around my age, hunched over a scattered agglomeration of papers. He was Asian and scruffy-faced, with long jet-black hair in a bun. My movements must have drawn his attention, because after a moment he turned to glance at me over his shoulder.

"How do you feel?" he asked, setting down his pen to cast me a cautious glance. "You've been out of it all day. I was just about to go give Fin an update on your progress—or lack thereof."

My eyelids fell shut again. "Damn. All day? Who's Fin?"

"The dorm monitor."

Which explained *everything*.

"Where am I?" I asked. "What time is it?"

I heard the rustling of papers and then chair legs complaining against the wood floor. When I opened my eyes again, I noticed him at the window, which was nothing more than a small hole woven into the wall.

"Close to dawn, I would say."

"Can you be any more specific?" I started to push myself up into a seated position. "Where am I exactly? What happened?"

"You passed out during a pranayama session," he said, returning to his seat. Without touching it, he spun the chair around to face me. My jaw went slack. "I don't blame you, though. Those things can be rough at first. Fin said that Hawk told him—"

My gaze shifted up to his at the mention of her. "Hawk?"

He nodded.

"Where is she?"

He shrugged. "Does it matter?"

I swallowed back my irritation, trying to keep my cool. "Okay, let me explain. I have no idea where I am or how I got here, but Hawk was the one who brought me—I came with her."

He looked at me blankly for a moment before a revelation seemed to strike him. "Oh, right. The fledgling from California. I'd heard the rumors, but I hadn't connected the dots. I'm Mitsue. Ion, right?"

I nodded slowly. "Where can I find Hawk?"

"She's probably up at her apartment. Good luck trying to get up there, though. I hope you're a good climber."

"Then where's Fin?" I asked, though I had no idea who he was. "I need to talk to him."

Mitsue opened his mouth to reply just as a new voice cut in. The canvas flap of a door I hadn't noticed before pushed itself aside.

"Who needs to talk to me?" An Irish accent entered the room only seconds before a tall, golden-haired guy who looked around my age strode in. "You're awake, I see."

"Barely," I confessed, dragging my legs over the side of the mattress. "Where am I?"

"Hawk didn't tell you?"

"Hawk never tells me anything."

"Can't say I'm surprised." He grunted a laugh. "Do you want me to fill you in?"

"Please."

He leaned back against the wall. "You're in a dormitory pod located on the cliff side."

"Cliff?" I asked.

Fin nodded slowly, studying my expression. "It's part of the Dimension. Which is where you are. Hawk brought you in through one of the portals."

"But it was a broom closet."

Fin laughed. "It was a portal."

I rubbed my eyes as everything that had happened prior flooded back into my recollection: watching Hawk eat ramen noodles, stabbing her hand, the closet escapade. Stepping out of what looked like a cave into what seemed like an entirely new world.

"You're here because…" He trailed off and gave a shrug. "You're one of us."

I looked up at Fin, feeling suddenly weak. "What do you mean, 'one of us'?"

He seemed to consider his words for a moment. "You're a slider. One of the protectors."

"Look, I don't understand what that means," I said. "But I can't stay. I need to leave."

"I'm afraid you can't do that until you speak with Hawk."

I felt my jaw tense slightly. I hated where this was going. "Then *where* is she?"

"She's not available right now—she left you under my supervision."

I shook my head. "No, you don't get it. I don't need supervision; I need to get out of here. That damn girl dragged me here—I didn't ask for this."

"You're staying where you are for now." Fin wore an irritating look of resolve. "Hawk is discussing your situation with Sensei presently. I'm sure she will fill you in."

"Is *everything* an uphill battle here?"

"Not always, no." He nodded for me to follow him to the doorway. "Come on. I can give you an orientation tour while you wait for the verdict from Hawk."

I was a bottle rocket full of doubt, but I kept my mouth shut and followed Fin outside. I had barely stepped past the canvas flap when he turned to me again, coming to a brief halt.

"And by the way—that 'damn girl'?" Fin's voice was severe as he gestured for me to step out onto the rope bridge in front of us. "Is my best friend. Watch your step."

I could tell by the way he'd said it that the last part had multiple meanings. I gave a brisk nod that satisfied no one.

Like an enormous spider's web, the rope bridges connected the pod to the dozens of others surrounding it and anchored the apparatus to the cliff side. The drop below it was extreme. I couldn't see anything beyond the blanket of gray fog rolling beneath us.

"These are the dorms," he explained. "This is where you'll be living while you're here. You said Hawk was your guide, so I take it you're not transdimensional yourself yet. Once you learn how to use the portals, you'll be allowed to come and go at will like the rest of us."

I glanced over at him. "You mean you don't live here all the time?"

Fin shook his head. "We phase in and out between this world and our natural one."

"So where's your 'world'?"

"Fairly close to Dublin, Ireland," Fin answered as we stepped out onto the pathway. "Sensei has an apartment close by. He set up a portal for me there."

I must have been staring because after a second Fin laughed.

"You thought he just lived in California, didn't you?"

"It seemed like a logical assumption."

"It is quite logical—and he does live there," he said as we walked. "But he lives in other worlds as well."

"You can't live in two places at the same time," I said. "That's not possible."

Fin gave a shallow shrug. "Perhaps you should reexamine your definition of that word."

The covered platform rose into view as we continued up the pathway. It was almost completely vacant now aside from a sparse scattering of students. Fin introduced me to several of them. Gaia, a young teenage girl of Ethiopian ethnicity, approached us to announce that Sensei wanted to speak with me.

My morale rose slightly at this. I followed Fin across the platform and down a different hallway.

"You'll soon learn that different things have brought each of us here, though we are all here for the same reason," he explained, keeping his voice respectfully quiet as we walked. "Slider, channeler, shifter, healer, so many other things—they're all abilities we each possess. It's because of them that we now find ourselves here. Gaia for example, she's so young and yet a *natural* slider. She's already helping to guide sessions."

"And you?" I asked, curious. "What's your thing?"

"Channeling," Fin replied. "You'll learn more about that soon. The platform is where you'll be spending most of your time. All studies and practices preceding your introductory lesson will take place here unless other-wise stated."

"Introductory lesson?" I repeated, attempting to match his brisk pace. "I thought that that already happened. The pranayama."

"Well, in case you haven't been paying attention, you failed."

"I held my breath for like three minutes, man," I retorted. "Doesn't that count for something?"

"Well, considering that most of us can push a half an hour, I'd have to say it doesn't count for much, no. Sorry."

"Half an hour?" I reiterated, stunned. "Are you frickin' kidding me?"

Fin paused at a humble mahogany door to the left, about halfway down the hall. "No. And just to brief you, expletives break the code of conduct here."

Instinctively, I rolled my eyes. Fin shot me a stern glance and lifted a hand to deliver a few rapid knocks to the hardwood.

"Sensei, I have Ion to see you."

There was a pause, then the familiar calm of Sensei's voice. "Let him in."

Fin glanced briefly at the brass knob and the door popped open. He gestured me inside. "I'll see you later, I'm sure."

I swallowed back my uncertainty as I stepped over the threshold. The door closed behind me.

Like Sensei's house, this room's interior was practically empty. The walls were white, and the floor was made of compressed bamboo, the same as the dorm. One wall had been replaced with sheer glass, overlooking the drop into the ravine. Small potted trees of various species grew alongside it, extending toward the sun. In the center of the room, a large red circle had been drawn on the floor. Sensei was seated cross-legged on the edge farthest from me.

He gestured for me to stop. "Take off your shoes."

I kicked off my Nikes unquestioningly and waited for further instruction. He gestured for me to take a seat in the center of the circle.

"It was not long ago that we sat across from each other and you asked if I was a teacher," Sensei said. "In turn I asked you what it was you wished to learn, and you had no answer to give."

"Yes, sir."

"Do you now have an answer?"

I reached up to rub my forehead, hesitating. I could hear raptor calls in the distance.

I had no idea where I was or who I was really speaking to, in fact. Up until the car incident, Sensei had simply been "the crazy old guy next door." Now he was beginning to feel like my only connection to sanity. I had no reason to trust him, but something in me gravitated towards it.

"Sensei, how did you know about me?" I asked. "Hawk said that you've been watching me—how did you find me? How did you know about my powers?"

His deep-set eyes studied my face. "You still have not answered the question."

I held his gaze for a moment, then let go of a sigh. "I don't know the answer to your question. I don't even know who I am."

"Would you like to know who you are?"

I nodded slightly.

"Then that is the answer to the question," he said. "You wish to learn who you really are. Where you have come from. And it is for that reason that you have been brought here."

"But why?" I asked.

"Because you were created to protect that which is to come, Ion."

I thought about it for a moment before shaking my head. "I don't get it."

"Every generation to walk the earth has, hidden within its repetition and pattern, a few who will resist. A few who will realize that they are inherently different from others," Sensei replied. "Most will follow the pattern cut through the density of the forest, because they are afraid to stray from that which is familiar. But a few will stray—the anomalies. Those who recognize their own powers and allow their abilities to guide them."

There was that word again. The word that had provoked me to the point of driving a knife through Hawk's hand only hours before. Coming from him, though, it didn't have the same effect.

"I created this dimension to protect you. Because you are the only ones who have awakened to protect the future from what it has become."

"How do you know what the future is going to be like?" I asked. "You talk about it like it already exists."

"Because," he said, "I have seen it."

"You've seen the future?"

Sensei nodded.

"So this whole…" I looked for the right word. "Dimension. You created it?"

"I am it."

I stared at him. "Wait, what?"

"When you healed Hawk, when you altered reality with your very thoughts, you projected that which is within you into that which is without. When you practice that for eternity, this," he gestured towards our surroundings, "is the result."

"You've found every one of us… every one of the anomalies?"

"From past, present, and future."

My head was starting to hurt.

"You were the one who fixed my face, weren't you." It wasn't a question.

Sensei nodded. "I could imagine how much it hurt."

"Yeah, well. You imagined correctly." I laughed mirthlessly. "God, this is *insane*."

"It is your choice to make, Ion. Hawk will teach you how to utilize the portals, and you may come and go." He folded his hands. "Or you may return to your world permanently—but you must tell no one what we have discussed or what you have seen here."

"I want to stay," I said, without hesitation, surprising myself.

Sensei nodded slowly. "The student body has established certain standards to aid in allowing initiates to fully hone their abilities. You do realize that you will be required to live by this code of conduct."

"Is there a curfew?"

"No."

"Then I'm sure I'll be down with whatever you throw at me."

"Very well." He gestured for me to rise. "You may begin training. Based on the results from the breathing test last evening, I was able to assess to what level you have manifested your power."

"Yeah? Fin said I sucked."

"Fin was accurate in this judgment."

I got to my feet. "So where does that leave me?"

"It has been said that when the student is ready, the teacher will appear," he told me, as if this was some kind of science. "Do you feel ready?"

"Honestly? No."

"I have found one for you, regardless." He rose. "She will provide you with an alternative introductory session and then bring you back to LA through the portal. She's waiting outside."

I watched him as he walked over to the glass wall to examine the foliage on one of the trees.

"'She,' Sensei?"

He ignored my question. "You may go, Ion."

I paused for a moment, attempting to pull myself back down to earth, then bowed my head in a somber nod and shimmied back into my shoes.

I crossed the room and swung open the door, letting myself out into the hallway. Hawk was waiting just outside. I stopped cold when I saw her.

"Where the hell have you been?" I demanded.

She was wearing a fitted gray muscle tank now, and her hair was thrown into a violent-looking bun.

"I was in conversation with Sensei, and then I went to LA for lunch." She folded her arms and leaned back against the wall, scrutinizing me.

"Lunch? What time is it?"

"Why? Are you hungry?"

"No, I'm just going insane."

She bit back a smile. "Good. Ready to start?"

I stared at her, confused. "Start?"

And then it clicked. She was the only one in the hallway—the only one who had been "waiting outside."

"Wait, no. You're my—"

She put up a hand. "Don't remind me, okay? You think I chose this? Now move your butt."

"Where are we going?"

"To the drop," she said, starting down the hallway and motioning for me to follow. "For your first lesson."

CHAPTER NINE
Hawk

"I saw the whole thing. I sat there on your shoulder and I watched you heal his face because he isn't even capable of healing himself, Sensei. Just like he's not capable of successfully finishing even a simple pran."

I leaned back against the translucent wall as I spoke. The coolness of the glass felt good against my skin, which had begun to heat with the desire to shift. Sensei was watering the plants.

"Yes, he's a slider. A healer, even," I confessed. "But does he actually have what it takes to become a protector? I'm not certain."

"Certainty is irrelevant to the matter."

"Is it? Is it really?"

"He's here."

"Yes, he's here." I reached up to stroke my forehead. "But is he going to keep his mouth shut? How do we know if we can even trust him?"

Sensei brushed aside some of the lower foliage on one of the trees and placed his fingers gently on the roots. Water gushed from his fingertips. "We don't."

"Then why are we risking it?"

"Because trust is built upon the basis of the unknown." He glanced up. "Risk, as you call it, defines trust."

"Then trust is dangerous," I concluded.

"Trust is a superlative. The result is never lukewarm: it is either an extreme producer of life, or death."

I blew out a laugh, fogging the glass. "And you think I should trust him? Put my life on the line for someone like him—someone who doesn't even know how to control their humanistic or slidatorial powers?"

Sensei straightened up. "It is your decision, Hawk."

My gaze hadn't moved. "Sensei, I trusted someone once before."

"I know, dear one."

"Do you think I would ever make that mistake again?"

He moved on to the next tree. "Our past can only follow us if we allow it to, Hawk."

"It doesn't follow me, Sensei, it haunts me," I said. "It lies in wait for me in the dark."

"A warrior cannot be haunted."

"What makes you think I am one?"

"Because when I look at you, I see nothing but a warrior who insists on wrapping herself in an unnecessary cocoon."

"When I shift, I feel it." I turned around to face the glass. "Somewhere deep down. But in this form I feel like I'm wearing someone else's skin, one size too small. I feel like a child packing her bags with a will to run away from herself."

"If you have a will to run, choose a direction and get to it."

I glanced at him. I could already see the answer in his crystal blue eyes.

"Alright. Alright, Sensei, I'll try it," I finally conceded. "When do you want me to start?"

"I'll speak with him now. Why don't you go get something to eat in the meantime."

"Why? I don't even need food."

"Yes, but you enjoy it." He nudged me aside to water the last tree. "And you're much easier to work with once you've eaten."

I crossed the room, but paused when I reached the door and turned back to glance over my shoulder.

"Sensei?"

"Yes, Hawk?"

I hesitated slightly. "You do know I don't trust him, don't you?"

"I know, dear one."

"Sensei, why are you doing this?" I finally asked. "You're the one who has seen the distant future—you're the one who has been there, and you're the one who has told us that we have the ability to change it. You're the one who has trained us for this—made us who we are. Are you seriously going to risk blowing the plan on some no-name college guy you picked off the street?"

A silence inserted itself, and for a few seconds it hung there. Sensei straightened up.

"Yes, Hawk," he said, still not having turned to look at me. "Because I did the very same thing for you."

I opened my mouth to reply, but no words came. So I stood there and watched him gaze through the glass, seeming to study the birds that were fluttering like scraps of paper in the early light.

I opened the door and left.

I met Gaia in the hallway. Her mood seemed to be seven shades lighter than my own.

"What's up?" she asked.

"Nothing's up," I replied. "Go and find Fin and have him tell Ion that Sensei is ready to see him."

"I can't believe this is actually real. I can't believe he created all this. It's insane."

"So you said." I withheld a sigh. "Two minutes ago."

"When did he find you?" Ion asked as we walked. "Are you from the future?"

"No."

"Present day?"

"It was present day at the time."

"Holy, fu—the past? Seriously?"

"Alright, just stop, okay?" I slowed to a halt as we reached the edge of the cliff. "I was okay with the question thing for a while, but now it's getting on my nerves. Let's just get this over with."

Ion came to a premature stop behind me. "Get what over with?"

"Your first lesson. I'm just going to have you jump off this cliff."

"*Just* jump off the cliff?" he repeated. "Are you frickin' mental?"

"I see we need to start with the code of conduct before we proceed," I said. "Sit."

He threw himself down on the grass, muttering unintelligibly.

"First, expletives are not permitted," I began. "Any form of violence or abuse, in even its mildest forms, is not permitted."

"I'm inherently violent—and I stabbed your hand. Does that mean I'm disqualified?"

I rolled my eyes. "That was different."

"Okay. What else?"

"Students are here to hone their abilities, and in order to do that, focus is required." I paused, considering how to break it down. "Which means that certain distractions are not permitted."

"Distractions like video games?"

"What are video games?" I asked.

Ion opened his mouth to speak, but then shut it again and gestured for me to continue.

"*Anyway.* Distractions like relationships," I went on. "Physicality, sex, and anything associated with the two. Purity is sacredly upheld within the Dimension."

He raised an eyebrow. "Isn't the point to create, like, a new subgroup of humans? Won't it fall apart without any means of reproduction?"

I shook my head. "It has nothing to do with creating a subgroup of humans, and even if this was the case, reproduction would still be unnecessary."

"And why is that?"

"Because we're immortal," I replied. "The only way we can die is if we are killed. You and the other fledglings—the other new students—are still adapting. It can be a bit of a shock, but in time you will understand."

Ion nodded slowly, still gaping at me as if I was a mirage.

"But points for trying to find a loophole for sex, Ion."

"Hey, I didn't say—"

I held up a hand. "Let's not belabor it. The point is you're here to train. You're not here to have fun or screw around. You weren't selected because you deserved to be, but because you *had* to be. You're inherently a slider, and that means that you have the potential to become a protector. There are different degrees of punishment for those who fail to follow the code—some being more severe than others."

He squinted up at me. "And what is a protector, exactly?"

"A creator and preserver of an alternate, highly improved future of the cosmos," I replied, sounding slightly scripted. "But only the best of the best become such. You have to be a certain kind of person to have what it takes, and to be quite honest, I'm not sure that's you."

"What makes you think I don't have what it takes?"

"Because you have a taste for the things of your world," I told him. "You cling to its material yielding. You're undisciplined, reckless, arrogant—"

"Well, apparently Sensei sees something in me."

"He does, in fact," I confirmed. "Which is why he has placed you under my tutelage." I paused and waited to see if he would say anything. When he didn't, I continued.

"Sensei suspects that there is a healer within you by natural tendency, and that I, by some magic, may be able to draw it out." I firmed my gaze, taking a step backwards towards the cliff's edge. "Which means that I will require your trust as much as you will require mine."

"You *don't* trust me, though," he pointed out.

"I'm afraid trust doesn't come cheap with me," I said. "You're going to have to earn it—starting now."

"You were kidding about the cliff-jumping thing, right?"

"I was not."

"I really don't like you."

"The feeling is mutual, believe me." I gestured for him to rise, then spun him around by the shoulders so that his back was facing the drop. "I'm going to count to ten, and you're going to walk backwards and over the edge."

"No way."

"You do realize you won't be able to get back to your own world without me, don't you?" I said, shooting him a sidelong glance. "You're not transdimensional; I am. Get the picture?"

"So basically you're blackmailing me."

"Basically."

I took a few paces back, stopping at an appropriate distance. Ion didn't move.

"One. Two—"

"No—no, no, no, no." He cut me off, shaking his head. "I can't do this. You don't get it."

"I do get it. I went through this too—we all did," I said firmly. "Do you want to be part of this? Yes or no?"

"Yes."

"Then suck it up and do exactly as I say," I said, picking up where I'd left off. "Three. Four..."

He hesitated, as I'd expected him to, but after that hesitation came an obedience I had not foreseen. He staggered backwards as I counted.

"Five, six," I continued. "Seven, eight... nine..."

I watched him carefully as I announced the final numeral. He took one last step backward, and his foot came down on nothing. He vanished abruptly over the edge.

His sudden bravado threw me off momentarily, but after a second I managed to follow suit, shifting as I threw myself over the edge. Flames overtook the surface of my skin.

I could see his pale arms beating wildly against the ashy gray fog below us. I was small in raptor form, but I was fast and strong enough to catch him by the back of his shirt before he was too far gone. Animalistic howls poured out of his lungs as I snatched him up. Had I any facial muscles in that form, I would have smiled.

Pumping my wings hard as he flailed, I rose back to the ledge and dropped him from about six feet up, letting him tumble into a disheveled heap, sputtering and swearing. I hovered a moment longer while he regained himself, and then landed gently in the grass. It took him what felt like an abnormally long amount of time to catch his breath enough to look up at me. His eyes went wide.

"You," he said, not seeming to have made the connection yet. "Where the hell did you come from?"

I narrowed my eyes slightly, looking back at him.

"I thought you were from the normal world." Ion pushed himself up into a seated position. "How did you... Wait..."

I could tell by the look on his face that it was starting to click. It was the sort of expression that would accompany a brain freeze.

"Oh my god. You're... Please don't tell me you're actually a bird. This has been demented enough."

I drew back my wings and returned to human form. Ion squirmed backward. His eyes looked as though they wanted to come out of his head.

"Don't look at me like that," I said, getting to my feet. "You're weird too."

"I'm not *that* weird. I don't turn into animals."

"I don't turn into 'animals,' either. I shift into one particular species of raptor."

"One more species than what I shift into."

I pressed my lips into the slightest of smiles. "That's because you can't shift, *period*. It's an extremely advanced ability. Sensei taught me personally."

"Is that so."

"He and I are the only ones who have proven ourselves capable of it thus far, actually."

Ion climbed to his feet. "Yeah, well. You said that if I jumped off the stupid cliff, you would take me home. I still can't believe I actually did that."

"Admittedly, I was surprised too. I didn't think you would," I confessed, glancing at my fingernails. "However, you've already broken the code of conduct several times in the last few minutes, so I can see we'll have to work on that."

"Yeah, sure." He sounded unconvinced. "Whatever you say."

I nodded towards the path. "You'll acclimate. Come on. I'll take you home for now. You passed your induction."

Ion didn't say a word on the walk back to the cavern, and my occasional glances at him confirmed that he was in some sort of daze. His eyes were hazed over and the blood had left his face.

"Does it hurt?" he finally asked once we were inside and I had shut the door behind us. "Shifting, I mean."

I thought about it for a moment. "No. Not really."

"Does it feel… strange?"

"It depends on how you define strange," I said, leaning back against the door and beginning to focus. "It feels good to me."

"Why do you do it?"

"Shift?"

I could sense him nodding.

"Because," I said, "Sensei believes that if I seek diligently enough, I can find myself."

There was a pause. I could hear him breathing softly.

"So you think you'll find yourself in a hawk?"

I didn't say anything for a moment. I closed my eyes and felt my eyelashes brush against my cheeks.

"I don't know that I'll find myself anywhere, particularly."

The answer was strange enough to quiet him while I focused on our transportation. I felt the texture of the wooden door behind me change slightly. After a few seconds of steadying my breath, I reached up to snap on the closet light. The numb expression had lifted from Ion's face, leaving only a thin sweat that coated his skin and dampened his dark hair. His eyes watched me as if I was dangerous.

"Upon induction, students are renamed," I explained. "The name, once given, becomes your sole identity. You no longer have a first or last name, title, or identification of any other kind."

"Do I get to choose?"

"No," I replied. "I do."

He opened his mouth to retort, but then closed it again, subtly kicking the wall instead.

I gave him a firm once-over. "Icarus."

He looked up. "I wouldn't have guessed you were into Greek mythology."

"I'm not," I said. "But I know that you are. And it does, after all, mean 'follower.' I think that's fitting, don't you?"

"How did you know that I was interested in the subject?"

"I know more about you than you realize."

I could see the uneasiness creep back into his eyes.

"Do you know about what happened at my last school?"

I studied his expression for a moment before giving a slow nod. "Yes. I know."

"Do you know *how* it happened?" His voice was tense.

"No," I answered. "But you're a shell, Icarus. One that can be opened. A darkness into which one can speak and call things out. You'll tell me about it one day, when you're ready."

A dubious smile passed briefly over his lips as he pulled his gaze from mine, shaking his head. "No. No, I'll never tell you. My only fear was that maybe you had already found out, by whatever witchlike methods you have already apparently utilized to learn everything else about me."

I opened the door, letting the natural daylight come pouring in from the hallway. "No, I don't know any of the details of the incident."

We stepped out into the hallway and moved into the kitchen.

"You'll find things have changed since you were last here," I explained, scanning the calendar that was taped to the refrigerator. "Time passage is far more prominent in this dimension."

He yawned. "Sure."

"Are you even listening?"

"Not really, I'm frickin' wiped," he said, messing a hand through his hair. "I just want to go home and sleep. Are you done with me?"

"Remember the code."

He threw me a look over one shoulder. "Oh, come on. Doesn't that only apply there?"

"Now that you're one of us, it applies everywhere."

"You've got to be kidding me—"

"And one more thing," I said before he could go further. "You can't tell anyone about the Dimension. You can't breathe a word about anything you've seen."

"I know. Sensei already told me."

I was still staring at him, not saying anything. I crossed my arms.

"What?"

"You may trust me enough to jump off a cliff," I said, "but that doesn't mean I trust you."

He shrugged, turning to leave. "Then don't. But I swear I won't let you down."

I stood there, watching him go. "Right."

CHAPTER TEN

Ion

By the time I got back to the house, it was almost noon. I couldn't believe I had spent an entire night in the other dimension. It didn't feel like that much time had gone by. I would have to rush if I was going to get to class on time. Ruger and West had already left. I shoved my homework into my backpack and went out to my car.

Ditching my Mustang in the parking garage when I arrived, I crossed campus and ran into Mel almost immediately, close to the trees where we'd last met. When she saw me this time, though, she turned away.

"Hey, Mel," I called, breaking into a jog. "Wait up."

She was carrying books under one arm and texting with her free hand. Her dark hair flowed down her back like ripples of silk, crowned by a pair of retro shades, which she promptly flipped down over her eyes as I fell into step beside her.

"What's your deal?" I asked, catching my breath slightly. "Are you ignoring me or something?"

She exhaled a laugh. "*My* deal? Shouldn't I be the one asking *you* that question, Ion?"

"What are you talking about?"

"Oh, I don't know," she replied coolly. "You just disappear for three days, miss our date without explanation, and don't even bother to get in touch with me."

I stopped dead, a sinking sensation forming in the pit of my stomach.

"What do you mean three days?" I asked, though she hadn't stopped walking. "I didn't disappear to anywhere—Mel, come on. What are you talking about? I don't understand."

"You don't understand?" she reiterated. "Haven't you checked your phone in the past few days? Haven't you gotten any of my or Ruger's or West's text messages?"

"No, I didn't have a chance to check my phone before I left the house."

"People have been freaking out about you, Ion." Mel finally began to slow down. "*I've* been freaking out about you. Do you even realize how this makes me look? Do you realize how much it took for me to dump Riley for you? How hard it was to keep my mouth shut during this whole thing, when I know…"

She shot a quick glance over her shoulder before lowering her voice. I could see the outline of her eyes vaguely behind her shades.

"When I know that you have… issues," she continued. "Here I was, thinking you actually trusted me, and then *bam*. You just take off one night and don't come back for a week."

My body felt numb as Hawk's words came rushing back to the front of my mind. How time was "more prominent" in this world than it was in the Dimension. How much time had gone by *here* while I was *there*? Had days actually passed in what had only felt like several hours in the Dimension? How was that even possible? How was *any of it* possible?

"Mel, look. I…" I drew in a long breath. "I'm sorry. I just… it's so hard to explain. I didn't mean to leave."

"Right. Of course you didn't." She turned to face forward. "That line is as old as the hills, Ion. You better give me something a little better than that. Right now they have no proof that you were the one who attacked Riley, but I'll give it to them if you're not honest with me."

I looked at her. "What do you mean they have no proof? What about the security recording? You said—"

"The recording was blank," Mel cut in. "How it happened, they have no idea, but when they reviewed it, they found nothing but static. No one believes Riley—he has a reputation—but they would if a witness came forward and backed him up."

"Witness?" I questioned, quickening my steps to match hers. "You?"

Mel shrugged flippantly.

"You would seriously turn me in?" I lowered my voice. "Do you know what they would do if they found out about me, Mel? I wouldn't go to prison—I would go to a *lab* for tests. Do you want that?"

She halted so abruptly I almost ran right into her. She flipped her shades up and her eyes drilled straight into mine. "If I had, I would have already told them what I know about you. I just... I need you to tell me the truth, okay? Relationships are built on honesty, right?"

I nodded. "Which is why I shouldn't be in a relationship. Not with you, not with anyone—"

"Ion—"

"No, Mel!" I cut her off this time, taking a step closer. "I hurt people, okay? You're better off staying away from me, for your own sake. I'm not capable of being honest with you."

"Okay, just calm down, would you?" she huffed. "Let me buy you a drink or something when we get out of class."

I shook my head. "I shouldn't, Mel. Really."

"Come on," she insisted. "One drink together isn't going to kill either of us, right?"

I weighed the possibilities. "I know what it is you want, Mel."

"I don't want anything from you, Ion. I just want to talk." Mel reached up to brush her fingertips back through my hair. "I thought you trusted me."

I glanced down again, pulling in an unsteady breath. "I do, Mel, really. I'm just..."

"You're just what?" she questioned, looking up into my eyes. "You're afraid that I'll tell someone? That I'll get hurt? Ion, you need to just loosen up."

I laughed mirthlessly. "You don't understand."

"I know," she said. "I know I don't understand, but I want to."

It was surreal. Only hours before, a girl had invited me to jump off a cliff in another dimension. Now I was back at school, in a very normal-looking world, being asked out by a very normal-looking girl. I wanted to laugh and scream at the same time. But instead I finally just broke down and said, "Okay. One drink."

And all would have gone smoothly, if it had, in fact, been one drink.

———————————

I received several warnings about my absence from my professors. My cover story was that I'd had to visit a sick aunt on extremely short notice. Afterwards, I met up with Mel in the parking garage, and she insisted that we take her car, teasing that she should drive. She put on the radio and we headed for the coast.

The sun was setting by the time we arrived, and Mel pulled up in front of a crowded, hipster-looking bar.

"You ever been here before?" she asked as we slid into stool at the far end of the long mahogany bar.

I shook my head. "I usually only drive all the way over here to surf, if the conditions are good."

Mel picked up a drink menu. "I love this place. I used to have Riley bring me here all the time."

"Mm."

"What are you ordering?"

"I'll have whatever you're having," I said. "It doesn't matter to me."

Mel grinned. The bartender came over and rested his forearms on the counter in front of her, and right away I detected that they knew each other.

They flirted back and forth slightly, and then Mel ordered us drinks in Spanish, which, judging by his accent, was the bartender's mother tongue. I glanced in Mel's direction as soon as he'd left to prepare our drinks.

"What did you just order?"

She waved it off. "Nothing too extreme; don't worry."

The place was filling up quickly. Someone prepped a drum kit on a stage at the back of the room for live music.

"So, do you want to start by telling me how you can even do these things that you do?" I could feel her eyes making a study of me. "Or maybe why you didn't care enough to let me know that you couldn't make our date?"

I pulled my focus back down to hers, becoming suddenly all too aware of her soft brown eyes.

"I'm sorry, Mel. I didn't have my phone with me."

"I know. Ruger told me he found it in your room, which he practically tore apart trying to find a trace as to where you took off to," she said, toying with the delicate silver chain that encircled her neck. "Why didn't you take it with you?"

I shrugged. "I was just going over to my neighbor's house. I didn't think it would take me that long."

"Your neighbor's house?"

I opened my mouth to respond, but closed it again as the bartender approached to slide two tall, slender glasses in front of us.

"*Disfrutar, señorita.*"

"*Gracias.*"

I reached up to run a hand back through my hair. "There's this girl next door, and she asked me over to talk about—"

"A girl next door?" she repeated, the tolerance in her voice beginning to dissolve. "Are you serious? That's what this is?"

"It's not like that. She wanted… it's…"

This was not coming out as planned.

"Mel, it's not that," I said. "It's really complicated. It's not even my secret to tell."

Mel didn't reply, but I could still feel the intensity of her eyes. I lifted my glass to my lips and downed half of it.

"Did it have anything to do with the car incident?"

I nodded slightly and swallowed.

"I thought that was the old guy's car."

"It is, but she's his…" I searched for the right word in the glass of amber liquid. "Student."

"And… his student lives with him?"

"It's complicated."

"Uh-huh. *Complicated*," Mel said, glancing at her drink. "You keep saying that, but so far nothing sounds complicated. It sounds like a love affair."

"Believe me, it's not like that." I tried not to choke. "I can't stand her."

"Was she with you when you went away?"

I took another long drink, stalling so that I could calculate a reply. It seemed like no matter what I said, I was digging myself in deeper.

"What is this, anyway?" I asked, setting the empty glass back down on the counter.

"You like it?"

I shrugged slightly. "It's… yeah. It's interesting."

"Good, I'll order you another."

I began to protest, but she was already rattling off something in Spanish to the bartender again.

"So she was with you?" She turned back to me.

I nodded hesitantly. "Yeah, but it wasn't like… what you're imagining."

"Then what was it like?"

I blew out a sigh, resting my temple on my fist. "I can't really say… She said I couldn't. I don't want to break my word."

A glass identical to the last slid in front of me, beaded with condensation. I started drawing circles on the wooden surface of the bar with my forefinger.

"Break your word to her?"

I nodded slowly, processing the question. My brain was beginning to feel like sludge, each thought like a ten-pound weight. Nothing moved very fast.

"I thought you said you couldn't stand her." Mel finally took a tiny sip from her glass. "Why is it that you have to keep your promise to her, Ion?"

I shrugged minutely, lifting my glass to take another sip. "I don't know. It's just like… right. You know?"

She shook her head. "No, I don't know. I thought your first loyalties would be to me, if it came down to it."

"I'm not a loyal person, Mel."

"Then who cares about the promises you made to a girl who doesn't care about you?" she said, lowering her voice as she leaned slightly closer. "I seriously want to help you, Ion. And I know you think that I can't, but I can if you just let me."

I glanced up slowly, my brain attempting to process her closeness. I felt the warmth of her hand on my thigh.

"My name isn't Ion," I said slowly, drawing circles again with my finger. "It's Icarus."

Her eyebrows met each other in the middle of her perfect forehead. "What?"

"You know, like in Greek mythology." I took another sip. "Son of Daedalus. Flew too close to the sun, and his wings melted and he fell into the ocean."

She stared at me.

"Have you ever wondered, like, what happened to him after that?" I asked, setting the half-empty glass down. "I mean, like… was his body recovered, or did the sharks eat him?"

"So that's your real name?" she asked, ignoring my question.

I shook my head. "No, she gave it to me."

"Who did?"

"The girl next door."

"The girl next door *renamed* you?"

I rubbed my eyelids with my forefinger and thumb. "There's this, like… secret society, but not really. She took me there."

"Where is this place?"

I drained the rest of the glass. "I don't really know, you know? It's in another dimension. It's for people who are like me."

I could still feel her hand on my leg, her fingers drawing vague circles now. She was leaning against the counter with her hair drawn over one shoulder. She looked so pretty.

"And what are you like?" she asked.

I watched the reflections as they played across her eyes. "I'm a slider, Mel."

The circles stopped. "What is that, exactly?"

I tried to refocus. Her hand moved smoothly to mine, gently opening it up to caress my palm with her fingertips.

"I can heal people," I said, noticing that my pronunciation had deteriorated, though honesty was becoming easier. "Weird things happen when I touch electronics… vehicles, stuff like that. I accidently fried a gaming console when I was younger, because I got too close."

"Seriously?"

I nodded. "That's why I had to transfer a few times. So no one would find out."

Mel's gaze hadn't moved from mine. "What about the people you've hurt?"

"I don't want to talk about that."

"Why?"

"Because I don't want to remember it," I said, trying to speak more clearly over the noise. The band was warming up by this point. "It makes me feel out of control, you know? That's why he chose me, I guess… So that I could learn how to control it."

My body felt relaxed, but something in my brain went haywire when I said this. In the mire that my thoughts had become, I questioned why I was even telling her this. How had the conversation evolved to this point?

A panicky feeling began to rise in my chest. I was about to ask her if we could go somewhere else to talk when she cut in with another question.

"Can you go there whenever you want to?" Mel asked, the light tone of her voice a stark contrast to the look in her eyes. "How do you get there?"

"I really can't say, Mel," I told her. "I promised I—"

"Oh, come on." She traced a heart on the surface of my hand. "You can trust me."

———————

When Mel finally dragged me out of the bar, it was late—well, after midnight. I barely comprehended the conversation on the drive back, but I didn't shut up. I answered every question she asked.

When Mel pulled her car into the shared driveway between my house and the neighbor's, ours was the only vehicle present. She turned to look at me.

"No one's home."

"Mmm. Guess not."

She unbuckled. "You have a way to get into his place, right?"

"Hawk said I have access to the portal whenever I want, so…"

I heard her door pop open. She got out.

"But—wait." I undid my seatbelt and scrambled out of the car. "What if he—Mel, what if he doesn't want me to take you there? I mean, there's a process and stuff."

"*Process.* Right." She pushed past me, crossed the driveway, and opened the gate leading into Sensei's front yard. "Ion—Icarus, whatever your name really is—you're either insane, or you're a stoner. I want to find out which."

I wanted to protest, but I was too busy trying to keep up. I stumbled on the way through the gate.

Mel skipped up the steps to the front porch and tried the doorknob. It didn't budge.

"Mel, seriously," I repeated, reaching up to rub the back of my neck. "I don't think we should be doing this."

She rolled her eyes and slipped her finger through one of the belt loops on my jeans, tugging me over to the door. She tapped the knob with one manicured finger.

"It's locked," she announced.

My hands, as if they were their own entities, ventured around her waist. Mel twisted around to face me.

"How are we going to get in?"

I looked at her for a second; then I heard myself laugh. "I don't know, but your eyes are really pretty."

She wriggled one arm free of my grasp to try the knob again. "Didn't you get really emotional the day you punched Riley?"

"Mm-hmm." I nodded slightly, brushing her hair back away from her neck. "I can't get emotional. I mean… I shouldn't."

"Why? Do your powers get stronger when your emotions do?"

"I don't know… Yeah, basically."

"Really?"

She seemed to contemplate this for a moment before shooting a quick glance over my shoulder as if to affirm that no one was around.

"What is it?" I asked, fumbling with the words as I tried to decipher her expression.

Mel shook her head, leaning closer to press a kiss onto my lips. "Nothing."

I wasn't sure why she had kissed me just then, but I was honestly too intoxicated to care. There was literally no one around, and I knew Sensei wasn't inside the house. At first her hands wanted to be in my hair, but when I started to reciprocate, pushing her up against the door, I felt her fingertips slip down my forearm and into my right hand. She eased my palm onto the cool, brass doorknob. I felt a slight shock tease my fingertips. They contracted—and blew a sizable hole through the hardwood, bulleting the knob onto the front lawn.

My heart rate instantly skyrocketed. I pulled back.

She slipped a hand over my mouth before I could say anything. "It's okay. Don't say a word. Someone might hear us."

I swallowed, feeling slightly dizzy as I tried to process what had just happened. She tugged me into the house after her and shut the door behind us.

"Mel, I have a really bad feeling about this," I said, trying to catch my breath as I followed her through the darkness. "I never drink this much—this is dangerous. I have a hard enough time controlling myself sober."

"You and this self-control thing," Mel murmured, finding the kitchen light. "What did I tell you earlier about loosening up?"

"You don't *understand.*"

"Take me to this other dimension and maybe I will."

Something inside me was screaming—warring against my rib cage to fight each of my pitifully inebriated decisions. But true to my new name, I did nothing more than follow.

Mel led me down the hallway I'd mentioned in what was now only a smudged memory of a conversation, and I opened the door to the broom closet. She turned to look at me skeptically.

"Are you serious?"

I nodded, feeling a warmth rising to redden my ears. "I know. It's weird."

"Both of us?" Mel laughed and playfully dragged me into the tiny dark space after her. "So your secret world is in a closet, huh?"

I fumbled around for the light but failed to find the pull chain. "Of course not. You have to transport there—or in this case, I do."

I had no idea what I was doing or why I was doing it. I had taken note of how Hawk had executed a transportation, but I had yet to even attempt it on my own. I had scarcely been in the Dimension long enough to understand what it even was. Mel's hands found my torso in the darkness and her arms wove around me, distracting my thoughts.

"So how does this 'transportation' work?" Mel asked, though apparently not expecting an answer because her mouth interrupted the mumbled beginnings of my response.

I fell back against the closest wall, feeling the air leave my lungs and flood into hers. I felt her fingers contract at the back of my neck, tangling with my hair. Feeling weak in every way imaginable and devoid of sanity, I gave in.

Blurry visions of the cavern and its sparkling interior made vague appearances in my mind's eye as I relaxed, pulling away from her slightly to take a breath. She murmured something inaudibly, and her hands slipped beneath my shirt, beginning to tug it off. That was when what felt like a sixth sense kicked in.

I tried to divert my focus, but I was a split second too slow. I felt my hands heat up, and as if an invisible force had inserted itself between us, Mel was pushed backwards into the wall opposite.

I wasn't sure what had happened or why. I wanted to apologize, but my voice had deserted me.

"*God*, Ion," she hissed, regaining herself. "What is wrong with…" She trailed off, and I attempted to slow my mind down enough to respond, but thankfully I didn't have to.

"Ion… the walls…" I could hear echoes in her words and slight movements now. Dimly, I became aware that the temperature had dropped again. "They're… *stone*. Ion, where *are* we?"

The fog that had been obscuring my every thought began to lift, leaving a sick feeling in the pit of my stomach. Things started to click.

"Ion, answer me." She sounded a little more frantic as she moved through the darkness, brushing past me to the door. "What just happened?"

I tried to process a response, but my brain was still out of commission. Mel flung the door open, letting the light spill in like water. The vast hall of windows stretched out before us.

I heard Mel exhale sharply. She turned back to stare at me, wide-eyed. I still hadn't moved.

"It's actually real?"

The three words nailed into my chest like bullets, and the gravity of my mistake began to sink in. I was about to answer when out of the corner of my eye I noticed a movement over Mel's shoulder. I glanced up just in time to see Hawk round the corner and start down the hallway. She stopped in her tracks when she saw me.

I was dead.

CHAPTER ELEVEN
Hawk

A twilight blemished with clouds mirrored itself in the hoods of the parked cars. I could make out their vague shapes through the window up against which my hands were pressed. My exhales made faded patterns on the glass as I breathed.

Sound, as if it hadn't been there before, began to slowly make its entrance, fading in as though breaking the surface of still water. Voices drew my attention from the sheen of the vehicles to the exquisite bodies emerging from them. Painted specters draped in silk, gold, and feathers, masqueraded in smoke. Limbs were curved, ivory, elegant, and set like jewels against satin.

I felt my heart losing track of its pace as I watched the familiar parade, steeped in all its barely post-war mystique. I became aware of a cigarette between my first two fingers and a voice like a gamma ray emerging from the black hole of my past. It spoke to me with words accented by poverty, and when I turned, my eyes found the shape of his face, his familiar features illuminated by the backstage electric lights.

I could hear the brassy tumult of instruments warming up on the opposite side of the heavy velvet curtain that stood to separate us from a society that would burn to the touch.

"And so we made it out alive." He passively made the same observation as he did every time. "A war to end all wars—theirs and ours."

Smoke sprawled up against the glass on my next exhale. "There is no 'our.' There's me, there's you—two fragments of carbon sent to drift in separate directions."

For a moment he didn't speak, and when he did, there was something strange hidden in his tone. "We're both cursed, you and I. Our patterns intertwine—converge."

"The markings don't mean I'm cursed," I said.

"A girl isn't just born with black bands around her arms as if she is permanently in mourning. That doesn't just happen."

"I don't care what they said. This place is temporary. By this time next year I'll be somewhere warm. Somewhere where fruit grows wild on trees and the sky comes up blue with the dawn."

My words felt scripted. The glances, the sounds, the flavor of smoke across my tongue—it was all a reincarnation. I was beginning to realize it as I stood there and listened to his voice. I knew what he would say next, what I would say. I knew what would happen.

"So you'll forget about me, then?"

I couldn't reply. I pulled away from the conversation, and I felt his eyes follow me.

"I'm the only reason you're here." His words stalked me along with his footsteps. "I'm the only reason you escaped, Charlotte. You owe me every-thing."

"I owe you nothing."

I couldn't stop the words from coming. They rushed out recklessly as if to speed up the progression of events and bring the unalterable end nearer.

The darkened hallway branching off to the dressing rooms swallowed me whole. I still recognized the faded red tone of the hardwood beneath my feet. I recognized the various doors and felt the burning sensation of the skeleton key folded into my hand.

"Charlotte."

My hatred for my own name overwhelmed me. I hated the way he said it.

"You need me."

My body halted numbly in front of a dressing room door. I unlocked it. It yawned open before me, and I slipped inside.

"I need neither you nor anyone," I said. "I don't trust you anymore."

I heard the door softly click shut. I felt my breath hesitate.

Two hands found me in the darkness and contracted around my arms. I felt his fingernails as they gently coaxed the blood from the blackened parts of my flesh. I stumbled violently backwards and the wall found me, pounding stars into my vision.

In the blackness my eyes searched for his, but found only mirages of what I remembered them to be. I felt his breath in my mouth as it bit down over mine. I drove the heels of my hands into his chest. His own countered by digging in deeper, like blades to a sacrificial dove.

We'd never been accustomed to words. Language had never come naturally, and violence had always been a stronger instinct. So my stream of consciousness allowed only exhales and rapid inhales as I struggled to sink my claws into his chest. I could hear the distant harmonies as they drifted rebelliously from the stage to slip under the door.

My heart thrashed at my rib cage, a trapped animal with no escape from my flesh. The body I, too, longed to leave—a cage with iron bars.

I felt his mouth against my neck, his teeth. His hands tore my clothing away and the heat of his body smothered the flame in mine.

I never found the light.

I was wrenched back into consciousness by a noise drifting in from outside. I was tangled in a stranglehold of sheets and saturated in my own sweat.

My apartment was freckled in patches of soft morning light reflecting off the full-length glass wall, as docile as moths. It was too early for the birds, too late for the orchestral evening winds, too still to feel unexposed in the silence as I attempted to regain my breath. My heartbeat was the only identifiable sound in the stillness—my heart, raging in my chest.

Forcing myself to rise, I stumbled slightly as vertigo kissed my sense of balance. I reached over my shoulder blades and drew my shirt off. The soaked fabric clung stubbornly to my skin. My hands drifted instinctively to the markings on my arms—the places where my flesh still burned with wounds that had vanished almost one hundred years earlier.

I undressed and stepped into the shower, avoiding the mirror. Shunning my reflection.

Though the water was lukewarm, it somehow managed to burn as it fell gently across my skin. I was hyperconscious of its heat, of my breathing, of the sick feeling that wouldn't leave me alone. The unfamiliar sensation of gathering tears startled me. I hadn't weakened to the impulse for the past century— I wasn't about to break that streak now. I shifted.

The water ran over my feathers, unable to penetrate to my flesh. I closed my eyes and let my thoughts focus on the impact of each drop. The way the spray gathered around me like the clouds did when I was in flight. The way it spoke to me, whispering how it was all just a dream, attempting to persuade me to believe in a fantasy just long enough for the blood to stop flowing from the wound. But I refused to swallow the consolation, as if it were poison.

I returned to human form and dressed, trying to ignore how painful it was to be back in my own skin. My former name reiterated in my mind, bathed in the tone of his voice.

Charlotte.

I twisted my hair back into a careless bun. Then I crossed the room and opened the window, easing out onto the ledge.

Dawn washed down the center of the ravine like floodwater, dousing the rocks in ripened yellow and tainting the fog that swelled up from what was believed to be the bottom thousands of feet down. My thoughts drifted to the amount of momentum at which one would reach the bottom, the intensity of the impact that would ensue.

The truth was, no one knew if such a place existed. It was likely that the drop was a bottomless one. The Dimension was, after all, projected from Sensei's deep consciousness, making it highly likely that nothing physically existed beyond the fog. This was why we used the drop for trust falls—because it was a wild card. The epitome of the terrifying unknown. Still, I couldn't help but wonder what it would feel like to free-fall either to eternity or to one's death—though I knew the latter was a physical impossibility for me.

I stared down into it. I could feel the coolness rising to caress my skin. I felt like a Juliet to its sadistic version of Romeo as it pleaded with me, tugging at my flesh, which ached to come off.

I diverted my focus as I slipped from the ledge and free-fell, shifting in the fog.

It was still too early for student activity; the platform was empty when I reached it. I dropped noiselessly from the railing, in human form, started across the platform and down the hallway leading to the cavern, and then came to an abrupt halt.

Icarus's gaze nailed into mine right away, and I could have sworn I saw the blood recede from his face. The cavern door was flung open, and he stood there looking like a train wreck while a girl I had never seen before stumbled over to one of the windows to stare out. She seemed to be hyperventilating.

Whatever scant amount of hope I'd had in Icarus vanished as I sized up the scene in front of me. My first experience in slider selection was turning out to be a true baptism of fire.

He attempted to speak as I approached, but nothing came out sounding especially human. I snatched a handful of his hair and turned to drag him back down the hallway with me.

"Ow! Hawk, wait. I-I swear I can explain—"

"You'll get your chance." I gritted my teeth.

The girl who had breached the Dimension with Icarus seemed spurred out of her trance by the sound of my voice. She turned away from the window and gaped at us in horror.

"Wait, wait, wait," she stammered, watery voiced. "Where are you taking him? You can't just leave me here! Where am I? What is this place?"

"It is of no concern to you where I take him." I spoke over my shoulder. "Someone will attend to you momentarily. Stay where you are."

She opened her mouth to speak, but when nothing coherent came out, she closed it again, slumping back against the window-pane.

I dragged Icarus across the platform and into the opposite hallway, where I almost collided with Mitsue. He was emerging from one of the safe rooms, and his attention was absorbed in a sketchbook.

"Mitsue, go find Fin and tell him I need him to deal with the girl in the northern hallway by the portal," I instructed, focusing open one of the sliding pocket doors. "Tell him it's a nonthreatening security breach, and he should keep her under observation until we have further information."

"Security breach?" He glanced up. "How on earth did that happen?"

I released Icarus and shoved him into the empty white room. "Just *go find Fin*, okay?"

I slipped into the safe room and closed the door behind me, locking it with a glance over my shoulder.

The room was completely empty aside from the *chabudai* situated in the center. The safe rooms were typically reserved for one-on-one teaching sessions with more advanced students, or other private meetings, but today it would serve as a tranquil little interrogation room for Icarus—and something of a torture chamber for me. I was more than ready to get this over with.

"Take a seat," I instructed as I did myself, gesturing towards the tatami chair at the opposite side of the little Japanese table. "You have about three seconds to start explaining yourself."

It took an unacceptable amount of time for him to process what I'd just said. He turned away from the glass and came sluggishly to the low-rising table, falling into the seat opposite mine.

"You swore that you wouldn't let me down."

His eyes closed under the weight of the words. "I know—"

"You've proven that your word means literally nothing."

"Hawk, I was wasted. I'm sorry, okay?"

"It's anything *but* okay." I was seething. "You've broken every rule, Icarus—fallen short of every standard. You have failed us in every possible way—does that mean *anything* to you?"

He reached up to press his forefinger and thumb to his eyelids. "It means that you should never have brought me here. I'm not cut out for this."

"You're not cut out for this?" I repeated. "Or are you simply unwilling to put forth the effort it will take to figure yourself out?"

He opened his mouth as if to speak, but then shut it again.

"Ion," I began, then corrected myself. "Icarus, do you know why I renamed you?"

He paused for a moment and then shook his head.

"I renamed you because when you entered the Dimension, you became a different person. Your cells, your DNA, your genetics had to recreate themselves. That isn't to say that you're a different human from the one you were before you came here, but you're… in a sense, a different version of you. A recreated version."

He squinted at me. I could tell this went over his head.

"Okay, never mind." I sighed, leaning forward to rest my elbows on the table. "I don't have the time—and you most certainly do not have the capacity to understand at the moment. You'll have to learn experientially."

"I don't understand."

"You don't need to," I said. "The only thing you need to understand is that you've proven yourself incapable of trust at this time. So now, unless you want to be exiled, you will do exactly as I say."

This caught his attention.

"Exiled? What are you gonna do, send me to some sort of deserted island?"

I shook my head slowly. "Do you recall Sensei mentioning cognitive readings?"

"Vaguely?"

"It's an extremely deep power that allows one to read another's cognitive—their thoughts, memories, and so on, and to remove such matter as necessary." I paused slightly, giving it a chance to sink in. "The Dimension is the only existing refuge for the anomalies of earth. If you prove to be a threat to the Dimension and its purpose, if you refuse to put forth the time and effort it will take to hone your abilities and become a protector, the rest of the student body has the right to decide what to do with you. Since you're still a fledgling, the easiest and most practical option would be simply to send you back where you came from."

I paused to gesture towards our surroundings.

"Sensei would take you to a room much like this one, and there he would give you a certain kind of sedative tea, which would put you into a comatose state. He would then focus on your subconscious thought patterns, find an inroad to your short- and long-term memory, and proceed to wipe out any recollection of having been here. You wouldn't remember hitting Sensei's car, you wouldn't remember meeting me or healing me or stabbing me—it would all be erased."

For a moment he said nothing.

"Would I still have powers?"

I nodded. "Of course you would. It would be impossible for anyone to cause you to part with them unless you allowed it. Not even Sensei can take those from you. But you would go back to being who you were before you came here—you'd be afraid of yourself again."

"What makes you think I was afraid of myself?"

"Because everyone is afraid of themselves. It's the way of humans," I said. "The question is are you ready to go back to that—yes or no?"

I observed his face for a moment to verify whether sincerity had finally made its debut in his icy blue eyes.

"I never want to go back to that."

"Then listen carefully." I folded my hands on the table. "Because I won't repeat myself. Since you have yet to prove yourself capable or worthy of taking part in the teaching sessions, you're going to have to work your way up to that point—which means you'll do whatever I tell you. I want you to familiarize yourself with every square inch of the Dimension and how everything works here."

"What about getting back home?"

"This is your home now," I replied firmly. "From here onward, you'll consider your natural world secondary. You may return there to attend classes at your school and to decrease any suspicions that may be raised by your long absence. You will, in essence, create a façade of a normal life, just as Sensei and I have done. Every moment that you are able to come into the Dimension, you will, and when you are here, you will do whatever tasks I assign to you, and work until I tell you to stop. I will assess your progress, and once you have proven yourself trustworthy, I will allow you to enter sessions with the rest of the students." I paused and scanned his face. "Don't expect the process to be quick or painless. You've seriously violated the code of conduct by breaching the Dimension with a non-anomaly."

The mention of the girl seemed to snap him back to attention. He leaned forward slightly. "What's going to happen to her?"

I leaned back a little, uncomfortable with his closeness. "Fin is assessing her. I imagine she will have to undergo the aforementioned process."

"Her memory will be erased?"

I nodded.

"Will she… remember me?"

I considered for a moment, calculating my reply. I already knew the answer was yes. She would remember everything up until the moment they transported. But I decided to leverage my answer to pump him for a little more information.

"No, she won't remember ever having met you," I said slowly, watching his eyes. "Were you both close?"

"Well, like… yeah," he answered, sounding disgustingly like a Western teenager. "She's a student at my school. She was dating this guy that I absolutely hate, but she broke up with him so we could go out."

"So she's your girlfriend?"

Icarus nodded, then immediately tried to retract his response, realizing what this meant. "Wait, no. She's just—"

I held up a hand for silence. "Thank you for the Freudian slip, Icarus."

"It wasn't. I—"

"Regardless of what happens to her, which will be based on Fin's analyses, you will break off any understanding you have with—what is her name?"

"Mel."

"You will end whatever relationship you have with Mel," I reinforced firmly. "This was, in fact, one of the first standards we went over, was it not? Relationships are a distraction, and they are not permitted."

"But that's so stupid—why?"

"Because what we're doing is *serious*." I felt my jaw tighten. "It's impossible for you to understand what's at stake here. It's impossible for any of us, really, even those from the near future, because no one but Sensei has seen the *deep* future—have you even wondered why we have no students who are from the distant future of Earth?"

"Why?"

My gaze drilled into his for a moment before I responded, "Because there are none."

"But I thought Sensei said that every generation has—"

"Not in the distant future."

"Why not?"

"No one knows. That's the point," I said, rising to walk off the restlessness that was settling into my body. "We know from the accounts of students here from the near future that humanity progresses towards deeper and deeper levels of darkness. Apparently a point was eventually reached where the dark energy became great enough to drown out the anomaly movement. I can't comprehend what must have happened to Earth."

I heard him shift slightly in his seat behind me.

"How you can talk about the future like it's the past," he said, half to himself. "It literally makes no sense."

I walked slowly to the window to gaze out at the cliff side opposite. I could see other raptors, full-time ones, rising effortlessly in the updraft.

"If you wait until things make sense, you'll never take action," I said, and my breath fogged the glass. "*You* don't make sense to me. You, and all that you are, yet I haven't given up on this idea of you, have I?"

"You talk about me like I'm some kind of theory."

"Precisely."

The conversation had sailed out of his depth. He said nothing else. Eventually I turned away from the window and came back to the *chabudai*.

"Do you understand the situation now, Icarus?"

He didn't look up, but he nodded. "I understand."

"Look at me."

He did as I asked. His immense blue eyes lifted to stare up into mine, and in that moment they were soft and childlike. They told me he was lost, and they begged for mercy that I refused to give. My tone instead firmed as I repeated the question.

"*Do you understand?*"

"*Yes.*" He swallowed. "I understand."

I let my gaze remain on his for a moment. Then I stepped back, breaking the lock. "Rise. You can go now."

"Go where?"

I crossed the room, sliding open the door again with a quick glance. "Wait for me on the platform. I'll assign you to your first task. Once you've completed it, you can transport back to LA before too much time passes there."

Not bothering to wait for him, I abandoned Icarus in the safe room and strode briskly down the hallway towards the platform, which was beginning to fill up. Sensei was engaged in conversation with a group of more advanced students, so I didn't disturb him. I would fill him in on everything later, once I had it sorted out.

Crowd-weaving, I quickly made my way to the railing, picking my pace up to sprint the last several yards. I grabbed the rail when I reached it and somersaulted over the edge of the platform.

I let myself free-fall to the fog before I finally shifted, grazing the cool wisps of vapor as I caught the updraft. My contemplations at the ledge that dawn swept back into remembrance. The haunting dream.

Barely having to pump my wings, I rode the current up the cliff side until I reached the approximate halfway point. When I caught sight of Fin's dorm, I angled out of it, slowing down only enough to focus on the canvas flap that served as a door, drawing it aside and gliding easily in. He was hunched at one of the desks, poring over a page covered in inky notations. I perched on the back of his chair. He inhaled deeply as I landed noiselessly, acknowledging my presence though it was scarcely detectable.

"Thank God you're finished with him at last," Fin said, pulling a hand through his blond hair. "I was starting to think he'd never let you go."

I rolled my eyes, trilling slightly.

"I know, I know," he murmured, jotting something down. "I was joking. It's only that I've been waiting to talk to you."

I tilted my head slightly to one side.

"I have Mel locked in one of the safe rooms. Mitsue's keeping an eye on her for the time being." He paused to scribble a final notation before setting down his pen and turning around to face me. "But I need to talk to you about something."

I gave him a questioning look and waited for him to go on.

"Are you going to shift back to a human, or am I going to do the talking?"

I gave him a look. And despite the seriousness of the situation, he grinned.

"Sensei had arrived on the platform by the time I'd managed to lure Mel away from the cavern," he explained. "So naturally I felt obligated to explain what I knew of the situation—which wasn't very much. I could see that Mel was shaken, so I said that I was going to take her to one of the safe rooms to be monitored until I could meet with you. Then as I was starting to leave, he said, 'Fin, I want you to test her.'"

My eyes must have gone wide, because Fin nodded his agreement.

"My thoughts exactly. But I wasn't about to protest, so I took her into one of the vacant safe rooms and put her through a *wide* range of channeling tests." He paused. "And you're not going to believe this, but her test results were positive."

I felt the tension leave my wings. I could scarcely believe what I was hearing.

"I know. I don't understand it either," Fin said, rising from his chair to stretch his arms overhead. "Slider selection—it's such a painstaking, touch-and-go process, isn't it? I mean, how long did it take for you to figure out Icarus was a slider?"

Unable to sufficiently answer his question in my current state, I lifted off the back of the chair and shifted into human form.

"Sensei knew long before I did," I answered. "Sensei has been watching Icarus since he was just a little kid. I would never have chosen him—I went ahead with his test only on the basis of Sensei's belief in him."

Fin was pacing now. "Then wouldn't it be extraordinarily unlikely that one of Icarus's friends from college would *just happen* to have slidatorial abilities? Mel seemed rather shocked by the entire ordeal."

"You mean she didn't know?"

He shook his head. "She said she had no idea. She was rather lightheaded by the time we had finished, actually."

"Have you told Sensei?" I asked, following him with my gaze.

"He was in a session," Fin said. "Besides, I wanted to talk to you first. Icarus is your student. You've spent more time with him than anyone, and I trust your judgment."

"To be honest with you, Fin, I wish I'd never brought Icarus here." I took a seat on the edge of the desk directly behind me. "He seems almost eager to prove himself to be the enormous waste of time and energy I fear him to be."

"You *chose* him, Hawk."

"And perhaps I chose wrong."

"This has nothing to do with him," Fin said. "However incompetent he may be, Hawk, you chose him. You saw something in him. Have faith in yourself."

"Yes, I did see something," I admitted, sarcasm in my tone. "Arrogance, self-importance, carelessness…"

Fin gave me a look. "He's still only a fledgling."

"A fledgling who has managed to break almost every rule in one day."

Fin came to a stop beside the desk where I was seated. "Then make him pay for it."

My gaze slid up from my hands to his eyes. I raised an eyebrow, feeling curiosity's teeth.

"What would you suggest?"

A smile teased at the corners of his lips. He placed a hand gently on the desk beside me. "I'm sure you'll come up with plenty of sadistic ideas without any help from me."

I pursed my lips to smother a smile. "Oh, shut up."

"Can I ask you something?"

"Shoot."

Fin looked back, his expression serious again. He studied my face for a second before he spoke. "Are you okay?"

I nodded unhesitatingly. "Mm-hmm. Why?"

"I'm sensing some kind of war raging under that skin." His hand followed his voice. I felt his fingertips gently come up to touch my arm.

I shied away from him, slipping off the desk and putting a few steps between us. I felt his gaze follow me.

"I'm fine, Fin," I said, not looking at him. "Really."

CHAPTER TWELVE

Icarus

I sat across the table from West and tried to explain that I was having an early midlife crisis. I apologized for vanishing without a word, and without my phone, but I was going out of my mind. I'd needed to get away from everything. And I could tell he didn't believe one syllable of it.

He folded his hands on the table and stared me square in the eyes. "Are you being blackmailed or something?"

I shook my head.

"What about school?"

I shrugged, feeling the weight of its sudden insignificance. "What about it? I'll be able to catch up. And if I can't, it won't even matter in the grand scheme of things."

West raised an eyebrow. "'The grand scheme of things?'"

I nodded, bobbing my foot compulsively under the table.

"When the hell did you start talking like this?"

"I'm not talking in any particular way," I said. "I'm just trying to give you an explanation."

West adjusted his glasses, leaning back in his chair. "You actually think I'm buying this little story about your nervous-breakdown, spur-of-the-moment getaway? Because I'm not. I think you're full of it."

West was tougher than Ruger. Not that Ruger had believed me either, but he'd grudgingly swallowed my story when I'd persisted simply to shut me up. Ruger wasn't the type to dwell, but West was a different animal—an intellect. He wanted to logically understand what was going on, and I couldn't let that happen. I started to get up.

"Is it that girl?"

Why does everyone think that?

"What girl?"

"Don't pull that card."

I sighed and got up to get myself a glass of water. "No, West. It has nothing to do with her."

West had a sixth sense when it came to liars. The truth was it had everything to do with Hawk. Hawk was my doorway into the Dimension and my slave driver once I arrived there. Whether I liked it or not, she was my teacher and my coach. She was all that I had.

I was a commuter now—a drifter between two worlds. I went to classes, then drove my car to a public lot and left it there, not wanting to appear to be home yet. I would walk to Sensei's and enter through the back door, which Hawk would leave unbolted for me. Transporting had become second nature. I didn't sweat it anymore.

When I arrived on the platform, Hawk would be waiting for me with a long list of chores. She would assign me surprisingly easy tasks, like waxing the platform, washing the glass walls, or patrolling the dormitories—which sounded more interesting than it was. Mel, however, had passed her induction and now commuted between the Dimensions just as I did. Though we were assigned opposing schedules, making it a rare occurrence for me to encounter her in the Dimension.

Discovering that she was an anomaly with slider blood had somehow changed her. Her reputation as the rebel beauty queen on campus was fading. Rumor had it that she barely went out anymore. She kept to her dorm and her headphones, ignoring everyone, including me. I approached her to talk on several occasions at school, but she made pointed efforts to avoid me.

"Ever since that night when you went over and talked to the old guy about his car, you've been acting really strange." West's voice pulled me back down to earth again. He watched me as I mechanically took a glass out of the cabinet. "What's up with that?"

"West, nothing is up. I'm just sick of my life, okay?" I said, turning back to the sink. "Get off my case."

There was a pause. A long one.

"Fine, whatever," he said finally. "Just know that whatever it is you're doing to Mel? It's not going unnoticed."

"What are you talking about?" I looked out the window, into Sensei's yard.

"Did you seriously think no one would notice that Mel's evolved into a hermit ever since she got involved with you?"

"That isn't the case."

"Isn't it?" West raised an eyebrow as I turned around to face him again. "I don't know her personally—we clearly don't run in the same circles—but I've heard things through the grapevine. People will assume you hurt her in some way—especially Riley. I would watch my step if I were you."

"What do you mean, exactly?"

"Oh, I don't know," he said. "It's just that she was dating Riley first, and the guy has a little bit of a hate issue when it comes to you. Maybe try lying low?"

His voice was dripping with sarcasm, but he had a point. It wasn't like I hadn't already considered it, but hearing it from someone else gave it fresh weight. The last thing I needed was for Riley to start plotting my demise. I had enough on my plate as it was.

I needed to talk to Mel—whether she wanted to or not. I decided to track her down after classes that afternoon.

I found her beneath one of the trees with her nose stuck in a book. She didn't notice my approach until it was too late for her to devise an escape. Her eyes stayed focused on the page as I sat down beside her, though I could tell she was no longer reading.

"Mel, talk to me."

She didn't look up.

"Please."

"Ion…" She drew in a narrow breath. "*Icarus*, you wouldn't understand. Just leave me alone."

"Of course I understand," I said slowly. "In case you've forgotten, I'm a slider too—I was a slider *first*."

"Yeah, but you *want* to be," she replied sharply as she turned to face me. "You were *always* weird, Ion. You were always an outcast—no offense. You were never like the rest of us."

"I know that, but you—"

"I have *always* fit in," Mel interrupted, finishing my sentence. "I've always been like everyone else. I've always had friends. I've always been normal. I *like* being normal, Ion—I don't *want* to be an anomaly." Her voice cracked slightly, and she trailed off. "God, why couldn't you have just been a normal guy?"

I looked at her for a moment before leaning back against the tree behind us. "Mel, you don't know how many times I've asked myself the same question."

A moment passed.

"Why didn't you ever tell anyone?"

I thought about it for a second and then shrugged. "I was afraid."

"Of what?" she asked. "Of what people would say?"

"Of everything," I said. "But especially of myself. What I was capable of."

She considered that for a moment. "Understandable."

I looked at her. "Did Fin give you a new name?"

She nodded after a second. "Mala."

"Not a huge difference," I noted. "Shouldn't be too hard to get used to."

"Mm."

We sat in silence for a few moments. The wind moved in the treetops.

"So you seriously didn't know…?" I trailed off, unsure how to finish.

Mel shook her head. From her expression I could tell her newfound abilities weren't something she was comfortable thinking about. Instead of answering my question further, she changed the subject.

"What about us?"

"Us?"

"You and me," she clarified. "I heard the rules—the code or whatever. What happens now?"

I tried to ignore her gaze. "Did you have to do a trust fall?"

"It was terrifying."

"Hawk has me do them every day," I said, looking up at the canopy of oak leaves above us. "She won't let me join the sessions yet. Not even the ones you're included in."

"Why?"

"Because I have to prove myself," I said. "I have to show her that I'm good enough. Mel, I can't break any of the rules. I have no option."

I could practically hear her thoughts.

She drew in a deep breath. "Ion, I need you more than ever right now. I feel so alone."

"Mel," I said, "we can't get involved. There's too much at risk. It's too important."

"Too much at risk for *you*."

"Mel, you don't know how hard this is for me."

She turned to look at me, her eyes steely. "Is it really?"

"Do you think I wanted things to end between us? You're the only person I trust."

She blinked, seeming a little taken aback. "You trust me?"

I *had* just told her that I did, but the truth was, I didn't. I didn't trust her because I didn't trust anyone. But I needed her on my side, and telling her that I trusted her seemed like a good place to start. So I nodded.

"Then tell me something." The way she said it was unnerving.

"Okay."

She studied me. "Tell me why you transferred. The student you said you almost killed—"

"Mel—"

She cut me off, raising a hand. "No, Ion. If you trust me and you want me to go along with this, tell me what happened to him."

Her dark eyes cut into my own.

"Her," I corrected quietly.

She turned to look at me. "What?"

"Mel, there are hundreds of things I could tell you about, but the one thing I can't tell you about is what happened at that school. It has nothing to do with you. It's just…" I bit my lip, searching for words. "I can't…"

Her gaze still hadn't moved from mine. "Why does Riley hate you?"

"I think it's because he knows," I replied. "He knows that I'm different— you heard him that day. I think he's known since I first came here."

"So Riley knows what happened, yet you won't tell *me?*"

"Mel, it's not that I—"

"You know what, Ion? Save it." She stood, gathering her things under one arm. "Go back to your mystical little world and rot there. I hope Hawk works you to death."

"Mel, please. It's not that I don't—it's not that I…"

I stumbled through sentences, with no idea how to finish them. There was nothing I could say that would redeem me. Mel stalked away without a backward glance, leaving me in the wake of her clicking high heels to regain myself. I knew that she wouldn't betray me even if she did hate me at the moment. To give me away would be to blow her own cover, since she was transdimensional too.

My consolation was in the breakup—at least it was over and I could give Hawk a report of my obedience.

I lingered there under the tree a while longer, lost in the haunting memory of Mel's words. I forced myself to gather up my books and walk back to my car. A feeling of déjà vu passed over me as I made my way through the garage. I thought about what West had said. About how people were starting to talk about Mel and me—how they would assume that I had wronged her in some way. How it was only a matter of time until Riley decided to carry out my execution.

Everyone thought Riley and I hated each other because we were both competitive and both wanted the same girl. They didn't understand who I was or how much Riley knew. I didn't even know how much Riley knew or how he'd even been able to track down the information about me that he had.

Something about it all didn't add up, but I didn't have time to think about it. A quick glance at my phone told me I was already running late. I couldn't leave my car in the driveway, not when I wasn't actually home, it would raise too much suspicion. So as usual, I paid to park in a lot a few blocks away from my house and then sprinted to Sensei's. I found him kneeling on the porch when I arrived, installing what looked like a new brass-plated doorknob to replace the one I'd annihilated. He looked up when he saw me.

"Icarus." He smiled placidly. "How are you?"

"Fine," I panted. "But I'll be in for a tongue-lashing from Hawk. I'm late by at least five minutes."

"This is why you have run here?"

I nodded and then gestured vaguely towards the door. "Sorry about that, by the way. It was an accident."

Sensei twisted the screwdriver. "You broke the doorknob?"

I nodded reluctantly.

"How did you manage it?"

"I was trying to get in one night," I explained, too embarrassed to go into detail. "When I tried the knob, I happened to be... emotionally preoccupied."

"Emotionally?" He continued turning a screw. "And it blew apart when you touched it."

"Yes, Sensei."

He glanced up at me. "And so your powers increase with your emotions?"

"It's always been that way."

"You cannot allow your emotions sovereignty, young one." He returned his attention to his work. "They will lead to your destruction. This is why you have had to run."

"Run here?"

"Run everywhere," he answered, moving on to the next screw. "From the homes you have lived in and the schools you have attended. From people who have loved you and tried to come close to you."

I watched him work for a moment before answering. "Sensei, no one has ever loved me."

"No. You have simply not received their love, Icarus," he said. "People have loved you. People have been close to you, even if you have decided to push them away in the end."

"I push them away because I don't want to hurt them."

"They would be in no danger had you control over your own thoughts." His voice was firmer now. "Hawk will teach you."

"By making me wax the floor?" I quipped. "Or wash the windows for the umpteenth time?"

Sensei tested the knob. It turned smoothly in his large, muscular hand. "What have you learned from these tasks that you mention?"

"That I am easily bored by the mundane."

"The door is found in the floor, Icarus."

"I don't follow."

"You find the high places within the lowly ones," he said, placing the tools back in the box beside him. "This, for instance—it was not necessary for me to repair this with my hands and these tools; I could have done it just as well with my mind. But it was fuel to my patience and my persistence. It left its inanimate state and became a teacher because I allowed it to become so. Hawk will only ever be an effective teacher if you allow her."

I looked at him, puzzled. "You say that like I'm in charge here. Hawk is stronger than me in every respect."

"And by embracing her strength, it may become yours." He closed the box and rose. "It is all yours to claim if you so wish. Hawk is merely guiding you to water. She cannot make you drink."

I thought about what he was saying, rubbing the back of my neck. "But she won't even let me join sessions."

"Only because she sees that you have no desire to."

"*No desire to?* Are you kidding?" I was stunned. "That's all I want—I've been waiting this whole time for—"

"'This whole time,' Icarus?" Sensei interrupted gently. "It was not long ago that you did not even know of the Dimension's existence. And if you truly desire to be taught and to join sessions, you will."

"But she says I haven't proven myself."

Sensei opened the front door. "Then have the intention to do so."

CHAPTER THIRTEEN
Hawk

"You're late."

I stood with my back to the glass wall and watched him close the cavern door. The expression on his face wasn't apologetic.

"I'm sorry."

"Just move," I said. "I'm going to have you wash all the glass in this hallway. Have you noticed how you can hardly see out?"

Icarus glanced in the direction I was referencing, looking somewhat skeptical. "It looks fine to me."

"We'll work on your observation skills, then—or lack thereof."

His focus shifted from the glass to me. "Why are you so mean?"

"Just go get the towels and cleaning solution," I said. "I don't have all day."

He begrudgingly did as he had been instructed. I settled cross-legged on the floor at the opposite side of the hall and watched.

"You getting tired of this, fledge?" It was a term of non-endearment that I'd come to feel suited him.

He drizzled the pool-blue liquid into the pail he'd dragged over. "Tired of chores?"

"If you choose to call them that."

His hand went up to fight against his hazelnut-brown hair. "Tired as hell."

"Hey—profanity."

His lower lip caught angrily between his teeth. "I am tired of it, yes," he rephrased, and submersed one of the small squares of cloth into the liquid. "To be honest, I hate it. I want to join sessions."

"You want to join sessions." I reiterated his words with no more spirit than he had.

"Yes."

"How badly?"

He glanced in my direction. He wanted to throw the sopping towel at me. I watched his hand quiver.

"Badly."

I looked at him for a moment and then nodded for him to start on the window. When his back was to me, I spoke.

"The last session in which you participated was a pranayama, correct?" I asked, though I knew the answer already.

"Yes."

"And—"

"And I failed, yes."

"Don't cut me off when I'm speaking," I said tersely. "I suggest that if you would like to join sessions, you master the art of the pranayama."

"I can't."

"Because that's what you tell yourself."

"You saw what happened—I could barely do *four minutes*, Hawk. The rest of you can do *forty*. Maybe more."

"But we didn't *start* with forty."

He stopped washing the glass. "What did you start out with?"

I opened my mouth to speak but then shut it again to bite down on a badly behaved smile. "Twenty-five."

"Does literally hating you break the code?"

"No. But it won't make your training go any smoother, I can tell you that."

He resumed his abuse of the window.

"Concept is everything," I said. "Concept comes first."

"Filling the lungs like a glass filling with water," he said. "I know. I heard."

"Then internalize that feeling," I replied firmly. "It's not just about air, it's about energy. It's about power—control. It's the first step to being able to control your powers. Everyone has to practice; it doesn't come naturally."

"It didn't come naturally to you?"

"I'm no different than you are, Icarus," I said. "Except for the fact that perhaps I was more eager to put forth the effort my initial training required. I had no pattern to follow. I was the first."

His hand froze in its motions. "You were the first slider? *You?*"

"I was."

Icarus turned around fully. "Where did Sensei find you? When?"

"Nineteen nineteen, in the back of a theater."

"The back of a theater?"

"Do your questions never end?" I tried to brush aside a feeling of tension that was beginning to creep in. "Take a deep breath and hold it. I don't have an infinite amount of time to exhaust on this lesson. You can keep washing the windows while you're at it; just keep your energy exertion in check. Focus on the movements of your hand rather than the feeling of dying that will most likely ensue in a couple of minutes."

I didn't want to overcoach, so I stopped talking and instead observed him quietly as he worked. My eyes traced the landscape beyond the glass and then moved seamlessly to Icarus's frame. It was only a matter of seconds before he was gasping for air again.

"I can't—"

"What were you thinking about?"

"How badly I wanted to breathe."

"That's your issue, fledge."

"Would you quit calling me that?" he growled. "I'm not a fledgling."

"Then prove it."

"Then *coach* me."

"I *have*," I said. "But it's not something I can talk you through. It's something that will require you to believe in yourself. If you don't trust yourself, then forget it. This isn't going to work."

Icarus glared at me. He pulled in another deep breath and went back to the glass. Sunlight stained the sides of the ravine and sneaked in through the windows, along with a new resolve that made its way into his posture.

I'd made him angry—he was finally serious.

I knew enough about him to know that he could do this if he truly applied himself. I knew what he was capable of. This was a test of his desires, not his abilities, and I think he knew it.

I watched his hand move over the tall plates of glass, making wide, listless circles. I counted the seconds and then minutes, observing his body language. He made it to six minutes before he finally breathed in again.

"Ow, man." His forehead made light contact with the glass as he leaned forward, drinking in the air. "That hurts."

"Where does it hurt?" I asked, not particularly interested.

His hand answered for him by finding his rib cage.

I sighed. "You're not focusing."

"I *am* focusing, Hawk."

"Not on the right target."

He straightened up, pressing the heels of his hands to his eyelids. "I don't know how."

I watched as he stood there for a moment in what seemed like a miserable, irritated contemplation of his own inadequacy. Then he bent down and dipped the towel into the window solution.

"I can't," he said. "I can't do it."

The tone of resolve was in his voice—he had decided. The test was over.

I rose, dusting off my thighs. "This has been a waste of my time, then."

He turned purposelessly back to the window. "I guess you're right."

I felt my jaw set, a feeling of irritation washing over me on a kind of cosmic level. I stepped closer.

"Icarus," I said, lowering my voice, "I tolerate many things, but I do not tolerate quitters. I suggest you take some time to examine your attitude and adjust it accordingly if you wish to continue."

"Hawk, I just ca—"

"You can, and you will." I cut him off, already knowing what he would say. "You give yourself whiplash, Icarus—you say you want something badly and then you give up on yourself as soon as you begin to stray from your comfort zone. You will remain here until I come for you. You will wash these windows and then move on to waxing the lower platform again. You will do this until you can hold a thirty-minute pranayama."

I paused beside him at the window. He glared at me.

"Then I'll be here until I die."

"If that's what you want." I shrugged. "Give me your shirt."

His gaze snapped back to mine. "What?"

"Your shirt," I repeated. "Give it to me."

"Why?"

My gaze hardened, and rather than obliging him with a response, I waited, hand extended.

Icarus finally reached back over his shoulder blades to pull the black T-shirt up over his head. He rolled the shirt into a ball and dropped it into my hand. "You're so weird."

I gave a solitary nod. "Have a nice time in the full sun."

He didn't say another word, but I could feel his eyes on me as I turned and walked away. A moment later I heard the sound of the wet towel against the glass again.

I reached up to pinch the bridge of my nose once I was out of sight, pausing beside the trays of plant life that now ran the length of the railing at the edge of the training platform. Fin had apparently been busy. I sensed his presence at the same time I heard one of the nearby safe room doors slide open.

I would recognize the tempo of his footsteps anywhere. I sighed and leaned forward onto the rail, resting my forearms there as he came up behind me.

"Hey."

That one word was like a thousand when he spoke it. It was a soft-spoken invitation to get everything off my chest, but I wasn't sure I had the energy.

I turned my head and looked at him. The sunlight bleached his tousled blond hair.

"Hi," I said.

His lips wanted to smile, but instead he leaned forward on the railing beside me. There was still enough distance between us for his presence to feel comfortable.

"What's going on?"

I returned my focus to the opposing cliff side. "Nothing."

For a moment Fin didn't say anything. The sound of the gentle overhead winds came between us. Violins.

I reached up to rest my fingertips against my eyelids. "Little bit of a headache."

"That's unlike you," he said. "You want to talk about it?"

I filled my lungs and released a sigh. The air was sweet with dawn.

"Mm."

"Yes?"

I smiled. "No."

I sensed him rolling his eyes.

"It's just that I'm tired, Fin," I said, exhaling. "I'm tired of banging my head against a wall. I'm tired of feeling as if I'm wasting my energy."

"We're talking of Icarus."

I nodded. "Who else?"

"How is he progressing?"

I turned and gave him a look. "Who said anything about progress? He's washing windows."

"At least we'll be able to see out."

My lips made a motion to smile. "I told him to move on to the gathering platform once he's through. I made him take off his shirt, so he should get a nice burn out there."

Fin shook his head slowly. "Wicked vulture."

"Hawk," I corrected.

"You're a vulture today."

I smiled. "I'm entitled to be. I've been burning at both ends for too long, Fin."

"Sounds like someone could use a holiday."

"Holidays are for Europeans," I retorted, biting back a grin.

He laughed. "So a day off isn't at all appealing to you, then?"

"I didn't *exactly* say that."

He seemed to study my face for a moment before biting down on the beginnings of another smile. "How about Ireland?"

———————

It was an interesting experience to cross dimensions with Fin. Naturally, I had been to Ireland before, but never to his apartment, which I discovered was more like a greenhouse. Practically every surface save a small area of the floor was covered in growth. Vines of ivy and wisteria covered the walls, moss coated most of the hardwood floor, and massive hanging baskets of lavender crowded the bay window at the far end of the room, all but blocking out the view of the sea.

Fin, too, had a peculiar broom closet through which we had entered. We had made our way downtown and into a pub, which, Fin promised, served exceptional human food. I wasn't disappointed.

"Hawk, there's something I've been meaning to tell you about Icarus." Fin made slow circles with his fingertips on the tabletop. "I didn't say anything for a while because I couldn't be sure. I didn't have enough to go on."

I raised an eyebrow. He looked up at me.

"But since then, I've spoken with Sensei about your test with Icarus—the details of it." He leaned forward slightly, looking down at his folded hands. "He told me that when you tested Icarus that morning in LA, he healed you."

I took a breath to respond, but stopped myself as the waiter came with our food. Baskets of fried fish and potatoes.

Fin waited until the waiter left to continue. He lowered his voice slightly, though it would scarcely have been heard above the pumping dubstep. "Is that true?"

I nodded. "It is true that he healed me, but it wasn't part of the plan."

"How do you mean?"

"I mean that I had contemplated allowing myself to be injured to see if he was a healer and then decided against it," I said, and paused slightly. "But I was perched in one of the trees, watching him while he worked, and I subconsciously drew in a wind. A branch broke and fell. I didn't move fast enough and it took me down with it."

Fin looked surprised. "And you got hurt?"

"It tore my wing," I replied, studying one of the skinny fried potato sticks. "He tried to go find Sensei, but I decided not to let him leave. I wanted to see if he could."

"If he could heal you?"

I nodded.

"Because," Fin hesitated slightly, "you think he might be the final piece to the puzzle?"

I immediately froze. My gazed shifted up and locked into his. "What do you mean?"

He gave me a knowing look. "Your other half."

My heart danced past a few beats, and I rapidly began to formulate a reply that would have broken the code of conduct, but Fin didn't let me get that far.

"Hawk, it's okay," he said, glancing over his shoulders as if aware that someone was listening in. "I'm the only one who knows. I swear."

I swallowed thickly as I studied his face. "You know that I'm the split soul?"

He nodded slowly, not taking his eyes away.

"How did you find out?" I paused for a shaky breath. "Only Sensei knew."

"Sensei told me."

My eyes widened. "W-why would he tell you?"

"Because he knows that I…" Fin trailed off, then stopped altogether.

I watched him close his eyes.

"That I have your best interest at heart," he continued, with a sigh hiding in the undertones of his voice. "The truth is, I figured it out myself—I know the prophecy by heart. It isn't hard to put two and two together—not when I know you as well as I do. I *see* the Sunrise in you. Sensei simply affirmed it when I asked—he too is subject to the code and cannot lie."

I pulled in a deep breath. "Then you know about the Sunset. My other half."

Fin nodded slowly. "Why do you keep your identity a secret?"

"Because…" I trailed off slightly, diverting my gaze to search for words. "I have a mission to fulfill. I cannot trust that everyone else's intentions would be as pure as yours, Fin. Sensei told me from the very beginning that my true identity must always be kept secret."

I could feel Fin studying me as I spoke. I could sense him processing it all.

"You're afraid someone would steal your blood and assume your identity."

I gave an affirmative nod. "Not afraid—but aware, yes. The method of entanglement has the potential of being a major threat if anyone finds out who I really am."

"Completely understandable," he agreed, finally taking a bite of the food in front of him. "Don't worry—my lips are sealed."

A pause.

"And so you think Icarus is…"

Fin tilted his head slightly to one side. "I didn't say that. I just meant that you should keep an open mind. We all know the end is near."

"The end of the gathering?" I questioned, picking up my fork.

"We both know Sensei has made it clear that he won't be gathering sliders forever," he said. "It's only a matter of time until Sensei chooses to send us back into our natural worlds to fulfill what we've been training for—even if we don't know what that is yet."

I thought about his words for a moment before giving a reply. "What do you think Sensei sees in the future?"

Fin didn't respond right away. "A darkness, he's said. A darkness we can apparently change by altering our present-day worlds in some way."

I swallowed, nodding. "And now you know that it hinges on me. Finding the sign that the end of the gathering has come—finding the other half of my soul."

Fin smiled slightly, taking a bite. "No pressure."

I rolled my eyes.

"Everything will happen as it is meant to," he said. "Perhaps Sensei appointed you to select him for a reason."

"He's failing miserably at everything he tries, Fin." I sighed. "He can't control himself. Besides, what about Mel—Mala? She came after him. He's not the last."

"It doesn't matter." Fin rested an elbow on the table. "We know that time isn't linear, you and I—time is in the eyes of the beholder. He could be the 'last' without necessarily being *last*. If you know what I mean."

I tilted my head to the side. "True."

"He could be bringing those who are preceding him for a reason," he said, taking a sip from the glass in front of him. "And I say 'those' because I think we both know it isn't over. There's a reason why Sensei has kept his location in LA for so long."

I was still surprised that Fin had decoded the prophecy, but my heart was comforted by the fact that our minds were in the same place. If I needed anything at the time, it was for both of us to be on the same page. I knew he was right. I knew something was coming because of Icarus—I could sense it. It was close.

We devoured the food, and Fin paid. We then made our way from the pub to his parents' home on the outskirts of the city. It was a small town house located at the end of a quiet street, sheltered by weeping willow trees and half-concealed by the fast-approaching dusk.

Two little girls were playing on a tire swing hanging from one of the lower branches of a tree. Only their little heads of blond curls were strikingly visible in the low light; their laughter swept melodiously through the cool evening air. I turned and looked up at Fin, who fell into step beside me.

"Are they your sisters?"

He smiled and I whacked his arm.

"You never mentioned."

Fin laughed, nudging me lightly back. "It isn't in our nature to talk about home. Besides, you never asked."

Touché.

I returned my gaze to the girls. We were nearer now, and I could see the features of their faces. They looked uncannily like Fin. They had his green eyes and his blush. They spotted us almost immediately as we approached, and scrambled up to attack their brother. They naturally asked who I was when the rush of his sudden presence had worn off, and Fin immediately turned to cast me a panicked sidelong glance. For whatever reason, neither of us had considered the fact that we would be in painful need of a cover story.

"Um, a friend," he fumbled, raking his fingers through his hair. "From… school."

Their small green eyes turned in almost frightening synchronization to give me a piercing once-over. The smaller one bit back the beginnings of a smile.

Fin sighed. "Alright, you two. Honestly."

He snatched up the smaller one and hoisted her up onto his shoulders. The other fled in a fit of giggles and darted into the house.

At the door, he set his little sister gently on the stoop. She scooted into the house, and I stepped in after her, followed by Fin. He closed the door softly behind us, and I paused to take in my surroundings.

We were inside what looked like a cottage warmly illuminated by the glow from table lamps and an antique-looking chandelier that hung from the vaulted foyer ceiling. Everything was soft on the eyes, warm to the touch, sweet to the smell. The room swelled with the scent of cinnamon and cedar, and I glimpsed a fire glowing in the hearth in the room adjacent.

Fin leaned slightly closer. "I'll let you do the talking."

I shook my head. "They're *your* parents."

He rolled his eyes. I elbowed him in the ribs.

I followed him into the kitchen, which was overrun with girls: the two we'd met outside and another one slightly older. Fin's mother seemed unfazed, and his father preoccupied, though both greeted me warmly. Their accents were thick and rich like Fin's.

His mother shooed the children out of the room and made us tea.

"You both met at school?" she asked.

I glanced over at Fin, who began toying with his hair again. "Yes."

She tsked. "Ronan, you should have mentioned."

I felt my eyebrows rise slightly as I turned to give Fin a look that splashed the hint of a blush across his cheeks.

Ronan. I tasted the name silently under my breath.

"I suppose I forgot to?" he fumbled.

I decided to help him out by changing the subject.

"You have a beautiful home," I said warmly, glancing around again. "I've never been to this part of Ireland before."

She raised an eyebrow. "Haven't you?"

I shook my head. "I'm not from around here."

"Where's home?"

"US of A originally," I replied smoothly. "But you could say I'm a bit of a restless traveler these days."

She handed us both mugs. "I was noticing the accent. You're an exchange student, I assume?"

I nodded slightly, withholding a smile, which I could tell Fin shared. "You could certainly say that."

"So you're living in Ireland now?"

"For the moment," I said truthfully, gingerly taking a sip of the tea.

She turned to give Fin a playful look. "Watch out, Ronan. You're going to lose her."

It took a moment for the tease to register. Fin opened his mouth, but nothing intelligible came out, so he closed it again and resumed wearing a hole into the back of his reddening neck.

We were eventually shooed off into the living room with the other children to enjoy the tea we'd been given. We sat cross-legged on the bare wood floor in front of the flickering flame. I watched, amused, as his sisters hung from him like he was a replacement for the willow tree they'd abandoned.

It grew later, we finished the tea, and eventually the girls were summoned to bed. With no one else in the room, Fin and I relaxed to our natural selves.

"So…" I gave him a sidelong look. "Ronan, huh?"

He grinned, glancing down at the floor. "Even I have a human name."

"Mm."

There was a pause, filled up by the quiet crackling of the flames.

"You've never told me yours."

I snapped out of the temporary trance into which the flames had locked my vision. The red-orange glow made vague shapes in the dark parts of his eyes.

"Haven't I?" I half-asked, not really expecting an answer.

He gazed into my eyes for a moment, then slowly shook his head.

I pulled in a breath. "Charlotte."

"Charlotte."

"Mm-hmm."

He considered it. "I think I like Hawk better."

I smiled a little.

"My mother was only teasing us, by the way," he said. "Earlier."

"I am familiar with the strange customs of humans, Fin." I tossed him an eye roll. "Now I know where you get it from."

He bit back a grin. "Guilty."

For a moment he seemed to make a study of me.

"Do you ever miss it?" he asked.

I leaned back on my palms. "Miss what?"

He pulled in a substantial breath, seeming to consider before he spoke. "Being human."

"Not at all."

"Mm."

"Why?" I asked. "Do you?"

He slowly shrugged one shoulder. "I miss what it used to feel like to be one of them. A member of my own family."

"They're still your family, Fin," I said. "They still love you—you still love them. Does it make a difference?"

Tension had begun to make its way across Fin's brow. He nodded.

"It's not the same, Hawk," he said quietly. "I see them with different eyes. I know they would never believe me if I told them who I really was. What I can really do."

"Have you ever tried to?"

Fin shook his head. "There's a reason why Sensei has told us never to reveal who we really are. It would be too dangerous."

I didn't know what to say to that.

"How do you see them?" I asked, turning to look at him. "Now that you're transdimensional, I mean... How is it different?"

Fin was silent for a moment. Then he shook his head. "It's different because I know something they don't. I'm the only one who knows what lies beyond the door they've yet to even realize exists."

I didn't respond verbally, but I could feel him reading the thoughts from my eyes. I knew exactly what he meant.

"Maybe it's not a struggle for everyone," he went on, his finger still playing on the rim of the mug in his hand. "Everyone sees situations—people—differently. Even as we all see Sensei differently. But I'm still haunted by an emotion left over from my former humanity. It's a hard thing to shake."

The sensation he described was unfamiliar territory to me. I'd never had a family. But I did know what it was like to be haunted. I knew the taste, the sound, the chills that accompanied what he was describing. But that part of me still refused to open up, even with Fin. It recoiled deeper into my chest as a vagrant clings to his shadows, refusing to listen to any voice, even a gentle one, that begged it to emerge.

I closed my eyes to clear my thoughts.

"How do you see Sensei?" I asked after a moment. "I mean, I know we all see him differently. But how does he appear to you?"

He set the mug down on the floor beside him. "Oh, gosh. How to put it into words."

"I know what you mean," I sympathized. "But try."

"Tall, Irish, with long hair," he said thoughtfully. "Golden skin, and eyes like the sea when a storm is coming."

"Is he young?"

He shook his head. "Aged. Experience—wisdom has always been the object of my searching."

"Understandable."

"What about for you?" One of his eyebrows rose slightly. "How does he appear to you?"

"He's not old," I said, taking my gaze back to the flame. "Asian. Dark hair, blue eyes. Soft-spoken, stable. Distant."

"Distant?"

I nodded. "We rarely touch. He's always at arm's length."

I felt Fin's gaze on the side of my face. "Really?"

I nodded.

"Why would you be uncomfortable with him touching you?"

I hadn't fully realized what I'd said until that question. A sudden tension began to creep in as I felt the black bands around my arms grow incrementally warmer. The places where fingernails had once pressed.

"No reason," I said dismissively.

He didn't question further, but I could sense that he wanted to.

"He's stable," I went on. "He embodies the stability I've searched a hundred years for."

Fin leaned back on his elbows. "That's a long time to search for something."

"It is."

He glanced over again. "What about Icarus?"

"What about him?"

"How does he perceive Sensei?"

"No idea," I confessed. "Probably old and hopelessly Western, with a clueless look in his eyes to match his own."

Fin swallowed a laugh. "You're rough on him."

"I was rough on *you*, wasn't I?" I tossed him a look. "When Sensei dragged you into the Dimension, kicking and screaming—"

"I was *not* kicking and screaming."

"Remember it how you would like."

He shot me a look.

"What?" I raised an eyebrow.

"You still know how to tease," he said. "There's still a human down there—"

"No way—"

"Mm-hm." He nodded playfully. "I've seen her. It's too late."

I rolled my eyes. "How did you find out that you had slider blood?"

He sucked in a long breath. "Oh, I don't know. I always knew I was weird—I never fit in with any of the other kids at school. I was always picked on…" He trailed off, and I could see in his eyes that he was back there.

"I always liked being around plant life," he went on after a moment, watching the now-dwindling flames. "One spring we were given this assignment—they gave us these trays that we had to fill up with an exotic kind of plant species and raise them for the science fair that autumn. They gave me some kind of aggressive, vine-like plant. I can't remember what it was called, but there was something about it."

I raised an eyebrow as he trailed off briefly again. Then he shook himself out of it.

"I don't know." He exhaled something like a laugh. "It was weird. I planted the seedlings and left the tray in the classroom with the rest of them overnight. The next morning, they canceled class because it had grown to about twenty times its natural 'adult' size and had overtaken the entire classroom."

I felt a smile ease over my lips. "Seriously?"

He laughed, touching the back of his neck again. "Yeah. Needless to say, I kind of realized at that point that something was up."

"It was a little obvious, huh?"

"Just slightly."

"What about you?" Fin glanced in my direction. "How did you find out?"

I hadn't anticipated that he would, of course, ask. I'd been so relaxed in the conversation and the warmth of the fire that my guard had slipped slightly.

"Well, nothing as exciting as that," I said, thinking rapidly. "I had the markings, so I just always... knew."

"But you didn't know you were a slider until Sensei found you."

"Yeah, I..." I considered my explanation carefully. "I was injured, and he found me. He brought me to this little abandoned place beside the railroad tracks. A shack, really. He talked to me there and..."

Pause.

"And revealed that you were a slider?"

I swallowed, giving a quick nod as I reeled my thoughts back in. "He pulled my hand over the wounds. When he lifted it away again, they were gone. The ability was familiar. It was like something I had dreamed of as a child, but forgotten until that moment."

I could feel Fin's eyes, though for a moment he said nothing. Then the question came.

"How did you get hurt?"

My voice sank back in my throat, pushing a sigh to center stage to cover for it.

"It was dark," I said finally. I realized I was biting at the insides of my lips. "I'd fallen."

I felt no regret for how I'd chosen to articulate what had happened. Because in its rawest sense, it was truth.

———————————

I hadn't realized it before, but that night in Ireland had been exactly what my soul desperately needed. I felt distanced from Icarus and the problems that waited for me only one dimension away. Though I still kept a great deal concealed, talking it all through with Fin was like breathing fresh air. My mind felt strangely clear.

When we finally returned, only a few hours had passed in the Dimension. The sun had made itself at home in the sky's zenith, and there wasn't a cloud to deter it from blazing down on Icarus, whom I could see from the tall windows as Fin and I emerged from the cavern. I felt Fin look over my shoulder when I paused.

"I have dorm patrol today." Fin took a breath and then continued down the hallway. "Come find me if you need me."

I nodded slowly, comprehending his words, but not moving my focus from the figure on the unsheltered platform below. As planned, his bare back now boasted an epic sunburn.

For a split second I almost felt something like remorse, but I quickly put the emotion to death. Footsteps sounded in the corridor behind me, curtailing any further thought. I turned and saw Mitsue, who waved curtly.

"What's up?" I arched an eyebrow.

His long hair sat in a messy bun on top of his head, and his forehead was creased with tension. He reached up to stroke it with his inky fingertips.

"Hawk, we have issues," he said, and exhaled meaningfully. "Again."

"Well?"

"Another human breached the realm."

"How?"

"Mala brought him, apparently," he said. "You know how humans work. I'm surprised Sensei hasn't cut connections with the portal in LA yet. Pretty soon we'll be overrun."

I immediately recalled my conversation with Fin, and I felt chills break out over my spine. I knew now that Sensei hadn't closed the portal for a reason. That all of this—this very incident Mitsue was informing me of—was happening for a reason.

"Where is he now?" I asked, refocusing. "Did you test him?"

Mitsue nodded. "He tested positive—flawless, actually. He said he's known of his abilities since he was young and just never revealed them."

I furrowed my brow slightly as I processed this. "And Mala brought him, you said?"

"Correct."

"Well, who is he?" I asked. "What's his name?"

"I don't know that much yet. Sensei took over." Mitsue shrugged slightly, tucking his hands behind his head. "But his name's Riley."

CHAPTER FOURTEEN

Icarus

I fried. She took the shirt off my back and I fried.

Sure, she could shift into a bird. But I was beginning to wonder if she also transformed into Satan during her free time.

I washed the windows and I waxed the lower platform, as I had been instructed. The sun was out in full force and I cooked thoroughly beneath its blaze. It was all part of her plan to slowly kill me. There was no way to get back at her except to succeed, which, I decided, was what I had to do, even if I died trying.

I practiced the stupid breathing technique until I was so dizzy and lightheaded I felt like vomiting. Yes, I limped my way there, I suffered, but I reached the benchmark—thirty minutes. And surprisingly enough, completing my first assignment as a slider made all the pain worthwhile.

At one point, I'd felt Sensei's presence behind me on the platform, but he hadn't said a word to me—nor I to him. I might not have known very much about student etiquette yet, but I had caught on enough to realize that you didn't question Sensei, first and foremost. My existence was an open book to him, and I *did* trust him—fundamentally. Maybe that was what pulled me through. What I couldn't seem to wrap my head around was the fact that holding my breath for thirty minutes was hardly possible. Yet I still did it.

Hawk was gone for a few hours, but fortunately it turned out to be for the best. She returned in a mood that was angelic in comparison to what it had been before. She seemed only intolerant of me now, not as if she were about to execute me.

She came to a slow halt several feet away, placing her hands on her hips as she scrutinized her surroundings. The sun made a halo around her hair, which spilled down over her shoulders, as I turned to squint up at her.

"It's not horrible, Icarus." She nodded in slow, grudging approval. "Not horrible at all. You did a fine job. You can stop."

"You sure?" I asked sarcastically, reaching back to gently touch my scorched skin. "I haven't died yet."

"Want me to bake a cake for your pity party?"

I grunted, dropping the rag I was holding and getting to my feet. "Whatever. I nailed the stupid breathing thing—"

"Pranayama?"

"That." I nodded. "I got it. Done. Finished. Perfect."

"I'm doubting the last one," Hawk said, looking at me dubiously. "Why don't you go get cleaned up and meet me on the training platform. I'll test you there."

She paused abruptly, seeming to have thought of something else.

"In fact, I have a new student for you to go up against," she continued, interlacing her fingers behind her back. "I have a feeling you may work harder with a little competition, yes?"

My brow furrowed as I stared at her. "Competition?"

"Just go get washed up." Hawk dismissed the question. "I'll help you put some aloe vera on that burn later."

I stared at her. "*Aloe vera?* Can't you just heal me?"

"I could." She shrugged one shoulder lightly. "But I'm not going to. It's high time you learned how to heal yourself, fledge."

The whiplash was setting in as I made my way back to my dorm. Hawk's mood swings were forces to be reckoned with, but I was getting the impression that she approved of my work that afternoon, however much she wasn't letting on.

For a brief moment, I was feeling fairly good about myself. Then I reached my dorm, and that moment came to a premature end as I closed the canvas flap behind me.

"Mala?" My voice tumbled out, surprised. "What on earth—"

She'd been standing with her face to the window as I entered, but there was no mistaking her flowing torrents of dark, wind-whipped hair. She whirled around before the words finished coming out of my mouth. That was when I noticed the tears streaking her face.

"Icarus, you have to believe me," she cut in, her tone unexpectedly frantic. "It wasn't my idea—it wasn't my fault—"

"You're not supposed to be in here," I said, putting a finger to my lips for quiet as I stepped farther into the room. "You could get us both in trouble for this. What's wrong?"

She reached up to dab her eyes. Mascara streaked her cheeks. "I haven't been in here long. I just—I had to talk to you. Where have you been?"

I shook my head dismissively. "It doesn't matter. Just tell me what's going on—why are you crying? Why did you transport in this early? You and I are never on the same schedules."

She stared at me for a moment. "You mean you haven't seen him?"

"Him?" I felt my brow furrow as I stood there and watched her cover her face with her hands. "Mala, who are you talking about?"

She said nothing. I heard her pull in a deep breath.

"You're going to hate me, Icarus," she said quietly. "You're going to kill me."

"I would never hate you or kill you," I said, though it was a white lie. Both were technically possible.

"You will, believe me."

"Mala," I exhaled her new name, exasperated, "just *tell me*."

"Riley."

My muscles suddenly slackened. My mouth went dry.

"*Riley?*"

Mala sobbed audibly and sank to her knees. "Icarus, I'm sorry. I—"

"You brought Riley into the Dimension?" I could hardly believe what I was hearing. "The guy I almost put through someone's windshield? The guy who literally wants me dead?"

"I am so sorry." She wept, letting her hands drop away from her face.

"Sorry?" I was unaware of how much my voice was rising. "You're sorry? Do you even understand what you've done?"

"Icarus, he forced me!"

"You could have said no!"

"I tried!" She struggled to keep her voice under control. "I really tried, Icarus. Please believe me."

"*Believe you?*" The words were bitter on my tongue. "Mala, you just gave my archenemy the opportunity to become immortal."

"I didn't know he was a slider. I didn't think he would test positive."

I looked down at the floor. "Well, it sounds like you were wrong."

She said nothing for a moment. I tried to gather my thoughts.

"How could you not have known, Mala?" I asked finally, looking up. "You dated him for *months*. If anyone were to find out, doesn't it seem most logical that it would have been you?"

Mala shook her head. "He never showed it. I never…" She trailed off. "I never knew. I swear."

"Then why the hell did you bring him here?"

She drew in a sharp breath, finally meeting my gaze. "He threatened me."

"He worships you."

She shook her head violently. "He doesn't worship me, Icarus. He used me—he used me in order to get to you."

My eyebrows came together as I stared at her. Something wasn't adding up.

"I never knew why Riley hated you, Icarus," she went on slowly, drying her eyes with the back of her hand. "I thought maybe it was just because he was jealous—he knew I always had my eyes on you. I thought maybe he just resented that. I didn't know that he hated you because you're a slider."

"Because I'm a slider," I repeated her words. "Or because... *he's* a slider." That was when it finally hit me.

The late-night race, the fight, the "background check" he'd run on me, how little he had fought to keep Mel from falling into my arms—it was all clicking into place, and suddenly I couldn't understand why I'd never seen it before.

"He hates me because... he's just like me." I spoke more to myself than to Mala. "That's how he found out about me. He knew I'd been initiated, didn't he?"

"Not right away." Her voice cracked beneath its own weight.

"When did he find out?"

"When I told him."

"*You told him?*"

Her head sank back into her palms. "I felt so alone, Icarus. I didn't even have *you* anymore. I didn't know what else to do."

I cursed under my breath and closed my eyes, fighting for self-control.

"That's why he didn't put up a fight when we started going out," she went on, pausing slightly. "He thought I would lead him to you... to this place."

I grunted. "Well, bravo. You didn't disappoint."

I heard her heave a sigh, and then soft footsteps, the rustle of cloth. When I glanced up again, she was closer.

"Do you think I would even *be* here, waiting for you, if I was still loyal to Riley?" Her eyes were intent, almost frantic as she studied my face. "I'm warning you, Icarus—I know why he's here. I know what he wants."

My gaze shifted back to hers. "And what would that be?"

Her damp brown eyes ran scared into my own. "Your blood."

"Okay. Show me what you've got."

Hawk kicked back in one of the two modern, classroom-style chairs. The only two pieces of furniture in that particular safe room. She watched me with eyes that expected very little.

I stood with my back to the glass wall facing the drop and stared back at her, trying to read whether she knew the danger I was in now that Riley was here. But staring into her eyes was like peering down into the darkness of the ravine; I had no idea what was down there. She was unreadable.

I took a deep breath and held it, letting my eyes roll shut.

"Thirty minutes," she said. As if I didn't already know.

The fight in the parking garage was proof that I hadn't understood, still didn't understand, what made Riley tick. If he had powers, why hadn't he fought back? Why had I been able to nearly kill the guy? Why hadn't Sensei chosen him long before he'd chosen me? Riley was obviously capable of keeping his abilities under control—I wasn't.

The longer I stood there holding my breath, the more confused I became.

Maybe the question wasn't even why Riley hated me. When it came down to it, maybe the question was why I hated him. Because I think we both knew that it had nothing to do with Mala, or who could be the most obnoxious overachiever. It had to do with the fact that something about him had haunted me since day one. A warning light had gone off inside me the first time I'd seen him, and that light had never gone out.

Mala was no longer the trophy I had once paraded. Her sweet doe eyes were now only a hollow reminder that she was an instrument. She was a string that Riley had pulled to trip me as I passed. When I looked at her, I saw my own downfall. All the places where I'd made a wrong turn.

Had Riley instructed her to get me drunk that night so that I would lead her here? I would never know whether she had been lying or not. But dwelling on the fact brought something inside me to a boiling point. I fell to my knees, breathing out, breathing in. Gasping. My head was pounding. I opened my eyes to immediately find Hawk's. She looked impressed.

"Where were you just then?" she asked, sounding thoughtful.

"Right here."

"No. I mean where was your mind?"

I raised one eyebrow, not following.

"That was *forty minutes*, Icarus," she said, with emphasis. "Forty. Your mind found its target. How did you do it?"

I stared at her for a moment, dazed and speechless. I pressed the heels of my palms to my eyelids. "I don't know. I just let my mind go numb," I lied. "I tried not to get distracted."

"Right," she said. She knew I was full of it. "Whatever. Keep working on it. You're finally getting somewhere. In fact, I've never seen a student make such drastic improvement in so short a time."

I took my hands away and gaped at her. "Seriously?"

Hawk nodded briefly, rising. "But don't get a big head. You're hard enough to deal with as it is. How's the sunburn?"

I glanced vaguely over my left shoulder, the rough sensation of the fabric against my skin suddenly coming to my attention. "It's nothing."

Hawk seemed somewhat surprised by my response, but then nodded. "Good."

The pocket door slid open.

"So I mentioned the new student," she continued, gesturing for the figure standing there to enter. "I gather you wouldn't mind some additional practice, would you, Icarus?"

The feeling went out of my fingertips as I stood there. Riley stood only a few yards in front of me. His gaze penetrated my head as if he could see through it to the glass behind me. His face was expressionless as he stared back at me, with seemingly no recognition.

"Of course I wouldn't mind," I said, swallowing back my own beating heart. "Not at all."

Hawk examined the two of us for a second. "I've been told that you both are aware of each other's existence from school, am I correct?"

"You are," Riley replied before I could. "Quite correct."

"Naturally you both have new names now," Hawk went on, circling slowly as if planning to devour us. "Icarus, 'son of Daedalus'—but not, in fact. And Mitsue has called you…?" She glanced at Riley.

"Raiden."

"Very well."

A red line began to appear on the floor and grew steadily into a circle much like the one in Sensei's office. I glanced at Hawk and realized she was drawing it with her eyes.

"You're both familiar with channeling," she said, taking a breath as she drew the circle. "At least somewhat. I don't think I need to refresh either of your memories. I would like to see each of you create an orb of energy, so to speak. After that, your goal will be to steal your opponent's and merge it with your own."

I felt my jaw tighten slightly. My gaze switched up to Raiden's, which remained neutral.

"Let's see who executes most naturally." Hawk finished her curt briefing just as the circle reached its completion. She gestured for us to step inside its boundaries. "To start out, I'll allow you both to see the colors of your energy, but the visuals will be limited—I don't want you to use them as a crutch. Remember the code."

The code of conduct? It was honestly the last thing on my mind, but I knew exactly what Hawk meant: no violence. She wanted to see if I could control myself.

Raiden stood opposite, positioning his hands like he'd been practicing since childhood. A glowing orange ball of what looked like a semitransparent flame immediately began flickering between them.

I began to panic; I had never successfully channeled before. Not on demand. My hands shook as I spaced them out in front of me and begged my mind to focus. I was still numb from my conversation with Mala, and I had yet to fully get my mind around the fact that Riley—Raiden—was *here*. I was still trying to puzzle out why he wanted to kill me—why he "wanted my blood" and what that even meant. Needless to say, focus was packing her bags and slipping out the back door.

"Concentrate," Hawk instructed, though it didn't relieve an iota of my stress.

By the time a dull blue glow had begun to swirl around my fingertips, I was drenched in my own perspiration and fighting off lightheadedness. I glanced up to find that Riley's orb had come to full fruition.

Internalize it, Icarus. Internalize.

It didn't even sound like my voice, but it played on repeat in my head like an earworm. I could feel the sunlight blasting in through the glass behind me, licking at my burns. I pressed my eyelids shut. A different kind of energy began to nibble at my fingertips. I could feel my own orb beginning to slip away. When I opened my eyes, the colors had vanished: Raiden was drawing my power away from me. I could see the faint glistening of sweat around his neck.

I sucked in a sharp breath; my lungs were still tingling from the pranayama. My knees were weakening.

Where were you just then? Where did your mind go?

I gritted my teeth under the pressure I was beginning to feel in my arms, thinking back to Hawk's question, which now bobbed listlessly in a mire of confused thought patterns.

Beginning to feel depleted, I rapidly visualized Riley—Raiden—in my mind's eye. His frame, his face, what he was wearing. When the image became saturated, vivid, my focus sank its teeth.

My eyes were still closed, but I saw the colors again.

Raiden's orb lit up bright orange in my mind's eye. His hands looked as though they were ablaze with a flame I could trace through his arms to the center of his chest. It flared there as if it were agitated. My attention shifted from the orb in his hands to the point of its generation. I locked my concentration there.

The room was deathly quiet. The warmth left my shoulders abruptly, as if the sun had hidden itself behind a cloud, afraid to watch.

My heart rate picking up, I began to draw the energy away from Raiden, starting at the chest and working my way out.

I heard his breathing deepen as he tried to cling to what was left in his hands. A pained exhale hissed past his teeth. With the voice still churning tirelessly in my head, I braced myself. Pulled.

I heard Riley cry out as the energy left his body. His orb shot across the span of the circle, crashing through my own and impacting into my chest.

It felt like a bullet. A very large, very hot bullet.

The air fled my lungs and I fell to my knees, clutching my rib cage. For a moment I could do nothing. When I finally brought myself to reach up and touch my face, I realized my nose was bleeding.

I hadn't opened my eyes yet, but I could hear Raiden whimpering like a child across the room. I would be lying if I said that it didn't bring me some satisfaction, even in the midst of my agony. I could feel the energy whipping around me as I forced myself up into a doubled-over seated position, finally opening my eyes.

The sunlight was back, and Hawk was staring at me from across the room with what I could only describe as an expression of shock, though it was partially obscured by the blur my vision had become. Raiden was sprawled at her feet. His lips were purple.

When I looked down at my palms, I found them both split open, my blood spilling out onto the floor.

CHAPTER FIFTEEN
Hawk

Sensei studied me for what felt like a long time before speaking. I could practically make out the elusive shapes of his thoughts as they took form behind his sparkling blue eyes. I stood at the opposite side of the circle with my fingers interlaced behind my back and waited.

Having just confidently emerged from an interview with Riley, I'd come directly to Sensei's office and made my petition. He busied himself by watering plants as he listened. When I finished, he took a seat across from me.

"You wish to use Riley as a tool to push Icarus." He raised an eyebrow at me.

I nodded.

"Do you feel there is a need?"

"I do," I replied confidently. "Icarus has spent a lot of time in the Dimension now, Sensei, and I'm not impressed by his progression—or obvious lack thereof."

He said nothing for a moment. "Is Icarus's chief end to satisfy you, Hawk? Is he to be pushed along, regardless of whether he is ready, simply because you require him to be?"

I looked at him for a moment before shaking my head. "I'm not sure you understand me, Sensei."

"Then expound."

"Icarus is the only slider of my own selection." I chose my words carefully. "You have appointed him my responsibility—my student. You have made me his teacher, Sensei. And as his teacher, I am telling you that Icarus is capable, but he's not applying himself."

"Did you apply yourself?" Sensei cast me a particular look. "When I found you?"

I immediately began a reply, but my voice froze in my throat. I swallowed the rest of the sentence and decided to start fresh. "That was different, Sensei."

"How was it different?"

"Because I was the first," I said, slightly louder than I'd anticipated. "Your Sunrise, remember? Your chosen one. I did all that you required of me."

"And what was that?"

I searched for words but found none. My heartbeat quickened in my chest.

"What did I require of you, dear one?" He repeated the question, gazing earnestly at me. "When I pulled your body from the darkness and brought you to that hidden place to heal you—when I kissed your hands and declared you my own design—what did I require of you?"

I felt my throat tighten, chills rushing over my skin. I wanted to take my eyes away from his, but I couldn't. They held me in a sort of inescapable gravity.

"Nothing, Sensei." The words came out softly, and I swallowed. "You required nothing of me."

"Nothing except that you discover who you really are," he replied softly. "The one whom I tell you to search for each day in the mirror."

"The one whom I never find." My voice clung to the darkness Sensei was attempting to disarm. "The one whom I've long since lost, Sensei—the ghost you urge me to chase."

"Hawk—"

"No, Sensei." I rose from the chair. "For once, just—just let me do this *my* way. Why have you assigned me this task if you don't even trust me?"

Sensei's eyes closed momentarily. And when the words finally came, they seemed weighted with something like hurt. "I trust you, Hawk."

"Good." I struggled to contain my frustration. "Because I think this would be good for Icarus. It will push him."

"It will *break* him, Hawk."

I exhaled, disgruntled. "How? Riley is just as much one of your initiates as Icarus is! They both have to abide by the code of conduct or be exiled."

"The exile system is one of your own invention—the student body's. Not my own."

"A system which you *allowed* us to create so that order may be maintained, Sensei," I said. "So that we may actually survive long enough for the gathering to come to a completion—for me to find the other half of my soul."

Sensei took a deep breath and looked up into my eyes. "Riley is not to be trusted with Icarus, Hawk."

I stared at him blankly. "Why on earth not? He's a slider—you've chosen him just as much as you've chosen Icarus or Mala."

"There is a difference with Icarus, Hawk."

I pressed the heel of my hand to my forehead. "Sensei, do not misunderstand me: I'm not in any way pleased by the fact that our Dimension has been rendered seemingly defenseless against outsiders since Icarus's initiation. But you also must be aware of the fact that there's no reason for me to treat Riley any differently. He's given me no reason to suspect him of anything unworthy."

"What is Riley's intention?" he asked. "As a slider."

"He made no mention of one," I answered, unfazed. "But he can be trained. Taught."

"With the same method you inflict upon Icarus?"

"Inflict?" I reiterated, astonished. "Oh, so now I am the perpetrator of some kind of affliction? Sensei, I am trying to teach him."

"Are you indeed, Hawk?"

I opened my mouth to speak, but no words came. Sensei's gaze pleaded with mine, attempting to disarm my hardened heart, though I gave not an inch.

"Hawk," he said again, and this time paused as if my name was almost enough. "Hawk, this is not who you are."

Sensei's words haunted me as I stood in the sterile white glow of the safe room, feeling numb as torrents of blood escaped Icarus's hands and spilled from his face.

The truth was, I hadn't expected him to get this far. I hadn't expected him to nail the pranayama or to rise to the occasion and beat Raiden. I had expected him to be motivated to try harder and ultimately to fail. But in the end, the only one who had failed was the girl in the mirror.

Internalize it, Icarus. Internalize. I'd been coaching him inwardly through the entirety of the match, watching—almost *feeling*—his stance and motions as if they were my own. Wondering where his mind had slipped to during the pranayama. Trying to decipher what exactly had made it a success. The sudden force that brought him to the floor had come as a shock to me as well as to him—nearly spiriting away my own sense of balance with his.

Raiden's massive orb of energy had merged with Icarus's and impacted into his chest. I'd expected the force to knock him down, yes—but I hadn't anticipated the blood. My heartbeat crept up into my throat when I realized just how much of it his lungs were expelling.

Icarus didn't understand the forces he was playing with. He didn't know because I hadn't taught him. Instead, I had fought hard to place him in an impossible and dangerous situation. Now he was being made to suffer consequences that bore my name. I could come to no other conclusion than the fact that this was my fault.

Icarus began to struggle to his feet. Raiden was still curled in the fetal position off to one side, his face ghostly white.

I struggled to refocus and started toward him. "Icarus, don't move." My voice sounded harsh in my ears.

Icarus attempted to shake his head. "I'm fine."

"You're bleeding," I snapped, quickly slipping an arm around his torso to support him, though I knew this only scratched the surface of what he really needed. "Talk to me—where are you feeling pain? Your chest?"

He began a reply, but the fluid in his lungs drowned his voice. He coughed violently into his elbow, staining it red. His knees buckled.

I already knew what his symptoms suggested. I popped the sliding door open with a glance and yelled hoarsely for Fin, panicking despite myself. I heard neither voices nor footsteps; sessions had yet to start and there was no one out in the hallway.

I knew exactly what I needed to do, but I couldn't focus. I could hear Raiden coming to behind me, coughing, sputtering curses. A sudden pain twisted through my midsection and I doubled over, bringing Icarus with me. It was obvious that he could no longer stand of his own accord—he was losing too much blood.

"Icarus, don't move," I said again. Leaving him where he was, I got to my feet, clutching my abdomen, and took a step towards the door—just as Mitsue reached it.

"I heard you yell," he said breathlessly.

"I need Fin. Immediately."

He peered over my shoulder, attempting to slide the door open even as I strained to hold it shut. "Why? What happened?"

"Don't ask questions, Mitsue. Just go get him."

Sensei had allowed me to train Icarus and Raiden against each other, because as the Sunrise, I'd been given some level of authority. But no one other than Sensei—and now Fin—knew my true identity. In the eyes of the student body, I was nothing more than a shifter—turned code-breaker. And I wasn't unaware that the outcome of the day's events would come with a heavy price.

I couldn't allow Mitsue to see what had happened. I could trust no one except Fin to conceal what I had done.

"What have you done with my student, Hawk?" Mitsue asked sharply, still trying to see over my shoulder. "Where's Raiden?"

"He's not nearly as bad off as you will be in a second," I told him, regaining my breath, "if you don't move. Now."

Mitsue's dark eyes narrowed, but after a second he obeyed. He spun back around and headed down the hall in the direction of the training platform. As soon as he'd vanished around the corner, I shot back into the safe room, slamming the door shut behind me and locking it.

Raiden was still in the process of regaining himself, with his head between his knees, and Icarus was exactly where I'd left him—now completely unconscious. Where his skin wasn't stained crimson from his own blood, it was stone white from the lack of it. It ran from his discolored lips and trailed down his neck.

I knelt down on the floor beside him and gently eased his head into my lap. "Oh, god, Icarus. Stay with me."

I was too scattered to focus. I needed to get him somewhere quiet— somewhere where I could actually hear my own thoughts. I leaned over his body and quickly made an assessment of the damage, checking his rib cage with my fingertips until I found the place where a rib had punctured his left lung. A split second after, I heard the pocket door unlock and retract behind me, and I didn't have to check the footsteps that followed to know whose they were.

I heard Fin stop short. "My god, what happened?"

"Icarus was hit during a channeling session," I explained, still out of breath for reasons I couldn't account for. "He extracted Raiden's energy too rapidly and drew it into his own body."

"You had Icarus and Raiden channeling *against* each other?"

I nodded, feeling numb.

"Hawk, are you out of your *mind?*" The tone of his voice cut deeper than the pain that was still coursing through my veins. "We never train students against each other. What the hell were you thinking?"

My throat tightened as I sat there, holding Icarus, and I realized that I had no words to give him. I'd never heard Fin curse or raise his voice before. He dropped to the floor beside me and tore off his shirt.

"We need to stop the bleeding. He's losing too much blood."

He rapidly shredded the fabric into a couple of strips and started tying them tightly around each of Icarus's paling wrists. He assessed the situation in the exact way that I had, examining Icarus's rib cage.

"A rib went through his left lung."

I swallowed and closed my eyes, struggling to refocus as the unexplainable pain in my own body intensified.

"Hawk, snap out of it!"

"I'm sorry, I—"

"Why haven't you healed him?" His eyes were vivid as I turned finally to meet them. "What is wrong with you today?"

"I can't focus." My voice sounded strained. "Not in here—not with Raiden. Not with sessions about to start out on the platform. I need to get him somewhere alone—I need quiet."

"Tell me what to do."

My mind churned as I tried to force myself into gear.

"Take him to Sensei, Hawk." He spoke again before I could reply.

I shook my head, working my hands farther under Icarus's torso to lift him a little more. "I can't do that."

I could sense Fin studying me, though he didn't stop moving.

"Why not?"

"Because I can't, okay?" The words rushed out, bitter as bile.

"So you're just going to sit here while Icarus bleeds to death?"

"Let's get him back to your dorm."

We were both on our feet now. Fin slung Icarus's arm around his neck to support him, taking on most of his body weight. I could hear noises echoing in the hallway now. The platform was beginning to fill up for sessions. Fin shot me a look.

"It's too risky to take him back to the dorms," he said, slipping a free arm around Icarus's waist. "If we get caught…"

He trailed off. He didn't need to finish the sentence—I knew what came next.

"If someone finds out what I've done…" I began.

"You'll be tried for breaching the code."

A knifelike pain hammered momentarily into my side, making me wince as I nodded. "I'll… I'll take him to my apartment, then.

No one can get up there except Sensei and me."

"How will you get him up there?"

I reached up to gingerly grip my left side, shooting him a look. "I have wings, don't I?"

"Hawk, it's hundreds of feet up."

"I can manage."

"How are you planning on getting him out of here?" He shifted Icarus's weight slightly. "The hallway's filling up."

I threw a hand in the direction of the glass wall, simultaneously reaching the other around Icarus's body. "Can you handle making me an emergency exit?"

I could see Fin's mind processing this for a second before he finally nodded and transferred Icarus's weight into my arms. "Watch yourself."

Checking over my shoulder, I reassessed Raiden's delirious condition once more before turning to face the sheet of glass. Fin rapidly back-stepped a few paces, circling his palms around a large mass of thin air. Then he halted abruptly, took aim, and threw. The delicate, translucent wall exploded.

The impact from the blast threw my balance off and knocked Raiden to the floor again. I felt Icarus's forehead against the curve of my neck, his body growing heavier in my arms.

Every color from outside came rushing in like a hurricane, spattering the walls like blood had done only minutes ago.

"Are you sure you can handle this?" Fin's footsteps traced mine as I dragged Icarus towards the now-gaping hole, where the cool evening air was washing in like a tidal wave. "You're small in hawk form—can you manage?"

I nodded, pulling Icarus onto my back and easing his arms around my neck. "I can manage."

"Hawk—"

"Stay with Raiden." I cut him off. "Make sure he keeps his mouth shut."

"*Hawk.*" This time his voice was firmer.

I turned and looked at him, my toes just over the edge, the wind gently licking at my skin. I couldn't read the look in his eyes. I'd never seen it before.

"Are *you* okay?"

I knew immediately from the way he asked it that he already knew the answer.

"No." My fingers contracted tighter around Icarus's cold ones, and I shook my head. "I'm not okay, Fin."

He said my name again, but this time it was swallowed by the rushing wind that rose violently up around me as my feet left the edge and I fell.

We fell.

CHAPTER SIXTEEN
Icarus

Darkness and cold. It was all my senses could grasp. The darkness took away my sense of sight, and the cold stole the feeling from my fingertips. I was blind and numb, staggering listlessly in the pitch black. Groping with both hands, reaching for something—for anything.

Sound was still there in full strength, so I clung to her. She was like music—a concert, instruments I couldn't identify. A muffled tumult sweeping in under the door.

The door.

I became aware of a golden blade of light unfurled across the floorboards. A shy patch of illumination in dark oblivion.

Stumbling, reaching, I found a wall with my left hand. My fingers danced across the wallpaper as I felt my way alongside it, choking on thick dust and what smelled like cigar smoke, progressing towards the light.

I heard my own voice come out to ask where I was, though there was no one to answer. The warmth of my breath retreated to my skin, leaving chill bumps.

Why is it so cold?

Vague shapes surrounded me like an army enshrouded in darkness, a host of lifeless forms reaching for me as I staggered toward the elusive light, which kept itself just out of reach, no matter how many fevered steps I took. I tripped over unseen obstacles in my pursuit, snagged my clothes, fell, and skinned the heels of my hands on the rough floorboards beneath me. I bit down on my lip as I felt the blood coming to the surfaces of my palms. The wallflower light kept her distance.

The music remained. A beat kicked in.

I tried to breathe, but the smoke was thicker now. I coughed violently into my elbow, and for reasons I couldn't understand, felt blood there and across my lips. My knees weakened under my weight.

Lightheaded now, I made a last-ditch effort to reach the light, the door, the only suggestion of escape. But the taunting ribbon of gold was fading, and in a moment the music followed suit, leaving me alone with the pounding of my own swollen heart.

The light vanished.

The air turned to ice and my voice caught in my throat. Suddenly I felt a pair of hands grasp me with a force like a punch. Hands that nailed me back against the wall. Hands that weren't like hands at all.

Claws.

Gasping for air, I writhed in their grip. I brought my leg back and threw blind kicks at the places its shins should have been, but never delivered a blow. I groped for its chest, its neck—any place I could find a sensitive point—but grasped only fistfuls of thick, smoky air. The razors sank deeper into my flesh.

It made no noise. No inhales, no exhales. It had neither body nor breath. The only sounds to disturb the unearthly silence were my own agonized screams. Screams that sounded neither like my own nor like any human's.

I swung desperately for its face and again connected with nothing. Did this thing even have a face? My answer came when I felt something sharp pinpoint my jugular and sink in.

I tried to scream again, but this time I couldn't. Frantically I flailed again, groping for hands, legs, anything at all. And at last, as my fingers clutched at the thin air, it seemed to slowly gain substance. Something tangible, something soft, took shape in my fists—and I clenched onto it with every ounce of strength I had left.

Whatever it was, it suddenly had breath. I could hear inhales, exhales, then a voice. The razors withdrew—the embedded claws, the sharp, unbearable pain.

"Icarus," it said, and sounded a thousand miles away. "Icarus... it's okay."

My mouth was full of words that were too heavy to come out. I sank back against the wall, and they spilled from my mouth in a sigh that wanted to be my last breath. My bones were heavy; my body was numb. I was done.

"Shhh, you're alright."

The voice was familiar, but my mind couldn't place it.

"Icarus."

That word. *Is it my name?*

"Icarus, wake up."

Breathing deep and feeling the cold recede, I opened my eyes. My fingers were clamped tightly around human wrists. Familiar ones. I loosened my grip.

"There we go." She spoke quietly, unwinding my fingers. Her hands were warm. "Can you see me okay?"

Though my breathing was still uneven, I managed a nod.

"How do you feel?"

I didn't answer right away. My eyes were too heavy to wander far, but I was beginning to perceive that I wasn't in the safe room anymore. The walls were pure white, and the light poured in through the window at the far end of the room.

"Little sore, I guess."

"Just a little?"

"Mm." I nodded slightly, though it made me dizzy to do so. My eyes lifted to hers. "Do I look bad?"

Hawk was seated on the edge of the mattress beside me, obviously somewhat amused by the question. "Hideous."

"Are... are my hands still bleeding?"

Hawk shook her head, picking one up. "I fixed it."

Her fingers were still warm against mine as she lifted my hand for me to see. The gash was gone, and my palm had returned to its normal state. When she finally dropped it again, it fell into her lap. I left it there.

I looked at Hawk for a long moment before attempting a reply. Her dark eyes silently studied mine with an intensity I didn't understand.

I attempted to gather my thoughts, to piece together everything I had obviously missed. "Where am I, exactly?"

"You're in my apartment," she said. "I... I couldn't concentrate back there. That's why it took me so long to heal you. That's why you lost so much blood."

It took my brain a moment to fully process what she was saying. "I didn't notice I was missing any."

A pause slipped in between us for several seconds; then she took a breath.

"Icarus." My name came off her lips quietly. "I really screwed up with you."

"You didn't screw up with me."

"I did." Hawk's voice was resolute. "I pushed you too hard. I wasn't thinking of you—I was only thinking of myself. It wasn't..." She trailed off, her voice breaking. "It wasn't loving of me," she finished, surprising both of us. "I'm sorry."

I said nothing. In my invalid, half-conscious state, staring like an idiot was acceptable, so I stared. And in that moment she wasn't Hawk, the shifter with fearsome superpowers. She was back to being the girl next door. The one who watered the lawn every other day—the one whom I watched from the kitchen window, making guesses as to her name. She was still someone to behold.

"Don't be sorry," I said at length, my voice oddly gentle. "I'm better for it. I'll be better for it—for you. I want to live up to your expectations, Hawk."

"This isn't about me, Icarus."

"It is," I corrected her, though I wasn't sure why. "It is about you."

I felt strangely as if someone else had spoken.

She smiled almost reluctantly. "Well, congratulations. You channeled."

I winced slightly, flexing my shoulder blades. "Does it always hurt that much?"

"Not always. But we can work on it."

I took a deep breath, then let it back out again. "My lungs don't really hurt anymore."

"They shouldn't."

"Yeah?" I reached up with my free hand to rub the exhaustion out of my eyes, peering at her between my fingers. "What did you do to me?"

Hawk shrugged one shoulder, finally seeming to notice that my hand was still in her lap. "You really want to know?"

"It won't be worse than my imaginings."

She smiled sideways at me. "I opened you up and pieced your ribs back together. With my bare hands."

"Are you serious?" Okay. So it *was* worse than my imaginings.

She pushed my hand out of her lap, rising.

"You'll never know," she said, rolling the stress out of her shoulder blades. "But the real question is—what is up with you and Raiden? I have a feeling I only know half of the story."

My muscles tensed. I wasn't ready to discuss this with her, or anyone. But we were treading new ground here, so I took a breath and waded in.

"Riley—Raiden." I forced myself to call him by his new name, though I resented the constant reminder that he was one of us. "He and I have been enemies ever since I transferred to college in LA. He dated Mala before I did. I almost killed him one time."

Hawk shot me a disapproving look, one eyebrow arched.

I shrugged—and immediately winced again. "It was an *accident.*"

"I'm sure."

"Anyway," I continued, "he's always been suspicious of me—he knows about what happened at my last school."

"The incident?"

I nodded.

"So…" Hawk was pacing. "He's been blackmailing you?"

"Tracking me would be a better way to put it, I think," I said. "Mala said he's here because he wants to kill me." For no reason, I laughed. I felt like I was high on painkillers. Hawk shot me a look that silenced me.

"Mala told you this?"

"Mm-hmm," I affirmed. "Today."

"And those were her *exact* words?"

"She said he 'wanted my blood.' Same thing."

"It's not the same—not at all."

"Everything's so complicated here." I sighed. "Why does everything have to mean something else?"

Hawk scrutinized me for a moment. "I'm not sure I fully understand your question," she replied. "But no matter. We'll get through this. Confusing questions aside."

"Cut me some slack," I said, feigning a sulk. "I just had my guts pieced back together by a teenage girl."

"I'm sorry—would you rather I'd left them how they were?"

I dismissed the question.

"And for your information—" she paused beside the window, bending one knee to rest it on the wooden sill, "—I'm a hundred years older than you."

"Nuance."

"*Anyway*," Hawk continued, irritated, "Slider blood is different than a human's. You know a little bit about particle entanglement, right? Did they teach you about that at school?"

"I honestly slept through most of it," I admitted, slowly reaching up to rub the back of my neck. "But I get the concept. Go on."

"Well, it's a bit like that, except…" She searched for words again. "Different. It's like a crossbreed between that and a blood pact—a ritual of the ancients. If a slider takes another's blood into his or her own veins, he or she essentially becomes one with that slider for the time being, unless that slider is killed—which is the only way you could possibly die, since you are immortal."

"So what happens if the slider is dead?" I asked. "The one from whom the other is stealing blood."

"If that's the case"—she turned to face the window—"then that slider essentially takes on the murdered slider's identity. He inherits all that that slider was and would have risen to become."

I swallowed, my throat suddenly dry.

"So if Mala told you that Raiden came here for your blood, and since he's a slider…" She went quiet for a few seconds, as if considering the implications for herself. "That means you have something that he wants."

The gears in my head were turning painfully as I tried to comprehend all of this. Pushing myself cautiously up into a seated position, I brushed aside the sheets. Something was not adding up.

"Why would Raiden want something from me? I'm a nobody."

"I know," she agreed, still gazing intently out the window. "I don't understand it either. But it's something you'll have to figure out yourself— he's *your* enemy. You know what makes him tick far better than I do."

I smiled a little, in spite of everything. "I love how you didn't even attempt to argue the point."

It took a moment for her to withdraw from her thoughts. She turned and glanced over her shoulder at me. "Hmm? Argue what point?"

"That I am indeed a nobody."

She opened her mouth, but no words ventured out.

"It's okay." I put up my hands in mock subservience. "I get it. You don't like me. Hint taken."

"Those are your words, not mine—"

"But they are *true* words," I said, cutting her off. I yawned. "You're just having a moment of weakness because you feel bad about me almost dying."

"I do *not* have moments of weakness."

I laughed. "Then why the hell are you being nice to me? Shoot, I'm not supposed to say hell."

"Can you be serious for two seconds? We're talking about someone wanting to kill you right now—do you get that? Even though you *did* almost die, you're better off right now than you would have been if Raiden had beaten you during the channeling session. Little bits of your insides would be splattered all over the safe room walls."

"Graphic."

Hawk gave a pointed nod. "But true. And if I were you, I would make it my personal mission to figure out what's going on inside his head. He's too powerful to simply exile—he's here for a reason. He knows the prophecy—"

"Prophecy?"

"Icarus, I'm serious." Hawk shot me a look. "I don't want to find your body somewhere."

"Why, because you wouldn't have any students left? You'd have to go look for a new job?"

Hawk's shoulders fell, and she wrenched her gaze away in obvious disgust. She was getting back to her normal self, which I didn't particularly mind anymore. It was growing on me, in fact.

"Seriously, I get it, Hawk," I said, swinging my legs over the side of the mattress. "I'll work on figuring it out—really. But I honestly still don't understand the whole..." *Words, words...* "Blood exchange deal," I finished, gesturing towards nothing in particular. "It doesn't scientifically add up."

Hawk threw me a look. "Does *any of this*?"

"You have a point."

"Of course I do."

"But I still don't get it," I confessed. "How does it work, exactly? Is it a commonly used method?"

Hawk started to shake her head, then stopped, seeming to have thought of something else.

"Because Raiden obviously gets it," I continued, mulling it over. "I'm not sure how he does, but... he knows the ropes—and I don't. And it *kind of makes sense* for me to at least try to grasp the concept of how this entanglement thing works, if that's what he's after. Because I would really like to, you know, survive? If possible?"

Hawk didn't say anything at first, but I could tell she comprehended. She nodded absently. "Understandable."

I waited for more than that, but nothing came. So I rested my elbows on my knees and gazed beseechingly up at her. "So maybe expound slightly more and slightly… slower?"

The absent look in her eyes lingered a moment longer, then vanished all at once. She was back.

"It's not something I can tell you," she began uncertainly. Something in her voice made me sit up straight. "It's something I have to show you."

I stared at her.

She sat back on the windowsill and looked at me. "How do you feel about shifting?"

CHAPTER SEVENTEEN
Icarus

"Is this going to hurt?"

"It might."

One of the drawers in the desk across the room slid open on its own, and I watched as Hawk walked over to it and drew out what looked like a penknife with a rough metal handle.

"Okay." I pinched my lower lip as I observed her. "Slightly nervous now. How's this going to work?"

Hawk flipped open the knife to examine it, sliding the drawer shut again with her hip. "Relax. It's not going to be a big deal."

"No offense, but you plus a knife doesn't equal me relaxing."

"Do you want to do this or not?"

"I'm not sure 'want to' would necessarily be the right way to phrase it," I confessed as she closed the knife and returned to the window. I was seated on the sill. "*Need to* would probably be closer to the truth."

"Give me your hands."

Anxiety was taking over in the pit of my stomach, but I did as she instructed. She flicked the knife open again and began to gently score the surface of my palm with the tip.

"It will be easier if you don't watch," she said, noticing my efforts to hold back a grimace. "It feels a little strange… messing up the work I just did on these."

I turned my focus to the partially open window. "I'm the one feeling it."

"We'll be even in a second."

The dawn beyond the glass was young and light pink as the sun began to sleepily reverse its path across the zenith. The gentle winds were beginning to awaken, sighing into the room to brush up against my skin. My jaw tightened as Hawk moved on to my other palm. I could feel a small pool of blood forming in the first.

"Okay." She placed my palms face up on my knees. "Since you mentioned that you slept through most of science class, I'll refresh your memory. You can look now."

I turned to face her as she started on her own palms. She spread the left open with her fingertips, warming it up slightly with wide, circular motions around her heart line.

"In quantum mechanics, entangled particles share a profound kind of connection. One that, in fact, allows actions inflicted upon one to affect the other—even if the two are separated." Hawk pressed the blade to her skin. "In laymen's terms, it's a phenomenon that occurs when a pair of particles interact physically."

A thin ribbon of crimson rose gracefully to the surface of her skin.

"We're not particles, though," I pointed out. "And that is hardly laymen's terms."

She moved on to the other hand, though this time the knife operated on its own. Hawk kept her opposite hand suspended face up to prevent her blood from spilling. "Of course we're particles—collections of particles, yes, but still particles. And we can still utilize such interactions if we so intend."

I wasn't following, but I nodded as I watched her.

"Of course, there's a lot more to it," she went on, staying focused on the handle of the knife. "I'm giving you the watered-down version. But you're more of an experiential learner anyway, right?"

"I would have to confess that this is a little over the top, even for me."

"It's not as scary as it sounds," she said. "Just jump when I tell you to. Keep your field of thought as empty as possible and everything will fall into place on its own."

I stared at her. "You think I'm just going to free-fall into an endless drop after you?"

"You practice this every day as it is, don't you—trust falls? This time will be slightly different, but the concept is the same."

She had a point. But somehow it wasn't remotely comforting.

Without using either of her bleeding hands, Hawk threw the knife back into the drawer at the opposite end of the room. She jerked her head in the direction of her left shoulder. "Rise."

I did and pulled in an uneasy breath.

"Nervous?"

"What do you think?" I shot her a knowing look. "I've never done anything like this before."

She lifted her hands so that they were hovering over my own, palms facing the ceiling; then slowly she inverted them and neutralized the space between hers and my own. I felt the warmth of her blood spill and mingle with mine.

"Neither have I."

I looked up from our hands at her. My shock must have been obvious. "Thanks for telling me ahead of time."

"I knew you would never go through with it if I told you."

"Shouldn't I at least have the right to make an educated decision?"

"Coming here was a silent acknowledgment of the fact that you no longer belong to yourself," she said. "You don't have rights."

"Who do I belong to, then?"

"You're a student, are you not?" she asked, letting her eyes close. "You belong to your teacher."

"This is slightly more than I bargained for, don't you think?"

"Deal with it."

My mind was full of retorts, but I couldn't bring myself to push the words out. I was beginning to slip into a foggy, sedated state, and both my tongue and my eyelids were heavy. I felt my eyes droop shut. I didn't realize Hawk's closeness until my forehead made contact with hers, which was warm with what felt like fever.

What had been only the mild warmth of our blood in my palms quickly escalated to a raging heat, as if a flame had slipped in between our clasped hands. I found myself biting my lower lip to keep the pain from verbalizing itself. Though I could tell that she was experiencing the same sting, Hawk only exhaled softly, and for an instant I felt her warm breath on my face.

My sense of balance began to slip again. A soft ringing teased my sense of hearing.

"You okay?" I heard her ask softly as she nudged a little distance between us. "You're kind of falling on top of me here."

I sucked in a breath, trying to snap out of it. "Yeah, sorry. I'm just kinda—"

"Tired?"

"—dying."

She laughed quietly, in that elegantly sadistic way that only she could. Then she slowly took her hands away, turning her palms face up. The cuts were completely gone.

I followed suit, checking my own. Same result.

"Was that… supposed to happen?" I asked, examining my hands cautiously.

Hawk took a few steps back, pausing beside the windowsill. She reached up and slid the panel of glass open the rest of the way, letting the fresh air roll wildly in. "Hopefully."

I stared at her for a second, then shook my head. "I honestly don't think I can do this. I'll die."

Hawk swung her legs out over the ledge, letting her feet dangle freely over the miles and miles of dawn-sprayed nothingness. "You won't die because I won't die—entanglement, remember? Do you want to figure this out or not?"

I swallowed back a rogue "not really." "Of course."

Hawk motioned rhythmically with her fingers. "Then get out here, fledge."

I eased myself out onto the window ledge beside her and tried hard not to hyperventilate.

This was different than a trust fall. The ledge I had jumped from before had only one small platform mounted beneath it, and the drop was obscured by a comforting gray mist. But here, now, from the window of Hawk's apartment, situated at the highest point of the cliff, I could see *everything*— the dormitories, the bridges and walkways, the platforms, the nearly microscopic people scurrying below—and it was terrifying.

I looked over at her. "You literally jump from here *every day*?"

"I'm used to it." She reached up to brush a strand of hair out of her face. "It will come naturally after a while."

I nodded, unconvinced, and watched as she shimmied closer to the edge.

"You ready?"

"Not really."

"Feeling okay?"

"Again, not really."

Hawk laughed. "Just don't think about it."

And then she jumped.

With one swift motion, she was gone. No countdown, no words of encouragement. Her body disappeared unceremoniously over the edge and plummeted downward. Just watching her made my stomach bottom out.

"Okay, okay, okay," I whispered frantically to myself, feeling free to hyperventilate now that she was gone. "You can do this, Icarus. If she can, you can. You *will* do this." It took me straight back to my high school running days, the psych-up before the ensuing torture.

Hawk's body was merely a speck contrasted against the fog below when I finally managed to swallow my palpitating heart and force myself from the ledge and into the fast-moving oblivion that yawned beneath me. I screamed like a small child the entire way down.

Hawk lied. I am going to die. She's going to die. We are both going to die.

The torrent of thought was still rushing through my head when a sound like an explosion burst above the rush of the downfall.

A burning sensation snatched me suddenly into a terrifying paralysis, blowing the tension out of my spine as it coursed through my body. For the second time that day, I tried uselessly to scream.

I felt flames licking at my arms and legs, climbing up my chest and into my face to fill my mouth like a burning soul kiss. I couldn't feel my limbs after that or my face. But I knew I was still alive, because the world hadn't gone dark yet—it was still flickering in shades of orange and yellow, and when that faded, it left an explosion of jet-black feathers in its fallout.

At first, nothing clicked. I fell a few hundred feet more until I heard a sharp, raptor-like scream erupt from above me. I glanced up and saw Hawk— in hawk form. Wings spread to full expanse, soaring circles above me. I looked down at myself again, still plummeting into the mouth of the ravine.

That was when it *finally* clicked.

I began pumping what I thought were my arms furiously, unfurling them to full length. The wind caught on immediately and launched me carelessly into the updraft. Yes, this time I could actually scream, but the voice that found its way out of my throat sounded frighteningly animalistic.

Holy crap, I am a literal freaking hawk.

The thought rewound and replayed like a broken record in my mind, matching the frantic rhythm of the dubstep beat that was slamming in my chest.

Okay. Breathe, Icarus, breathe.

I'd recovered about ten percent of my cool by the time I reached Hawk's altitude. She said nothing when she saw me, naturally. But something was going on in her eyes. I couldn't figure it out.

She threw herself into a stronger updraft, climbing rapidly higher, and I quickly followed suit. Trying to get a feel for my wings. Oddly enough, it wasn't all that different from arms and hands.

Together we rose to the top of the cliff, which boasted a gradual peak that tapered off into what seemed like flat, empty space. Bellows of ash-gray clouds obscured any view there might have been, mirroring the fog masking the massive ravine below us.

I wondered what was at the top.

There Hawk paused, hovering. She made no sound, but seemed to evaluate me for a moment with her sharp golden eyes. I attempted to copy her finessed maneuvers, but instead faltered and plummeted. I heard what could only have been the raptor equivalent of laughter in my wake.

I was able to regain myself as the training platform rushed up, feeling a set of sharp talons coming down playfully across the top of my left wing. I could practically hear Hawk's human voice telling me, *Slow it, you idiot.*

And I did—or at least attempted to. Luckily, it was still early enough for the platform to be empty. I landed on the railing, and Hawk soared past it. She slowed up when she noticed I'd stopped.

She shot me a look. Trilled.

I'd made it to the railing alive, and I didn't really feel like leaving it again. But she was my teacher. So I bit the lower lip I no longer had and tentatively followed her, sailing quietly into the coolness of the shadows.

The sun hadn't climbed high enough yet to spray-paint the platform in the shades of an ambitious new day. Everything still slept beneath a soft, ambiguous blanket of dusty silhouettes. Hawk dipped one wing gently down to graze the floorboards as she passed over them, leaving a temporary trail of colored light that rose and drifted away like breath in cold air. She let out a long shrill call that echoed eerily through the opposing corridors.

I pumped my wings to keep up the pace as she made a sharp turn and shot down the glass-lined hallway leading to the portal. The light crashed down through the glass like atomic bombs to burst and drown us in the electric yellow fallout. We rocketed through it, and the door swung open on its own to whisper us inside. Hawk tipped her wings back slightly to slow herself, slipping effortlessly into the darkness. I chased after her.

The door closed, sealed. Swallowed.

With my sense of sight taken away, I became hypersensitive to the sound of our wings stirring the cold oxygen around us. We hovered in the darkness for a moment that stretched lazily into two, then three. I felt her feathers brush accidentally against mine once or twice as the walls seemed to close in on us slightly.

I could still feel my heart hammering in my chest. Breathing felt somehow different in this form and perhaps just a bit harder.

My attention was snared by a beam of light that materialized suddenly through a keyhole that had not been there before. It shot a laser-point streak of illumination into the opposing closet wall, setting a whirlwind of tiny dust particles ablaze as they danced to the motion of our beating wings. Brief flashes of rust and white downy feathers flickered in the vibrant projection.

The door burst open. I heard the brass handle hit the wall.

The sudden explosion of golden California sunlight burned my eyes and I turned away. The impact didn't seem to affect Hawk half as much. Calling quietly, she pumped her wings a few times and coasted the length of the hallway on the momentum. Blinking, I lifted into the air again to follow her, and we sailed through the empty kitchen and living room, passing windows with curtains drawn over them.

Hawk focused on the front door and the lock retracted, allowing it to fling wide open.

A blast of late summer warmth hit me in the chest—the scent of fresh earth, wisteria. The distant sound of pounding bass in passing cars.

The sky was a violent shade of red-orange, opaque and unfurled like thousands of blank pages. Without hesitating we rocketed up into it like we were the story it had been waiting for. The sun was just beginning to set.

Seasoned as she was, Hawk barely had to move her wings to catch an updraft. I had to fight for it, though the wind eventually decided to play along, making it slightly easier.

I didn't realize how high we were until I glanced down and noticed the shrinking roofs of houses and apartment buildings—thousands of them. LA had never looked so tiny and crowded. People were fading into invisibility, and cars were glossy specks contrasted against the raging rivers of asphalt, reflecting broken pieces of a burnt-out sun.

Hawk called again and diverted my attention. She was flying at a slightly higher altitude, shooting occasional glances down in my direction to make sure I was doing okay. She tipped her wings slightly and swung for the skyline.

A thin blanket of smog had nestled in among the palm trees, an eraser smudge out of which skyscrapers rose like glass giants, throwing sunbeams around like strobe lights.

Like a moth attracted to the luminescence, Hawk burst from the air current into which we had flown and let gravity channel her in the direction of the glow. She fell a few hundred feet, then flared her wings open like a freckled amber parachute. I shadowed her with less grace.

With my senses overwhelmed and my perception lagging, the buildings seemed at first to approach slowly, but then as if a switch had been flipped, they came on in a freight-train rush that had my heart instantly up in my throat. Mimicking Hawk as she tilted her wings again, I followed her as she cut through the spaces between the towering buildings like a knife.

To my left was glass. To my right was glass. We were running in the veins between high-rises, and whichever way I turned to look, there were reflections of wings, and feathers, and eyes that were braver than what I knew to be my own.

Currents of pale yellow headlights pulsed beneath us, rattling the atmosphere with the growl of engines and shrieking brakes. Hawk had dropped to my altitude, flying directly in front of me. The wind ran its fingers through her primary feathers like a lover, coaxing her a little higher. She glanced over her left wing and met my eyes for a moment with her golden ones. I couldn't read them.

She shrugged her wings into a tight fold and bulleted downward, free-falling past hundreds of windows ignited red by the sun, and slowing only to make a low swoop over the traffic below. I stayed where I was, but my eyes followed.

I couldn't believe she did this all the time! I was seeing a side of her I had never seen before. I'd been aware of her abilities, yes, but actually experiencing what it felt like, what *she* felt like... I was looking at her through new eyes. Both literally and figuratively.

The sky was a pinkish amber now, graffitied in unruly streaks of purple, maroon, and gold as the sun sighed lower. The US Bank Tower had crept up to split the view in half, just beginning to glimmer awake with lights that were still subtle in the evening glow.

Pumping my wings harder, I soared over its roof and sensed Hawk following. A massive number 12 spread slowly out in front of me, framed in what looked like a giant red bullseye: the helicopter pad—and all was quiet.

It was just too tempting. We exchanged a glance, a tacit agreement. We dropped together at breakneck speed to crash-land like two teenagers abusing a trampoline, our bodies tumbling back into human form as we hit. The impact wasn't significant, but I still found myself lying there panting and stunned. I could see the vague pulsation of my heart through my T-shirt. I closed my eyes and let out the breath I'd been holding for what felt like an eternity.

"Holy crap."

The breeze, which had softened somewhat now, swept my words away as they came off my lips. I heard Hawk hum a quiet laugh again.

"You enjoy that?"

"Understatement of the century."

"That's what shifter blood feels like."

"I'm definitely a fan," I said, stretching my arms out over my head, creating some movement in my fingers. "Can I have more?"

"What are you, a vampire?"

"You've discovered my true identity."

"At least we won't have to worry about you flying too close to the sun, then, will we?"

"Very funny."

"But in all seriousness…" She turned towards me. "You did really well. I'm proud of you."

"That's a first."

Her face turned back to the sky above us. Neither of us had moved yet. "First time for everything, right? Isn't that what you humans always say?"

"I'm afraid I wouldn't know," I said. "I'm not one of them."

I hadn't taken my eyes off her yet. I caught a glimpse of a smile on her lips, though she never replied. She sat up and ran her hands back through her hair. "You know, I'm pretty sure they have security cameras up here."

"Excellent."

"There's no way to trace us," she explained, getting to her feet. "Besides, you could always just cause connection interference. Mess with the security recording."

"Yeah?" I raised an eyebrow as I gazed up at her, still sprawled out on my back. "What makes you think I could do that?"

"You did it before, didn't you?"

My eyebrows came together. I shook my head.

"Parking garage incident? Ringing any bells?"

Windshields, broken glass. Mala's piercing scream. My mind reeled back to that day. The split second between the hammering of my own heart and the impact of the punch.

"How did you know about that?" I asked, puzzled. "I never told you."

She interlaced her fingers to stretch. "I have ways of knowing these things."

"Scary."

"Mm-hmm."

"I didn't even try to do that," I said, finally pushing myself up onto my elbows. "I didn't realize I was the one who erased the recording. It was an accident."

"I know it was." Hawk took a few steps closer to the edge of the helicopter pad. "You were emotional—you panicked. Things happen almost by themselves when you lose your focus—I've seen it happen. That's why you have to be careful of how you handle the next few days, because I can already tell it's not going to be

easy for you."

My eyes followed her as she walked to the edge of the roof and paused there. The sun had slipped away now, but there was enough light to silhouette her thin frame.

"I'll try my best." I got to my feet now too. "I don't have the best history of controlling myself. But you just said I was improving, right?"

"Those weren't my exact words." She tossed me a pointed glance as I approached. "But yes. You have improved. Far more than I expected."

"Does this mean I've earned the right to rejoin sessions?"

Hawk tilted her head to the side contemplatively, just to drag the moment out. "It might…"

"I'm sensing a 'but' coming on."

A ghost of a smile traced her lips. "*But* I want you to tell me something first."

I shook my head. "No."

"Why not?"

"Because." I shot her a knowing look as I took a seat on the very edge of the helicopter pad, somehow no longer intimidated by the altitude. "I already know what the question will be. I know how the words will sound when you say them. I know the look you'll give me."

"No, you don't," she retorted, stepping closer to the edge.

"I know you—at least a little, anyway," I said as she sat down on the ledge beside me. "I know better than to let you inside my head."

The city was igniting beneath us. I watched as the damp asphalt melted gradually into a warm river of gold, coursing its way through the city's veins to light up all the windows. A soft, cool breeze wove its way around us, filling the significant gap Hawk had pointedly left between us. She leaned forward and peered down at the world below.

"I didn't ask to get inside your head," she replied at length. "I just know what it feels like to carry something around."

I rested my elbows on my knees. "So you think this is a weight I drag around with me everywhere, then, huh?"

Hawk tilted her head and looked into my eyes. "Is it? You tell me."

I said nothing. Truth be told, I had no idea what to tell her. We sat for a long time in silence, but I felt her eyes on me, waiting patiently.

I heard her inhale. Then her voice, soft in the dusk. "Jump," she whispered.

And in that one word she told me ten thousand other things. It was like a punch, a kiss, a push from a high place. A shiver ran down my spine and my heart threw itself against the inside of my chest. My vision filled with the first time Hawk had dragged me to the edge of the ravine and told me the very same thing.

I let go of the breath I hadn't realized I'd been holding and let the words come.

"My first year of college," I began quietly, "there was this girl. She was *explosive*. There was a darkness inside her that scared me, but also attracted me like light would for normal people. But I wasn't normal."

"So she got close."

I nodded slowly. "I didn't even notice it happening, but eventually she got to know me well enough to know that something was up—that I was different somehow. I knew she was only in it to figure me out, use me—whatever you want to call it, but..." I paused, attempting to stay focused.

"We were spending a lot of time together, getting more and more involved," I went on. "I knew I would eventually have to push her away, but I'd never had anyone that I could really... talk to before. I let her think there was more to us than there was just so I could hang onto that for a little longer."

Hawk nodded thoughtfully, seeming to understand. "So what happened?"

I took a shallow breath, letting my gaze rest on the thousands of lights flickering below our feet. "We were out late one night, and when it was time for me to take her back to her apartment, she asked if she could spend the night with me instead."

"And you said no?"

I nodded. "I told her I couldn't go there. I… I didn't even know *why* at the time, but it was like… this force inside me had made a promise that I wouldn't cross that line, with her or anyone."

"And I'm assuming she didn't take it well?"

"She *blew up* at me. And it didn't help that we were in a dark parking lot behind a club and both fairly intoxicated. I can't even *remember* what I told her, but she got really aggressive, and…" I trailed off as memories, like black water, poured in. I could feel the ghosts coming back to wrap their fingers around my throat.

"She swung for my face," I continued finally, pushing the words out. "And, like a knee-jerk reaction, I hit her back. The impact slammed her into the back of the brick building—exactly like what happened with Riley, except… she didn't walk away like he did."

Hawk's voice was quieter when she spoke. "What happened to her?"

"Her skull was fractured in two places," I said, pressing my eyelids shut with my forefinger and thumb. "I would have been arrested had it not been for the fact that she couldn't remember anything when she came out of a coma three days later."

"What did you tell the police?"

I shrugged slightly. My shoulders felt heavy. "That we'd been drunk and she fell. I transferred soon after. I was afraid someone would connect the dots sooner or later. I wasn't about to wait for that to happen."

Hawk said nothing at first. She turned her gaze back to the skyline. I looked down at my hands to find they were shaking slightly.

"I'll just never forget that feeling of being back there," I continued, swallowing back the tension that was forming in my throat. "Behind that building, holding onto her while she bled—having no idea how to heal her… being completely unable to even come to terms with what I had just done. I couldn't even comprehend it." I gathered my courage and turned my face to her. "Do you think less of me, Hawk?"

She shook her head. "No, Icarus. I don't think less of you." After a few moments, she turned to look at me. "And even if I did, that would be a fault in my character, not a black mark on yours." She spoke gently, but her gaze was serious. "It's neither my place nor yours to judge your past. Ion died when you assumed Icarus's identity. Don't carry his corpse."

I wanted to look away, but I couldn't take my eyes from hers. There was still something I needed to know.

"How did you stop carrying yours?"

"I—" Hawk hesitated, then glanced down for the first time "—haven't stopped."

"How do you mean?"

"I mean that I dream of her ghost and awaken each morning to bury her again, because I—" Her voice faded abruptly, running out of breath.

"Because?" I prodded gently. "Because you what?"

She let her gaze return to mine. "Because I was raped when I was seventeen."

The words poured off her lips like a dam had broken, and looking into her eyes, I couldn't help but feel as though she was more caught off guard by her confession than I was. If anything, her words actually felt familiar to me as they hung heavy in the air between us.

"I know," I said.

I know? Who is using my voice?

She rested her forehead on her fist again, not looking at me. "You do?"

Of course I didn't! What was I saying?

I nodded slowly, mechanically. Like I had no control over my own body.

"I have no idea why I just told you that," she said finally, staring out into the deepening night sky.

"Does Sensei know?"

Hawk nodded, and we sat in silence once more. For what felt like a long time neither of us said a word. When Hawk finally spoke again, her voice was different. It bled a kind of vulnerability I had not heard before. I had expected it to come out with claws—defensive. Instead it was like a child's. Limping, wounded.

"It was right after the war," she said. "I'd finally made it out of the orphanage. The two of us had 'escaped,' we always said."

"We?"

Hawk nodded. "He was my refuge… the first person I ever really trusted. And one night he just…"

She let the unspoken words hang in the air.

"Sensei tells me that the past is not who I am," she continued quietly. "He tells me there's a warrior under my skin, waiting to be let out. One that he tells me to search for every time I look in the mirror."

I studied her silently for a moment. "Have you found her?"

Hawk hesitated, then shook her head. "That's why I asked Sensei to teach me to shift."

There was more, I could feel it, but she held it back for a moment. I saw the words making their way through the filters behind her eyes. I could see the tension in her fingertips as she dangled at the edge, trying to decide whether she could really let go. Whether she really wanted to. Finally she spoke again, her voice resigned, as if she had stopped fighting.

"Because I feel lost in my own skin."

My head was a hurricane. I wanted to tell her that I saw the warrior she was describing. I wanted to tell her that I knew her, because she was my teacher. I wanted to tell her that I *hadn't* known that she'd been raped. That I had no idea why I had told her I did. That I felt as if someone else had taken over my body and used my voice to tell her things that I didn't understand. I wanted to tell her how afraid I really was—because something was happening to me, and I didn't know how to explain it. I wanted to tell her something, *anything*, that would reseal the wound I'd just torn open without even knowing what I was doing. There were a thousand things I wanted to tell her.

Instead, I tore my gaze away from those green-gold eyes of hers that were cannibalizing mine. We sat, unspeaking, the sound of our steady breath rising and falling over the hush of the traffic far below.

CHAPTER EIGHTEEN
Hawk

I knelt in the grass and picked tomatoes that were still warm from the afternoon sun.

My eyes absently monitored Sensei's movements as he pruned the arborvitaes. Sweat stained his white T-shirt and beaded at his brow. The shears in his hands were rusty, and each time the two blades passed over one another, the slight friction was audible. I became almost hypersensitive to its rhythm and the accompanying *swish* of each branch as it tumbled to the ground. It took a moment for me to become aware of the fact that I had been holding the same tomato for some time now.

One long California night had passed since my flight with Icarus and our conversation on the helicopter pad. The conversation in which I had divulged the darkest part of my past to the guy I had nearly neutralized earlier that day, leaving myself open, vulnerable, and with a question that haunted me unceasingly: *why?*

Why had I told him?

I had never willingly shared that part of my history with anyone. It was something that fought me, lashed me, and *never* came easy. Why had it spilled from my lips so suddenly, so effortlessly? I felt like a daughter who had failed to conceal a secret from her father's eyes or her mother's warm arms. I had never even experienced either of those sensations, yet somehow Icarus's eyes and words and very presence that night had become both to me. His voice had picked a lock that had long since rusted.

The fact was, I hadn't told him willingly. The truth had pounded its fists against the inside of my chest and fought its way out.

I was raped when I was seventeen.

I'd never said it aloud before, and the words had shocked me. I'd been overwhelmed by a familiar darkness as soon as I'd spoken them; for a moment I'd felt as if someone had walked in on me while I was undressing. I felt naked, and I could tell Icarus knew what I was feeling—which made it even worse. His eyes had wandered deeply into my own and lost themselves there. I had evicted them as fast as possible, and shifting again, we'd flown back to Sensei's house. The potency of my blood in his veins had already begun to wear off by that point; I could tell by how difficult it was for him to keep up.

Icarus had muttered something about how he'd lost track of time, and I'd gestured for him to go—after one last reminder to control himself with Raiden. He'd nodded and left. Once he was gone, I'd collapsed into one of the kitchen chairs and taken my face into my hands. Asking myself the same question I was still asking as I sat there in the garden the next day.

Why did I tell him?

Or maybe the real question was, how on earth had he known?

Part of me wanted to assume that he was lying. But there was something in his eyes that told me he was real—honest. And that was what terrified me. Because only one other soul in the universe knew about my past and that was Sensei. *Sensei.* My savior, my love, and my teacher to whom I had pledged my unreserved allegiance. The architect of my spirit, skin and bone, the one who had never forsaken me. He was the only one who possibly could have revealed my secret to Icarus. I could hardly bring myself to believe it.

Hadn't Icarus himself asked if Sensei knew about what happened to me? Why on earth would he ask such a thing if Sensei had been the one who had told him? Something didn't add up.

My eyes still followed Sensei. His skin sparkled in the sunlight. I couldn't decide if it was from the tiny prisms of perspiration that were forming there, or if it was something else. I wanted to approach him, to stop working and simply sit at his feet. I wanted to ask him why he had told Icarus—why he would tear the rug out from under me like that. I wanted to cry, I wanted to scream, I wanted to punch something. I was a bundle of confused emotions and I wanted him to be the outlet. But something inside me wouldn't allow it. The light emanating from him now seemed to push me away rather than draw me closer as it always had. Suddenly, it was no longer something I wanted to run towards, but rather a presence from which I sought escape.

I rose, lifting the basket of ripe plum tomatoes.

"I'm taking these inside, Sensei." Though my voice was hardly loud enough for someone at that distance to hear, I felt as though I could have spoken in a whisper and he would have heard.

He nodded and I started for the house, taking the steps two at a time.

"Hawk."

I stopped short, fingertips touching the knob. "Yes, Sensei?" I asked, not turning around.

Metal on metal. *Swish.* "You wish to speak to me?"

I opened my mouth to reply, but words abandoned me. My heart barricaded my throat as I shook my head and shifted the basket to my hip. "No, Sensei."

I could feel his subconscious mind reaching for my own, straining as if trying to make sense of badly penned cursive, though verbally he prodded no further. My fingers contracted and I let myself inside, evading him.

How does he always know?

The house was sweet with the scent of incense: myrrh and dragon's blood. I breathed it in and gently stretched my shoulder blades. It hit me that I hadn't slept in two days. Not having had the mental capacity to transport back to my quarters in the Dimension, I'd spent the previous night in the guestroom no one ever used.

I'd lain awake and listened to the music pumping next door. I had pulled the curtains closed over the windows, but not before noticing Icarus crossing the driveway to vanish into the house, where a fairly wild party was going down. I'd chided myself for having watched him.

My consciousness questioned all of my actions in painful repetition: *Why had I told Icarus? Why had I broken the code and pitted Raiden and Icarus against each other? Would someone find out what I had done? How could I claim to be a teacher when I did that which I taught against?*

As I made my way down the length of the hall now, I noticed that the light was on in the kitchen. I found Fin at the counter as I entered. He was all tousled hair and white tee, leaning there like he owned the kitchen—pint of ice cream in hand and a serious expression on his face. It was an interesting combination, and I was only a little surprised to see him.

"What are you doing here?" I asked, my voice neutral, as I set the basket down on the kitchen table. "I can't remember the last time you transported in."

Fin dug his spoon into what I could now see was chocolate ice cream and shrugged awkwardly. "It feels like we haven't spoken in a while, you and I."

"I was assuming you were probably still angry with me."

"Who said I was angry with you?"

I turned around, placing my hands on the back of the chair behind me. "You did."

"No—"

"Mm-hmm."

"*Disappointed,*" Fin corrected, with emphasis. "Which is different. I was shocked and disappointed."

I watched him look at the ice cream in his hands as if he didn't understand the concept of eating it. "So… you came here to tell me that?"

"I came here because I was concerned about you," he said. "You didn't transport back last night—why?"

"I guess I didn't feel like it."

"Since when do you not feel like transporting back for dawn sessions?" he asked skeptically. "And since when do you not feel like following the code—which strongly discourages pitting two students against each other?"

That struck a nerve. I threw my hands up, turning away from him. "Look, I'm sorry, okay? I screwed up. What do you want from me? I can't go back and do it over—if I could, I would, but I can't. I was doing what I… what I thought was best at the time."

"Perhaps you're unaware of the fact that suspicions have been raised," he said.

"Suspicions about what?"

"About you." He pulled out a chair at the table. "About what happened to Raiden. About everything that went down yesterday."

I drew my lips into my mouth, thinking hard.

"No one knows what really happened," he said slowly, resting his elbows on the table. "To anyone who's asked, I've simply said that Raiden overdid it."

"So… you lied?"

A pause. Spoon against his teeth. "Call it what you like."

"That's just as much breaking the code as my error is."

"But in this case I regard your standing as the Sunrise above the code."

I temporarily lost the capacity to speak. I tore one of the chairs out from the table and sat down across from him.

"Ronan, you are a walking, breathing contradiction," I said, shaking my head. "You rebuke me for breaking the code that you yourself break in order to conceal my shortcomings."

The slightest of smiles passed over his lips. He pulled his gaze away from mine. "Alright, can you just, like… not do that?"

"'Just, like'?" I repeated, shooting him a look. "You sound like a *teenager*. Not do what?"

Fin rolled his eyes. "Say my name and look at me like that."

I leaned back in my chair, folding my arms.

"I lied because I know that you're someone to be protected," he went on. "We need you—even if Sensei and I are the only ones who know it thus far."

I leaned forward on my elbows. "I really screwed up this time, didn't I? I let you both down—hugely."

He stabbed the spoon into the pint container and pushed it in front of me. "Welcome to the world where screwups happen sometimes—we have ice cream."

I finally felt a smile creep onto my face.

"And just for the record," he continued after a few seconds. "You may do wrong and I may be disappointed in you, but you've never let me down. You're not the only one who's broken the code before—I have. And not just on this occasion."

I carved out a scoop with the spoon and glanced at him suspiciously. "Are you just saying this to make me feel better?"

"No, I'm serious," he said, and then faltered. "It's not even so much something I've done as it is something I find myself continuously doing."

"How scandalous," I teased dryly, checking to see if he was actually serious—and he was.

He pressed his lips together, a distant look in his eyes. "It's my one weakness."

"You know I'm really curious now, right?"

"That's all I'm saying, so don't even try."

I made no further response, forcing him to start fresh.

"Did you get hurt the other day?" he asked, making circles on the table with his fingertip. "During the session, I mean. Did you get hit?"

I shook my head. "No. No, I was fine. I just..." I thought back to the incident, the strange hammering pain in my side. "It was just the shock of everything." I twisted the spoon between my fingers. "I feel fine now."

It wasn't strictly true. A dull ache spanned my forehead and throbbed gently at my left temple. I chalked it up to sleep loss.

I could tell Fin wanted to question further, but instead he let me change the subject.

"Fin, can I ask your advice about something before you go?"

He rested his chin on his fist. "Before I go? What, are you kicking me out?"

I withheld a groan, spoon in my mouth. He chuckled.

"No, I know. I have to get back," he agreed, clearing his throat. "But of course you can—shoot."

Turning to anyone besides Sensei for advice felt strange, but in this case necessary. Sensei was, after all, the reason I needed it. I fumbled with the spoon, contemplating the container in my hands. "Fin, what if, say, I knew something about you… something that I knew you would never want anyone to find out about—and I was the only one who knew it?"

Fin said nothing, but held my gaze, following me.

"And what if you realized that someone else, other than just me, had found out about—" I paused as I thought my own words through "—whatever it was you were concealing."

I looked up. Green eyes made a study of mine.

"What would you think?" I finished.

"I would assume they learned this information by some other means," he said finally. "I would place my trust in you above what 'reason' might point to. Because if I trust you, that means I believe you would never turn your back on me, correct?"

"Of course."

"If I say that I trust you, I mean that I'm willing to risk being let down," he said. "It means that I've made a conscious decision to believe that you *wouldn't* let me down."

"So trust is commit flight?"

He nodded. "Commit flight whether it's take off or crash-land."

I had to admit, I'd never thought of trust on those terms before. I'd been too occupied with putting my defenses up, thinking about how much of myself I could salvage before someone noticed I was falling apart under my armor. But now, listening to Fin, it made perfect sense.

"So I wouldn't become a suspect in your mind?"

"That wouldn't even be an option for me," he replied. "But since you're asking this question to begin with, I would suggest you simply ask him."

So he knew.

"Just talk to him, Hawk."

I wanted to say something that made sense, I wanted my words to be organized, but I was losing the talent for that.

"I'm scared to," I said simply.

"Then this will be a trust fall, will it not?" he asked, though not looking for an answer. "We live for the things that scare us."

I thought about what he was saying. It was what I had been communicating to Icarus all along, but somehow it felt fresh coming from someone else. Trust, I was beginning to realize, was more complex when observed through the eyes of a student. Yes, we lived for things that scared us, because all that was real *was* scary. The Dimension, who we were and who we would become, our purpose… it was *all* terrifying.

Fin was right. Questioning Sensei was my opportunity to jump—*again*. It was a choice between courage and cowardice, and I knew which option my heart required.

I was opening my mouth to respond when, as if on cue, Sensei entered the kitchen. I hadn't even heard the back door open.

"Ah, Fin," he said placidly, "it has been some time since you transported in, has it not?"

Sitting up a little straighter, Fin nodded briskly. "That it has, Sensei. I was just leaving."

I heard the tap turn on behind me as Sensei washed his hands. "Stay for the evening. I've just finished with the garden."

"Wish I could," Fin responded, beginning to rise. "But I wouldn't interrupt you and Hawk." He cast me a brief, pointed glance as he spoke my name. "Besides, I have a session this afternoon that I should get back for." He pushed his chair back in

to the table. "Thank you for the offer though."

Sensei said something else, and Fin replied, a conversation that trailed off and faded as Fin's voice echoed in the hallway and then muted into the broom closet. I heard no actual words or sentences. The dull ache in my head became my only awareness, the twinges of pain with each beat of my heart.

All was quiet. Then there were small sounds, water being poured into glasses and Sensei's bare feet creating a gentle rhythm across the floor. A deep and soothing inhale as he seated himself where Fin had been.

Just talk to him, Hawk.

"You and Fin were in discussion?"

"We were, Sensei," I said.

His blue eyes were bright—almost iridescent. His hair was tousled and shimmering with sweat.

"We were speaking of you," I said.

"And you wish to speak to me?"

"Yes, I wish to speak to you."

Sensei leaned back in the chair, holding his glass in one hand and gesturing with the other for me to let the dam break.

In my mind's eye I could see the drop into the ravine yawning before me. I couldn't see the bottom, but it was time for me to jump. And I would have— I was so close. But the chance vanished as the sound of fists against the front door abruptly echoed in the room around us.

Startled, my train of thought derailed. Sensei didn't seem surprised by the sudden interruption and began to rise.

"I'll get it," I said quickly, and jumped to my feet. I cut briskly across the living room, which was still brushed in wisps of smoke from the incense smoldering on the mantel. I threw open the door and Mala nearly fell inside. Her face, neck, and arms were marked with tiny scratches and her eyes were wild. She looked as though she'd just been through a war.

"Hawk, thank god you're around," she gasped before I could speak. "I… I just…" She paused to catch her breath. "We just came from campus," she finally blurted. "There was a fight and—"

"We?"

"Icarus and I." She leaned against the doorframe for support. "There was a fight—Raiden just would not give. I—we couldn't get him to stop. I tried…"

I could see the whole thing replaying behind her eyes as I watched her. I had no idea what had gone down, but I could tell right then that we were in deep.

"Did anyone witness this?"

She froze for a moment before giving a grave nod. "Everyone. We managed to escape just as the police were arriving," she said, quickly glancing over her shoulder. "But it's not like they don't know where we are."

My heart began to pound.

"Where is Icarus?" I asked, following her gaze. "Why hasn't he gotten out of the car?"

Mala's eyes finally turned back to my own, still frantic. "Because he can't."

CHAPTER NINETEEN
Icarus

On more than one occasion I'd been asked why there was no grass left in our front yard. My answer was always the same: Ruger liked partying. And partying to him meant inviting over more people than the driveway could accommodate. As I left Hawk and cut across the driveway that Sunday night, I noticed the yard was packed with cars.

Windows were flung open and music was pumping through the screens. Inside, the kitchen was a chaos of bodies, Solo cups and roaring conversation. Typically, I would have been seething with annoyance by that point, but having disappeared without explanation for the second time, I was relieved. This was exactly the kind of diversion I needed.

I squeezed my way through the crowd, making my way in the direction of my bedroom. The last thing I wanted—or needed—was to run into someone I knew and feel obligated to answer the onslaught of questions that would surely ensue. I needed quiet. My head was still spinning from my flight and the conversation with Hawk. Only a half hour before, I'd been atop the Bank Tower—and the adrenalin rush had hardly worn off. So I wove through the kitchen and almost made it into the hallway. Almost.

Ruger was at the counter, shirtless, red cup in hand, and locked into conversation with a lavishly pierced girl whom he was sporadically making out with. His hair was now a shade of navy blue. He must have dyed it over the weekend.

The meaningless distraction delayed my progress for a split second too long and I winced as he glanced up as if on cue.

"Whoa, look who's here." He brushed the scantily clothed girl aside. "Ion, dude, like, where the hell have you been, man?"

I groaned inwardly.

"You've been gone like, what?" He slapped me on the back, nearly spilling his drink down the front of my shirt. "The whole weekend?" he said, laughing. "Like… poof. You vanished off somewhere. Did this happen before or am I hallucinating?"

"The latter," I said, my voice dripping with sarcasm as I glanced around.

Ruger nodded slowly and then stopped to squint at me. "Wait, the what?"

I rolled my eyes, deciding that he was drunk enough for me to make it up as I went. "So remember I told you about that one cousin I have in San Francisco? Her cat broke its foot and… she didn't want to leave it by itself, so I drove up to deliver groceries to her and stuff—remember? I told you before I left?"

He nodded, seeming to recall this utter nonsense perfectly. "Right, right."

I smiled and gave him a shoulder punch. "So, yeah. There you go. Okay, have fun."

I started walking away, but he grabbed me by the arm and pulled me back over to the counter with him.

"Dude, it's, like, the weekend," he said, pouring me a drink over my protests. "You can't always just hole yourself up in your room—you're getting to be about as boring as West."

So West was locked away studying. I took mental note of this as Ruger pushed the cup into my hand.

"I have a lot of homework to catch up on," I explained, shooting him a serious look that he took no notice of. "I have a really big secret about this semester."

"Yeah?" He made a vain attempt to focus his bleary eyes.

I lowered my voice conspiratorially. "I'm failing."

Ruger laughed. "Join the club, bro."

I set the cup down on the island behind me. "Look, Ruger—"

"Why don't you go find your girlfriend or something," he mumbled, gesturing vaguely towards the entire room. "I don't think she's left yet."

My eyebrows shot into my hairline. "Mala—I mean Mel? She's *here?* Where is she?"

He shrugged. "Go figure it out."

I didn't need to be told twice. Leaving Ruger to reoccupy himself with what he'd been doing previously, I dived back into the crowd again and made my way towards the back door.

I was no neat freak, but I couldn't help but cringe inwardly as I considered what the house was going to look like the following morning. I couldn't remember the last time I'd seen this many bodies crammed into so small a space. It took a ridiculous amount of time to get across the house, pushing and shoving my way in the direction of the back porch.

Despite the noise and confusion, my thoughts kept drifting back to what had happened on the helicopter pad. Our conversation, Hawk's confession, what I'd said. I could still scarcely process that it had all actually happened. It was like a blur I couldn't seem to get my head around.

How had I known that she'd been raped? It was like I'd known… yet I *hadn't.* It was an uneasy sensation that I both loved and feared at the same time. In a sense, I'd been relieved to get away from Hawk, hoping that escaping her would mean escaping the rogue waves of emotion that were taking me under with them. But I was beginning to learn that this wasn't the case. If anything, the storm inside me grew only stronger with the separation. I found myself wondering whether she'd transported back to the Dimension or stayed in the house. My brain was measuring the possible distances between us, playing her voice like a soundtrack on repeat.

The back porch wasn't as crowded as the rest of the house, and I found Mala almost immediately. In a short black dress, she stood leaning against the railing, her face illuminated by the light from her phone's screen. She didn't take note of my presence until I was right in front of her.

"She kept you in there awhile," Mala said as she glanced up. "What's with that?"

I tried to calculate how much I should tell her. But she cut me off at the pass.

"Forget it," she said, looking back at her phone. "I already know what happened. You can spare yourself the struggle."

I looked at her, surprised. "You know about what happened with Raiden?"

Mala nodded.

"Who told you?"

"Who do you think?"

For a split second, I thought the question was genuine. Then I caught on.

"I can't believe you still go to that dirtbag for information." The words caught in my teeth. "I thought you said he used you."

"He did."

"Yet you still talk to him?"

She nodded. "You actually thought I was going to be the nice girl who let him get away with it? I'm going to use him back."

"I'm pretty sure this whole revenge thing would be breaking the code."

Mala rolled her eyes. "You wouldn't be talking that way if you knew what he's been planning to do with your head once he's severed it."

I sighed and leaned back against the railing, glancing down at the deck. The music wasn't as loud out here; I could finally hear my own thoughts—though I couldn't decide which was worse. "I don't want to hear about it."

Mala laughed softly. "Keep your friends close, Icarus—but keep your enemies closer."

"What's that supposed to mean?"

"It means that you'd better watch your step tomorrow," she said, and finally pocketed her phone. "At school. Raiden knows you can't control your emotions, and he's going to push you until you snap."

"That would be breaking the code," I said mechanically. "He'll be exiled."

"You actually think Raiden cares about the code of conduct?" she asked. "He cares about getting his way, Icarus, that is all. And what Raiden wants is to wipe you out."

She had a point. Whether Raiden was exiled or not, it wouldn't affect me very much if I were dead.

"Okay," I said. "Okay, I get it. But why does he want my blood? That's what I'm still trying to figure out—I know more about… what could happen if he kills me, but I just haven't

grasped *why* he wants to."

"He hates you."

"No kidding." I rolled my eyes. "We're both sliders. He's jealous. Whatever. But there has to be a bigger reason. I feel like I'm overlooking something."

She said nothing for a moment. I watched her expression closely.

"If you knew something, you would tell me, wouldn't you?"

She shrugged. "Maybe."

My jaw tensed. "Mala."

She ran a hand back through her hair. "Okay, honestly? I still think you're kind of a jerk. I have a *real* love-hate relationship going with you right now. Does that mean I would withhold information from you that might cost you your life? No. I don't know anything beyond what I just told you." She stepped closer. "My best advice would be simply to watch your step," Mala said again. "Don't lose your cool."

Don't lose my cool. It was exactly what Hawk had also advised, and it was exactly what I was afraid I wouldn't be able to do.

I wasn't ready for what the day would bring—I wasn't ready for *anything*. But the sun came up anyway and left me no choice. I showered, shaved, and worked on yet another excuse for my absence to feed my professors—and West, who I knew would read me the riot act anyway. Thankfully he'd left earlier than usual, and I was spared the confrontation.

I studied myself in the mirror as I got ready, looking for something behind my eyes. Asking myself questions I couldn't answer.

I had become used to living as a stranger in my own body. I was not a friend, I was not an enemy, I simply… was. I felt nothing when I looked in the mirror, not hate, not love, just neutrality. I was a reflection of a shell with something inside it—something I didn't understand.

Icarus, you were found in a car. You have no parents. You have nothing to your name. Who on earth are you that the blood in your veins is worth so much? Who are you?

I'd tortured myself with those three words for as long as I could remember. I'd cringed inwardly when other people asked them, my heart banging in my chest as I groped frantically for an answer, any answer at all, that would get me by.

The truth was, I had invented my life as an author invents a fairy tale. I was made up. Faux. Nothing about me was real. I was as much a legitimate human as the stars on my ceiling were actual stars.

I decided to run to school that day. I wasn't sure why; maybe I felt the need for some order, some familiarity, something resembling my old life, such as it was. On Monday I had morning classes, and campus was crowded, as usual. Cliques of students with coffee cups congested the walkway. I stepped off the path and cut through the trees. My footsteps made vague impressions in the soft grass as I slowed my pace. I was slightly out of breath from hurrying, and since I had barely caught any sleep the previous night, my body was beginning to complain.

You're not tired, I told myself. I needed to be on guard.

Almost immediately I spotted Raiden outside one of the auditorium halls, lighting a cigarette and chatting with two attractive females. He said something I couldn't hear, and one of the girls gave a reply and laughed. After a few minutes the girls walked away, leaving Raiden to browse his phone through faint plumes of gray smoke. Students were sluggishly beginning to file into the building behind him. My anthropology class was in that building.

I passed him calmly without uttering a word. Raiden, likewise, said nothing; I merely felt the stab of his gaze in my back as soon as it was turned.

The truth was, it wasn't necessary for either of us to speak. The communication between us didn't require words. In light of my conversation with Mala the previous night, it wasn't hard to guess what was weighing on his mind.

I left him outside, and the double doors swallowed me whole.

I couldn't concentrate at all during class. The professor was talking and other students were asking questions, but I didn't hear a thing. Raiden was seated across the room, and my peripheral vision wouldn't leave him alone.

Raiden was looking for a way to expose me. It made sense that he would want to make an example of me before he siphoned away my power. He had, after all, waited a long time to beat me at my own game. On top of it all, he had the upper hand because he obviously knew something about me that I didn't.

But how was that even possible? How could an enemy know me better than I knew myself? What was I missing here? I needed to watch him closely, just as Mala had suggested: friends close, enemies closer.

As class let out, I mechanically gathered up the papers splayed out in front of me. I was just beginning to think that I was going to make it out unscathed when something tore my desk and chair out from underneath me. Papers flew everywhere, and I fell sideways. I landed on the heels of my hands and, biting back a profanity, got to my feet again, avoiding the stares of the other students. Someone asked me if I was okay, and I must have responded in the affirmative because after a minute I was left alone. My heart was pounding as I bent to pull the desk upright. Across the room, Raiden was placidly gathering his things, pretending not to have noticed. I swept up my papers and unzipped my backpack to shove them inside. The classroom slowly drained until there was no sound left except the rhythmic thundering in my chest. Then I heard footsteps behind me.

"Need help with that, Ion?"

My jaw clenched. "Get the hell away from me." Something inside me threatened to boil over. I grabbed my things and stalked out the door before that had a chance to happen.

Outside, I found Mala in conversation with a circle of other girls, though when she noticed me, she tore herself away and caught up with me.

"Hey, are you okay?" I felt a hand on my arm. Warmth. "Icarus—"

"Don't." I brushed her away. "Don't touch me right now. I'm fine."

"I heard about what just happened."

"I can deal."

I could sense her giving me a dubious look. "Can you, though?"

I glanced over my shoulder and saw Raiden coming down the path, chatting with a few other students. He was headed in the same direction that we were, but the walkway was congested with students rushing to make their next class. I quickly calculated the distance between us and tried to gauge how involved he was in the conversation.

"You know I came to the party last night specifically to see you," Mala went on, and I half listened. "I was concerned that maybe…"

I let her words wash over me and zeroed in instead on the conversation several yards behind us. Raiden was watching me closely, although he, too, appeared to be listening to his friends talking.

The sea of students had swept us all along to the front of the auditorium building. We milled in with the jam of bodies waiting to climb the steps.

Over the babble of voices, I became aware of the fact that Mala was still talking. She stopped and put her hands on her hips. "Are you even listening to me? Seriously, Icarus, I—" Suddenly the blood drained from her face and she clutched her right wrist. "Ow. Oh my god." She was holding her wrist so hard that her fingertips were turning white. *What the hell?*

"Icarus, what's happening?!" Her voice was a strangled squeak of pain.

I quickly turned and located Raiden just a few feet away now. His dark eyes were narrowed slightly in concentration—and locked on Mala.

"Icarus!" Mala cried again. "What's going—"

Pushing the other students out of the way, I threw myself on top of Raiden. The impact of my body broke his channel, and a burst of orange-yellow energy ignited around us, burning my skin as he swung for my head. I jerked backwards to avoid the impact and dove to pin his hands down. My left hand found his and slammed it into the cement, and immediately a searing heat ripped across my palm.

I recoiled, sucking in a sharp breath, and saw the same orange flicker dancing over his palm for a split second before it vanished back into his skin like a trapdoor spider.

How on earth...

I stared, stunned, for a second too long.

"Icarus, look out!"

Mala's voice wrenched me back into reality just as Raiden managed to drive a kick into my stomach, throwing me off him. He wound back his fist and hurled what looked like absolutely nothing right into my face. Thrown into the air like a toy, my limbs flailed as I crashed onto the walkway with a thud that knocked the breath out of me. Raiden scrambled to his feet and turned to face me, knees bent, his face a mask of cold fury. Over the ringing in my ears, I could hear a confusion of noise, yelling, and frantic footsteps. Raiden raised his fist, and I dodged to the side a split second too late. A bullet of energy cut like hot iron across my left temple.

Clenching my jaw against the pain, I rolled to the left and jumped to my feet. Racing to the steps, I grabbed the railing and vaulted myself to the top. The rest of the students had scattered. I had hoped that Mala would run, but instead she raced up the steps after me and ducked behind one of the massive steel support pillars in front of the entrance. I dove behind the one opposite, feeling the cold steel against my back.

Breathing hard and attempting to zone out of the unfolding chaos, I turned and glanced over my shoulder to find that Raiden had remained where he was, having chosen an efficient vantage point. The other students had dispersed to alert security or escape. A handful of energy swirled visibly in his right palm, and he shot it at me as soon as he caught a glimpse of my face. Bracing myself, I pulled back and felt it explode through the steel just above my head, tearing a jagged bite out of the pillar.

I glanced at Mala. She was staring at me, her eyes enormous. Her fingertips, which had been stone white only a moment ago, were now scarred with first-degree burns. I pressed my eyelids shut, refocusing.

Some of the students had fled into the auditorium building and locked it down—I'd heard the dull *click* of the tumbler. I couldn't blame them. But the only escape route for Mala and me was through that building.

Mala seemed to read my thoughts. "Icarus, go!" She jerked her head in the direction of the door. "I'll cover for you."

I shook my head violently. "No, Mala—bad idea—"

Ignoring me, she brought up both hands and formed a ball of energy, stepping out onto the top step to take aim at Raiden, who was crouched in the grass, forming his own orb. Mala ducked as it rocketed towards her, and then threw her own, hard.

I heard a small explosion of concrete and the clattering of rubble falling onto the walkway. Raiden cursed, caught off guard.

Now.

I brought my hands up in front of me as I stepped out of cover and quickly took aim. The glass doors imploded, sending a shower of tiny glass particles scattering into the empty hallway. I stepped through the mangled door frame and ducked into a doorway to my right.

I was unfamiliar with this building and suddenly realized that I had no idea where the emergency exit was. Dimly lit hallways twisted off in two opposing directions, and neither looked promising. My head was throbbing, and I fought down a wave of queasy lightheadedness.

I heard a rush of footsteps in the hallway and Mala scrambled to a stop on the rubble of glass in the foyer as an orb rocketed past her head and slammed into the opposing wall, where it burst into flames. Emerging from the doorway's temporary shelter, I sprinted to the opposite side of the hall where the stairwell opened up, grabbing Mala by her unburned hand.

"Icarus, we can't go upstairs!" she yelled, refusing to budge. "There's no way out. We'll be trapped up there—"

"Just trust me on this one, okay?" We took the stairs together, two at a time.

The second floor was nothing but a long glass-lined hallway looking out over campus and branching off into various labs and classrooms. Panting, I halted for a split second to get my bearings.

Suddenly I felt Mala stiffen beside me. Wordlessly, she pointed at the glass. Raiden was pacing on the ground two stories below us; he had clearly anticipated my next move and circled around to regain his vantage point. I threw myself on top of Mala and rolled both of us to the side as a cannonball of fire blew the glass in. A wave of heat washed over us and the air seemed to vacuum away.

Mala screamed and I clamped a hand over her mouth as another fireball came thundering through one side of the building and crashed out the other. "Quiet!" I hissed.

We scrambled to our feet and began to run, staggering and slipping on pebbles of glass and chunks of brick and metal. I found a doorknob and turned it, and we tumbled together into a utility closet. I yanked the door closed behind us and everything went dark.

For a few moments everything was quiet. I could hear my heart hammering in my ears and the sound of Mala's labored breathing. I listened for sounds beyond the door. I could hear the fire murmuring hungrily on the first floor as it fed along the walls.

Finally she spoke. "I told you Raiden wanted to kill you, you idiot."

"Give me your hand."

"Why?"

"Just let me see it."

Grudgingly, she slipped her hand into mine and then sucked her breath in sharply as I ran my fingertips gently over her skin.

I closed my eyes and focused on what I was feeling. The shape of her fingers, the lines running across her palm. I let the warmth pulsing in my forearm flood down into my hand and filter into hers.

"Ouch!" she whispered. "Your hands are so hot."

"I know." I released her hand. "Just close your eyes for a second, okay?"

Mala hesitated. "Why? What are you going to do?"

"Shhh."

I had a hunch—a strong one—and I needed full concentration to test it.

I had never attempted transportation outside of Sensei's or the Dimension before—in fact, I didn't even know if it was *possible*. I knew I would have to pick something extremely fresh in my mind in order for success to be even a possibility.

I pressed my eyelids shut and attempted to calm my racing thoughts, fighting to focus… *focus…*

I visualized the building where I'd just had an anthropology class. Near the emergency exit was a large walk-in supply closet like the one we were standing in now. I'd only caught a glimpse of the interior, but now, as I stood there in the dark with the sounds of alarms wailing downstairs, I found I could recall the details vividly. As soon as I had the image, I locked in on it.

Suddenly the air around us grew cooler, and the sound was the placid hum of an air conditioner.

Hell yes.

The silence lasted only a moment longer as we regained our breath; then I cleared my throat.

"You know," I started feeling around for a light switch or a doorknob, "last time we were stuck in a closet together, we were making out."

Mala gave a wry laugh. "Don't get any ideas—I'm *so* over you."

"Good to know."

My fingers found the switch and I flipped it.

Mala brought a hand up to shield her eyes from the sudden flood of illumination—a hand that now looked completely normal. She glanced around for a second before saying anything, looking vaguely puzzled.

"Is this even the same closet?"

I stepped past her and opened the door. "How about we save questions for later?"

We emerged into the hallway, where a small cluster of professors were loitering, chatting over cups of coffee as if the world wasn't ending outside. One of them, a middle-aged woman in a tweed suit, glanced up when she noticed us, clearing her throat.

"Um, excuse me?" She looked pointedly at us. "This building is closed to students at the moment. May I ask how you got in?"

There was no point trying to explain, so I merely grinned as Mala and I started back-stepping towards the emergency exit.

"Closet—long story. By the way—" I paused to gesture in the opposite direction "—the building next door is kind of on fire. Just FYI."

That was all it took to divert their attention. Mala and I fled the building, leaving the door swinging violently on its hinges as we broke out onto the green. I quickly sized up the situation as we ran. The good news was that the trees were in front of us, offering ample cover.

The bad news was that Raiden had moved to the front of the building from which we'd just emerged. He paused for a moment to admire the plumes of smoke billowing up overhead before turning and taking note of our position.

Mala cursed. "He just saw us."

Picking up speed, we bolted for the trees just as the first orb came sailing through to find us. Mala darted behind a massive oak and yanked me down with her. An explosion of leaves and small branches rained down on us as the orb impacted into the canopy overhead.

Shielding her eyes, Mala glanced up. "This is going to get messy."

I turned my attention back to Raiden, who was only across the green now, fighting off a couple of male students who had attempted to tackle him.

With one quick, sweeping touch, he lit their clothes on fire and moved on as if nothing had happened.

The guy was *insane*. Relentless, deadly, insane.

My head was throbbing. Exhaustion was setting in, and I could feel the power in my body depleting. I started manifesting the last of my energy, blitzing him with it as I peered around the trunk of the tree—and came close to getting decapitated.

I threw myself to the side, into Mala, as a huge portion of the tree was blasted into hardwood shrapnel. I felt several oversized splinters nail smoothly into my right thigh with a sickening sound like meat being skewered. I swore through my teeth.

"You okay?"

I shimmied up into a sitting position, trying to ignore the agonizing pain in my leg.

"Y-yeah," I stuttered, breathless. "I'm solid. You have to move—this tree is only going to take so much."

As if on cue, another blast shot away a sizable portion of the tree's trunk. This time the impact was on Mala's side, but she responded quicker than I had and missed the fallout. With two large bites taken out of it, only a small middle portion of the tree remained intact. I was quickly catching on to what Raiden was planning.

"Do you think you can make it to the next one?" Mala asked, breathless, as she scanned the green.

I shook my head. "I'll be okay—it's better if we split up."

She stared at me. "I can't just leave you here."

"I'll be okay," I said. "I'm fine. I'll follow you—I just need a second."

"You're not fine," she said, stealing a quick glance around the tree before turning to lock eyes with me again. "Don't do something stupid."

"I'm incapable of stupidity," I told her, still gritting my teeth slightly as I rolled to my knees and shot a blaze of energy through the void Raiden's first blast had created. "Now go!"

My aim was good this time; the blast thudded into his shoulder, and he roared in outraged surprise.

Finally.

I knew he was about to let go with everything he had. He took a moment to regain himself, and I took that opportunity to check on Mala; she had positioned herself behind an oak tree about fifteen feet away and was getting ready to throw, spinning the ozone rapidly around in her fingertips. I could smell smoke and heard sirens in the distance.

Even if we didn't die, we were *so* dead.

Yes, Raiden was the "bad guy" in the situation—a complete given. But all three of us were responsible for breaking the code of conduct practically in half. If we actually made it back to the Dimension alive, I had no idea how the student body would handle the situation. We had each been instructed never to use our powers outside of the Dimension unsolicited. And now there were countless witnesses to our blatant disobedience of the order. *Everyone on campus* had seen.

Edging out slightly from her cover, Mala took precise aim and hurled her orb at Raiden, catching him on the arm just as he blasted one in my direction. An unhealthy cracking noise in the tree above me told me that it was time to move, injury or no injury. I somersaulted to the side, landing beside Mala's oak tree. She slipped out from behind it to cover me, firing relentlessly.

I heard Raiden cry out as he was hit. Mala quickly ducked back beside me, breathing hard.

My ears were ringing from the explosions; her voice sounded like it was underwater. "Brace yourself," she said, clutching my arm. There was a deafening crack as the tree I'd just rolled away from came crashing down like a dying giant.

The impact shook the ground, and its massive branches raked the air. A whirlwind of leaves showered down around us.

"You good?" Mala asked a moment later, brushing twigs out of her hair.

I quickly blinked back into focus. "Set."

She leaned back against the tree and peered around the side. "He's limping now," she whispered breathlessly. "He won't be able to catch up. We have to run—now. Can you make it?"

"Yeah—yeah, I can make it." I pulled in a sharp breath through my clenched teeth. "Just go. I'll be right behind you."

Mala shook her head. "You go first and I'll cover for you. If I get hurt, you can heal me—you can't heal yourself."

She had a point there.

"Where did you park?" We ducked through the fallen branches, using them as cover.

"The garage. First level." We burst out of the fallen tree and took off running across the green. The sirens were louder now—on campus, I could tell. I had no idea how much time had passed. It felt like a small eternity.

It didn't take long for Raiden to recover and start pursuing us again, but apparently he wasn't a healer either, and he soon lagged behind, limping badly. A few last-ditch orbs sailed uselessly past us, and at last Mala half-dragged me the rest of the way into the garage.

Her maroon Saab was waiting only four spaces in. She unlocked it and swung into the driver's seat, wincing as I took shotgun.

"You're a mess," I heard her murmur, almost more to herself than to me as she shoved the key into the ignition.

"What are you talking about?"

"You're bleeding everywhere."

Up until then I'd barely even noticed the pain—my mind had been tapped solely into that primal "don't die" instinct, high on an adrenalin rush—but now, in the sudden calm of the car's interior, it came clawing its way front and center. I was afraid to look down, but did anyway.

"Oh wow," I mumbled, looking down and feeling suddenly nauseous. "You're right."

My body was on fire with pain. During the battle, the constant fight to stay in one piece had engaged my mind completely. But now my head was pounding in agony, and my leg ached and stung where splinters of wood were embedded. Adding insult to injury, something that sounded like heavy metal rock started pulsing through the speakers as Mala put the car in gear.

"Ow," I complained. "My head."

"Shhhh." Mala shifted into drive and floored it. "It helps me concentrate."

Raiden was standing dead center in the entrance of the garage, hands up.

"Seriously?" I heard Mala groan softly, not slowing down. "Why do all my boyfriends have to suck so much?" She shoved my head down and floored it.

Raiden threw himself out of the way but not before hurling a fiery ball of energy through our windshield.

Payback.

CHAPTER TWENTY
Hawk

I didn't say a word. Not when I pulled his body out of the car, which was missing a windshield. Not when I dragged him through the house. Not while we transported. I spoke only to tell Sensei that I was transporting back with Icarus, and to tell Mala that she should stay in the house with Sensei and await further instruction.

The platform was in session upon our arrival, so we were able to slip past almost unnoticeably. I made brief eye contact with Fin, who was leading one of the larger groups positioned off to the right. He hesitated mid-speech when he saw me. I shook my head, lifting a hand slightly to communicate that I could handle it.

I pulled Icarus into the corridor at the opposing side of the platform and unlocked the safe room at the far end as we approached it. The pocket door glided open, and I gestured tersely for him to enter first.

He was holding his head, reminding me that my own was still achy from earlier, and taking a breath for what I presumed would be an apology.

"Save it." I cut him off before he had a chance to start, and gestured for him to take a seat in one of the two *zaisu*, the only pieces of furniture in this particular room. "There's nothing you can say that will change what has happened."

Icarus sank onto one of the floor chairs, sighing heavily. I pulled the other up alongside his. Tiny flecks of broken glass peppered his shirt and glittered in his sweat-soaked hair.

"How did the windshield burst?" I asked.

"Raiden shot a mass of energy at us as we were leaving the parking garage."

There were a thousand things I could have said, a thousand things that were bringing my blood to a boil and my heartbeat up into my aching head, but I controlled myself.

"Take off your shirt," I told him, steadying my breath.

Icarus did as I'd instructed, removing his T-shirt, balling it up, and tossing it aside.

"Talk to me about where it hurts," I said, noticing the impact wound across his left temple and the minor cuts running down along his neck and chest. His leg looked as though it had borne the real brunt of whatever had gone down. "How did you end up with pieces of a tree in your leg?"

Icarus winced slightly as I slid my hand over the left half of his face, letting my fingertips press slightly into the wound. "A tree fell."

"A *tree* fell?"

"Raiden was attacking us… we were behind one of the oaks," he replied. "It was the only cover we… had at the time."

I had been focusing on his head wound up until then, watching it slowly decrease in size, then vanish altogether, but when he said this, my focus immediately went to his eyes.

"Other students saw?"

Icarus nodded.

"How many?"

"Everyone," he answered, sounding numb. "Everyone present."

I swallowed, at a loss for words. I moved my hand across his jawline and to his neck. My fingertips found one of the deeper cuts and gravitated to it.

"Mala told me Raiden wouldn't care about breaking the code," he continued, still sounding as though he couldn't comprehend the words that were coming out of his mouth. "She told me he would

do whatever it took, but I didn't listen."

My eyes stayed trained on my fingers. "And why didn't you?"

"Because I thought I would be able to take it," he responded. "Because I thought I was better than that—I thought... I thought I could control it no matter what happened."

A quiet fell over the room. I said nothing in response as I watched the thin trail of blood steadily recede beneath my stained fingertips. I could feel the rapid thumping of his pulse.

"Well, apparently you couldn't." The palm of my hand slipped to his chest. "You couldn't handle it, you couldn't control yourself, and you were far from being better 'than that.' You *failed*, Icarus. Some would say it's cold of me to say so, and perhaps I would concede that it is—it's not like you made it out unscathed. But I think we're beyond concealing what we actually feel, you and I."

"I understand," he said. "I know you're disappointed in me, Hawk."

I shook my head. "That doesn't even cut it this time—I am *beyond* disappointed with you. I am *done* with you."

At this he finally turned and looked at me, shocked. He wasn't the only one.

"Done?" he repeated the word in a voice so strained I wanted to take it all back, but that was something my pride simply wouldn't allow.

I took my eyes away from his. "I can only give you so many second chances, Icarus."

Dead silence. Then a tentative breath.

"What about the other day?" he asked, like this should mean something. "What about rejoining sessions, everything we talked about—what about us?"

Us.

The word, for reasons I couldn't understand, was sharp. It stung, and it beckoned my gaze back into a lock with his own.

"*What about us?*" I repeated, the words rolling bitterly off my tongue. "What *about* us? Icarus, you are a student to me, and *nothing* more. I was a fool to have poured my soul out to you like I did the other night. I was stupid to ever think that I could trust you—I *can't believe* I trusted you."

"Hawk, please—"

"No." I cut him off before he could get further. "I don't want to hear it, okay? I don't want to hear it. You have *no idea* of the consequences that we will all be forced to face because of your actions. Your errors no longer affect only you but *all of us*, Icarus. You bring this suffering down not only on your own head—"

"I didn't know! I wouldn't have even done anything if it wasn't for the fact that—"

"There's no excuse for breaching the code! I know that the ways in which we are obligated to conduct ourselves are just so much white noise in your mind, but do you even know what they actually mean—what they mean to *me?*"

I didn't intend to wait for an answer, and I could tell that he didn't intend to give one. Our eyes were still locked.

"It's not a set of rules, it's not about deprivation and death, it's about living in such a way that actually brings one's true identity to the surface," I continued, and my voice calmed itself for a moment. "It's about *everything*—everything that's important. Waking up from this stupor—this illusion we've all been living in and told to accept as though it's reality! It's living like you *actually believe* what the prophecy says—like you actually believe that we are worthy to rise and reclaim that which is ours."

I paused, breathless now and feeling a lump beginning to form in my throat. For a split second I feared that I would cry. *I wouldn't cry.*

"I told you no one could know about us," I said. "I told you never to use your powers in the world beyond this Dimension. I told you…"

I told you, I told you… The words felt more and more hollow each time they fell from my lips. Because, like his apologies, they could do nothing to repair the damage that had been done. We were both standing at the scene of the accident, and the vehicle in which we'd traveled this far was totaled. There was nothing left to say. Yet I kept speaking.

"You have no idea what this means." My voice had dropped involuntarily to a whisper, as I spoke more to myself than to him. "You have no idea how dark this place is about to become."

My emotions, like disobedient children, were becoming harder and harder to keep under control. I felt like I was holding back a waterfall with both hands. My strength would only last so long. I wanted to let go, but I was more afraid to than ever—I had new burns.

We had perched on the edge of a thousand-foot drop, overlooking a city of flickering gold, and I had finally unclenched my hand from the wound to show him the place where the bullet had found me. Now I could feel something inside myself receding back into the darkness. Telling me to run instead of jump, telling me to take a deep breath and hold it back. Telling me to take death before letting go.

For a moment, I forgot how to breathe. I lost track of where I was and what was happening. My awareness rendered itself incapable of anything beyond my own heartbeat… then his. Suddenly I realized that my hand hadn't moved from his chest. Together our pulses were like explosions. Like two cannons taking aim and firing, relentless in their pursuit of breaking through the fortress and into the other's soul. Each attempted to tear off the other's armor, though neither surrendered.

"Hawk." His voice was softer. "Please forgive me."

My focus swam to the surface to break into his eyes, I'd lost track of them somehow though our gaze had been locked the entire time. His icy blue eyes looked somehow different when they were this close. Like mines, there was gold lost in that darkness, glimmering as the illumination from my own swept past like a searchlight. Looking for something.

In that split second my soul was no longer my own. I was standing outside myself, watching like a spectator as it took off on its own. It was pure, innocent, staring, reaching, wanting to feel something for the first time. *Yes*, it whispered. *Yes, I forgive you.*

It was the closest thing I'd ever felt to losing control. And it terrified me.

Icarus's heartbeat was still echoing under my hand, pounding up against my flesh. His gaze melted from my eyes to my skin, to my lips, seeming somehow to reach—pull. I felt it. I saw his eyelashes against his skin and felt chills over my own.

My soul was fire, then ice. I caught my breath again and pulled away, forcing my eyes to let go of the things that they'd found inside his. My hand slipped from his skin, closing into a fist to suppress my trembling fingers.

"No, Icarus," I told him, in a voice that was hardly my own. "I can't."

"I'm guessing Mala has filled you in, so please debrief me on everything you've learned thus far." I threw myself down in the middle of the red circle on Sensei's office floor. "I've finished with Icarus."

Sensei was standing in front of the glass wall with his back to me, his fingers laced. "Did he not fill you in?"

"I didn't ask him for the details. I can't say that I felt like discussing it with him. I need to know what *you* think—that is all that is relevant to me."

At first Sensei said nothing, and for a second I wondered whether he would answer at all.

"Shall I start from the beginning, the end, or shall I answer the questions you will inevitably ask before I can convey even half of it?"

He knew me well. A thousand questions were percolating through my head, but I gestured for him to continue in whatever way he deemed most coherent.

"Raiden desired to make an example of Icarus before carrying out his plan to execute him, and thus pushed him to the breaking point."

"He did tell me that much."

"Apparently after having already provoked Icarus, he shifted tactics and targeted Mala, whom Icarus then violently acted to defend." Sensei paused, his back still to me. He glanced off to the left and I saw the profile of his face.

"Apparently there was a crowd and thus many witnesses to the fight that proceeded. Mala explained that there was considerable damage."

I barely heard the second half of Sensei's explanation. My attention had been snagged by the first item.

"Icarus defended Mala?" I asked, incredulous. "How… why? I thought Raiden was set on attacking Icarus personally. Why would Mala be a target?"

Sensei turned slightly and looked at me, hands still behind his back. He looked surprised. "What would be the surest way of provoking your aggression, Hawk?" he asked, studying me. "Would it be by attacking my character or your own?"

I wasn't sure why he was asking, but the answer was obvious. "Yours, Sensei."

"And why is that?"

"Because I would defend you above all else," I answered matter-of-factly. "You are my creator. Mala is no such person to Icarus—"

"Now place Fin in the same situation," he cut in. "What if the same verbal or physical attack had been perpetrated on Fin—what then?"

I opened my mouth, but my words had frozen in my throat.

Fin? Why had Sensei brought Fin into this?

"Am I to understand that your reaction would be disassociated and neutral in order that the code might be upheld?"

My mouth was still open. I closed it and swallowed the rest of what I had been about to say, pressing the heel of my hand to my forehead.

"Am I to understand that you would do nothing?"

I shook my head. "No, Sensei."

"You would act to protect him, then?"

"With my life, Sensei."

"Mm." He turned back to the window. "Then we cannot punish an act that we ourselves would commit."

"You have never and will never commit fault, Sensei," I said, speaking into my wrist. "But Icarus, Mala, and Raiden—they've all fallen short of the standard. They each exercised their powers beyond the walls of the Dimension. They've exposed us."

"They have indeed."

"And you have no problem with that?"

"It is not that I find no fault in their behavior, Hawk," he said. "It's that I see the greater issue, which I have brought to your attention before: the fact that we need them. Yes, they have all missed their mark, but they too are necessary brushstrokes towards the painting's completion."

I frowned, struggling to get my head around what he was saying.

"So, in essence, you forgive them," I concluded. "You count them all as having merely fallen short? Even though Raiden acted with such violence? That doesn't make sense."

"It doesn't now," Sensei said. "But it will eventually."

There was nothing left for me to add to that. "So what now?" I asked. "What of Raiden? If there are witnesses to what happened, they'll easily identify him to the authorities unless you plan on finding him first."

"He's capable of transporting in," Sensei replied. "He will locate us before anyone locates him."

He had a point. Raiden knew his way to Sensei's and wouldn't have any trouble transporting in. What still wasn't adding up in my mind was the fact that Sensei wasn't acknowledging that we had a fairly large problem on our hands—one that, by the standards of the student body, could be punishable by exile.

"Sensei, Raiden is trying to kill Icarus," I explained slowly. "I haven't figured out why yet, and I don't think Icarus has either, but... how do you plan on handling that situation?"

"Is Raiden not Mitsue's student?"

I nodded.

"Then Mitsue will keep him under his supervision, I am certain," he said, as though this settled the issue. "And you will keep your own student under yours."

I felt my muscles tense slightly at the last part of his sentence, my mind immediately recalling my heated declaration. I made no mention of this, deciding that now wasn't the time to inform Sensei.

"You say that as though we will have the power to keep constant watch over them, Sensei," I said. "Our supervision is inevitably cut off as soon as they decide to transport back into their own world."

A silence I hadn't anticipated filled the room in response. Sensei neither spoke nor turned to look at me.

I eventually prodded, not sure of what to say but too anxious to stay quiet. "Sensei, what is it?"

I heard a raptor call distantly beyond the glass and then saw it for a split second as it passed—a blur. I sensed that he was watching it, too. He took a breath.

"They won't be transporting back into their own world, Hawk," he said, and turned to look at me over his shoulder. "No one will be."

Something inside me froze.

"Don't ask anything yet," he said, his voice heavy as he turned away again. "I've called a meeting this evening. I will explain everything then."

CHAPTER TWENTY-ONE
Hawk

I left Sensei's office and returned to my own apartment. The effects of sleep deprivation were beginning to take their toll. The sun was at its highest point in the cloudless sky and moving steadily onward toward the opposing horizon. It would be evening soon.

Aware that I would need to be in full focus for the meeting, I attempted to rest, but I slept little and restlessly. I awoke in a sweat, breathing heavily. Nightmare fallout. I lay there for a few moments, feeling more exhausted than I had before.

The window was open, and a soft breeze swept into the room. The sky was pink now, staining the rocky cliff face and silhouetting the trees a little farther below. I listened for the quiet sighs of violins, but they never came; it was as if even the wind was holding her breath, awaiting Sensei's word.

The conversations from earlier that day came rushing back to my mind, giving fresh weight to the seriousness of the situation. My heart felt like lead in my chest. My soul murmured an almost clairvoyant message of what was about to take place, but in a language I couldn't translate.

Accentuating my markings, I dressed appropriately in all black, zipped on a light jacket and pulled my hair back into a tight bun.

I stood by the window for a moment. My breath clouded the glass as I drank in what I well knew could be the last glimpse of normality I would have for a long time.

The meeting was being held on the lower gathering platform. Beyond the window I could already see the thin strip of flame flickering along the platform's edge. Students were emptying out of the dormitory pods and making their way toward it.

As I flew in, the sense of déjà vu was strong. It was impossible to miss the similarities the gathering platform shared with the helicopter pad at the top of the Bank Tower. A bullseye—red brushstrokes replaced by war-paint white ones, and the number at the center with a dancing flame contained in a levitating half sphere. The platform's edge, overlooking the drop, was trimmed by a long conduit filled with fragrant oil on which rust-colored flames also fed. There was no overhead shelter, leaving us exposed under the dull crimson sky. A few faint stars were just visible in the zenith.

The space was packed nearly to its capacity. Everyone seemed to be present except for Sensei.

Glancing around as I flexed the nerves out of my fingers, I spotted Fin almost immediately. He was locked in conversation with Gaia. We made brief eye contact, acknowledging each other's presence before I vanished farther into the crowd.

As Sensei had predicted, Raiden was indeed back. My scanning eyes found his sharp ones in the crowd and froze there.

He was seated beside Mitsue and dressed in what were obviously borrowed clothes: black jeans and a Japanese graphic tee. His hands, I could tell, were bound behind his back and gloved to the forearm. His expression was neutral. Mitsue, in contrast, was wearing a trench coat, and a look of intense displeasure on his face. I decided to sit with them because I knew Icarus would strategically find whatever place was farthest away from Raiden.

"This seat isn't taken, is it?" I asked, sitting down beside him.

Mitsue glanced up from his notepad to toss me a brief, irritated glance. "I was saving it for someone."

I ignored him. "Did Sensei fill you in about…?"

Raiden didn't seem to be paying attention to our low-spoken exchange, but I knew better than to finish that sentence in front of him.

Mitsue gave a single nod. "He did. And Mala informed Fin."

I wasn't exactly surprised, just slightly taken aback. Word about the day's mishaps had spread more quickly than I'd anticipated.

Given the casual hum in the atmosphere, I got the feeling that I was the only one who knew the real reason we'd been summoned. It was a strange sensation. I felt like I was in a room that was about to be fired upon, and I was the only one who knew what was about to happen. And I remained silent.

"Where is Sensei?" I asked, almost to myself. I heard none of the answer Mitsue gave.

Icarus walked onto the platform. He entered at the opposing end and remained there, just as I had suspected he would. He, too, was dressed in all black; his hair was messy and contrasted against his skin, which seemed paler than usual in the glow of the flames around us. His eyes avoided mine, but I could feel he knew exactly where I was and that I was looking at him.

Breathe.

Though I'd neither seen nor heard him make his entrance, Sensei was now standing in the center of the innermost circle in front of the suspended flame. It took a moment for everyone to become aware of his presence, but gradually a hush washed over the platform.

Without speaking, Sensei gestured for someone in the front row to rise. I couldn't see who it was until she stood. Gaia's petite frame was unmistakable. Her dark, dreadlocked hair was twisted into a thick, elegant braid that lay between her small shoulder blades. Sensei motioned for her to enter the innermost circle.

Gaia was our youngest initiate—affectionately referred to as "the child among us"—and as such, the demands of the ritual fell upon her to open the gathering. I could tell from a quick glance that Icarus had no idea what was going on, though immediately after this thought, I felt a sharp pang of guilt. *Whose fault is that?*

Gaia took a deep breath and closed her eyes. She brought her palms face up in a position that suggested she was holding a light, invisible weight.

"The heavens and the earth were born unto us, a supernova," she began, her voice velveteen soft, but intensely audible in the silence. "A soul split in two. Thus we poured forth: one."

Having attended countless other gatherings, I was already focusing on the empty space on the floor where she stood slightly in front of Sensei. Already anticipating the verses of the prophecy that would appear as she spoke them.

"Stars in need of no darkness to shine, trees in need of no light to grow; the sun and her children find voice between a sunrise and a sunset."

White brushstrokes began to appear across the floorboards around her, flowing like water from her feet to the perimeter of the circle, slowly making their way around its circumference—brushstrokes that formed words.

Though the sky still glowed red with the sunset, the verses, as though penned by some invisible author, glowed with such an intensity that all else in contrast seemed suddenly dim.

"For the universe exists between two halves of the same spirit…"

I zoned out of Gaia's voice and allowed myself to become absorbed in the verses as they appeared. Reading them, though be it for the hundredth time, never failed to inebriate my soul.

A sensation of ecstasy overtook me, and for the duration of the prophecy's recital, I could do little else beyond stare in awe as the luminous words painted themselves across the platform.

A sunrise marred by the fruits of the earth,
A sunset marked by all that it could become,

A beginning, and an end,
An eternity birthed in a state of possibility;

Unobserved, hidden from our vision,
A universe that is a question.

An infinite existence that is both alive and dead,
Until we make the decision,

And open not the darkness, but our eyes
To create that reality.

Every nerve in my body was humming. Hearing the prophecy was like listening to a lover's poem, each verse ripe with details of the beloved, each penned specifically with the receiver in mind.

I was the subject of the story—*one* of them. I was the first half of a sacred book torn asunder at the binding.

I watched as the darkness dissipated along with the words, which remained only a moment longer before fading away. Sensei and Gaia exchanged reverential bows and she returned to her seat. Sensei stood directly in front of the flame, facing us.

"I believe most of you may already be aware," he began calmly, though I could sense the gravity hidden in the undertones, "but this gathering is not of an ordinary nature. It is, in fact, an emergency."

A vague hush of whispers arose from the audience. Sensei lifted a hand for silence.

"Please." He glanced briefly around at all of us. "Do not make this harder with speculation. The situation, I will confess, is grave. A tragedy has undeniably befallen us, but it is not insurmountable. There can be redemption."

He paused there, and for a moment I felt the heavy pull of his grief. A sensation that sent chills over my skin. I hadn't felt that from him since the day he found me.

"But redemption, I'm afraid, does not come without a cost," he continued. "It is a quenching of a thirst, and one cannot both provide one's self as the sacrifice to be drunk down and still continue to exist in the same way. One cannot redeem the future without losing a part of one's own past—or present."

I stole a glance at Icarus out of my peripheral vision. His elbows were resting on his knees, his fingers interwoven and his forehead pressed against them.

"At the dawn of your gathering, you petitioned that there be set in place a system of order—a means through which peace may be maintained. I granted you this right and gave you the freedom to do what seemed fitting," Sensei went on. "And thus you all have striven to abide by the code of conduct. A set of standards that are indeed worthy, honorable, and for your own preservation. Citing the first and foremost item, you each have 'wholly sworn to keep your abilities a secret, never at any time exposing your true nature to the human world.' You each agreed to this upon initiation."

There was a murmur of agreement from everyone present except a few— and I was one of the few. Although I was not guilty of the same breach, my hands weren't clean.

"It is with deep regret that I must make known that some of you, several of you, have betrayed this agreement, and in doing so—" Sensei raised his hand again for quiet "—*and in doing so* have exposed us."

The platform exploded in a swell of voices.

"Please, everyone." Sensei raised both hands now. "Please. Allow me to continue."

Mitsue was grumbling under his breath in Japanese. Beside him, Raiden wore a neutral expression. For an instant I could have sworn I saw the slightest of smiles flicker across his lips, but when I looked again, it was gone.

Someone yelled above the noise and asked Sensei to reveal the identities of the traitors. Another voice retorted that it was "already obvious."

And it was—painfully so. Raiden was sitting there with his hands tied behind his back, under strict supervision, and I could already tell by how students were interacting with Icarus that they knew. The only one who seemed to have been spared the humiliation was Mala. She was an unlikely suspect, so apparently she had slipped under their radar.

I knew that Sensei wouldn't reveal their identities, but I couldn't help but also notice that there was little to actually be revealed even if he so chose.

I glanced again at Icarus, and our eyes locked, his searching mine for answers. I quickly looked away, but the damage was done. I felt as though I'd been burned.

Sensei began to speak again. "Our purpose—*your* purpose—is to be this redemption of which I speak," he said. "You were born for such a time as this. You were designed with the power and the ability to lift all that is to come from the jaws of death itself. For you are life—all of you. Each one of you. Though I fear this error has altered your path. Therefore, both a present and a future sacrifice will be necessary. For in order to defeat that darkness which is ahead, you must first preserve yourselves now." He paused to let his words sink in.

"Without the protectors, there is no redemption—no hope for that which is to come. The world has now been exposed to your powers in ways that they have never experienced before. They have seen your light and cannot unsee it—"

"But not *all* of us broke the code," said an indignant voice. "Why should we all be obligated to bear the blame?"

"Perhaps you did not, of yourself. But does the prophecy not state that each of you is interwoven into the tapestry—does it not state that you are all one?"

No one answered.

"Therefore, you fall together," he continued more quietly now. "And therefore you will face redemption together." He paused. "You can no longer save the future by altering it in your own individual worlds, as we had hoped. Humans know what you are capable of now—not just in one dimension but in all present and near-future dimensions, which have been altered because of this event."

"Forgive me, Sensei," Fin said from his seat in the front row. "But... what does this mean exactly? For us?"

Sensei gazed at him sorrowfully. I felt a sick feeling settle in the pit of my stomach.

"I'm afraid it means evacuation," he said. "Withdrawal into the Dimension—permanently."

I thought I'd been ready for this news—I thought I'd expected it and prepared myself accordingly. But hearing the words actually coming off his lips, I felt my mouth go dry. The feeling left my fingertips.

This is actually happening.

"The portals will be closed, and entrance into the cavern for transportation will be prohibited," he intoned, his voice growing louder over a chorus of stunned, frantic whispers. "This will take place three dawns hence. You all may transport freely in the meantime."

"But, Sensei." Fin spoke again. "What about… what about our families?"

A barrage of voices echoed him.

"I understand this is a shock," Sensei replied. "This is a heavy blow—I do not wish to convince you otherwise. I wish only to protect you."

"By forcing us to leave behind our entire world?" someone else shouted. "Our families, our lives—everything? Just because Icarus and Raiden disobeyed?"

Sensei raised his hands for quiet. "You are no longer safe in your natural worlds," he said. "There are those who would search for you—those who would capture and hold you in attempts to understand your abilities. There is no way to eliminate the suspicions that have been raised. There is no way to neutralize this danger."

Mitsue stood suddenly and turned to face the crowd. "If one of us was captured and forced to divulge our knowledge, all other protectors would be put at risk," he explained. "We cannot afford that—especially not now. The police are already searching for Raiden—and undoubtedly for Icarus too."

Mitsue's argument made perfect sense—it would be an enormous risk to allow anyone back into the natural dimensions, where humans were now on high alert for the slightest anomaly. And Raiden had already proven his disloyalty: he, especially, was not to be trusted.

What about Icarus? said a nagging voice at the back of my mind. *Do you trust him?*

Sensei resumed speaking. "Mitsue is correct. You must now consider the Dimension your home. But this will not be the end of your earthly dimensions—you will return to them, but when you do, much of what is known as time will have passed for those who live there. Your world will be almost unrecognizably different, older, upon your reemergence."

Mitsue raised a hand briskly. "I am from what is considered by most to be the future, Sensei. Will my natural world also be affected?"

Sensei nodded. "All dimensions are connected, Mitsue, as I know you are already aware. Just as the mistake of one student effects all, a catastrophe in one dimension affects and alters the others—whether for better or for worse. The 'future' in which you live is not as distant as that future into which you will emerge. Your world will quickly fall to the sword of the past."

I could tell Mitsue was affected by this news, though he did an efficient job concealing it. I had a hard time attempting to follow suit. The sick feeling in my stomach was still there, and chills were beginning to reach across my spine as I considered what this meant.

So, in effect, we were to be sealed, all of us, into a time capsule. My head spun.

"Your purpose, be assured, has not changed," Sensei continued, gesturing again for silence. "You wish to restore peace to the universe—you will. You wish to reverse the unbridled advancement of its entropy—you will do that also. But the means by which you will do this have changed. You will no longer battle this darkness from a distance. You attempted to alter it at the roots, in your own worlds, but now you will be made to face it head-on. You will emerge within it. All that you see and hear and taste will be the enemy against which you have remotely fought. Everything around you will be the machine you've been destined since the sunrise to disarm."

"What if..." Another hand went up. "What if some of us don't want to do this? I mean... we're talking about leaving everything we've ever known behind."

Fin stood now, with fire in his eyes. "Do you doubt our purpose? Have you learned nothing during your time here?"

"In the face of tragedy, faith—and doubt—are both reasonable re-sponses," said Sensei. "None of you will be forced to partake. How you proceed from this point is indeed your choice."

I felt the need to speak. "Sensei, how do you mean that?"

He began to pace contemplatively around the center flame. "I mean that as protectors—and also as living, breathing beings—you each have the right to determine your own destinies. You have three dawns to decide whether that destiny will be in the future, in the darkness of that which we do not know–"

I saw Fin's jaw tighten.

"—or if it lies in your natural world, with your family," Sensei finished, though the words came laboriously. "And if the latter is indeed where your desires lie, you will not be prevented from returning to your own world. Your memory of the Dimension, however, for your own protection and ours, will be carefully erased, and you will be given unconscious transportation back into your natural world. However—" He raised his voice over a clamor of questions. "However," he began again, "whatever your decision, it will be final. Once you have made it, there will be no going back."

Unlike other gatherings, this one had no official adjournment. Together we were a cauldron of questions; students surged forward and crowded around Sensei, looking for answers. Fin stood at the front of the platform, similarly engulfed in a sea of anxious students. Even from a distance, I could see the storm behind his eyes. Everyone else in the crowd was obscured. The sound died away, and his gaze lifted to meet mine. For a moment the only con-versation on the platform was the one that exchanged itself between us without a single word being spoken.

Something inside me couldn't take anymore. I knew I wouldn't get a chance to talk to him, not yet. And something in the dark parts of his eyes had pulled me closer to the edge of a precipice I wasn't ready to face.

For a long time I sat there alone, a spectator to the unfolding turmoil. Several times students came and spoke to me, and in turn I must have replied because after a while each went away, leaving me again to the black water of my own thoughts.

Eventually I realized the platform was nearly empty. Mitsue and Raiden were gone, and Icarus was nowhere to be seen. The sky was pink with the beginnings of dawn. I rose stiffly and headed for my quarters. I needed to be alone. I needed time to think everything through.

Back at my apartment, I drew the shades over the windows and receded into the darkness of my own thoughts. My body pleaded exhaustion, but I gave no heed.

My mind was engulfed in a tempest.

I wanted to empty myself—I needed to sort everything out, to analyze. I needed to understand what I was feeling about all of this. Why was I so afraid, so burdened with guilt? Why could I not rid myself of the pain in my heart?

You're strong, my head told me. *You can figure this out for yourself. You can make it out unscathed—you need no one's assurance.*

But my heart argued fiercely against it—and in the end it won.

I lifted the blinds from the large window, slid it open, and slipped out onto the ledge. The flame had burnt out on the lower platform, which was empty now, as was the training platform. The air was still. A soft, warm mist swelled up from the belly of the ravine below. It clung to my skin as I sat there. If everyone else was sleeping, I knew exactly where I would find Fin.

I shifted on the way down to the training platform, landing silently on the railing.

Fin was there, as I had known he would be, but he wasn't channeling as he usually was. He was seated on the floor off to the side, with his back against the railing. He was holding sheets of paper in his hands, and a messy stack of it lay beside him. There was an ocean of empty, dew-kissed floorboards between us.

I stepped softly into the shadow of the platform's shelter, human once again. He didn't look up, but I could tell he knew I was there.

I sat down quietly beside him. "What are you doing?" My voice sounded oddly shaky.

"Reviewing assignments," he answered. "I meant to make time for it before now, but…"

"Can't it wait? You've been up all night."

Fin shook his head. "I'm fine. I'm…" He turned the page. "I'm not tired."

I stared at my hands, void of words.

"Mala is improving," he said, sounding numb. "With sessions…"

"Is she…" My voice. A question, but not.

I heard his fingers turning pages, a rough sound as he swallowed.

"Gaia is, too." He gestured to the pages on the floor with his free hand. "And so many others. We're solid."

"We are."

He sighed. "It's strange… realizing so many people are depending upon you for guidance."

"People depend on those whom they respect, Fin."

"Don't say that."

I turned to look at him. "Why not?"

"Because it… it wasn't one-sided. I depended upon them more than they could have possibly imagined." His words hung softly in the humid air. "They meant everything to me."

Depended, imagined, meant… Past tense.

I pulled in a shaky breath. "Fin—"

"I was your student, Hawk," he cut in gently, his voice scarcely above a whisper. "Remember? You took care of me… you taught me everything I know."

I shook my head. "Not everything."

He laughed softly. "Hawk…"

I could already hear the question he would ask before he had even spoken the words.

"You would take care of them for me…" He pulled the words out of my thoughts and left them in the space between us. "Wouldn't you?"

I shook my head again, though now the motion became more deliberate.

"Fin, don't say that," I said, my voice small. Tight. "Please."

Feeling the warmth of his sigh, I realized that he had turned to face me. "Hawk, you're the one they really need. You're the one we all need," he said quietly, his words tangible on my skin. "I listen to Sensei speak of the future, I hear others voicing their doubts, and none of it matters. You *are* the future."

"You are too."

"Not in the same way," he said softly. "Not like you."

I turned to look at him for the first time since stepping onto the platform. "I knew you would leave me one day." My voice was almost a whisper. "I knew I would lose you somehow."

"No." He shook his head fiercely. "No, you could never lose me. I'll always be with you. Even if it's not physically… even if we're worlds and light-years apart." He stopped to steady his voice. "I will always be with you, Hawk."

My vision blurred with tears. I wanted to say something. I wanted to speak words that would make sense, words that would match his own. Words that wouldn't die painful deaths in my throat before they had a chance to break the surface.

Something inside my chest was on fire, dying, falling—so many things at once. A bullet had pierced my armor and I was quietly fighting for my life. Trying to breathe in and out as if all was normal, everything was alright.

Nothing is alright.

Something inside me had stretched too far. I broke. My arms fell around his neck. I pulled him into an embrace, and he pulled me tighter into his own. He leaned forward slightly, allowing my body to spill into his.

I felt the warmth of his hands move gradually to the small of my back, and the softness of his next exhale against the curve of my neck.

For the first time in what felt like an eternity, I let myself cry. I cried, and my tears rolled down my cheeks and onto his skin, staining the collar of his T-shirt.

"My little sisters told me they loved you," he whispered softly, one of his hands going gently up into my hair. "They told me I should marry you."

I couldn't help but laugh slightly, though it came out sounding more like a sob against his chest. "Did they?"

"I tried to explain that it didn't quite work that way, but they would hear none of it."

"They're going to need you so much, growing up," I said. "Someone who will always be there for them—someone they can count on. They love you, Fin."

He sighed shakily. I heard his heartbeat—closer than I ever had.

"I know they do," he whispered in reply, so softly I could scarcely make out the words. "And I love them." A pause. Another breath—deeper. Gently, he pushed himself back and stared into my eyes. "But is it wrong that I love you more?"

I opened my mouth to speak, but my voice was absent. A tear trailed down my cheek. I felt his fingertips softly brush it away.

"I told you of a weakness," he whispered softly. "A weakness I've yet to overcome."

I heard him take a shallow breath. I could almost feel his heart reaching for the one I didn't have.

"You." He let the word break away from him. "You are my greatest weakness." His voice cracked.

I took his face gently into my hands and lifted it toward my own, leaning closer to let my forehead make contact with his. "Whatever you decide," I said quietly, "I will support you. I promise."

We sat there for a time, not speaking, our foreheads touching.

"I'm transporting back tomorrow," he whispered, and I felt his fingertips brush away a strand of hair that had fallen into my face. "Would you come with me? One last time."

Something inside me was dying. The bullet wound had bled me out completely.

"Of course," I whispered, broken. "Of course I will."

CHAPTER TWENTY-TWO
Icarus

The darkness was familiar. I knew it as one recognizes a face they've seen before in a crowd. We were not acquainted, yet there was an intimacy between us. I couldn't help but feel, as I stared into it, that it stared back, that it recognized me too.

The same music played. The same ambiguous shapes surrounded me, looming and silent. I knew where I was, though at the same time I didn't. I had no idea where I was, but I had been here before and I knew what came next.

I saw the light through the crack under the door. The light that would flicker and fade as I made my approach.

This has happened before. I'm dreaming.

As if being pushed by some invisible force, I stumbled through the darkness towards it. I groped restlessly for something to brace myself against, but found no such object. The light reeled me in closer, as if I were prey.

A cold trail of sweat made its way down the back of my neck, traversing each vertebra and leaving a tension across my skin in its wake. The instruments sang out in more fevered repetition.

I tripped on something and fell, bruising my hands as they absorbed the impact. When I glanced up to search for the light, it had vanished. My heart beat wildly against the inside of my chest. I heard the softness of muted footsteps across the floor, over the sheets that had slipped and fallen from the objects they had covered. I struggled to get to my feet, but familiar, icy hands found me, lifted me, and pinned me back against the wall. The fingers morphed into claws and sank into my skin.

The pain that followed, the warmth of my blood in my mouth as my assailant sank its teeth into my neck—it was all so vivid, too real to be a dream. Only reality could ever hurt like this.

But this happened before.

This time, though, there was no possibility of gaining the upper hand. Before, the claws had melted away into hands that were Hawk's, struggling to awaken me.

Hawk isn't with you, Icarus.

The thought was clear and deliberate. I no longer seemed to be dreaming: was I awake? No—I hadn't awakened from the dream: I had awakened *within* it.

My hands battled fruitlessly with the thin air in search of an unseen body. Blood spilled from my mouth, choking me. The music, which up until then had been only speeding up, finally crashed into silence. My arms were burning, seared about halfway up by a pain I didn't remember from the first time. It was a detail I must have overlooked.

I began to realize that I'd breached the point at which I had been awakened last time. I felt as though I was locked in the trunk of a car—I had no idea where it would take me from here. The intensity of the pain seemed to reach its climax, and then rather than gradually fading, it abruptly stopped, just as the music had. The wall behind me disintegrated, and I tumbled backwards into a new and yawning void. A cry rose in my throat, but no sound came.

I could have been falling for hours or merely seconds. I had no way of knowing. I felt my muscles tense for an impact that never came.

Now I was lying down—had I ever been falling at all? My body was sprawled out across something soft, worn, curved in a familiar way. My eyelids were too heavy to lift, so my left hand drifted up and over my body to investigate, and my fingers closed around something cold, metallic...

A seatbelt buckle?

My brain fumbled with this information as I began to focus my attention on opening my eyes. When I did, I was nearly blinded by vivid shades of orange and red, sunlight blitzing me in large shafts.

I was in the backseat of a car.

For a split second longer I lay there, not moving a muscle as an eerie feeling of déjà vu seized me from the inside. Pressing up into an awkward seated position, my legs cramped in the small space, I quickly assessed my surroundings while still attempting to ignore the frantic beating of my heart up in my throat.

The car's interior was small, every window was fogged with the color of age, and the windshield was shot. In the two front seats, subtle plant life was pushing its way up from the decaying upholstery. Several jagged pieces of glass tangled with the vines that had crept in from outside.

My gaze journeyed beyond the windshield to the surrounding forest—a thick spread of towering pines and birches closing in from all sides, seeming to bend slightly toward the vehicle as if longing to gaze inside. The foliage was a blend of various golden shades, frosted in what looked like a first snowfall. That was when I became aware of how cold it was.

It was no longer a question. I knew exactly where I was.

I have to wake myself up.

I groped for the passenger door's handle, but couldn't find it. When I turned around to look, I discovered there wasn't one. Not wishing to cut myself on the mangled windshield, I kicked out the rear passenger window, reached through, and grasped the external handle. My fingers contracted, pulled, and the latch gave.

I shoved the door open, kicking and struggling against the brush that leaned in like an attacker. Thorns raked my legs and tore at the palms of my hands.

I stumbled from the car's interior and began struggling through the dense vegetation. My sudden movements spurred a tumult of black feathers as a murder of crows sprang from the canopy overhead. They were like splotches of ash against the patches of sky where branches failed to reach.

My vision faltered like a skip in a record as I gazed around me, searching. About ten yards ahead lay a dirt road, narrowed with time and lack of use. The setting sun glittered off the thin layer of snow that covered it. I pushed my way toward it, shivering. Overgrown roots reached and snagged my shoes, tripping me and causing me to fall. My hands were bleeding now, sending flickers of pain up my arms, though this still wasn't enough to wake me.

I reached the road and found to my dismay that it stretched on into oblivion in both directions: an endless corridor of trees allowing in only the filtered light the sunset provided. It was an eerie replica of the endless tunnel of arborvitaes that had kept me from leaving Sensei's house that one day that felt so long ago.

Breathless, I drank in the cold air and listened to my terrified heart as it struggled like an animal caught in a trap. Blood dripped from my hands, staining the snow.

You were found in a car; you have nothing to your name… the ghost of my own voice whispered in the emptiness. *Who are you that the blood in your veins is worth so much?*

I fell to the cold ground, into the stains of my own blood. My breath made faint plumes in the freezing air.

"Who are you indeed, Icarus?" answered a voice, soft in the dusk. "Who are you that the earth opens its mouth to receive your blood and groans in long anticipation of your awakening."

I knew the voice and turned my face away, unworthy of meeting his gaze.

"I cannot awaken," I said. "This dream—this place. It is my prison."

"I do not mean from this dream. That is all this place is, Icarus," he answered. "A dream and nothing more. It is a past that you have kept alive only in your own mind—a prison indeed, but one of your own making. A cell that you have maintained and chains that you yourself have created and chosen to return to. *Why* have you chosen to return?"

I swallowed back bitter tears, willing myself to reply though my thoughts were crumbling. "You ask that as if you know this is where I came from."

He said nothing, and finally, I gathered my courage and turned to face him. He seemed merely a reflection of the sun.

"How is it that you know I have *returned?*" I asked, looking up into Sensei's face. "How did you know they found me here?"

Still Sensei gave no reply. He stood silently, studying me intently. I wanted to tear my gaze from his, to stare deeper into his eyes, to run and to draw closer, to awaken from the dream and to stay in it forever. His body seemed to flicker between a state of translucence and solidity, each giving way to the opposite as soon as my thoughts drew nearer to analyze. Then seemingly without transition, he was darkened in silhouette, for though I could still feel the vaguest hint of warmth from the setting sun at my back, a new light was piercing through the trees ahead, forcing my bleeding hands up to shield my vision.

The sun that I'd perceived only moments ago as setting was now somehow dawning.

"They..." Sensei said, the sound of his voice seeming to emit from the light as it rained down on me. "'They' did not find you, Icarus."

My hands came down. I knew what he would say before he had even spoken the words. I finished his thought for him.

"You..." my voice came out in almost a whisper. "You found me."

A pause.

"Icarus."

I wanted to respond, but I could not.

"*Icarus.*"

It was no longer Sensei who spoke; it was a different voice.

As abruptly as he had appeared, Sensei vanished. As did the light, the cold, and everything else save an echo of what I'd just spoken. *You.*

"Icarus!"

I startled awake, gasping for air, and an instant later the woven, basketlike ceiling of the dormitory pod came into focus. I struggled to a sitting position and saw Fin at the desk.

"I thought you would never wake up," he said. "Sensei's called an emergency gathering. If you want to make it on time, I suggest you start moving."

"An emergency meeting about what?"

He gave me a hard look. "Take a guess."

———————

The following dawn, I found myself wrestling with the aftermath of the gathering, boiling over with mixed emotions. This was all actually happening—because of *me*.

Sure, I hadn't been the only one involved in what happened on campus that day. Perhaps I hadn't perpetrated the greatest acts of violence, but my hands still weren't clean. Nor was my conscience.

It had been impossible for me to see Sensei in the same light as I sat there in the darkness and listened as he earnestly forewarned us of what was about to happen. My thoughts were haunted by my dream and the revelation that he had been the one who found me all those years ago.

How was that possible? How can I believe in something my subconscious merely projected into a dream? I can't.

I grappled for something that made sense—for something that felt even remotely stable, but nothing did. My struggle was swept abruptly away when Gaia rose and recited what I realized was the prophecy. *The* prophecy—the one everyone seemed to mention but never explained. The prophecy that Hawk had assumed I knew. Seated in the unearthly quiet that had befallen the crowded platform, I finally heard it in its entirety, and the effect it had on me was difficult to comprehend.

If I could compare it to anything, I would say it felt like falling in love. I could even liken it to the helplessness I'd felt during my first trust fall as the colors of the Dimension had swept up around me. But the feeling was so vastly beyond it that attempting to even understand it seemed almost to diminish it.

I was compelled at last to simply call it what it was: an incomprehensible ecstasy. Something of which I was simply the dependent, passive recipient. I couldn't grasp it, but it had clearly grasped me.

I couldn't help but feel that Hawk had somehow spoken prophetically when she told me I had no idea "how dark this place was about to get." Yes, the darkness was real—a force to be reckoned with, but somehow it also became the vehicle through which a renewed strength had been permeated. Everything had fresh weight and meaning. I left the meeting with a deeper consciousness of our purpose and of what being a protector actually meant. Because according to Sensei, its definition did not lie in that we did not fall, but in that we fell together and would rise together. I had a choice to either stay at the bottom or start climbing, and I chose the latter.

Yes, I had majorly screwed things up. But mourning my own inadequacy was not brave.

Sessions that day were canceled. Few students besides myself left the dorms. I spent as much of my time outside and away from everyone as I could.

The following day, everyone was back to routine, and for the first time since my initiation, I was allowed to join in the dawn sessions. I gave it everything I had.

Hawk was nowhere to be found. I heard someone mention that they had seen her transport out with Fin. A strange sensation bit at my heart. Yet I was almost grateful for the lack of her presence. I didn't need the hurricane that she was to destroy what little focus I had.

Going through the motions of the pranayama, the sense of familiarity was strong, though this time the outcome was entirely different. Utilizing everything Hawk had taught me during my numerous window-washing sessions, I executed the practice almost flawlessly. It was no longer a meaningless struggle—I had stopped playing. My brain went into autopilot and I just *did it*. I left myself with no choice.

In the back of my mind, though, were the words that Sensei had spoken in my dream.

Who was I indeed, that the earth opened its mouth to receive my blood… groaning in long anticipation of my awakening?

What did that even mean, "my awakening"? *What am I meant to awaken into?*

I had told him I couldn't awaken myself from the dream. He had answered that it was not the dream to which he was referring.

What, then?

I needed to talk to Sensei again.

After sessions ended, I made my way down the hallway towards Sensei's office. With dismay, I saw that Mala was there waiting for me.

"Icarus," she said, "I need to talk to you."

Reluctantly, I followed her outside and onto one of the walking paths, which was basically deserted. A cool, gentle breeze wafted up from the ravine, caressing us as we made our way downward towards one of the lower platforms.

"I want more than anything to blame you, Icarus," she said at length. "But I know that I can't—I'm just as much at fault. I was there, I participated, but now we're talking about something more than a slap on the wrist for bad behavior—we're talking about leaving Earth. Like, holy f—do you even get that?" Her hands were shaking.

"I do, Mala. And I'm-I'm sorry—" My voice broke.

"*You're sorry?* Of course *you're* sorry." She looked at me over her shoulder. "You who have no family or home to return to. You have no earthly ties, Icarus. Maybe a few friends, I'll give you that. But you have no parents—"

"I know—"

"You've never shared… *life* with people like I have." Mala's voice hardened. "I have a *family*, Icarus. I have two parents and a brother and a home filled with memories—I was going home in a few weeks! I was going to go home to *them.*"

"You can still go back," I said.

"The authorities know I was involved, Icarus. My face is already plastered everywhere, along with yours and Raiden's. Just because no one in this dimension seems to realize that I was involved doesn't mean everyone outside is just as ignorant—they *know*."

"I didn't mean for you to get caught up in it, Mala. I didn't mean for any of this to happen."

"Well, it *has* happened, and now they're looking for us... for *me*," she said. "Now I can't go back."

"If you *could* go back, would you?"

"Of course I would! Didn't you hear anything I just told you?" Her voice cracked with outrage. "Do you actually think that I would—that I would choose *this place*—" she gestured wildly around us "—over my own flesh and blood? I *hate* this place. I wish I'd never come here—I wish you'd never brought me here!"

I could have pointed out that if she hadn't gotten me wasted that night, it was highly probable that neither she nor Raiden would ever have discovered the Dimension at all. But I couldn't pass judgment on her actions when I was just as much at fault.

"But this place is... *truth*, Mala," I said. "This place, when it comes down to it, is... actually reality itself."

For a moment she fell silent, seeming completely disgusted. When she finally spoke, there was ice in her voice. "We ignore truth on a daily basis, all of us. 'Reality' is in front of our faces all the time—it's displayed everywhere. It's on the Internet and in printed word and rolling from the lips of the brave, but we ignore it so that we can lead a normal life. Because if we were to stare it in the eyes, we would find something that frightens us. We don't want to be frightened, Icarus—*I* don't want to be frightened."

"So you want to live your life blind, then? You want to just go on living in a world even if reality as we know it is actually a lie?"

"Those are your words, not mine," she said. "All I know is that I don't want to be here—if I can't return, I would rather die."

"You don't really mean that."

"I mean it more than I've ever meant anything."

She didn't. I could tell that she didn't—she just wasn't thinking this through, but rather than fight her, I took a different approach.

"Okay," I said after a moment, falling into step beside her. "Then if that is actually the case, why don't you go back? Return to our world, go home to your family, and wait for the police to find you—because they *will* eventually."

Mala said nothing, so I went on. "You'll live in a lab, connected to an assortment of monitors—undergoing various scans and tests. You will no longer be considered fully human anymore, but a valuable artifact of progressive research—"

"Icarus—"

"You wouldn't be dead," I interrupted her. "You would merely be a prostitute to 'science'—"

She halted, flipping around so suddenly I almost collided with her head-on. "Enough, Icarus! I get it."

Her eyes were wild and tears were cresting at her lower lash lines now. The color had drained from her face.

"I get it," she repeated quietly, faltering for an instant as a student passed us on the walkway. She lowered her voice. "I get it. But what if… what if I can get my family to believe?"

I stared at her for a moment. A strange sensation tugged at my heart. "What are you talking about?"

"Sensei says the anomalies are those who realize they are different," she replied. "I didn't even know I was an anomaly until Fin *made me* realize that I was different. I would never have found out otherwise."

"So what are you implying?"

She cast a quick glance over her shoulder and then mine, checking to see if anyone was approaching us. No one was.

"What if there are more of us than we realize?"

Dread and expectation filled her eyes in equal measure.

"Mala, I've heard Hawk speak about slider selection. It's not a simple process," I explained. "I mean, simply consider the fact that there are only a few *hundred* of us. Out of the *billions* of people that have lived in the past, present and near future on planet Earth, that is a fairly *minute* assembly."

She put up a hand for me to stop, stepping closer. "And that being so, have you considered how strange it is that *all* three of us turned out to be sliders—you, Raiden and I? Have you yet to hear any other students speak of a portal from which *multiple* sliders have come to join the Dimension—all within the same time frame, each unrelated to the other, and all just happening to be enrolled at the same school? Am I the only one who senses something odd about that?"

The truthful answer was yes. Having been so overwhelmed by the shock of my own initiation into the Dimension, my mind had never fully sunk its teeth into just how strange that coincidence was. Something about the tone of her voice sent a chill down the length of my spine.

"So you're saying, like..." I swallowed, still trying to process everything she'd just said. "What are the chances that we would all... *just happen* to be anomalies?"

Her eyes were still wide and locked with mine. "Exactly—what if sliders aren't born." She glanced up at me. "What if they're *made*? What if... what if it's possible that an anomaly sleeps inside every single person who has ever lived?"

My mind reeled. "That can't be true, Mala," I said, keeping my voice low. "It defeats the very definition of anomaly. And if it *is* true, then why isn't *everyone* born knowing that they're a slider? Or at least slowly awakening to the fact that they have powers?"

Another student passed us, and for a moment we fell silent.

Mala's next words were almost a whisper. "I don't have the answers, Icarus. But I certainly have a lot of questions."

CHAPTER TWENTY-THREE
Hawk

If I could have changed one thing I did that day, I would have avoided seeing Icarus before transporting out with Fin.

The fallout from the last few days had been etched into Icarus's features. His face was like a page where a story had been written and then quickly erased, a void where something had once lived, not long ago.

Why seeing him had such an effect on me, I couldn't understand. Yes, I'd been a subpar teacher, a less than flawless example of what it meant to abide by the code, and I'd said things that I had lived to regret—all of that was true, but was that really what was bothering me?

Like a splinter in my mind, there was something about Icarus that I couldn't escape from. Something that haunted me the entire time I was away. I felt almost ashamed that my thoughts even had the capacity to focus on anything other than the gravity of the situation at hand. I was on the brink of losing Fin, yet my thoughts still managed to whisper "Icarus" between every line.

We'd transported into Fin's apartment and taken his car to his parents' house to whisk his sisters away for "an adventure"—something Fin had kept even me in the dark about.

I'd shot him a questioning glance as the girls situated themselves in the backseat, raising an eyebrow as our eyes met over the roof of the car. He'd only smiled in that particular way and shaken his head.

Howth wasn't far from his family's home in Dublin City, and the view from the cliff walk made the moderate drive worth it for the girls, who quickly reached that elated state of intoxication that only fresh sea air and open spaces can provide for a soul.

For me, it wouldn't have mattered where we went. Riding shotgun in a car with Fin, watching the way the sunlight lay across his wrists and shadowed the veins in his arms like he was a sketch, listening to his sisters chattering in the backseat, speaking a language known only to children—it was all so visceral.

Their voices, and then Fin's in response as his hand went over to the radio, touching buttons; music, soft. A window rolling down, a gentle breeze playing with the golden heads of hair in the backseat, and Fin's glance brushing across my cheek.

It turned out to be something of a picnic. I'd never been on one before, so I was unsure what etiquette would be expected, or what exactly the event would consist of. This one had food that hardly anyone ate—the girls because of their excitement and Fin and I because we were sick in the soul.

Stretched out on the blanket, we watched his sisters play amongst the overgrowth that dominated the rolling hillside, and drank in the view. We avoided words and eye contact.

Finally Fin spoke. "I used to come here when I was a kid," he said. "Before Lara—my youngest sister—was born. My father used to come here to talk to God. He believed He 'dwelt most in the seas' or something like that."

"What about you, Fin? Did you think God dwelt in the seas?" I asked. "Did you come here to find Him?"

I watched the girls frolicking, heard their shrieks of laughter. White and blue sundress smudges against a richer shade of green. Pastel apparitions.

"No," he replied quietly. "I would come here to be overwhelmed."

There was a long pause. The sea boomed below us.

"I was in a meeting with Sensei before you arrived on the platform," he continued. "To go over the details of today. My decision."

I felt the ghost of a familiar ache beginning to creep back into my chest.

"He reaffirmed something to me," he went on, speaking almost to himself. "Something I've always heard but never listened closely to—something we've each been told since our initiations."

"And what would that be?"

Fin's eyes remained on the ocean, and for a moment he fell into a silent contemplation.

"That the Dimension is an open reality to those who believe," he answered finally. "That it is water from which anyone can drink if they only believe that it exists."

"Sensei told you this?"

He nodded.

"But that would imply…"

"That anyone who believes can be rescued from what's about to happen." He turned finally and looked at me. "The key has been under our noses this entire time."

For a second I was speechless. I knew exactly what Fin was talking about because I had heard it many times before—we all had. Each one of us had heard Sensei speak of the anomalies—"those who believe." But never had I considered it within this context.

"But that disagrees with what we know to be the order of selection," I protested. "A student is chosen and initiated based upon the fact that they have powers. Thus, they believe in the Dimension because of the evidence of their own abilities—"

"Or so we thought," Fin interrupted gently. "I can't say that I understand it either. But wouldn't it almost… make sense?"

"Expound."

He squinted out again at the horizon. "The universe is a question, both alive and dead…"

He didn't have to finish.

Until we make the decision.

"But in the most literal terms," I said, stunned, "that would literally imply that everyone is… that everyone could *become* a protector. That everyone *could* develop powers."

"Exactly."

"How *on earth* is that possible?"

I couldn't swallow it—not yet. If anyone could enter the Dimension simply by belief alone, then why had Sensei chosen to monitor specific students in specific locations for as long as he had? Why would we have a system of selection if all humans possessed the same potential?

"As I said," Fin went on, "I don't pretend to understand it. I also don't find myself in a place to question Sensei's authority. I heard the questions students were asking him after the gathering—I heard the answers he gave them and the one he gave me: if anyone believes in what we know is in fact reality, they can ultimately become part of it."

I knew what this implied: that the families and friends of students could be rescued from the fate discussed at the gathering if they could be persuaded, so to speak. But I could still scarcely believe it.

"I'll be the first to confess that I never imagined that we were to take it so literally. And were it not for the fact that I know that my family does not believe, I would have counted it the greatest gift imaginable—a chance to redeem those I love most in this world."

His face was etched with pain. I could hear the sound of his sisters' laughter coming in snatches on the wind.

"What makes you think they would not believe if you told them who you really are?"

"I've tried, Hawk. I've tried to tell them in every way I know how to, and they've never understood me."

The waves crashed below us.

"My parents only know that I'm different, and they don't know how to handle me because of it. They can only see my shell, not who I am underneath."

"Then you still face the same choice," I concluded quietly. "To remain here with them, or to leave with us."

He nodded. "I can't help but wonder sometimes if they would have heard me out if I'd been more open from the beginning. Maybe I would have been able to articulate it in a way they could comprehend. Maybe if I had done something differently..."

"Fin, we can't know what would have happened," I said quietly. "That way of thinking will torment you."

"I'm *already* tormented, Hawk." He tilted his face toward the graying sky. "I am the embodiment of torment; I am in hell with a choice to either remain here intact, or to return to paradise with only a fragment of my heart still beating in my chest."

I had no idea what to say. Though I knew intellectually that my own feelings weren't relevant in this case, I still had to fight against my aching heart. This wasn't my decision to make—there was nothing more for me to say.

I left Fin at the edge and retreated back to the blanket where the girls had gathered. After a few minutes of needed solitude, he rejoined us.

There was something about Fin that ignited his little sisters. He was a spark, and they were the dancing flames which it sourced. As soon as he ventured close enough, the two youngest attached themselves, weighting him down until at last he surrendered to them. He took one down in a playful neck lock and they tumbled backward into the grass. The remaining two pounced in attack.

I couldn't help but smile, watching the scene as it unfolded, a tangle with shocks of blond hair and grass stains beginning to weave through the fabric of their clothes. It was laughter, playful screams, words so intertwined that no one voice could be separately distinguished. It was multifaceted, transcendently beautiful, yet soul sickening in the same moment. My mind was plagued by types of fears I had never before experienced.

We started for home soon after. Heavy clouds had begun to roll in, and by the time we reached the car again, the first drops of rain were beginning to fall. Fin rolled up the windows as the storm began in earnest, and after a while the girls fell asleep, their cheeks rosy in the cool, damp air.

I leaned my head against the window and listened to the muffled pattering of the rain on the roof of the car and closed my eyes. When I opened them again, we were back in the driveway of his parents' house. We carried the two youngest girls inside, letting the oldest trail groggily behind us.

"My goodness, you tired them out," said Fin's mother affectionately as she ushered us inside. "Stay for tea?"

Fin and I exchanged uneasy glances, and his mother raised an eyebrow.

"We have to be heading out," he said. "I just wanted to say goodbye."

His mother looked puzzled. "Goodbye?" She chuckled and mussed his hair. "You sound so formal. It's not as if you'll be gone long. Go enjoy the evening, Ronan—both of you."

Fin pulled gently away from her. "Is Dad around?"

"He's out at a jobsite, I'm afraid."

"Where at?"

"The church today." She replied. "Is it important?"

Fin gave a strained nod.

His mother peered at him more closely. "Is everything alright, Ronan? You seem out of sorts."

I stepped away to give the two of them space. I stood near the door and waited. Out of the corner of my eye I saw Fin pull his mother into a tight hug. I could sense the effort it took for him to keep it together, yet he still managed somehow to keep his voice steady.

"I'm fine, Mum," he said quietly. "Really."

Kissing her on the cheek, Fin drew back and calmly said goodbye. I opened the door and we made our way down the path and got into the car. I had no idea what to say, and I didn't want him to feel obligated to answer, so I said nothing.

He turned the key and the engine came to life.

Though I was hardly familiar with Fin's hometown, I recognized the road that brought us back to Fin's apartment as we blew past it. I turned and looked at him questioningly, though he gave me no explanation.

The quiet hum of the engine absorbed the silence as Fin drove to the city's outskirts where the lush green grass dominated the landscape and the breeze pressed in through the slightly open windows. The gentle rainfall had yet to let up.

Fin turned the car into a dirt parking lot. It was empty save one vehicle which Fin seemed to recognize. He pulled up alongside it and stopped the engine. A quietly looming, white church stood contrasted against the gray sky.

Across the church yard, in which a beautifully maintained garden grew, I could make out an outline of a figure. A familiar, Fin-like figure. Weathered hands pressing fresh earth around a sapling. Blue eyes turning from the earth to acknowledge us and wave.

I heard Fin breathe an aching sigh and for a moment he just sat there.

"Do you want me to come with you?" I asked gently.

He shook his head slowly and reached over to open the door. "I'll…"

He stepped out.

"I'll be back in a minute."

Weakly, he swung the door shut again, leaving me to watch him make his way through the lush ivy and wild roses alone. The fatigued pattering of the rain filled my ears.

Fin carried himself through the garden as though his body were made of lead. When he reached the place where his father knelt, he stopped. I saw his lips move with the rhythm of words, and his father turned to look up at him.

He said something in reply, though the expression on his face seemed confused. Slowly he got to his feet, but before he could finish dusting himself off, Fin, as though no longer able to hold it together, folded him into an embrace. A long, tight hug that ached with a thousand words he couldn't say. The rain rolled gently down the windshield, momentarily obscuring them from my view.

After a moment they parted. I heard the muffled sounds of words, footsteps. Then the driver's side door opened and closed again, and once more Fin was beside me. His father was still standing and watching as the engine started again, as Fin put the car in gear and pulled away. He watched us, and waved.

Fin said nothing for the entire ride. It wasn't until we parked in front of his apartment again that he let out the breath I could tell he had been holding. His forehead touched the steering wheel for an instant; then he leaned back, closing his eyes.

"That was *so* hard."

"I know," I said softly, surprising myself. "I'm… I'm so—"

"Don't." He cut me off, shaking his head. "Don't say it." He opened his eyes again and turned to look at me. "Don't say that you're sorry, Hawk. It was my decision."

"One that you shouldn't have had to make. And it's partially my fault."

He shook his head. "You cannot take responsibility for all of Icarus's actions, Hawk. He has made his choices just as I have made mine. I cannot bear the burden of living as one who is blind when I have been given the gift of sight."

He opened his door and got out of the car without waiting for a response. I followed him. He took out a key and let us into his apartment. I glanced around the room as he fumbled with a pad of paper in the kitchen, scratching something out across the first blank page.

"Fin, is that the only reason?" I asked. "Are you sure?"

Ignoring me, he tore the page off and placed it on the counter. Then he strode to the closet, opened the door and gestured for me to step inside with him. I did.

"You'll never know, Hawk," he said now in the darkness. "But, yes. I am—I am sure." I heard his voice crack slightly. "Can you get us home?"

Home. That was what the Dimension was now—for both me and Fin. This was the last transport we would be experiencing together for a very long time.

The temperature in the room changed slightly, the damp scent of the cavern drifting in. Fin opened the door and a thin shaft of light cut into the darkness. The hallway was vacant. We stood together for a moment and stared into the thin air where the closet had been only moments ago. Something that he would never see again.

"If you need me, I'll be in my dorm," he said, forcing himself to step out into the empty hall. "I just need to... I just need a few minutes."

I closed the door behind us, reaching for his forearm. "Fin—"

My fingers made contact, but he pulled away. "I can't... Hawk, I just can't right now."

And like an apparition, he was gone.

I lingered in the hallway several moments longer, attempting to regain my composure. As always, hardly any time had passed while we were away. Sessions had only just been dismissed; I could still hear voices on the training platform. This meant that Sensei would be free.

I reached back and twisted my hair into a careless bun as I headed for the familiar door to his office. When I reached it, however, rather than tossing it open with my usual resolve, I halted and listened. Over the general hum emanating from the platform, I could identify two distinct voices inside, engaged in conversation.

Icarus. *Why is he meeting with Sensei?*

My thoughts halted at the sound of approaching footsteps. Mitsue, dressed all in black, stopped several yards away when he realized he'd caught my attention.

"Hawk, I need to speak with you," he said gravely. "Immediately, if you're not otherwise occupied."

My questions for Sensei would have to keep.

"What's up?" I questioned, stepping away from the door.

He shook his head, spinning back around to retrace his steps. "I can't explain now. You'll see for yourself in a minute."

Though my curiosity was immense, I didn't ask anything further. I was cleansed temporarily of everything else that was on my mind as I followed

Mitsue across the platform and into the opposing passage where the safe rooms were located.

He unlocked and opened one of the doors at the far end of the hall, gesturing for me to follow him inside. I did.

Raiden turned as we entered.

I raised an eyebrow, glancing from Mitsue to his student. "What's this?"

Mitsue slid the door closed behind us, locked it, and then turned to Raiden. "Show her."

Raiden looked caught off guard by the command. "Why?"

"Because I said so," Mitsue replied firmly. "Now show her."

He manifested a blue circle on the floorboards and Raiden reluctantly stepped into the center of it. He brought his hands up and began to focus his energy into them. At first the results seemed typical. The energy wavered between his hands in a semi-translucent orb, then slowly began to glow yellow. Then orange.

Surprised by how quickly he was transitioning energy types for such a fledgling initiate, I began to study him a little more closely. I watched as he passed the orb off into his left hand and balanced it there. That in itself was fairly impressive, but the rest of his actions reduced this to mere child's play. The flickers of yellow and orange energy quickly morphed into a violent shade of red, which seemed to increase rapidly in temperature before bursting into what looked like an actual flame dancing in a controlled fashion over the palm of his hand.

I felt my eyes widen. "Is that… fire?"

Ignoring me, Raiden threw the small mass of burning energy across the room. It impacted into a midsized potted tree that stood against the glass wall, and to my astonishment it burst into flames.

I turned to stare at Mitsue. "How long has he been doing this?"

"I wasn't aware that he was even capable of the ability until today," Mitsue replied. "He immediately attempted to recant that he possessed the ability."

My attention flickered back to Raiden, who watched the burning tree with almost childlike fascination in his eyes.

"My question for you, Hawk," Mitsue said, "is when was the last time you saw someone who could channel fire?"

"I can't say I have ever witnessed such a thing."

"Not with any student?"

"I've only ever heard stories," I said. "Legends. It's a rarity, like shifting. It takes a certain kind of person to even begin to learn how to facilitate it."

"So can you explain how that would even be possible for a new initiate?"

I glanced over Mitsue's shoulder at Raiden. He hadn't moved.

"Can I have a second to talk to him, please?" I asked, lowering my voice. "Alone?"

"Why?"

I gestured toward the door. After a moment, he moved himself begrudgingly in the direction of the threshold.

"Five minutes." He rolled the door gently shut behind him. "Make it quick."

I nodded, though I had no intention of following his orders.

As if the day hadn't already been difficult enough, this was the proverbial frosting on the cake. To say I was stunned by what I had just witnessed would be an understatement.

"Raiden, take a seat, please," I said, snapping him out of his trance. I gestured toward one of the levitating metal half-shell chairs as I smoothly drew it into the center of the room with my gaze. "I want a word with you."

His gaze lingered on the flames a moment longer before he turned to me. "Why?"

"Do as I say."

He sank down reluctantly into the seat across from me and leaned heavily forward to rest his elbows on his knees. "What do you want to know?"

I ignored the question, continuing with my own. "I'm assuming you overheard what Mitsue and I were discussing just now, did you not?"

He shook his head slowly—bluffing. I decided to roll with it.

"There are certain abilities, powers if you will, that are more difficult and take more time to attain than others," I began, making solid eye contact with him. "For example, I shift into animal form. How many sliders have you seen within the Dimension who possess this ability?"

"Based on my limited observations?" He tilted his head slightly to the side and gave a low shoulder shrug. "Only you."

"Exactly."

"So… what is your point?"

I stared at him for a moment without answering. There was something about the way he looked at me that set me on edge. I didn't know what it was.

"My point is that I find myself extremely surprised—shocked even—that you apparently have the ability to channel your personal energy into flame," I replied, leaning slightly closer. "Mitsue was essentially asking me whether it was feasible that a student as inexperienced as yourself would come to master this particular type of power with such ease."

"And how would you answer that question? I'm curious."

I still hadn't broken eye contact with him. "I find it extremely difficult to believe that you've acquired this ability on your own."

He looked at me for a moment before giving me a faint smile. "You're very perceptive, Hawk."

"Don't digress. I want an answer."

"Then ask me a question."

"You're the most aggressive slider this dimension has ever seen, Raiden," I said slowly and deliberately. "You know how to drain life and energy from others and utilize it to your own advantage. You can channel fire—you do things that only the deeply advanced among us, such as myself, find themselves able to do. How did you come to learn all of this so quickly on your own?"

I could see the gears turning behind his eyes. I knew that anything he told me would be manufactured, not raw.

"I didn't," he said finally, leaning back and crossing one leg smoothly over his knee. "I didn't consciously learn any of it."

"How do you mean?" I asked cautiously. "Of course you would have had to learn it, unless you…"

I never finished my sentence. Because it had finally hit me.

I broke the lock between our gazes, pressing my eyelids shut with my forefinger and thumb. "Unless you stole your powers."

"Perceptive."

"Don't say that again." I rose abruptly. "You know how to channel life out of other people, other *sliders* whose lives you've taken and whose identities you've assumed. That's what you were implying by—"

"By the fact that I didn't *learn* this?" he said. "Yes, that's exactly what I meant. Except, had I not slipped up during the session earlier, I would have kept the fact contained a little longer."

I stared at him. "Until you could kill Icarus?"

He shrugged.

"So you're not exactly the average college student I initially took you for, then, are you?" I was thinking out loud now. "You've known about your abilities for a while… You haven't merely been stumbling across other people with slider blood: you've been tracking them down and using them to your advantage."

He watched me, his expression slightly bemused.

My gaze fell to one of his hands resting loosely on his knee. I reached down and lifted it, pressing my fingers into his flesh. "You're not one student… you're many. You're an ensemble of powers that others spent lifetimes developing."

He looked at me for a moment before speaking. "You think I've admitted everything, don't you? You think you know the whole story, but you don't, Hawk. Believe me when I tell you that. I've earned the right to become who I am—I've *fought* for it."

I stared at him for a moment, noticing the strangeness biting at the undertones of his voice. Then I dropped his hand.

"I'm sure you did."

I reached my fingers back through my hair, thinking. I passed him and rounded the back of his chair, turning my focus to the burning tree. The majority of the foliage had all but disintegrated by this point.

"But if you're merely collecting the lives of other sliders—hoarding their powers to become who you are—" I squinted at the embers "—why haven't you killed, say, Mala—also a powerful slider? Why haven't you sought the life of anyone else within the Dimension?"

"Because…" He seemed to consider his answer for a moment. "They don't have what would satisfy my desires."

I glanced over my shoulder. "And Icarus does?"

Raiden's eyes remained focused in front of him.

"Answer me."

"Icarus has something I want," he said, more to himself. "He's led me to something I've spent a very long time looking for."

"And what would that be?"

For a moment the room was filled with only the crackling of the flames and the muffled sounds of voices from the platform. I knew Mitsue was still waiting just beyond the door, so I bit back the urge to let my voice escalate. I circled to the front of his chair, stopping abruptly to place my hands on either side of the metal rim. I spoke directly to his face, not even taking note of how little space was left between us.

"Why does Icarus's blood mean so much to you?"

Raiden studied my face for a moment, seeming slightly taken aback. His gaze flickered over my facial features for a split second; then he shook his head slowly. "Tell me why you want to know."

"I will not answer to you," I replied tersely. "I have Icarus's best interest at heart."

He raised an eyebrow. "Do you—do you really? And is that why you dropped him from your mentorship?"

I opened my mouth to speak, but no words came out.

"The interesting thing is you probably wouldn't have made that decision if I gave you the answer to your question," he said softly, studying my eyes. "If you knew who Icarus really is."

"I know exactly who Icarus is," I said with a confidence I no longer felt. "I don't need you to cite anything about him to me. I know his past in its entirety."

Raiden raised an eyebrow, though I could tell his surprised expression wasn't genuine, it was calculated. It was searching for something. "So you know that Icarus is the Sunset that the prophecy speaks of?"

My heart spilled into the pit of my stomach.

"No one knows who the Sunset is," I said, a certain fierceness in my tone. "Nor the Sunrise. It's not for us to know."

Raiden shifted his gaze up to mine. "But you know the prophecy."

"What do you mean?"

"I mean that you know exactly what would happen if someone were to discover who the two halves of the split soul were," he replied slowly, watching me closely. "What if someone found them before anyone knew who they were? What if they simply vanished off the radar—what if their blood ran in the veins of a single soul…" He trailed off, and I felt a swallow slip quietly down my throat as I became suddenly aware of just how close we were. I pulled away.

Raiden didn't react. His gaze remained unfaltering.

"That one person," he continued softly, "would hold the culmination of the universe within their physical body. The blood of the cosmos would flow through their veins—they could influence the outcome of the future itself. They could control it."

Against my will, I could feel the warmth of a sweat prickling the back of my neck.

"If this is indeed your plan," I said, watching his expression closely, "why on earth would you divulge it to me—when I have the power to expose you?"

"I have my reasons," he replied, sounding as if he wanted to say something else.

"You do realize that you have critically violated the code," I said. "You will undergo trial. The student body will determine what to do with you from this point forward. Do you understand?"

"Fine."

I knew that his compliancy wasn't sincere, but I didn't question it. I started toward the door, but before I reached it, I slowed to a stop once more and turned to glance back at him. His eyes were still fixed on me.

"Though your assumptions cannot be accurate," I said, clearing my throat. "Do you have any inkling as to who the Sunrise among us may be?"

"No," he replied, trailing thoughtfully. "No, I don't."

I stood there a moment longer, considering the reply. I gave a solitary nod to acknowledge the response and left the room.

Brushing past Mitsue, I told him I would meet with him later for further discussion. I barely comprehended his response. I attempted to steady my fiercely wavering heart, but I couldn't prevent the reality of the situation from coursing through my veins.

Icarus was no longer the only target.

CHAPTER TWENTY-FOUR
Icarus

"I feel like I have literally nothing but questions right now. I have nothing to give, nothing to offer—I *am* a question. I'm confused, I'm a mess, I need help—I need *something*."

I was babbling. Sweat was biting at the back of my neck.

"Sensei, were you the one who found me—all those years ago?" I asked, my voice cracking. "The forest… the car abandoned on the side of the road. Were you the one who found me there?"

Sensei turned from the window. "Do you believe that it was me, Icarus?"

"Yes," I said. "I do."

"Then I need not strengthen your case." He met my gaze squarely. "There's nothing stronger than one's belief resolved."

I was still unsatisfied.

"But you've always known who I really am," I said, allowing my thoughts to empty out across my lips. "That's something *I* don't even know, not even now. Not even after everything that's happened. Even after the distance I've covered, and the things I've learned, and the ways in which I've changed… I still don't know who lives inside the mirror and stares back out at me."

"I didn't choose you so that you would no longer have questions, Icarus," he replied. "On the contrary, I chose you so that you may be provoked to ask yet more. To probe further—deeper than you ever have."

"But probing deeper is pointless if I never find anything in that darkness."

"You wish for an answer, then?"

"Sensei, I cannot believe that Mala, Raiden and I all merely happened to be in the right place at the right time. It cannot have been a coincidence that we all possess power. But—" I groped for words "—if it is not merely coincidence, then that would mean—"

"It would mean that your horizons must be stretched," he finished. "It would reveal that power does not, in fact, activate belief, but rather that belief activates power."

"So everyone is a slider."

Something like a smile passed across Sensei's face. "Everyone is a *possibility*, Icarus. Everyone is a question—both alive and dead until they make the decision to open not the darkness but their own eyes to create that reality."

"I don't understand."

"It does not require your understanding," he said. "But if understanding is what you seek, for the sake of your own solace, test it. Press it from all sides—push it until you can force it no further and see which walls have tumbled and which still remain—whether they are of your own creation or otherwise."

"I have your permission to search this out, then?"

"Do not underestimate the fact that as a protector you carry some authority, Icarus." Sensei placed a hand briefly on my shoulder as he passed me. "This dimension is no longer your classroom. It is your haven—your home."

I stood facing the glass wall, watching the light spill across the floor. I heard the door roll open behind me, letting in a tumult of conversation from the platform.

"Is that what so many of the others have been asking about?" I turned to look at him. "Is that what the buzz has been? Whether we can convert other 'normal' humans from our worlds into anomalies and take them with us?"

"Convert?"

"To make people like us."

Sensei paused in the doorway. "You cannot make anyone become something that they truly are not, Icarus. A mirror does not change the person who looks at it; a mirror simply reflects an image that is already present."

I knew that everything he was explaining was true—even if I didn't fully comprehend it all, I could *feel* it. Sensei was right, I did want answers—I wanted them straight up, yes or no. But apparently he didn't believe in making it that easy.

"So… you're saying that everyone is a slider: that it's possible for everyone to 'see the reflection of who they really are' and awaken their powers."

"Just because a mirror exists does not automatically mean that everyone looks into it—and just because someone looks into their own reflection, as you do your own and as Hawk does her own, does not mean that they see the warrior beneath their skin."

I stared at him for a moment, not fully understanding this clarification. "The warrior beneath my skin?"

Sensei gave a slow nod.

"I don't know that there *is* a warrior beneath my skin, Sensei."

"An echo of one hundred thousand other voices if I ever heard one," Sensei replied quietly. He stepped out into the hallway, leaving me standing there in the middle of his office, alone with my thoughts.

The discussion hadn't been a consolation. If anything, it had only created more turbulence in my mind.

Mala was right. There was something bigger going on here than we had initially realized. Not only had her instincts been accurate, but like a ticking time bomb, she would have an opportunity to test this redemptive theory, just as I would. For Mala, I knew it was more urgent. She had a family, a home— people whom she loved and missed. I didn't have any of this… but I still had a subject with which I would be able to experiment. Two, in fact.

Lost in the fallout of my own thoughts, I managed to snap out of my daze, making the decision to transport back to LA for my final visit.

I couldn't deny the fact that the mirror analogy got under my skin in ways that I couldn't understand. It was only another strong reminder that I was walking around with a mask over my face, wondering what was really underneath. Wondering why it was that sometimes even my worst enemy seemed privy to information about my true identity that hadn't even been disclosed to me.

Raiden apparently knew me well enough to want to become who I really was. Sensei spoke to me as though he could see straight through the mask I wore. Even things inside me seemed to nudge at my heart, whispering secrets about my true identity.

Though everyone addressed me as Icarus, I still struggled to feel that I was anything more than Ion. Ion in an Icarus shell, trying hard to feel like I even belonged in there at all.

I pressed the heel of my hand to my forehead, trying almost in a tangible way to clear the chaos of thoughts. I made my way down the hallway and onto the platform to find Mala and fill her in before I took off.

Hawk, emerging from the opposite corridor, stepped out onto the vacant platform at almost the exact moment I did.

Our eyes locked into each other like fighters. Hers were dark, and they looked across the expanse between us and into mine as if she had never seen me before. She approached and came to a stop in front of me.

"You were meeting with Sensei," she said, coming straight to the point. "What about?"

"Everything. Everything that's been going on these last few days."

Hawk, seeming to have been expecting something more intricate, hesitated.

"I understand," her words replied, while her tone said a thousand other things.

I had no idea what to say or how to take my eyes away from hers. I hadn't been this close to her since our argument.

"Icarus, can I ask you something?" she said after a moment.

"Of course."

"The prophecy," she began with difficulty. "Before the gathering the other night, had you ever heard the prophecy before? I know I never told you—I'd always just assumed that Sensei had, but did anyone else?"

"The recital at the gathering was the first time I'd ever heard it in its entirety."

Hawk looked at me for a moment. "Raiden never mentioned it?"

"Raiden? No," I said. "Why would he?"

"I was just wondering," she said, glancing down at the toes of her black boots. "I was just talking to him."

"To Raiden?"

Hawk nodded. "He's known the prophecy for some time."

"That doesn't add up," I said, thinking out loud. "He's a new initiate. I was never exposed to it before I came here."

"A lot of things aren't adding up right now, I'm afraid." She blew out a sigh. "Why didn't you tell me that Raiden channeled fire?"

Her gaze was still on the floor. I watched her eyelashes.

"Does it matter?"

"Very much so, since he likely attained both the knowledge of the prophecy and his channeling ability through the same method."

I squinted slightly, trying to catch up.

Her eyes flickered back up to mine again. "So quickly do you forget the things I've taught you. Entanglement, remember?"

My jaw tensed. "I never forgot."

Hawk's hand passed over her eyes. "My point, Icarus, is that yours would not have been the only life Raiden has taken for his own."

"You're kidding."

Hawk's gaze swept away from mine, wandering to the platform's edge. "I wish I was."

"Raiden has killed other people?"

"Other sliders, yes," Hawk replied, lowering her voice a little. "He's... I don't know, honestly. He's a freak of nature, so to speak. I've never encountered anyone like him—he's not just one person. He's a whole blacklist of sliders. You were merely at the top of his list, Icarus."

"Why at the top?" I asked, attempting to keep my voice low. "I mean… it *would* add up that Raiden is on some kind of power trip and I was just one of the many anomalies he's encountered and wanted to take out of the picture—"

"That *is* the case."

I stared at her for a second, then shook my head. "No, it's not. You said I was at the *top* of his list."

"I meant that—"

"Because Raiden knows who I really am." I cut her off before she could say more, stepping closer. "That is the reason, isn't it?"

Things were finally starting to click. It was almost like her eyes were giving me the things she didn't verbalize.

"He… told you, didn't he?" I asked quietly. "He told you whatever it is that he's never told me."

Hawk drew in a breath. "It's not like that, Icarus. It's—"

"It's what?"

"It's complicated, okay?" Her voice escalated, and she stopped herself. "Raiden is not just a powerful slider," she said, more quietly now, "he's a murderer—I don't even know how the student body is going to handle getting rid of him, or if we can even risk doing that right now. Do you actually expect me to believe a word he says?"

"No," I said, exhaling the word as I reached up to press my fingertips to my forehead. "But I would expect…" I trailed off. "I would *hope* that I don't mean so little to you now that you would withhold what he told you about me—even if it turns out to be a lie."

The look in Hawk's eyes changed; something seemed to draw back. "It's not that, Icarus. It's just—"

"We argued," I interrupted. "You disowned me, and now you don't want to tell me anything anymore. You don't trust me because I screwed this entire thing up and basically totaled the system."

"Just stop, okay? That's not why."

"Really?"

"Yes, really." She spoke through her teeth, then glanced over her shoulder and stepped even closer. "And if you would just shut up for more than two seconds, maybe I could explain."

I said nothing. I was painfully aware of how close she was.

"I know that we argued and that I recanted being your teacher." Her voice was a whisper now. "And I… I'll admit that I have lived to deeply regret the things that I said to you that day. But that's not the reason I cannot repeat to you what Raiden has claimed to know about you—not yet."

My mind was a chaos of questions, but I could only manage to blurt out one word. "Why?"

"Because," she said finally, taking a resolved breath, "I can't be sure that it is, in fact, a lie." She paused. "But I can't say anything until I have proof."

I wasn't sure how to respond. I searched her face as if I would somehow find answers in her eyes.

"Do you trust me enough to give me some time?" she said at last.

Trust her. After everything—the arguments and the whiplash and the silence between us, after all of that, Hawk was still asking the same thing she had been asking since the beginning. She was still counting down, telling me to jump.

I weighed my options—basically, I was damned if I did and damned if I didn't. "Of course I trust you."

I could hear voices, footsteps of students arriving for class, and I knew our conversation was over.

"Okay," she said. "Thank you."

———

"Ion, do you realize the police are looking for you?" West's voice was terse.

I nodded. "I'm aware."

"Do you realize that I've undergone *thorough* interrogation because of you—that I've been strictly ordered to report it if I so much as clap eyes on you?"

Again, I nodded. "It's not like I meant to drag you into this, West. I'm sorry. I didn't mean for you or Ruger to find out about it, but... I guess it's too late now."

I was sitting at the kitchen table across from West, who was less than thrilled to see me. I had no idea where Ruger was.

"Ion, look." West cleared his throat, leaning forward on his elbows. "I don't understand what kind of drugs you're on, but I need you to leave. Like, right now."

"I'm *not* on drugs."

He sighed, exasperated. "Dude, look. I heard about what happened—I saw, in fact. I was in the crowd that day at school."

"You were?"

West nodded. "I'm not going to lie. I'm honestly scared of you. Everyone I know is scared of you—you have some serious issues."

"I know."

"I mean, it's not like I *want* to see you get arrested, but... I hardly know what to think anymore, Ion."

Join the club, I wanted to say.

"West, something happened to me," I said, studying the creases that ran across my palms as I considered how to put the last several weeks into coherent words. "I can't say that I understand what's going on, or why I was chosen to do the things I'm doing, but—"

He raised his hands to shush me. "No, seriously, Ion, save it. I'm not interested in your cult, okay?"

"It's not a—"

"Ion, look." West swept his arms in a wide gesture that included everything in the room. "Do you even see what I'm doing here? Do you even *get* any of this?"

I looked at the papers scattered about, the coffee pot, the stack of textbooks. "Homework?"

"Exactly! Ion, I am a frickin' college student—I'm just a normal guy who somehow got sandwiched into a house with a party animal and some kind of cult member. I don't even want to think about how things got to this point without my notice. I feel like a frog in boiling water."

"West—"

"I should have just bit the bullet and lived on campus." He cut me off to continue, still making exaggerated gestures with his arms. "That would have been a hell of a lot better than this nightmare that is now my life."

"Come on, West, seriously. Do we have to make this dramatic?"

"Oh no, you—" he stabbed a finger in my direction, a wild look in his eyes "—*you* are the one who has made this 'dramatic.' I've just been sitting here."

"That's my point!" I retorted. "Don't you ever get tired of this?"

"Of what?"

I snatched a fistful of papers and shook them in the air. "This."

"Dude, that's my chem test. Drop—"

"Come on, West!" I said, frustrated. "Seriously… haven't you ever found yourself wondering what on earth we're all doing here? Haven't you ever wondered about what all of this even means?"

He leaned back dejectedly in his chair, thumbing his glasses back up the bridge of his nose. "Of course I have, Ion," he said, sounding almost hurt. "Just because I don't talk about it, or run around fighting people with fireballs like you freaks do, doesn't mean that I don't…" He searched for words. "That I don't feel like I'm missing something," he finished. "Because I think everyone feels like that sometimes. But that doesn't mean that I'm going to go jump off the deep end."

"I don't think anyone would expect that of you, West. You and deep ends don't exactly go hand in hand."

"Whatever." He shrugged. "That thing I mentioned earlier about you leaving? It still stands, you know."

"Yeah, yeah. I know." The words tumbled out in an exhale.

My gaze wandered to the kitchen window. California sunshine was streaming in from outside. Beyond the glass I could see Sensei's front yard. I had to bite back the feeling of nostalgia.

"West, I know you think I'm crazy," I began again, laughing slightly. "And I probably am. But can I show you something?"

West's eyes narrowed into a distrustful glare.

"Come on, it's nothing weird," I said, trying for a reassuring tone.

West didn't move.

"Okay, so maybe it is," I conceded. "But I swear it will only take a second—and you'll like it."

West folded his arms over his chest again. "Why am I seriously doubting that last part?"

"Because you don't have enough faith," I replied, pushing back the kitchen chair to get up. "Come on."

He shook his head.

"Come *on*."

"Ion, you're insane." He sighed, slipping his fingers under his glasses to rub his eyes. "Didn't I just tell you that I didn't want to have to call the police? Do you actually want me to do that? Because if you keep talking like this—"

We were interrupted by a commotion of footsteps on the stairs. A second later the door burst open. Ruger stood on the threshold for a moment, sizing up the situation, before stepping inside.

He tossed me a glance. "Look who's back."

I lifted my hand into an awkward wave and heard West mutter something under his breath about how he hated his life.

"So are the rumors true?" Ruger crossed the room and lazily swung open the fridge. "I won't believe it until I see it with my own eyes—I'm a skeptic."

West rolled his eyes. "Haven't you been watching the news, you idiot?"

Ruger's head was in the fridge now, so his laugh was muffled. "News? Like, who even watches that anymore."

"Okay, you know what?" West threw his hands in the air and leapt to his feet. "Forget it. I am taking my homework to my room and I am locking myself in there. Ruger, you can deal with the police when they show up. Have fun."

I heard the sound of a can popping open as Ruger slammed the refrigerator shut. "Police?" He took a generous mouthful of beer.

I reached out an arm to bar West's escape route. Which didn't amuse him. At all.

"Ion, get out of my way, alright?" he demanded, trying to shove past me. "I'm sick of this crap."

"West, *please,*" I pleaded. "All I'm asking is for two seconds of your time."

"And your answer is no."

"*West.*" I clamped my hands down firmly on his shoulders. "*Please.* I need you to come with me—this is the last chance I have."

West's eyes were wild. His mouth opened and closed, but no sound came out.

"Last chance to do what, exactly?" Ruger took another swig of beer.

"Not just my last chance." I sucked in a breath. "*Your* last chance."

West's eyes grew even wider. "What are you talking about, Ion? You say that as if—"

"As if I'll never see you both again?" I finished for him. "That's because I won't."

I could practically hear the gears in Ruger's head spinning.

"Where are you going?" West brushed my hands away. "Are you seriously going to try to run away from this? Because it doesn't work like that, Ion."

I shook my head. "Not running away, no. But I am leaving." I stepped back slightly, glancing at the two of them.

They were the perfect candidates. Strange, quirky, *perfect.* West was still looking at me like I had escaped from an insane asylum, and Ruger was holding his can of beer, clueless as usual.

I bit back a smile. "And I'm taking you both with me."

CHAPTER TWENTY-FIVE
Hawk

The sun rose and set—then did it all again several times over. Days had swept by, and everything that we'd been told to expect gradually came to pass.

I'd transported back to California one last time to visit the garden—to run my fingertips along the limbs of the arborvitaes, to water the front lawn and feel the morning sunlight on my skin one last time. It all went by in a blur, and before I knew it, I was back in the Dimension again, watching as the last student transported back and Sensei sealed the cavern.

Our tether to Earth had been cut. We were on our own now.

And so were they—everyone who had been left to the version of Earth they had created. Everyone who, in the blink of an eye, would become part of the past, mere monuments of things that were no more.

Like the darkness of dusk, a state of what felt like mourning fell over the Dimension. No one was left untouched.

Over the previous three days the Dimension gained twelve new initiates—humans who had been recruited to join our movement and leave their natural dimensions before the portal was closed indefinitely. Each of these new students, though through a slightly more gradual process, had come to assume a various form of slidatorial power. In different circumstances, this progress might have been celebrated. But as it was, most of us simply carried on, half sick with grief and too shaken to dive for a deeper analysis of the situation. For now, in this state of chaos, things simply were what they were. It was almost as if we were temporarily embracing the fact that nothing made sense.

Except me. I wasn't as easily satisfied. I wanted to puzzle it out—and soon, but for now I had no opportunity. As I had predicted, the council had agreed to a trial for Raiden, and it was in full swing now. My mind kept circling back to what he'd said about Icarus and his potential identity. The things he'd said and the questions he'd asked echoed in my thoughts almost without ceasing. I had no idea what to think or feel anymore.

Things were moving too fast for my comprehension—I couldn't keep up. First the evacuation, then the unforeseen rescue of those who had come to "believe," now the discovery of Raiden's true identity—or in this case, *identities*—and to top that off, a bold indictment that Icarus was in fact the other half of my own soul.

My brain was in overload.

I'd spent the past two afternoons sitting at the back of the gathering platform, listening to testimony, making mental note of anything that could possibly give me a clue as to how Raiden could have known that Icarus was the awaited, symbolic "Sunset." How could Raiden know this? More to the point, how could I trust *anything* that rolled from the lips of someone who had taken other sliders' lives—someone who had killed to get what he wanted? And even if it was true, and Icarus was the Sunset, which I still couldn't bring myself to accept, why would Raiden choose to tell *me*, of all people?

At first I assumed Raiden would use this information, fabricated or otherwise, to leverage some kind of upset among us; something that would cause a distraction and provide him with an advantage of some kind. But after our discussion and a later follow-up with Mitsue, I quickly came to the realization that I was the only one Raiden had told. Neither Mitsue nor anyone else involved in evaluating the case knew anything beyond the fact that Raiden was a killer. For everyone else, that was what the case was about: serial murder.

I was the only one who could see the bigger picture. Raiden wasn't just a murderer—he was a searcher. And I was fifty percent of what he was searching for.

Why had he told only me? Why?

There was a strange familiarity about Raiden that I'd noticed when he'd initiated. Though our discussions were heated, we conversed easily, and strangely it almost didn't feel unnatural that he should divulge something of such magnitude to me, though the sensation made no sense.

Frustrated and—if I were honest with myself, slightly afraid—I sat at the back of the gathering platform, hour after hour, listening and trying fiercely to figure out how I was going to fix this. I needed a plan.

Fin was absent from the proceedings; he had originally been selected to be part of Raiden's jury of peers, but Sensei had exempted him, given that he was grieving the loss of his family and his earthly life. He hardly left his dorm now, and I hadn't had a real conversation with him since the day we'd transported. Though I knew it had been his decision to remain in the Dimension, I couldn't think about it without a feeling of guilt in the pit of my stomach.

Did Fin actually tell me that he loves me? Is that really why he chose to stay here?

I wished there was some way I could tell him not to love me, some way to tell him that there was nothing inside me that could do the things that the insides of him were doing, but I knew I couldn't. My only hope was that he would eventually hear the echoes from the hollow place where my heart wasn't. And, selfishly, I wished that Fin had found the emotional capacity to take the position he'd been offered on the council. More than ever, I needed someone to help me make sense of what was happening.

In the end, Raiden confessed to his guilt, and it was determined that his long-term memory would be selectively erased. Sensei usually handled this procedure, but to my surprise he instead commissioned Mitsue and me with the task.

It was late in the day when the event transpired. Sessions were over and the platform was empty. The sun was just beginning to slip over the top of the ravine, painting the cliff side red. We convened in the largest safe room. The floorboards at one end of the room faded and sank gradually into a stone half-sphere in which a small cluster of flames fed on thin air. Opposite this was a rigid wooden examination table. Raiden was seated there, staring down at his folded hands. At my signal, Mitsue lifted his free hand into a gesture that tinted the glass wall at the far end of the room a darker shade. The interior of the room was thrown into a wash of wavering rust hues, leaving everything in deep shadow.

I set about brewing what looked like a type of tea in a small silver bowl, which I held in levitation over the flames.

"Hawk?"

I glanced up.

Mitsue shot me an inquisitive look from across the room. "Are you paying attention to that?"

I nodded, though it was a partial lie, slipping the small silver bowl away from the orange tongues of flame.

Mitsue was busy checking things off on the page in front of him. He set his pen down on the table. "Let's get this over with."

Still allowing the metal bowl to hover just above my palm, I drew a small handleless cup off a shelf nearby and strained the pale gold liquid into it. I carried it across the room to Mitsue, who in turn extended it to Raiden.

"Drink it."

Raiden took it and peered uneasily at the contents. "What is it?"

"It's a sedative," I replied, watching him examine it. "You'll be out for a few hours."

Slowly he drew his gaze up to meet ours. "So you can remove the things I've learned?"

I knew exactly what he was alluding to. I said nothing.

Raiden turned to Mitsue. "Will she be able to read my long-term?" he said, inclining his head towards me.

"Only I will," Mitsue replied.

Why would that matter?

"Are you positive?"

"Enough," Mitsue replied firmly. "Just do it."

Raiden turned back to me for a moment, and then, without a word, he brought the cup to his lips and drained it. Mitsue instructed him to lie down, and to my relief he was out within a few minutes.

"Okay." I gestured for Mitsue to take over. "He's all yours."

I wanted to get as far away from Raiden as possible. I knew Mitsue had been selected for this task because he was Raiden's teacher, but why had I been chosen? Though Raiden had confessed to having no knowledge of who the Sunrise slider was, I felt unnervingly exposed around him, and the less time I had to spend in his presence, the better.

Mitsue stood alongside Raiden and placed his index and middle fingers on the appropriate areas of his student's forehead. Focusing, he went completely silent, and in that silence I slipped and fell into my own thoughts again.

After my conversation with Raiden that day in the safe room, I'd run into Icarus on the platform. He was coming from the direction of Sensei's office. His hair was a mess and his eyes were wild with things that were still trapped inside. He was Icarus, but he was also, in some terrifying way, somebody else too. Somebody I'd never met before but somehow knew perfectly. He was the slider I had trained, the guy next door who drove too fast, my constant opponent in the ring; he was all of this but something else besides. He was a nightmare that both terrified and attracted something inside me like a moth to a flame.

I couldn't really remember what I'd said to him, what words I'd chosen, how I'd phrased my questions or what he'd said in reply, but the look in his eyes was burned into my brain. I'd looked away, down at the floor, my shoes, anything to keep my gaze away from his, from reading what they were telling me louder than words ever could.

He couldn't be what I was looking for. It was impossible.

I knew who I was waiting for, deep down. I knew what I would feel and how it would happen. I would find someone, something that would fill the emptiness inside me, not dig the black hole even deeper. Someone who would see me for the inside-out star that I was. Someone who would push back against gravity, someone who wouldn't get too close.

Icarus *had* gotten too close. In fact, he was already gone. The only thing left for me to say was that I was sorry. That I hadn't meant to swallow him—that he should have watched his step. But the truth was, none of it mattered anymore. Like the darkness that was taking over around us, there was no way for me to reverse what I had done.

"This isn't working," said Mitsue.

I snapped back into awareness. I had no idea how long I'd been standing there mindlessly watching him.

"I don't know what's wrong," he muttered, his forehead beaded with perspiration. "It's not working. I can't see anything."

"What do you mean?" I asked.

"I mean that it's all a tangle," he snapped. "I can't get past his surface-level consciousness. I can't see any of his long-term."

Mitsue stepped up to the table and started rifling through the agglomeration of papers he'd brought in. I could tell by his expression that he was at a complete loss. "Well?"

I raised an eyebrow. "*Well?*"

He threw the papers down on the table, letting them scatter and fall to the floor. "Are you just going to stand there and stare at me, or are you going to help me figure this out? It's not like he's going to wake up anytime soon!"

What is wrong with me?

"Yes." I cleared my throat. "Yes, of course. I'm sorry."

"I don't want an apology," he shot back. "I want you to help me."

"I don't know what to do! I've never done this before."

"Neither have I!"

Raiden stirred slightly, attracting our attention.

"I'm sorry," Mitsue said, lowering his voice. "I'm just starting to panic. I don't want to look like a failure."

I pursed my lips, still watching Raiden as his chest rose and fell with the gentle motions of his breathing.

"Tell me what you saw," I said quietly, kicking my brain back into gear, "when you tried reading his thoughts."

Mitsue wiped the sweat off his face with his forearm. "Nothing beyond the day's events and even then... there were parts that were obscured."

"Obscured?"

He nodded. "I've taken cognitive readings before, and I've never experienced anything like this. His memory is more expansive than what would seem possible for someone his age; I was able to observe that much. But he's still keeping things under wraps, almost like he's still conscious—how strong did you make that tea?"

"Are you blaming me?"

He shook his head. "No. I just don't understand how this is happening. I don't understand why I can't break into his mind."

I stood there for a moment, unsure of what to say or do with myself. I studied Raiden's body for a moment to confirm that he was, indeed, unconscious.

"You've read minds before," I repeated slowly, my voice coming out soft as I turned to face him. "But have you ever read more than one at the same time?"

Mitsue turned to stare at me. "What are you talking about?"

I closed my eyes for a second, trying to focus on the larger picture with deeper clarity.

"Have you ever navigated the inner workings of not just one, but several people's minds simultaneously?" I rephrased. "Maybe three or four people?"

I could tell he wasn't following. His eyes flicked back and forth from the flames to my face.

"Of course not," he said uncertainly. "That's impossible. No one's ever done it."

I gestured toward his unconscious student. "Well, that's what you're dealing with here."

Sensei's office looked different now that the portal had been closed. Since he had spent most of his time at the California house when he wasn't in the Dimension, the room had been in a constant state of sparse organization. Now there were trees and wisteria vines climbing along the glass wall at the end of the room.

Incense burned in an iron plate on a stone mantel to my left. A tatami bed and a set of floor chairs to match had been adopted into the office-turned-apartment as well, and the atmosphere was bright and sweetly scented, an embodiment of Sensei's persona.

Although he maintained his usual calm, I could sense that he was grieving inwardly. His grief, however, was of a different kind, deeper somehow than what the rest of us were experiencing.

I'd been the one to bring him the report about the unfolding situation with Raiden.

As soon as Raiden had awoken, Mitsue had taken him back to the single-person dorm in which he was being kept temporarily under guard. I'd waited until dawn to go and report to Sensei. To my surprise, he seemed to have been expecting what I reported.

He was seated now on the end of the thin beige mattress and I was sitting on the floor, my back to the wall. I was tired—drained. In fact, I couldn't recall the last time I had felt such exhaustion.

"I need to know your thoughts on all of this, Sensei," I said, tipping my head back against the white wall. "I don't even know how to put what I'm feeling into words."

"What you are feeling in regards to Raiden?" he asked.

"Yes and no." I ran my tongue briefly over my lips, debating. "It has to do with Raiden, of course. What he's done is absolutely abominable. I listened to every moment of his trial, and unfortunately the results of his actions have us up against a pretty serious wall. There's no foreseeable way for us to neutralize him."

"Because of your failed attempt to eradicate his memory?"

"That, and the portals are closed. Our options are running out."

"The situation is difficult, I agree," he submitted, sighing. "I'm afraid it's not my place to advise the case, though, Hawk. I've given the student body the authority to act as they see fit. I cannot impose myself upon them."

I straightened to look at him. "Since when does anyone ever consider your advice an imposition?"

He said nothing. Unable to read his eyes, I closed my own.

"Anyway, in truth, yes. It has much to do with Raiden," I continued. "But not because of the trial, because of something else—something he told me and no one else."

"You don't have to tell me, Hawk."

I glanced at him. His eyes were filled with something I couldn't identify.

"Why do you say that?"

"Because you are no longer a student, Hawk." He folded his hands. "Have you been with me this long yet continue to seek my judgment in every situation?"

"Sensei, I ask your advice and seek your judgment because I know it is sound." His words had come as a surprise to me. I sat up a little straighter. "Would you rather I didn't?"

"I didn't say—"

"Am I a burden?"

Sensei flashed me a stern look. "You are not, nor could you ever be, a burden, Hawk."

"Then why wouldn't you want me to come to you?" I asked. "Why would you say I'm not your student anymore?"

"I say it because it's true," Sensei replied, rising. "A student is a soul in training—an apprentice. Someone who is learning to carry the weight of something larger than themselves, a spirit in preparation."

"Exactly."

"And now the time has come for you to assume your position as someone who has reached completion." My eyes followed him as he paced the room. "I tell you that you are no longer a student not because I've grown weary of your audience, Hawk... but because I see within you not a fledgling but a fully matured individual who hesitates at the ledge."

"The ledge?"

"Hawk, the prophecy is encoded even into your heart. You have learned it experientially."

"Yes, but—"

"We have been cut away from Earth, Hawk," he interrupted, pausing to touch the foliage on one of the trees. "Have you never considered what was meant by a 'culmination'? Or what exactly that would be like?"

I sighed, refocusing. "Are you saying..." I groped for words. "How can this be the...? Sensei, you *knew* that it would happen this way?"

"I didn't say that."

"But that *is* what you're implying."

"I am implying that you are ready," he replied in a voice that was both gentle and firm, satin and steel. "Did you think you would be a permanent understudy? Did you think this moment would never actually come, Hawk?"

I had no response for him.

"Didn't I once tell you that I designed you?" he asked, still intent. "Didn't I destine you for such a time as this?"

"Sensei, I'm not ready. And I'm not just saying that—I am sincerely *not ready*," I told him, though I spoke the words to the floor. "I'm a mess. I'm in transit—I *haven't arrived*. What Raiden said... what he told me, it could change everything. I don't know what to think."

"Or are you merely *afraid* to consider it?"

I swallowed. "So... you know, then?"

"No," he said. "But I know you... I know that you are capable of searching this out."

I didn't want to be hearing this—not from him, not now. I needed him, and all he was doing was nudging me closer and closer to the edge of the precipice.

"But I'm—I..." I trailed off, pressing the heel of my hand to the space between my eyes. "I feel like I'm fumbling around in the darkness, searching for something that still evades me."

"And what would that be?"

I sighed in frustration. "Sensei, how will I know? It's been... it's been a century. I feel like all my life has been is a search for something that would complete me—that part of my soul. My missing piece." I paused, gazing up at him through the haze of chaos in my head. It was almost a visible presence within the room. "I trust you, Sensei. I trust that you know me better than I know myself," I said. "I won't ask you to figure it out for me, but... I need you to tell me something else. Something important."

He took a seat beside me on the floor, the subtle repositioning somehow shifting everything into a completely new perspective.

I was no longer looking up and into his eyes like a child at a towering father. His blue eyes were level with mine—soft, present, waiting for me to go on without knowledge of what I would say next. He was no longer above me, but beside me.

"How will I know?" The words I needed were running, hiding. I had to grab them by the wrists and drag them out. "If I ever find them..." I swallowed back the rest and rephrased. "*When* I do... how will I know they're the one? Will it be a word—a look? Something they do?"

I was avoiding the word *he* for the sake of my own sanity.

"Will I feel something inside me change?" I continued, my voice cracking slightly. "Will something just... click? Will there be any room for doubt left in my heart?"

"Doubt and faith are the very language of the heart, Hawk," he answered softly, and a smile passed briefly over his lips. "Would you expect that by finding the other half of yourself, its voice would be lessened? On the contrary, its volume will only increase. The storm will become a hurricane—the embers a forest fire. Yes, you will still doubt—hard and strong. But it will only mean that you are that much more awakened."

"But doubt is questioning."

"And questioning is faith that there is an answer. And that you will one day find it."

I hung on his words, trying to grasp their meaning. I felt as though I was overlooking something that he was holding right before my eyes.

"But will finding them cause me to stop doubting myself?"

"If that's what you believe the purpose of your other half to be, you have a misconception of your own soul," he said. "You cannot find fulfillment for yourself in another—nor can they find their purpose in you."

"I don't understand."

"No one will ever be able to make you stop doubting yourself except the person in whose skin you awaken each morning," he said. "Neither half of a being torn in two is complete. It's a fallacy to search for one hundred percent within fifty. It cannot be found—it will not be."

I stared at him for a moment without saying anything. His expression was soft.

"How will I know?" I repeated my earlier question like a child desiring a simpler answer. "How will I know when it's real?"

He took his eyes away from mine, gazing towards the glass wall where the shafts of dawn were filtering in. I watched as his thoughts took form, and then again he smiled.

"You will know it's real when you find that your eyes are fixed on the same end," he replied softly, as if considering the words in a new way himself. "It cannot be based on external signs, for there will be none. Like an actual sunrise and sunset, you both will be the same, because you are one and share the same purpose—to continue eternity."

I felt my muscles relax slightly as I inhaled, taking his words in with the sweet-scented oxygen. Up until then I'd been studying his face. The familiar, knowing eyes. The skin that seemed somehow iridescent in the soft lighting.

"To share the same dreams and the same nightmares," he continued, lowering his voice slightly, as if he were imparting a secret. "To be, together, the set of hands that hold between them a spinning, dancing, longing universe—one that has been yours from the beginning."

For the rest of the day, we talked—about anything and everything. My wounds began to heal. His words stayed with me—haunted me, in fact, over the next several days. Sensei had given me no direct answers, yet in doing so, had given me everything. He had given me the invaluable knowledge of my own authority.

Over the course of a few weeks, Icarus had gone from a merely passable student to an absolute powerhouse. It was as if he'd waited until I'd taken my eyes off him to tear out of the cocoon. He'd moved his way up through the ranks when I wasn't looking, and suddenly there he was, coaching fledgling initiates alongside Mitsue and me and other more advanced students.

He had brought in his roommates—two teenage guys called Areos and Runner (formerly "West" and "Ruger"). Although they struggled to adapt, understandably, they were coming on shockingly strong, both of them possessing surprisingly expansive capacities for such new students. Areos was reserved and attentive, while Runner was the opposite in every respect. They melded easily into the flow of daily sessions and quickly gained momentum.

Mala, Mitsue, and Fin, oddly enough, hadn't succeeded in retrieving anyone from their home dimensions. How on earth was this fair? We had been taught that slider selection was an ancient art, something monumental—yet here was Icarus bringing in his friends seemingly effortlessly. Where did that put the many of us who had worked *so hard* to achieve the level of power we had come to hone? Something wasn't adding up, but I could sense that Sensei wanted me to arrive at the conclusion on my own.

Icarus and I had barely spoken since that day on the platform, but now it seemed we'd outgrown the need for words. Our conversations were in the giving and tearing away of our eyes. Each time we were together, it became harder and harder not to think about Raiden's words and my conversation with Sensei. Each time we parted ways, it became more difficult for me to ignore the storm that was gaining strength in my chest.

Since Sensei had bowed out of the picture, and with Fin out of commission, I had no one to turn to besides the voices in my mind, and each night I found myself lying awake, listening carefully to what they had to say.

Someone to share your dreams—your nightmares...

"But what does that mean?"

The sun was rising, bathing everything in tones of faded amber. It was lonely, talking to the ceiling. But there were things inside me that needed to be spoken aloud.

Icarus was the perfect storm. He was everything I never wanted. His entrance into the Dimension, no matter how much it had been supported by Sensei, had flipped reality as we knew it on its head. I'd gone from feeling as though I was on top of the deck to being lost in the shuffle. But... Sensei had chosen me to select Icarus, hadn't he? He'd urged me to—told me that it was meant to be. This was *meant* to happen.

And if this was the culmination of the gathering, of everything that we had been working towards, that meant that finding the missing half of my soul was at hand. It meant that he, whoever he was, was already here, sealed into the Dimension with us. With *me*.

The thought alone was enough to keep me awake, thinking, and wrestling with the things that lived silently under my skin like abandoned furniture beneath dusty sheets.

Eventually I brushed back the blankets. An almost unreal stillness hung in the thick, humid air below; my windowpane was thick with condensation. I crossed to the wardrobe and took out a few items of clothing. As I dressed, my thoughts wandered back to that day in the pub with Fin. The day he had told me that he could see the sunrise within me and suggested the possibility of a hidden identity in Icarus.

What did he see in me that gave it away? What does he see in Icarus?

I went to the window. I slid it open and the warmth pressed in, whispering. I sat there on the ledge for what felt like a long time. I studied the mist below, the dormitories, the emptiness. I watched how the wind gently swayed the bridges made of rope. From my perch I could see the isolated dorm where Raiden was being kept under guard until the council came to a decision as to what to do with him. The light that had been in the window earlier was gone now, leaving the place looking absent of life.

How am I to know? What will confirm whether any of this is true?

I knew what I had to do, but I was afraid. Discovering how Raiden had come to know what he knew wasn't my real task. He wasn't the one I needed. I had believed that evidence was what I needed, but my own soul had proven me wrong. I didn't need proof, or faith, or even confirmation—I needed to *feel something*. Because I had felt nothing for the last century.

We were split, Icarus and I. Our friendship had been fractured without either of us knowing exactly why, but the fact resurrected itself each time we were together on the platform, each time we groped, fruitlessly, for a common language.

I needed to talk to him.

Far below I could see a faint bluish light flickering alive on the lower gathering platform. A dim illumination, so fleeting that I wondered if it was a mirage. *No.* I squinted and the light flickered again. Someone was there.

I dropped down, free-falling and shifting silently.

Twisting through the dense air, I spread my wings to slow myself as the pathway carved along the cliff side came rapidly up before me. I landed close to the training platform. I couldn't see who the figure was.

Returning to human form, I followed the path quietly, hyper-cautious in the low light. My footsteps were loud in the absence of all other sound. The reflections of the light cascaded up the smooth cliff side like a hazy waterfall in reverse. The path curved, and growth reached down to obscure my visibility. Through it I could see glimpses of the figure in the distance, silhouetted against a familiar blue light. I halted, still concealed in the foliage, my hand slipping up to touch the cold, smooth stone.

I was still about fifty yards away, and with the trees I knew he couldn't see me. But I could see him perfectly.

Icarus.

He was pacing, head down, intent on something only he could see. His lips moved, but I couldn't make out the words. I edged closer and then stopped, bewildered.

He was reciting the script of the prophecy.

I'd seen it a thousand times before at gatherings, but never like this. Never in the solitude of a quiet morning, pulsing behind the hushed voice of a single curious soul, spilling out to gather around him like maternal wings. I stood rooted, watching him, holding my breath.

Icarus had gravitated toward the prophecy as a thirsty soul stumbles toward a spring.

Did he feel anything when he recited it? Did it ignite anything in him like it did in me?

Doubt held me fast. Doubt, suspicion, complacency—all of it. I waited; I watched him pace—and at last watched him leave. My chance and my courage slipped away.

How could I possibly tell him? How would he possibly understand?

I *wanted* to trust. I wanted to jump, to dive, to reveal myself to Icarus, but my heart refused to let down the shield.

I had flown under the radar so long I had no idea how to emerge again.

I realized suddenly that moments had passed and I was standing there alone.

As I stepped lightly onto the platform, the words immediately gravitated in my direction, flowing like a stream to sweep around me and stain my skin in the afterglow. At first they were jumbled, unintelligible, but then they shuffled back into a coherent state and I felt chills break out over my skin.

I tilted my face towards the sky and breathed it softly in, aching inwardly.

"Why does this have to be so hard?" My voice sounded plaintive, beaten, in the stillness. "How on earth can I know for sure?"

"You know because you feel it," replied a quiet voice behind me.

He spoke softly into my right ear, and I felt his face in the curve of my neck as he pulled my hair back. I writhed violently and then froze as I felt the coolness of a blade on my throat.

"And you feel it because you are the missing piece, Hawk."

The pressure increased as the blade began to bite down. I struggled again, but gained only the sensation of his nails sinking into my skin, a wave of déjà vu, and hot blood as it broke the surface around the blade.

"You're the one I've been looking for."

CHAPTER TWENTY-SIX
Icarus

Time passed me by, though I hardly perceived it anymore.

I lost track of how many times dawn and dusk came, how many days were ticking gradually by. My only motivation was to work as diligently as I could. I carried the guilt of what had happened with me everywhere—it was a constant reminder of the fact that this storm was mostly of my own creation.

Areos and Runner, though they had been dragged into the Dimension and renamed with much kicking and screaming, had proven themselves to be assets. This confirmed my suspicions that something more was going on here—the fact that there didn't *have to be* so few of us. I didn't know whether to be excited by the implications or heartbroken.

Mala had left the Dimension for a full dawn cycle before the portal was closed to spend time with her family, though she, like Fin, had returned solo. The empty look in their eyes was my memento mori.

For me, the most disheartening consequence of everything was my rift with Hawk. I couldn't tell whether she was avoiding me or if I was avoiding her, but either way it felt like a sort of death. I would have preferred the firestorm of her presence to her absence. I was so tired of seeing her back as she turned and walked away; I was tired of fighting her ghost.

Sleep abandoned me; I wrestled with the person I was becoming. I went for long solitary walks in the predawn so I could talk to myself without anyone around to hear. I felt like I had in the dream, when I'd awoken in the car. I was scared and lost in my own skin.

Who the hell am I?

The prophecy had been a shot to the chest. It had made me feel something I couldn't quite understand. I couldn't even say that I cared to understand it—I just wanted to feel it again. I wanted another dose.

So I had retraced my steps.

I'd first been exposed to it at the gathering platform, and as if the remnants themselves might be lingering there, I visited in the lonely time between dusk and dawn, spending hours in silent contemplation of the words and the round sky and the brilliant stars, my feet dangling over the expanse of an endless pit. I never did anything else there; I merely contemplated the words and what they meant and why they had such an effect on me.

And at last, it made perfect sense: the prophecy was a servant bound to the voice of its masters. Like Gaia and every other student who had ever recited the ancient script, I too had the authority to summon it.

At first I hadn't noticed the words as they appeared around me. A bluish glow emanating from behind me startled me to attention. Seated at the edge of the platform as I spoke, I'd nearly slipped and fallen into the abyss.

The words appeared exactly as they had before, in the order that they were spoken and manifesting in shades of blue-tinted light. I'd stood, then, and begun to pace as I spoke, and they had adjusted their position so as to be constantly facing me, gravitating toward my every footstep as if they were not words but living beings.

And so while the Dimension slept, I escaped to a secret gathering of one. Evening after evening reeled in by a blurry dance, my voice a backdrop as the verses awakened out of the floorboards. The starlight itself seemed to dim in comparison. It was as if something was drawing me in and holding me down. With each recital, the rush came on stronger. It became an addiction. With each experience, the effect seemed to double.

But one evening as the sun fell and began to rise once again, something felt different. Something was coming. I had no idea what, but the wind spoke of it in whispers as I left the platform that morning.

Taking the opposite path, I made my way back up the cliff side. I could see my exhales painting the air in front of me. A prickling sensation kissed the curve of my neck and I felt a light sweat breaking the surface of my skin though I ignored it and focused instead on the ground in front of me, my fingertips running over the smooth surface of the stone, then brushing against the limbs of trees as they reached down.

Suddenly I froze in place: a shrill cry pierced the silence. A moment later it came again—a voice that was neither human nor tame, but I knew it better than my own. A shrill, frantic cry that summoned my heart up to my throat. It cut through the air yet again, clearer now, giving away its location. Shoving branches away from my face, I began to struggle towards it.

When I reached the first clearing, I broke into a full run, my heart pounding and my breath coming in ragged gasps. I rounded the last corner and the platform rose into view. A thin veil of mist wasn't enough to hide what was now there.

A circle had been drawn—a dull red one, in the dead center of the platform's open expanse. In the center of the circle was a dagger reflecting the first fragments of the sun, a sharp angle of light like an artifact from a dream. The tip was embedded into the platform. Splayed out across it was a layer of flesh and blood and feathers tangled in splotches of crimson. A wing—a body.

Hawk.

She was stretched out on her back, pinned to the platform, her eyes meeting mine through an upside-down world as another cry escaped her. I couldn't tell if the vocalization was one that was meant to beckon or deter me, but I wasn't thinking about it anymore because something inside me had just met its death.

I ran to her. I fell to my knees before her and my fingers contracted around the blade's handle.

"My *god*, what happened?" My voice sounded muffled; I could barely hear anything beyond the thundering of my own heart in my throat. I tore the knife from her flesh, a pained cry escaping her lungs again. I cursed and reached out to touch her wing, but she wrenched herself away, fighting me—and trilling a broken warning call. Tiny droplets of blood flecked my skin as she beat me away with her wings.

"Hawk, *stop*!" I shielded my eyes with one hand and reached for her with the other. "What happened?"

She didn't answer—not in human words. She didn't shift.

"Hawk." As gently as I could, I grasped her right wing. "Who did this?"

She responded with only more of the same warning calls—shrill and frantic. She bit my hand and I tore away with a hiss of pain, the blade slipping from my opposite hand as I fell back. It clattered to the platform's smooth surface.

"Why are you doing this?" I yelled at her. None of it felt real. I felt like we were in a dream—another segment of the nightmare from which I could never awaken. "Why are you fighting me?"

Her eyes were wide with terror. I pushed myself up to my feet, and she backed frantically away, dragging her bleeding wing. She shook her head violently and shrieked again, her eyes darting frantically to something behind me. I reached again for her, and again she dodged me.

"Hawk, if you don't let me touch you, I can't heal you. Why aren't you shifting?"

And this time, finally, a human voice responded.

"Because she can't, Ion."

I felt the droplets of sweat that had formed at the back of my neck slip beneath the collar of my shirt to roll down my spine. I started to turn around but stopped dead at his command.

"Don't," he ordered, and I heard the subtle crackle of flame in the palm of his hand. "Don't turn around."

I looked back at Hawk. She'd frozen, her gaze riveted on Raiden. I could see the gears turning, and a feeling of fear rose in my chest.

Don't, Hawk. Don't move.

"If you want her to live, do as I say." Raiden spoke loudly. "Understand?"

"I understand."

The dagger, which had been lying where I'd dropped it on the platform, lifted suddenly into the air and gravitated to Raiden, handle first. A split second later I felt its tip at my back.

"She can't shift," he said slowly, returning to my question. "Because she no longer has the capacity. She doesn't have another form to shift into."

Hindered by her wound and the speed at which Raiden reacted, Hawk was barely able to execute a liftoff, let alone the attack I'd seen festering in her eyes. When he threw the flame in his hand, rather than igniting her body, the impact took her to the floorboards and set fire to them, creating an encompassing ring around her. Something like invisible energy seemed to billow up in the shape of a cylinder, deflecting her as soon as she touched it.

"Tell me why you need my blood," I said, my voice was surprisingly steady again, almost commanding. "Why is it so important to you—why did you involve her in this?"

I felt the blade slip up to the back of my neck. "Your blood? You think this is just about you?"

"I'm only repeating your words."

The blade pressed into my skin. I glanced over at Hawk; her eyes met mine through the wavering mirage of energy.

"Isn't that what you've been telling me?" I demanded. "Didn't you say you knew something about me that I didn't know?"

"I wanted you only because I wanted her," he replied. "Because I knew you would lead me to her, and she would confirm whether you were the one."

Hawk's eyes pleaded with me not to listen to Raiden, but I needed answers.

"I don't understand."

"You read the prophecy each night, yet you grasp none of its meaning." Raiden sounded almost taken aback by my ignorance.

"And you claim to know its meaning?"

One of his hands went to my shoulder and clamped there, cold. He pulled me firmly backward several paces. "It's not that I claim to understand it," he replied, jarring me abruptly to a stop. "It's that I *do* understand it—fully. Unlike you, I've been privileged to know who I am—who I was born to be... and I am not afraid of it."

"I still don't—"

"I know, Ion," he said. "I know. And now it doesn't matter. It won't matter—not for you, because this is the end of your chapter."

Hawk threw herself again at the energy barrier, but her efforts still proved fruitless.

"Yes, your chapter," he repeated. "Because in the grand scheme of things, that is all you ever were. We are all chapters, segments of a more expansive journey, you and I—and Hawk." He said her name almost reverentially. "The great difference between us is that I am completed, whereas you are not. I am whole, and you are merely a fragment—a half. A veil torn down the center."

"What the hell are you talking about?"

"Think, Ion. My god." He sighed, driving me to my knees. "Or don't. It will be over for you both soon."

Suddenly the stars in my head aligned and ripped open the darkness I'd lost myself in so long ago.

Both of us.

That was why Raiden had baited me here—why he had taken Hawk's blood only in portion, waiting to execute both of us simultaneously; because that was the only way it could be done.

I whirled around, knocking his arm to one side, and lunged for him.

Raiden's reaction to my touch was instinctive and startlingly fast. His free hand clamped down over mine, lighting into my flesh with his—which was now dowsed in flame.

My fingers wound around his wrist and my nails sank into his skin, twisting the blade backward along with his arm.

I threw myself backward and on top of him, turning to nail him to the platform. The dagger was still firmly in his grip, still pointed toward me, and

I had no free hands with which to wrench it from him; I kept it momentarily frozen in its pursuit as I grounded his wrists to the floor.

"You can't kill her without me," I said through gritted teeth, my face just inches from his. "You can't take my blood unless you take hers too—why?"

His expression turned to puzzlement: clearly, he had not expected this.

"You've known who I am for a year," I went on. "You've followed me, you've had hundreds of opportunities to take my life—yet you *haven't*." I forced the heels of my hands down harder into his wrists. "Because you couldn't—because you didn't have *her*."

The flames flickered and died beneath my skin, which felt as though it had been scalded off, and for the first time since I'd met him, a look of unexpected defeat overtook his expression.

"You knew she was the missing piece," I whispered. "And if you killed her…"

"Then you would have died too," he hissed. His eyes locked onto mine. "Just as she will die with you now."

The strength suddenly returned to Raiden's body as if he had been electrified. His right hand wrenched itself out from under mine and the blade came for my face. I watched the violent red flames travel from the palm of his hand to the blade in his grasp.

Raiden was right. I was merely a chapter in a larger story. A story that was about Hawk—I was beginning to understand that she was the one he wanted the most; I'd simply been the arrow pointing her out. Whatever happened, whatever the outcome, I wouldn't be the only one bearing the consequences. It wasn't just my life that I was fighting for. It was hers.

I jerked back and threw myself to the side as Raiden sprang to his feet. He took aim and threw—hard. The blade rotated through the air as if in slow motion, slicing a collision course toward me. Patches of morning light glinted off the burning steel.

Fully focused now, I waited until it was only several inches away. Then, with my right hand I reached up and let my fingers brush the handle. It settled neatly into my palm, and I closed my hand around it, testing its weight.

I closed my eyes and took a long steadying breath. The world seemed to stand still as I drew my arm back, aimed, and threw.

The blade twisted through the air towards him, exceeding the speed at which he was capable of reacting, and glided into Raiden's chest. The color draining from his face, he stumbled and fell hard on his knees, then doubled over and stiffened. I couldn't ignore the sick feeling that instantly bit into my stomach.

I reached him in two long strides and stood over him.

"This isn't the end of my chapter," I said evenly. "It's the end of yours."

Raiden lay motionless, a pool of blood spreading across the wooden surface under him. Then suddenly he moved. His left hand was white and trembling as he lifted it and reached for the knife handle. With a sound like tearing fabric, he pulled the blade from his chest. Almost quizzically, he studied the droplets of blood that clung to it, the crimson stains soaking the front of his T-shirt.

My mind flew back to the day when Hawk had commanded me to drive a knife through her hand. How I had stared, breathless, as her blood had retreated up her forearm and into her hand.

The circumstances couldn't have been more different, yet more the same as I watched Raiden's blood gather itself and recede into his body.

Raiden was carrying Hawk's human half just below his skin—and her abilities in the wrong hands posed a greater threat to me than anything I had ever known. I knew what Hawk was capable of, and not only Hawk, but the others Raiden had absorbed: I wasn't fighting just one individual now, I was up against an army of ghosts—a graveyard of powers buried beneath ordinary human flesh.

"Props, Ion." Raiden was short of breath as he climbed to his feet. "You've shown me a new side of you—you've proven the rumors to be true."

I retreated backwards, and Raiden matched me step for step.

"You *would* kill if the opportunity presented itself—if someone pressed the button hard enough." He used his fingertips to wipe his blood off the blade. "If you were given the opportunity. If I didn't have her blood in my veins—" he jerked his head at Hawk "—I would have died just now, and you would have been responsible for my death, Ion—my blood would have been on your hands."

"I didn't want to kill you," I said, still backing away.

He grasped the dagger handle more tightly. "Didn't you? Haven't you waited for it—thought about it?" He took a long step forward then and whipped the blade against my throat, holding it there. "You think I'm the one responsible for this. You think I'm the one who brought all this about—but it's you. This is your own doing, Ion. Your life has culminated in this."

I felt a draught of air at my back and realized I was nearing the platform's edge. I tried to step forward again and felt a kiss of renewed pressure from the tip of the blade.

"I've never wanted to hurt anyone—I've never consciously hurt anyone," I said, staring him directly in the eyes, searching for some fragment of a human that I could reason with. "Not that day in the parking garage, or now. I—"

Raiden cut me off, seizing me by the wrist in a motion so rapid I scarcely comprehended it. My reaction came just as quickly as I attempted to tear away, but he had my hand in a vice grip. He forced open the palm of my hand and pressed the blade to my skin.

"You've never consciously hurt anyone." He repeated my words slowly, watching as warm red blood rose to pool in my palm. "What about her?"

I froze, my gaze lifting to his. I knew to whom he was referring. He wasn't speaking of Hawk.

"Your last school—that night you completely lost it. That poor girl you almost killed…" He had sliced his own palm now. He switched the knife to a levitating positioned and used his free hand to lift mine, bringing it up over his own open palm. "Was that conscious or subconscious?"

I felt blood trickling from my palm and into his own, where it pooled and mingled. My eyes closed, and I breathed in. Then they flew open and I snatched my palm away from his as if I had been burned. My fingers locked around his wrist and my other hand closed on his throat.

"No," I said, in a voice I didn't recognize. "No, that wasn't conscious."

The knife clattered to the platform, distracting Raiden for a split second. I back-stepped and felt the edge at my heels. My eyes locked onto his for a final split second, and what I saw there was something I knew I wouldn't understand for a very long time.

"But believe me when I say that killing you is."

I leaned forward, hard, throwing him off balance long enough to step around him, reversing our positions so that he was at the edge, not I.

For a split second his dark eyes filled with terror.

I took a breath. I pushed.

His hand became a ghost—an apparition void of substance, swallowed up by the thick sea of white fog. He vanished over the edge.

My focus, dizzy and weakening, found the floor as I collapsed back onto the platform. My breathing was my next awareness, my lungs reaching for air, then the knife lying lifeless beside me, still laced with blood.

"Hawk." A blur of motion, and I was suddenly beside her, kneeling in ashes that had only moments ago been flame. Her form was human now, a girl, her face stripped of color and her body still as stone. I pulled her into my lap, staining myself with her blood. Her left hand and her neck were still bleeding, as mine were, but I knew there were deeper wounds.

"Oh god, stay with me." The words rushed out as I brushed her hair away from her face. "Hawk."

I wove my fingers through hers, letting our wounds bleed into each other, healing hers instantaneously. I tugged my right hand gently out from underneath Hawk's body, staring it as if it wasn't my own. And in a way, it wasn't my own. Nor was the blood beneath my fingernails.

"Icarus." Her chest rose slightly and fell again. Her face was drenched in sweat. "Icarus, I…"

"Yes, Hawk?"

She exhaled softly. "I should have told you."

My arms wanted her closer though I didn't comprehend their actions. If I had, I would have prevented them. I was afraid of what they would do to her.

"Icarus." She spoke again, softer now. "Are you alright?"

I nodded, and she opened her eyes.

"Icarus." She said my name again, though I wanted to stop her. It sounded so pure when she said it, yet it was tearing something inside me apart. Her voice was a god who had searched and found me vagrant in the desert. Her voice was the mark on my forehead.

"Where is he?" she asked.

"He's gone now." A voice came out of my body, trembling. "He's gone."

CHAPTER TWENTY-SEVEN
Hawk

I was submersed in darkness. A voice that sounded like my own, but different somehow, was asking "Where is he?" I had no idea what I was asking. I was dizzy, falling, and my body was like lead in his arms as he pushed me back against the wall.

I heard the music fade as the air rushed out of my lungs and into his mouth as it closed over mine. My hands fought against his chest and his own groped for my waist and pulled. I felt his fingers against my hips as if I had nothing on. The light hadn't quite disappeared yet. I could still see the thin shaft as it cut its way through the darkness around us. I writhed in his grasp and tried fruitlessly to break free, as I always did. But unlike every other time, his hand eventually slipped from my skin and found my own.

Unlike what I remembered, his hand was warm, soft, and his fingers were gentle as they tangled with mine. Warmth and softness—my two innermost longings—and then something beyond that. I wasn't up against the wall anymore, and the hand that had mine in its gentle grasp was bleeding.

I tried to say something, but the words wouldn't form on my lips; they crawled back into hiding. His forehead was warm as it gently made contact with my own. He was touching me, yet somehow I felt no impulse to pull away. I heard him take a breath, and I knew before he had even spoken a word that his voice was different.

"Are you okay?"

I did nothing and then perceived that I was shaking my head.

"Why do I have to come here?" My voice was a tangle and my words scarcely made sense. "Why do I always have to come back?"

His fingers traced along mine and droplets of blood fell delicately across my open palm, spinning across my skin and cascading downward.

"You don't. I've been here before too. I know what it's like."

"No," I said. "No, you don't know what it's like."

My wrist was bent into his and I felt the bass rhythm of his pulse against my veins.

"Maybe not completely," the voice replied again, soft and familiar. I tried to place it, but I could not. "But I know that you don't have to come back."

I shook my head. "I don't know how to escape it."

The feeling of his fingers began suddenly to fade.

"Wake up."

My fingers contracted around his, or tried to, but found only thin, cold air.

"I can't…"

I couldn't discern whether the voice had been my own or his, or which belonged to whom, or if they were even different. I'd felt his hands, his body, his presence; these were the things that led me to believe that there was someone in that darkness with me.

"Wake up, Hawk."

And I repeated, more softly, that I couldn't. Again and again, I wrestled with this voice. I told it that I couldn't. I couldn't.

Then suddenly the hands were again changed. They'd been soft and warm and between my fingers, and now I became aware that it was only one hand. It was still warm, but in a different way, and clamped lightly down on my shoulder, with a thumb touching my collarbone. All at once the darkness was now a shade of blood orange, like light pressing passionately up against my eyelids and tugging at my lashes.

"Hawk."

This time the voice was distinct. The hand became familiar again as it shook me gently. I inhaled deeper, stretching my shoulders.

My eyelids were heavy as they lifted to let in the secondhand hues of light and a world of unfocused shapes. I exhaled and quickly shut them again.

"How do you feel?"

I lifted a hand heavily out from under the sheets and ran my forefinger and thumb over my eyelids in lethargic circles, dampening my lips. "I feel like I'm forgetting everything."

"Mm." Fin's weight shifted slightly on the mattress where he was seated. "What about your body?"

An unhappy laugh pushed softly past my lips. "What about it?"

I closed my eyes. I didn't want to open them again, not for a while. I wanted to live in that moment of imagining the blurry apparitions that the room and Fin had been. That place in between unconsciousness and the light of dawn, where everything exists but nothing is real yet. I knew what would happen when I opened my eyes again, and I knew the look I would find in his eyes.

"I'm in the dormitories, aren't I?"

"How did you know?"

"I can feel the movement of the wind beneath us."

"Icarus brought you here," Fin said.

He was looking down at his hands, which were folded together over his knees. As my vision cleared, his features came in clearer and I realized that we were in the dorm pod that belonged to him, Mitsue and Icarus. Aside from us the place was empty.

"How long have I been here?"

"About two days," he replied. "Raiden drained a great deal of your power."

"Two days?" I repeated, shocked. "My god, he must have…"

Fin turned so that he was facing me. "Do you want me to fill you in now, or…?"

"Now," I said, pushing myself up into a seated position. "But tell me something first—"

Fin lifted his hands slightly. "Let's just take it slow, alright? You're still weak, Hawk."

"From the sound of it, I've spent far too long in bed. I need you to tell me everything you know, but first… where is Icarus?"

Fin's lips parted slightly as he stared at me. "He's been on trial, Hawk."

"Already?"

"The first session was held the same afternoon that the incident occurred; the council didn't see a point in postponing it," he said, seeming to consider his words for my sake. "Since Icarus himself pleaded guilty."

My heart sank to the pit of my stomach. "He *pleaded guilty*?"

"He confessed to having pushed Raiden from the platform—intentionally."

"But it wasn't intentional." I swallowed back the sudden tightness in my throat. "Icarus was defending me, Fin. I was the one Raiden wanted… I don't know how he figured out who I was, but he did. He attacked me and drew enough of my blood that I could no longer shift into human form. Icarus was the only one close enough to hear when it all happened."

"So he fought for you?" Fin looked confused.

"Raiden was using me to bait him there—he needed Icarus too in order for his plan to work, and I played directly into his hands."

"What do you mean 'baiting him'? Why would Raiden want both of you?"

The blood, the hands, the dream. It all flooded back to me in a blurry, sweeping motion. Everything that had taken place on the platform, Icarus's voice, his arms around me. It was like a wave crashing up against my consciousness.

I swallowed, feeling suddenly sick. Feeling suddenly as though my messy, confused stars had finally aligned. Everything clicked into place. My eyes locked into Fin's, which still stared into mine as if he was looking for a missing piece. "Why, indeed."

"I don't follow."

"It doesn't matter," I said, brushing back the sheets. "Not yet. When are they holding the final session?"

"Tonight," he replied. "If you feel up to it. You're the only witness, Hawk."

I froze, my legs half over the side of the mattress. "So you're saying they're waiting for *me* to give an account of what happened?"

He nodded. "I'm afraid so, yes. I was trying to break it to you gradually–"

"*Gradually?*"

"You know I have a difficult time with words." He sighed. "With things like this."

"So what's going to happen?" I rose slowly, steadying myself. "I'll be interrogated and prodded until I say something that confirms Icarus's ineptitude?"

"We're not talking about ineptitude."

"What, then?"

"Hawk, he *killed* someone."

"He *defended* me, Fin."

He stared at me. "And are you saying there was no other way for him to do that without murdering Raiden?"

I opened my mouth to reply, then closed it again, turning away from him.

"I'm not taking sides, Hawk," he went on as I started across the room. "God knows I would have fought for you. But I wouldn't have killed someone."

I swallowed down a bitter taste in my mouth. "You still haven't answered my question. What will happen at the session this evening?"

"Since you're recovered enough, you'll be required to give an account of everything you witnessed on the gathering platform three days ago."

"And what if I refuse?"

A pause.

"Then the council will be forced to make a decision based on unclear evidence."

"Which is Icarus's word alone?"

"He pleaded guilty, Hawk."

I stood in front of the small circular window. Beyond it was a dull purple dawn, one that matched so many others I had seen, with nothing to make it stand out from the rest. It was a dim, complacent shade—it was calm, and everything inside me wasn't. And for that contrast, I hated it.

"I don't care what he pleaded." I spoke more to the glass than to him. "I know what happened."

"Then I heartily suggest you state your case for his sake, if not for your own," Fin said, his tone full of a resolve that only further unsettled me. "You cannot expect his trial to be a fair one if you're withholding information."

I closed my eyes. "What will happen if he's proven guilty?"

I heard Fin pull in a breath. "With transportation from the Dimension prohibited for the time being, I can only tell you for certain that they won't exile him. It won't even be an option."

"Then they'll erase his memory."

There were a few seconds of quiet contemplation. "Perhaps."

I glanced over my shoulder. "You know something I don't, Fin. You can't hide that fact from me—I can hear it in your voice."

He stared at me for a moment as if he had no idea how to respond. "I cannot tell you things that I do not know for certain."

"But you can tell me whatever it is you suspect."

He pressed his fist to his forehead, blowing out a frustrated sigh. "Mitsue is on the council, Hawk. I cannot betray his trust."

"Mitsue?" I repeated. "Mitsue, Raiden's former teacher?"

He nodded, and I spat out a disgusted laugh.

"No conflict of interest there." I flipped back to the window, to the view I was growing to resent even more. "And you hold his trust in higher esteem than our friendship."

"That has nothing to do with it."

"It has everything to do with it!" My voice cracked as it rose, as I whirled around to face him again. "Don't you understand what any of this means to me, Fin? You sat across from me in a pub not long ago and told me that you thought Icarus could be the one—"

"I didn't know—"

"Well, he *is*!"

I practically shouted the words, my voice hot not with passion but with something like hatred. Not hate for their meaning, but for the fact that I was speaking them too late.

"He is the one…" My voice broke off. "The other half of my soul. The half that is a fighter, a murderer, a savior—the half into which my own scars extend. The wild, stupid, flawed, arrogant but teachable half. The half that *would* kill to fulfill the wishes of the other who has merely desired to."

Fin said nothing.

"Yes, Fin," I continued, my voice stronger now. "I watched him lose it, I watched him attack Raiden, I saw every detail. I saw Raiden's body as the ravine swallowed it—I saw all of it. And I saw the blood in Icarus's hand when he pressed it to mine and healed my wounds, although he is not even capable of mending his own."

"So you pardon his behavior because he healed you?"

I pressed my fingertips to my forehead. "What can I say that will make you understand?"

"Hawk, please believe me, it's not that I don't understand—it's not that I don't *want* to understand, it's that…" He looked at the floor.

"That what?"

"That I cannot *believe* this is what Sensei has planned for you…" He trailed off. "For us. I don't know Icarus, not really. I thought he would be different. I thought that perhaps he would be—"

"Perfect?" I cut him off, my hands falling away from my face. "Without blemish or black marks? Because if you imagine me to be even *remotely* free of those vices merely because I am one of the chosen, you do not truly know me, Fin." I took a few steps closer. He held my gaze.

"If I am the standard of 'perfection' against which you compare Icarus," I went on, "then indeed you have never really known me at all, Fin. You have no idea who I truly am, and if you did, you wouldn't love me. You would despise me about as much as I despise myself each time I look in the mirror merely to see two voids staring back into my eyes."

"Hawk—"

"No, Fin!" I cut him off, my voice rising again. "I can't bear the burden of your doubts right now—I don't want to hear all the reasons why you think you were wrong when I know now… I know for sure."

"Hawk, you have no proof," he said. He lifted a hand to touch my shoulder. "Please don't tell me you're going to go into this blind—that you're going to risk so much on someone who could be your greatest mistake."

"Fin, if only you knew how deeply I envied you." My voice was barely a whisper. "The violence of your affection for others—your declarations of the innermost workings of your heart, your grief, and the pain you felt in ripping yourself forever from your world's womb, from the arms of your own flesh and blood." I reached up and placed my hand gently over his, grasping it, lifting it. "I hold your hand in my own and feel nothing more than skin on skin," I said quietly. "A hand, yours. Fingers and muscle and flesh, and nothing more."

He made no response. I lifted my gaze from his hand and met his green eyes.

"If only you knew how much I have longed to feel something, Fin," I told him, letting my fingers intertwine with his. "If only you knew what it was like to exist merely as the absence of someone who used to be."

For a long moment, Fin's eyes pressed deeper into mine, as if searching for a false bottom under which he might find what he was looking for. Then finally, after a length of time I couldn't account for, he drew in a deeper breath. "And you feel something with Icarus."

The words were heavy, and I wanted to push them away, but instead I nodded.

I felt Fin's fingers loosen slightly in my grasp, as if the strength within them had withdrawn. He closed his eyes, and when he opened them again, the look that had been in them before was gone—replaced by something wilder that I could not describe.

"Then fight for him," he said, taking his hand away from my own and reaching up to brush a strand of hair away from my face. "Fight for him as you would fight for your own life—because god knows, that is exactly what you'll be doing." He stepped back. "Fight for him as I would for you."

"Fin—"

He shook his head. "You owe me no explanation, Hawk. It's okay."

That was it. Those quiet words, and then he was gone.

For a long moment, I stood there, staring at the thin sheet of canvas as it wavered slightly in the kisses of the morning air. The ghosts of everything we'd just said twisted and chanted around me.

A fresh change of clothes had been laid out for me at the foot of the bed. Resting on top was a folded sheet of parchment with my name scrawled across the front in thick ink. Picking it up, I unfolded it and found a set of instructions in regards to my summons and what was expected of me. Though nothing about it came as a surprise, my chest felt heavy.

On one of the desks at the far end of the room, there was a basin of water set in a stone bowl. The cold water was precisely what my foggy head needed. I let down my hair and washed it. As the torrents of water trickled over my scalp and down the back of my neck, the events that had led to Raiden's death came rushing back to me in full detail. The fight between him and Icarus— every step, every instant of brutal contact. The look that had risen like black water from behind Icarus's eyes, overtaking him in the second before he'd grasped Raiden by the throat and dragged him to the edge of the abyss. Even from where I'd been trapped, I'd witnessed it as clearly and intensely as if my own wild hands had carried out the actions themselves.

I couldn't help but wonder if it was wrong that, in seeing him vanish, I'd felt as though I'd seen not a death but my own life redeemed. Raiden had not died: I had lived. I had lived because Icarus had lived.

How would I tell them? How would they possibly understand?

I spent the day trying to answer those two questions, but in the end found myself still empty-handed.

A purple sunset was ripening on the horizon when Fin returned to escort me to the session. The platform was full almost to overflowing when we arrived.

"I've never seen it so crowded for something like this," I said to Fin as we jostled our way to the front.

"No one has ever murdered anyone here before."

"Raiden killed before."

Fin shot me a glance as we made our way along the left railing. "In other worlds and other times."

That was the extent of it—that this was simply a fresher wound? To me, this seemed juvenile and unfair. Were we all merely children who were more affected by a tragedy if it took place in our own backyard and involved individuals we knew? I remembered my conversations with Sensei, the endless discussions we'd had about how we governed ourselves as a student body, how fervently I'd rallied for our admittedly imperfect system. I felt my faith slipping further with each footstep as I followed Fin and took my place behind the black brushstroke that had been drawn alongside the long *chabudai* at which the seven-person council was assembled.

Where was Sensei in all of this chaos? Where had he been through my injury and days of unconsciousness? If ever I needed him, this was the time; I needed him desperately.

Mitsue was seated with the council; I glanced at him and he glanced away almost just as quickly.

Beside me stood Mala.

"What's happened so far?" I asked her, raising my voice only as much as I needed to in order for her to hear me over the chaos. "Why isn't he here yet?"

Mala stared straight ahead. "Who?"

"Icarus."

"Oh, I don't know, Hawk. He asked to be excused briefly."

"So they're waiting to resume?"

"Yes," she said. I could see now how pale she was. "They gave him a few minutes."

"Did they finish with you?" I asked, casting a quick side glance in the direction of the table to see if our conversation had been noted. It hadn't.

Mala nodded slowly, seeming elsewhere.

"And…?"

"I can't really talk about it."

I felt something in my chest tighten. "Why? What happened?"

"They push so hard." She stared at the ceiling, blinking back tears. "They ask so many questions, I hardly knew what I was saying after a while. I don't even understand why I've been asked here, Hawk. Why are they making me do this?"

I placed a hand on her shoulder. "You went to school with him, Mala— you dated him. They think you may be a possible source of information."

"But I dated Raiden too," she protested. "I went out with both of them. And now they're both dead."

A chill traveled down the length of my spine.

"Mala." I lowered my voice. "Icarus isn't dead."

A sudden uproar rose now from the sea of students. Icarus had returned. His face was bruised, and his forearms were scarred with burns. Tied at the wrists. Mala stared at him, wide-eyed, and then, composing herself once more, leaned closer.

"But he will be," she said softly, the tears gathering in her eyes glimmered in the firelight. "He will be, Hawk."

I wanted to object, but the words died in my throat.

Mitsue rose, silhouetted against the flames at the platform's edge, to call for attention.

"Silence, please," he said. "Be seated, everyone." He turned and gestured for me to step up. "Come forward, Hawk."

I stole a glance at Icarus as the whispers died around me. His eyes were like ice, cold and empty, and I realized he'd been staring at me for some time.

I swallowed and felt my lips part silently in the shape of his name. He looked away.

"Your attendance tonight is necessary and appreciated, Hawk," said one of the older male students at the table, whose face I couldn't easily identify in the dim lighting. "I trust you are recovering. Thank you for making the effort."

This was pure formality, so I made no response. I folded my hands behind my back and I waited.

Azalea, one of the female students on the council, spoke now. "Since you are the only remaining witness to Raiden's death, we ask that you answer each of the following questions with simply a yes or no. Do you have any objections to this?"

"I do."

"Would you please state your objections?"

I took a deep breath. "Depending on the council's questions for me, I feel that certain clarifications may be required in order to properly communicate the facts."

Whispers erupted vaguely behind me. Mitsue gestured with his hand and an instant later they faded.

"If what you choose to communicate is indeed simply fact, Hawk, then elaboration will not be necessary." His voice was sharp, as if daring me to make a comeback. "Would it?"

I bit my tongue and said nothing.

"No other objections, then?"

I shook my head, trying to ignore the sick feeling in the pit of my stomach.

"Do we have your word that, according to the dictates of the code, any and all information you provide us with will be strictly factual?"

"It will."

"Very well." Azalea consulted her papers and cleared her throat. "You were present on the gathering platform the morning of Raiden's death?"

"Yes."

"And you will confirm that this location was the place of Raiden's death and that you were present at the exact time of his demise?"

"Yes." I glanced again at Icarus.

"Will you confirm that Icarus was on the platform also, at the time of Raiden's demise?"

"Yes, he was."

Mitsue spoke next. "And was Icarus indeed responsible for Raiden's death?"

I stole a glance at Icarus; he was staring back at me now. *Tell them*, his eyes seemed to say.

I can't.

I took a breath. "I was attacked. Raiden attacked me—"

"We have already been made aware of that, Hawk. Thank you," Mitsue cut in curtly. "Had Raiden survived the incident three dawns ago, he would be on trial for this transgression. However, the fact remains that my student is dead. Therefore, we must require that this session pertain solely to Icarus."

Tell them. It's okay.

Why are you giving up? Why are you giving up when you know that I need you?

The feeling inside me was so strong—he had to be feeling it too. Or were those illuminated, sacred words still nothing more to him than a puzzle that he still didn't comprehend?

"Hawk." Mitsue's voice drew me out of my thoughts.

"I can assure the council that Icarus did nothing beyond acting to protect me—"

"Yes or no, *please*."

I closed my eyes to hide from the ones that were still reaching into mine. A war was raging in my chest. "Yes."

Blue. It collided with my vision as soon as I allowed the darkness of my eyelids to part again. Blue stained by the fire and the fear he tried to conceal.

The platform exploded. I couldn't tell whether it was from the heightened volume of everything, or if it was merely an effect of my injury, but the violence in the voices around me became muted by a soft ringing that seemed to bite at my ears from the inside. Time progression seemed to lag as I watched chaos taking hold around me. Even in the dimness of the sparse firelight, I could still make out the outlines of bodies gripped in the throes of hatred, and eyes that glistened not with a desire to understand, but a desire to believe whatever flowed smoothest around the rocks.

How far we have come.

Mitsue ordered silence, and after a moment a hush fell across the platform.

Another student began questioning me now. "You've stated that Icarus's assault on Raiden was directly in your defense. Was Raiden touching you physically at the time of the assault?"

I hesitated, then shook my head. "No."

"He was physically touching Icarus, then?"

"Yes," I said heavily.

"But you said that Raiden followed you to the gathering platform, correct?" Mitsue spoke again.

"Yes."

"That noted, I will agree that it fits within our understanding of Raiden's character, that he should desire to obtain the identity of a slider as advanced as yourself, Hawk." He rose from his chair and began pacing. "Of course, the findings from our interrogations have not been cleared for release, but without violating any restrictions, I can also add that for Raiden to follow and attack another slider would not disrupt the pattern we've seen in his behavioral tendencies."

I felt something inside me falter at this new piece of information, though I couldn't immediately identify why and I was given no time to ponder.

"That said, would you say that he was merely utilizing your student in order to further injure you?"

"No," I said.

Mitsue gestured for me to expound.

A hurricane was raging inside me: things were beginning to fall into place now. I'd promised Sensei that I would keep my identity a secret, but now I realized that this might be the only thing that could save Icarus.

"Raiden wanted me… that's true," I said, my voice coming out softer than I expected it to. "Raiden had kept track of me—I don't know for how long, and I don't know how he discovered me. But he wanted Icarus too. He suspected that Icarus was… he baited me with Icarus in order to…"

I hesitated and looked at Icarus again. His eyes were wider now, staring into mine. He shook his head almost imperceptibly.

Don't.

I pulled my gaze away. "In order to see if he was accurate in his assumptions about my identity," I finished. "When he realized that they were, he then used me to lure Icarus back to the gathering platform in order to fulfill what the prophecy required."

I could have heard a pin drop.

Mitsue turned fully to look at me, seeming caught off guard. "What are you implying, Hawk?"

I locked eyes with Icarus again. "I think you know."

The whispers resumed. Mitsue took a few steps closer and stepped between me and Icarus.

I slowly lifted my gaze to meet his. "Or is it too hard for your heart to believe anymore?" I said. "Have our own conventions, our own rules and regulations, stripped us bare of what faith we had left in who we were?"

A hush fell over the platform again.

"Have we so long guarded ourselves, so long sought to do what is right, that we've forgotten what actually *is* right?" I felt almost as though I was trying to convince myself, too, cynic that I was. "Have we so deeply buried ourselves in our own interpretations of the prophecy that we're blind to the manifestations of it around us?"

Mitsue stared at me coldly. "You refer to yourself?"

"Yes," I replied. "To myself, to Icarus, to every single one of us."

His lips parted slightly as if to say something, and then he closed them again.

"Has it never occurred to you that we've been gathered—culminated— as much as we ever will be?" I turned now to face the rest of the students, and my voice rose. "Or have we become so closely acquainted with our purpose that we've forgotten what it even means?"

Mitsue shook his head, taking a step back. "No. No, I won't allow you to derail the intentions of this gathering—"

"And what if the intentions of this gathering should be wrong?" I stepped forward, over the line on the floor. "What then? What if we've been wrong about what this all means—what then? Are we to simply keep marching when destruction is the only possible end? We're the ones creating it—that ever-looming 'darkness' that lies in the worlds that 'are to come'—we are, in fact, that darkness! It's us."

"Your illness has clouded your judgment, Hawk."

"I have no illness!" I shouted. "I have no illness other than the sickness my half-soul has had to endure in its chains for the past century. No, my judgment has not been clouded."

"You expect us to believe that you are the Sunrise—*you?*" He spat the words out. "The only teacher among the protectors whose one and *only* initiate into the Dimension not only upset our entire system and tore us away from our own worlds, but also went on to violently murder another student?"

His words echoed in the air around us. He turned to face the council, though speaking to everyone. "I could cite the prophecy to support my point. I could simply bring one thousand other practical reasons why this is false to the attention of the gathering, but I feel we've digressed quite enough as it is, so I'll be brief."

Mitsue shot me a glance. "If this were true—if we were standing now in the presence of our two saviors—our patriarchs since the beginning of time, the two 'bookends of the universe,' if you will—do you not think that Sensei would have deemed this trial worthy of his presence and input?"

My heart skipped a beat at the mention of his name, then sank in my chest.

"Don't you think he would be here to defend your case and Icarus's, Hawk?"

My hands, which had been subconsciously contracted into fists, slowly fell open.

"Do you actually attempt to justify Icarus's actions on the basis that he was a soul attempting to deliver his other half?"

I made no response.

"Very well," he replied. "Since you've chosen not to answer, perhaps Icarus can fill in for you. Let this be the final word on the subject." He turned to Icarus now. "Icarus, did you attack and murder Raiden solely in defense of Hawk, because you believe her to be the Sunrise?"

My eyes begged him to say yes—to say yes even if it wasn't true for him. *Say yes.*

· The light from the flames played across his skin, shadowing the bruises and the outline of his collarbone. He remained silent for so long I began to doubt whether he would answer at all.

Then his eyes lifted to mine and slowly he shook his head. "I killed Raiden because I wanted to." His voice was like velvet wrapped in razor wire. "I killed him because I hated him."

The platform erupted in a flurry of shouts.

In the chaos that followed, I heard nothing except the slowing beat of my own heart and the apologies that his eyes made.

"It has been predetermined by the student body and this council"— Azalea's voice rose in a tone of finality—"in light of the fact that we no longer possess the capacity to exile, that the guilty be inflicted with the treatment bestowed upon the victim in order that peace may be maintained."

Hawk, I'm sorry. I'm so sorry.

I closed my eyes.

"Icarus, by your word and by the evidence that has been brought against you, Raiden's blood is found on your hands. With the arrival of the coming dawn, you will be executed in like manner."

I opened my eyes again and found Icarus staring at me. His lips moved silently in the shape of my name.

I turned away.

"This session has concluded."

CHAPTER TWENTY-EIGHT
Hawk

"Hawk."

It was the third time Fin had spoken my name. The earlier storm between us had melted away to nothing in the fallout of the verdict. The things we'd said felt old and far off. The sun had set, painting the sky a shade of red that embodied everything I was feeling below the skin. We were on the rope bridge behind the dormitory, wrapped in the shadows from the cliff side.

"Hawk, what are you going to do? They can't kill him. If he dies—"

"I'll die?" I cut him off. "I'll die because the Sunrise cannot exist without the Sunset—a half-soul cannot survive without its missing piece? I'm afraid you weren't listening, Fin. How could someone as 'flawed' as I am be the Sunrise? Someone who 'initiated a traitor'—a murderer. God, what on earth was I thinking!"

"If you expect me to pity you, Hawk, because no one believed a word you said, I'm afraid I'll have to disappoint you," he said evenly. "You can't afford to waste time feeling sorry for yourself right now."

"I don't know what to do, Fin! Okay? I have no idea anymore." I covered my face with shaking hands. "I hate him."

"Icarus? Why?"

"Because he knows now," I said, my voice coming out between my fingers. "I saw it in his face that morning—in his eyes. He doesn't understand it completely, but he knows that we're both

part of it, somehow… and he gave up anyway."

"And now you're both going to pay the consequences." Fin cursed and leaned heavily on the railing. "You said that Raiden was following you—that he knew who you were." He paused. "How did he find out about you?"

"I don't know, Fin."

A quietness settled between us.

"There's something very strange about that."

"Have I fought so long merely to die because someone else refuses to pick up their sword?" I mused quietly. "Was this really what it was all leading up to? A culmination that would eat its patriarchs alive?"

"You tell me. You're the one Sensei wrote it about."

I whipped around to face him now. "Then where is he? I needed him at the trial, Fin—I need him now! And he's keeping himself as far away from me as he can."

Fin was anything but sympathetic. He turned and looked me squarely in the eyes. "You don't know why he's not here, Hawk?" he asked. "I can tell you why."

My mouth went dry. I waited.

"He's not here because he believes in *you*," he said, with emphasis that cut. "He believes that you can do this without him holding your hand, telling you what to do—without a set of regulations to guide you. He believes in who you were before all of that—in who you were when it was just the two of you and no one else… before the code, before anyone else was initiated. You were the *first*—you *are* the Sunrise, you *are* the chosen one."

He paused, waiting to see if I would respond. When I didn't, he went on.

"And I suggest that you start acting like that is indeed the case." He took a few steps closer, pausing in front of me. "Because you don't have a lot of time to work with. The sun's going to be up soon."

I closed my eyes, swallowing back a lump in my throat. "I need to talk to Icarus, Fin. I don't know what I need to do, but I know that I… I'm so angry with him right now."

"Then tell him."

"They gave him Raiden's dorm," I said. "It's guarded. I doubt they would make an exception, even for me."

Fin shrugged. "Then I'll distract them."

"How?"

"Don't worry about it," he said. "Just wait until the sun has peaked enough to blot out the light of the Chief Star, then go to him. I'll have diverted the sentry by then, and I'll unlock the door for you. Are you strong enough to manage shifting?"

"Yes, but—"

"But nothing. Just be ready."

His eyes faltered on mine for a split second before he turned and began to walk away.

"Fin." His name tumbled out of my mouth abruptly.

He stopped and looked at me, his eyes questioning.

"Do you believe in him, Fin?" I asked quietly.

Whether he had expected the question or not, I couldn't tell. His expression kept it hidden.

"*You* believe in him," he replied finally. "And I believe in you."

Back in my room, I stopped quietly in front of the window. My hands began going through the motions of lighting the torch mounted to the wall. I struck a match, then stopped myself. The hiss from the flame as it ignited kissed my sense of hearing. My eyes lingered there a moment, then shifted to the glass. To the stained atmosphere beyond it, the stars.

I have to be able to see them.

I felt the heat as the fire fed its way down the match toward my finger and thumb. I pulled in a breath and let it out. The flame vanished.

Minutes felt like hours. I paced the length of the room; my fingers blazed trails through the length of my hair. The noise from the platform, which had been faintly audible from the dorm upon my return, had faded to nothing. A soft wind took shape and whispered between the folds of the canvas. The Chief Star held me in its gaze, watching me.

Finally, dawn began to break, and the stars faded to invisibility against the lavender gray of the sky. My heartbeat stumbled—caught itself.

I slipped outside again and made my way to the bridge. I hoisted myself up onto the railing. My feet dangled over the absence of anything below me. Far off, I could see the soft light that still burned in Sensei's apartment. I swallowed a bitter taste.

I gazed along the agglomerations of winding rope pathways and found the outermost dorm, bathed in the washed-out hues of pre-dawn. Two torches burned at either side of the heavy oak door, but the flicker of the flames was the only movement. The guard was gone. Far below me I could see vague movements on the gathering platform, where preparations were under way for the execution.

I shifted, dropping silently into the air and falling towards the dorm. My talons found the threshold with a muted clatter, and I shifted to human form once more.

Fin had been good to his word: the door was unlocked. Quietly turning the handle, I slipped into the darkness that yawned incrementally open before me.

A striped canvas mattress lay in a simple frame at the far end of the room. Icarus was seated on the edge opposite, his bare back to me. I saw the vague outlines of his vertebrae shadowed in the dull purple light as it filtered in.

I closed the door softly behind me, and he turned slightly.

For a moment a silence hung between us. When he finally spoke, it was a barely above a whisper.

"I'm so sorry, Hawk."

"You're not," I said quietly. "Don't say something you don't mean."

"What could I have done?"

"Lied," I said. I saw him breathe a little deeper. "And I don't believe it *would* have been a lie for you. I don't believe that you're still completely in the dark—I know you better than that."

One of his hands lifted and went back into his dark hair, gripping. "You know me about as much as I truly know you, Hawk—very little."

"Apparently so," I conceded. "Because if you had any idea who I am— who you are—you would never have made that confession."

"And if you truly knew *me* at all, you would have some level of trust in me." I watched as he rose, but scarcely noticed the gap between us narrowing with his steps. "You have no idea how much I *suffered* saying those words— you have no idea how much I regret all of this."

A bitter tone returned to my lips. "Icarus, what have you ever done to earn my trust? You've done nothing but bring out a greater

darkness in me than I ever thought possible."

I saw the muscles in his jaw tighten. "Oh, and that's my fault—your darkness?"

"It is," I replied sharply, stepping away from the door now. "Because you *are* my darkness, Icarus. The larger part of it, though it's a fact I've had to force myself to accept. Do you think I *wanted* to believe that your wounds are capable of bleeding me out, or that your past haunts my own?"

The look in his eyes turned cold. "My past haunts me more, I promise you."

"So that's why you're doing this?" I whispered harshly. "You're throwing our lives away because you can't let go of who you were."

He shook his head, swallowing. There was less than a foot between us, though I scarcely processed this.

"No," he replied, lowering his voice to match my own. "I'm doing this because I still *am* that person, Hawk. I am *still* the same person that I was, in a different place with a different name—and I still have no idea who that is or how to control that person…" He trailed off and looked into my eyes with his goldmines, which had given up trying to conceal the fear now; they were wild with it.

"I hate that person, Hawk."

I dug my nails into my palms. "I hate him too," I said softly. "But I need him."

"You're not listening—"

Before I could comprehend my own actions, I slapped him—hard. The impact threw his head to the side.

"I *am* listening," I said icily. "You know you're the Sunset. You know you're the chosen one—the one I've been searching for *all this time*, and you gave up—you gave up on everything I've been fighting for. Didn't you listen when Raiden told you that I would die when he killed you? Didn't it ever occur to you that he needed to execute us together because he *couldn't* take our lives separately—because our lives, yours and mine, are halves of one whole?"

His gaze slowly returned to mine, one hand pressed to his cheek. "You actually think I would take your life, Hawk?" His voice was barely a whisper. "Do you think I hold you in such low regard that I didn't consider this? Do you think so little of me?"

I tilted my head slightly, looking up at him. "I can't say that I think of you at all, Icarus. Only the fact that I will die with you today at dawn."

He shook his head. "I'm not taking your life."

"It's too late. There's nothing—"

"You're taking mine."

The rest of my sentence froze in my throat.

"I know I'm the chosen—the other half of your soul," he said. "And I have no idea how or why or *what that even means*." He stopped, searching for words. "But what I felt on the platform during the fight… when I pushed him… Something fell into place. It's like a fog I can't seem to see through, yet I know what's hidden inside it. And I know that something is wrong—"

"What do you mean?"

He opened his mouth to speak, hesitated, and then closed it again. Though it was scarcely audible, he sighed, and his forehead made light contact with mine. I felt a strange sensation pass over my heart, quickening its pace.

"Hawk, I didn't kill Raiden for you. I killed him because I *did* hate him." His voice shook slightly. "If I stayed, I would tarnish *everything* you've worked for, everything you've fought for, Hawk. I would be a black mark to you, not an asset."

"But that isn't true."

"It is." He pulled away. "You were born for this. And perhaps I was too, in another life, in another place. But the test is up now, and when it comes down to it, they need you—not me."

"They need *both* of us. Haven't you read the prophecy? Haven't you understood the meaning of any of it?"

"And they *will* have both of us." He grasped my arms. "Because I'll be in you."

It took a few seconds for his words to sink in. I froze. "What are you talking about?"

"I think you know." He replied softly. "You're the one who taught me."

My mind immediately flashed back to that day in my apartment; the day we had cut our hands to temporarily entangle so that Icarus could shift. I started to back away slightly, shaking my head—not because I didn't understand, but because I did. A sick feeling began to settle into the pit of my stomach.

Icarus wasn't talking about entangling temporarily.

"Hawk, if anyone else took my life they would kill us both," he explained quickly, before I could object. "But you—you would *save* yourself and everything we have fought for! You would assume my identity; my blood would flow in your veins—"

"No, Icarus—"

"—And you could *do this*." He persisted. "You could save *everyone*."

"*No*."

"Hawk, it's the only way you're going to survive this—"

"I said no!" I bit down on my lip, suddenly aware of my voice's volume. I pressed the heel of my hand to my forehead. "*No*, Icarus."

For a long moment neither of us said a word. I strained to hear sounds beyond the door, but there were none.

"I confessed at the trial because I had to, Hawk. I deserve to reap the death I have sown." He stared at the floor. "I knew I could spare you by surrendering myself to you. You're deserving of life, because that's all you've ever given to the world. I've never given that to anyone." He paused for a breath though it only rushed back out. "I'm asking that you allow me to give that to you now."

"And I've already given you my answer."

"Hawk, I can't let you die. Not when you can save them." His eyes sought mine.

I shook my head, avoiding his gaze. "*We* could have."

"Hawk—" He stepped suddenly closer again.

"You don't understand, Icarus." My hands were shaking. "I can't..."

A pause. His hand on my arm; warm skin.

"Yes, you can," he replied, his words barely audible. "You're the only one who can take my life without extinguishing your own—because I belong to you."

"I know." My gaze lifted to his. "But I can't."

His eyes suddenly softened. His hand fell away from my arm.

And suddenly it made sense. How I'd felt pain with each of his injuries, how apparitions of Icarus had invaded my dreams, how he'd known that I'd been raped without Sensei having told him. At any other time, in any other place, this revelation would have intoxicated my soul, filled me with ecstasy. But now, here, it was like bitter poison.

Because now there was an unsurpassable and ever-rising wall between us, one that wasn't solely of his own creation. We'd built it together. Working side by side, we'd constructed our own demise like a star reducing itself to a supernova. Now he was offering to tear open a wormhole large enough for only my body to pass through—and I was turning him down. Because I couldn't leave him there.

"You were right," I said at last. "I didn't know you. I don't… I don't know you."

"Hawk." The warmth of his hand went to my face. First just one, and then both. "Please…"

I felt the pressure of his fingertips, the stinging heat of tears as they pressed past my eyelashes and rolled gently down my cheeks.

"It isn't how I thought it would be." I forced my voice to hold steady. "It isn't how I thought it would end… but this is how it will end, Icarus. This is what we trained for. This is where we jump."

He softly brushed my hair back with his fingertips. "I'm so afraid, Hawk."

I opened my eyes again. "I am too."

Icarus's lips moved slightly as if he was searching for words. He let his forehead come gently against mine again, and I was suddenly aware of his breath and the warmth of his skin. One of his hands trailed slightly to rest against the curve of my neck. He neither pulled me closer nor himself nearer; he merely drew the space between us closer together until it was no longer there.

At first, his lips merely touched mine, making contact that was so light it could almost have passed for no contact at all; it was like that moment that water touches the skin, when one almost becomes the other. I felt his next breath as if it were my own.

My heart was racing, abandoning me for elsewhere and taunting me to follow—to search the graveyard inside my chest for a sign of life, for a fragment of something that was still alive, still breathing.

The tension left my body under the soft pressure of his hands, and I felt the space between our bodies melt. A split second inserted itself there and stretched. I felt his collarbone beneath my fingertips, his lips moving over my own, his hand settling gently in the small of my back.

A space eventually pressed itself between us, leaving us both breathless.

"I had a nightmare about a place like this," he said quietly. "About a dark place where the light is present but never reachable."

Something inside me skipped a beat.

"Have you had it more than once?" I asked, though I already knew the answer. "Do you feel as though it keeps coming back—that you can't get away from it?"

Everything outside was beginning to awaken. I could hear it on the wind.

"How did you know?" Our foreheads were still touching. His voice felt like my own.

"I didn't," I said. "It was just a guess."

I left Icarus before anyone returned. I didn't want to be discovered there with him; I'd already brought enough shame down on my own head at the trial. I already had enough fallout to deal with—my only dark consolation was that I wouldn't have to endure it for long.

Sessions had been canceled for the day, leaving the training platform abandoned and echoing. I'd escaped to my apartment and everyone else was either in the dormitory or making their way down to the gathering platform for the execution.

My execution.

I sat in the silence that bathed my apartment, losing myself in my thoughts. After a while I sensed a presence on the other side of the wall that I was seated up against. I heard the familiar sounds of his footsteps through the open window.

"I needed you. I needed you so much and you weren't there. If you had been there, none of this would be happening… everything would be different, Sensei." I leaned my head back against the wall. "I trusted you… I trusted you with everything that I was and you never came. You lied to me."

A silence inserted itself where his reply should have been.

I pressed my eyelids together against a flood of hot, bitter tears.

"Why have you abandoned me?" I whispered, knowing he would hear regardless. "Why didn't you come? When you could have saved me."

"I have saved you, Hawk."

"From what? From a death in the past so that I could die a slower, more agonizing one in the future?" My voice rose and echoed in the emptiness of my apartment. "You saved me from nothing, Sensei—I wish I had died *there*. Then none of this would have happened."

"It has happened because you have chosen it."

"I have *not* chosen it!" My voice cracked. "I haven't chosen it, Sensei, *you* have! You created me—you created me for darkness and that is exactly what I have become."

A pause. I could hear faint voices outside now, far below.

"Did you speak to Icarus?" Sensei asked quietly.

I felt a sob tightening in my throat. I pressed a hand to my eyelids.

Icarus.

"No."

Silence.

"Icarus is to be executed, Sensei," I said, and felt my jaw tighten. "Or did no one tell you?"

"I knew before you did, Hawk."

"Then there's nothing else to be said."

"Hawk, please… let me in."

I shook my head, biting my lip. "Why should I? You didn't come to me when I needed you. Why are you here now when it's too late?"

"Have you already lost faith, Hawk?"

I shook my head. "I've preserved my faith since I arrived here," I said, the words bitter in my mouth. "It's the one in whom I had faith that I've lost."

"Of whom do you speak?"

I said nothing.

"Hawk?"

I put my hands over my face.

"Of me?" Sensei asked gently.

The question was like a knife in my heart. A soft-spoken memorial of everything I had ever believed in, everything I had ever fought for. Two muffled words, heavy with pain and reaching for a reply that I never gave.

Because the answer was yes.

CHAPTER TWENTY-NINE
Icarus

It would be a lie to say that I couldn't believe it—I could, but I didn't *want* to.

I didn't want to believe that I'd actually given voice to my confession, even if it had been true. I didn't want to believe that I'd been stupid enough to put her life in jeopardy under the pretext that she would accept mine as compensation. *She wouldn't.*

In her heated words there had been truth: I'd done nothing to earn her trust. I'd manifested nothing but destruction in her world. I was powerful now because of her guidance, and I'd used my abilities to usher in death. I'd taken everything Hawk had, and given her nothing in return. I didn't understand the prophecy, and I didn't want to because something inside me knew that it would tell me things I didn't want to hear. I didn't want to believe that I was who she had been looking for, because I knew in my heart that I wasn't worthy to be that person. I wasn't worthy to touch her, let alone stand beside her in any position of power.

I would die eventually—I already knew that. I felt it in the hollow place where my heart used to beat. I would die because I was destined to, or at least that was what I would tell myself when I saw her face. I would tell myself that there was nothing I could do, and it would be a lie—a shot of fantasy to drug away the pain that I couldn't bring myself to face head-on: the fact that I had cost Hawk her life. That I was connected to her even if I couldn't fathom how, and that death would swallow me only to turn and prey upon her, though she'd done nothing to deserve it.

But if Sensei had taught me anything at all, it was that the Dimension was not a place of fairness. In fact, the opposite was true: it was a place of divine unfairness. Only truth could exist here, even if it took some time to penetrate the mosaic of corruption to which we'd each contributed fragments. And truth, I found in the end, couldn't coexist with fairness; put together in a room, one would always put to death the other.

Throughout my confession, I'd clung to a solitary consolation: her cold, sharp inhumanity and how much I loved her for it. That ability she had to see clearly, through lenses that weren't battered by the flaws of a mortal mind. Hawk had set the standard.

She could cut my heart from my chest and drink my soul away from me and do so ceremoniously—mechanically. She was self-sustaining and in need of nothing, no one. I'd seen what she was unflinchingly capable of. I could live, die, despise her, or kiss her lips and she wouldn't waver because she was the chosen one—she'd been created to fulfill a specific purpose, and she'd shot all the wolves that stood between her and that destination.

I was one of those wolves.

I was already dead in her eyes. All I asked was that she take my life—and there was no logical reason for her not to accept my offer. It was hers to take and dispose of as she saw fit, but she refused it. She told me she couldn't, and let my lips touch hers.

When I'd needed her strength and severity the most, she had ripped it from me and instead slipped into my hand the skeleton of her humanity, like a note she'd hoped to pass without drawing any notice.

She couldn't have chosen a worse moment to let me down—because she was letting herself down too, and she knew it.

Hawk had struck me and told me she hated me. I could have told her that the feeling was mutual. Because as fiercely as something inside me had fallen in love with her, I hated her because of the unstable ground that she was. I hated her for allowing me to destroy her, for watching at a distance as I burned to the ground everything the stars had destined us to be.

She hated me for giving up, and I hated her for the very same reason. We'd fought, clung, clawed, and in the end, given up on each other. It was a strange, incoherent story, and this was how it ended.

With the dawn, Hawk left me. A door opening and closing—the sound of wings. That was all. She escaped unceremoniously before anyone could discover her presence in my room and tarnish her further than her own confession at the trial had done. She would go down in fewer flames.

Two students came soon after to take me to the gathering platform. They were teenagers who seemed filled with almost as much dread as I was.

The sun had halted on the horizon, tilting back in the direction from which it had come, rising in an uncharacteristic wash of muted blue-green pastels, as if it were hesitating.

I became acutely aware of the sound of my own footsteps, my bare feet softly making contact with the ground as the path bent downward, stretching itself out before us and coaxing me closer to what at first looked only like a darker patch contrasted against the forest. But as we came upon it, I became aware of life-forms along with streaks of blood that had pointedly not been washed away.

The gathering platform was crowded, though in contrast to the trial, there were far fewer attendees. I could identify several peers from sessions, but aside from those few faces, almost everyone else was my superior by standard of experience. These were the elite—the ones who had reviewed my case, or at least heard the more refined details that the others hadn't been privy to. The clean, strong, and immortal among us—these were the ones who had gathered to witness my death.

This, I supposed, was the reason why Areos, my roommate, had been obligated to wait beside the stairs leading up to the plateau. I noticed him almost immediately. His breath made shapes in the morning air, which had cooled dramatically with the lifting of the fog.

One of the two student guards broke away now as we reached this set of steps and climbed them. "Wait until you are called for," he told me.

As soon as he was out of sight, Areos came closer.

"I'm sorry, but you'll have to leave," said the remaining student. Her voice sounded too young to be giving orders. "No interaction."

"I'm about to die anyway," I said, sighing. "Does it matter?"

"It breaches the orders we've been given."

"Then you can tell whoever is above you that I don't give a damn about your orders," Areos cut in. "I have something I want to say, and I will say it. This is the only chance I will ever have."

There was a certain finality in the tone of his voice. I felt sweat break out across my skin. The guard fell silent, and Areos came to a stop in front of me.

"I want you to know that I met with the council and then privately with each member afterward," he said, looking me squarely in the eyes. "I said everything I could, I pleaded with them, Ion, and they wouldn't be moved. I tried *everything*."

"I didn't expect you to, Areos—you didn't have to."

He looked at me for a second. "You surprise me, Ion."

"What do you mean?"

Areos seemed disappointed and said nothing. For several moments the silence was filled with the distant sounds of a voice as, down on the platform, someone from the council recited a final, almost detached overview of my sins.

"Ion, we've been good friends, you and I," he said, looking at the ground. "If it wasn't for you dragging me here, I never would have found this place. This... this extraordinary... *fundamental layer* of reality. You've introduced me to something that my classmates would have *killed* to come in contact with."

Areos paused, lifting his gaze to mine once more.

"This is what the greats were searching for—the physicists, the philosophers." He shook his head in amazement. "The legends of the scientific field—this is what they spent their *lives* searching for, Ion. Do you even understand what that means?"

I nodded. "It means you bear a great responsibility, Areos."

I lifted my one free hand and placed it on his shoulder, as I used to do when we were friends on Earth.

"You're a new person now," I told him quietly. "Learn from the mistakes I've made. Protect this place in all the ways that I've failed to—guard it. Pour yourself into it, search it out… find yourself in it." I swallowed back the pain in my chest and continued. "I never did any of those things, Areos, and now my chance has passed, but your time here has just begun."

Areos's jaw tightened. "Your time here shouldn't be up either."

"You say that as a friend, Areos," I said. "But if you were to consider it without bias, you would agree that it has to be this way—that it *should* be this way."

"Why are you bent on playing the martyr?" He narrowed his eyes at me. "I don't understand you, Ion."

"I'm the furthest thing from a martyr, and I would never pretend to be one," I replied, pressing my eyes closed for a moment. "I lost my grip on what I'd been given. I lost sight of everything that mattered—I took someone's life, Areos. That is, and should be, deserving of death."

"Ion—"

"My only regret is that I can't seem to do anything without hurting someone else," I said. "I can't even die without hurting someone else."

"What do you mean by that?"

The voice on the platform became more pronounced now, and we both glanced in its direction.

"Nothing." I said, retreating. "You'll find out soon enough."

Areos studied me for a moment, and I studied him back.

"You want this," Areos concluded finally, his eyes devoid of sympathy. "Don't you? You *want* to die like this—you want this to happen and that's why you aren't fighting it."

"Areos," I said firmly, "you don't understand."

"I don't. Not at all."

"And it's better that you don't," I said with finality. "It's safer for you not to. I don't know what's going to happen, but I know that if you do what I've asked, you'll be safer. Everyone will be—because I won't be here."

He stared at me as if he couldn't believe a word I was saying.

"Please, West," I said, reverting to the name I'd called him for so long. "Just..."

I never finished. I didn't need to. I saw in his eyes that he understood at last. The speaker on the platform had concluded, and my guards returned to grasp my arms once more. I was pulled up the few steps and into the open space, though dragging me there was hardly necessary. I would have gone through the same motions of my own free will.

I kept my eyes trained on the platform as I crossed it, avoiding the blur of faces around me, afraid of finding her eyes there.

At last the hands released my arms and the two young guards stepped away. Waiting for me at the platform's edge was a small figure silhouetted against the dark shades of the forest.

"Come forward, please, Icarus." The voice was female, young, but hard.

I forced myself to continue until I was standing before her, only a few feet from the place where the platform ended. The place where nothing began.

I hadn't been this near Gaia since the day we'd been introduced. I'd forgotten how large her dark eyes were, and the effect they had on me. Her hair was a twisted nest of dreadlocks, woven together to crown her small, heart-shaped face.

"Icarus, kneel," she instructed, her voice cold and steady.

I did so. I noticed from this vantage point that her child-sized feet were bare.

"Though our perspective is not restricted to the dimensions of age, it still stands that I am the youngest student here," she began, "the last to have opened a gathering and, therefore, the appointed for the task of delivering you into the hands of the death you have chosen."

She paused.

"If you have withheld any details of your case, if you have kept anything back, go to your death knowing that you have, even at the end, been given one last chance to bring any hidden truths to the light. We do not deprive you of it."

"Nor would I accuse anyone of that."

"Yet you have nothing further to say on the subject?"

I nodded. "That is correct."

There was a short silence. Gaia exhaled softly.

"Then I am required to reconfirm to you, Icarus, the reasons for which you have been condemned."

"For willful murder and for treason." I completed this formality for her. "Yes. I am aware."

The look in her eyes asked *had I no shame?* I wanted to tell her that the contrary was true: I was an embodiment of what it meant to be ashamed.

"Rise, Icarus," she said now. "Stand facing the platform, please."

I stood at the edge of the drop, with my back to the ravine.

My eyes scanned the platform and found Hawk's. The emptiness of our interlocked gaze reached past everyone in the crowd.

I didn't care about this half of who I was: I cared about the other half of me more than anything else in the universe. The girl whom I'd watched for so long through my kitchen window. The girl who had refused my life to sacrifice her own instead. I wished, even now, that I could say I was sorry—but I knew that this would merely have served to ease my own conscience, not hers. She already knew that I wasn't sorry.

I wasn't.

If I was honest, I felt as though I was standing, finally, at the edge of the nightmare. I'd finally reached the light, and my hand was closing around the handle of a door I longed to open. I was no longer standing in the center of that snow-covered road in the middle of nowhere, with both a sunrise and a sunset closing in on me from either side—I'd chosen a direction. And I was running.

Gaia placed her hand gently against my chest now. Her voice trembled slightly. "By the authority given to the governing student body, it is with a heavy heart that I confirm, again, the accuracy of their ruling, and therefore..."

I heard nothing else. Nothing beyond what Hawk's eyes were communicating to mine, almost against her will, and the words they tore from the folded fists of my own. Three words.

Then I closed them, and she was gone. Replacing her behind my closed lids were ghosts, words. His. As clear as if there was no one there but him.

Who are you indeed, Icarus, that the earth opens its mouth to receive your blood?

Gaia's hand tensed against my chest now. She was so young, so afraid.

I took one last breath and relieved her of the burden she feared. I took one step back.

Then, there was nothing.

ABOUT THE AUTHOR

When she's not hermiting away in her colorfully-painted home office writing her next science fiction, passionate storyteller and adventurer K.A. Emmons is probably on the road for a surf or hiking trip, listening to vinyls, or going for a power run. Emmons' debut novel *The Blood Race* is the first book in her YA science fiction/fantasy thriller series. She lives in the often-snowy hills of rugged Vermont with her husband and dog named Rocket.

Also follow Kate on:
- youtube.com/kaemmons
- facebook.com/kaemmonsauthor
- instagram.com/lonehawkwrite